GROWING UP O'MALLEY

MARY FRANCES FISHER

GROWING UP O'MALLEY

The 1920 picture above was the alternate family portrait without
Mary O'Malley's mother (aka Nana Ginley).

"Days became whimsical over the ensuing years as the symphony of
life played out its tender notes. Life, laden with memories over the
vestiges of time, repeated itself as the O'Malleys experienced the
beauty of living through their children and grandchildren."
- *Growing Up O'Malley*

AUTHOR'S NOTES

This novel is based on true events and stories passed down by the author's family. Events surrounding the Great Depression, World War II, and others are factual based on numerous books, documentaries, and research. Certain experiences and fictional characters have been added for creative purposes and entertainment value.

If you read my first novel, *Paradox Forged in Blood*, my mother, Ellen Grace O'Malley, was cast as the eldest sibling to honor her memory. This rendition contains the actual order of birth in the O'Malley clan. With the number of descendants bearing the same first name—Mary, Margaret, Patrick, etc.—many subsequent names have been changed.

PRAISE FOR MARY FRANCES FISHER

"This book is so much more than historical fiction; it's about the characters that are described so well you begin to believe they are real and that you are a part of the family. To say this is a mystery about a murder on Millionaire's Row is to oversimplify the complexity of the story. One tends to have to think back a few pages when another character is introduced, and there are a lot of characters. There are stories behind the main story, but without complicating it too much, I was amazed at how it all came together at the end. I fell in love with everything about this book and eagerly await *Growing up O'Malley*, Fisher's companion book to *Paradox Forged in Blood*. If this book is an indication of things to come, we will be hearing a lot about Mary Frances Fisher – she's that good." —Linda, Host of *The Authors Show*

"Mary Frances Fisher took all these scenarios and put them together to create a murder mystery with a twist, a love story, and historical fiction. *Paradox Forged in Blood* will make you mad, it will make you cry, and it will make you cheer for the good guys. The story of the lives of these people will warm your heart and leave you shocked. The twist was well played and you will not see it coming. I was completely caught up in this story and could not put it down. There is something for every reader in this book."
—*Reader's Favorite, 5 stars*

"*Paradox Forged in Blood* has intrigue, but it's much more than a murder mystery or a war novel. It's a family saga about self-discovery and coming to terms with the past while looking toward the future." —*Books & Benches*

"I really enjoyed this book! Even though there were several story lines, the author managed to weave them all together masterfully. This story has something for everybody-mystery, historical fiction and mystery.

This book kept me hooked from the beginning and the ending really was a paradox. It was also interesting because the author is the daughter of the main character and the story was based on true events. A great book-highly recommend!" *–NetGalley and BackLit PR Reviewer*

"A wonderful read! From start to finish, you won't be able to put it down. The story has all the ingredients of a gripping yet accurate look at life in Cleveland, as well as WWII and Europe. Forging into nationalities is another rich part of this novel. If you love a good read, don't miss *Paradox Forged in Blood." —Amazon Reviewer*

"I thoroughly enjoyed this book because it kept me guessing until the very end! Clues are there in character development but the mystery sustains itself. For anyone interested in a mystery, a history, a romance, or a psychological study, this tale weaves them all together. Bravo!! I look forward to more good reads by this author."
—Amazon Reviewer

Copyright © 2023 Mary Frances Fisher
First Edition: October 2023
Second Edition: November 2024
Published in the United States of America
Cleveland, Ohio
Growing Up O'Malley/novel; Mary Frances Fisher

www.maryfrancesfisher.com

DEDICATION

To my "fairy" godmother, Veronica O'Malley Collins, who expired in 2020 at the age of 96. She was the youngest sister of my mother, Ellen, and a loving inspiration to us all. With her passing, all the original O'Malley clan and members of their greatest generation have now been reunited to forever wreak havoc in heaven, just as they did in their youth. Each of you will be missed, but your shenanigans will live on forever.

PREFACE

After much contemplation, I fully appreciate two indisputable facts about my life. First, I would still be an angel, floating on a cloud and playing a harp except for one thing—the potato. Yep, a vegetable is the reason for my entrance into this world. However, I'm not referring to any contemporary forms prevalent in today's society—baked, fried, mashed, or even Mr. Potato Head. I'm referring to an ordinary vegetable, with the good sense to carry its own jacket, graced with numerous nicknames—spud, chips, tuber, murphy, crisps, and fries. By now you're wondering how a potato could be responsible for my existence. The simple answer is the Great Potato Famine of Ireland, sending my ancestors from the land they loved in search of prosperity and freedom from tyranny.

Second, fate has chosen me to be the Storyteller of my family's century-long chronicles. 'Tis a grand journey filled with a sprinkling of smiles, love, heartache, laughter, and tears.

Centuries ago, the Storyteller wandered the Auld Sod to share Irish legends passed from one generation to the next. Stories imparted by the Storyteller surely would have included folklore from the exploits of the infamous pirate queen Grace O'Malley (*Granuaile or Ghrainne Ni Mhaille* in Gaelic) whose love of adventure was passed down through the generations to my grandfather, Michael O'Malley. In the fifteenth century, Grace earned the respect of hundreds under her command as they pillaged and fought the British, earning the motto of "Powerful by Land and by Sea."

A gifted journeyman, the Storyteller traveled from village to village to provide entertainment combined with history and a healthy dose of blarney. Crowds gathered from nearby villages, hungering for stories to connect them with their past and tales to brighten desperate times in their retelling. From his bag of tricks, he plied his rapt audience with just the right combination of enticement to delight listeners in a singular way. His mastery of words magically blunted the pain of poverty. When food became scarce and the days insufferable, food for the soul was readily available by sharing stories imparted by the Storyteller. His only payment was food and lodgings as he regaled his audience with tales to fill their hearts with pride and ignite their imaginations. When walking the earth was no longer possible, he would pass the mantle to an apprentice.

Unlike the traveling Storytellers of old, only your imagination and a few moments are needed as we travel back in time to discover life *Growing Up O'Malley*.

Mary Frances Fisher
Cleveland, Ohio
2024

1

'Twas a beautiful summer evening in 1885. The sun, deep in its slumber, was illuminated by the moon shining through the dark velvety sky casting hope and possibilities on mortals below. Elizabeth Ginley, oblivious to nature's resplendent beauty, sat alone in her favorite rocker. As darkness descended, she removed the clear glass chimney from the hurricane lamp and gently turned the knob to advance the wick steeped in kerosene. A lit match touched the wick before the lamp globe was replaced to give a controlled burn and fill the room with light. In spite of light and warmth provided by the lamp, it was insufficient to ward off her internal anguish.

Elizabeth lived in Polranny, a tiny village in County Mayo on the western seaboard of Ireland, in a one-room stone cottage with a thatched roof. Oblivious to its deterioration by the ravages of time and nature, Elizabeth often escaped the confines of their home to sit on the tiny patio out front.

Despite her devastating losses, Elizabeth's mood was uplifted when she returned inside and gazed at the sparsely furnished rooms offset by flowers, homemade afghans in bright colors, and a warm, sturdy hearth glowing with the promise of hope. During her life, Elizabeth discovered beauty in small pleasures to sustain her soul through life's tragedies and provided an inner strength that remained hidden until tested by fate.

Elizabeth listened to the sound of her three sleeping children in the next room and pulled a shawl around her shoulders to warm herself from the chill penetrating her bones. She glanced sadly at the photograph above the fireplace, the last picture of their happy family of six. Weariness from life's burdens were becoming daily occurrences, but she refused to give in to self-pity. Work, caring for her family, and a profound faith sustained her throughout the day and brought some measure of peace during lonely nights.

At the beginning of each day, Elizabeth watched neighborhood men and children from the village drive their horse-drawn carriages to the coast where they picked up stacks of seaweed used as a fertilizer for their potato crops. Ironically, they were ignorant that this practice resulted in destroying their harvest, which contributed to widespread famine.

In the evening, Elizabeth's mind clouded over as terrifying events from the past two years refused to fade into the recesses of her mind. Everywhere she looked, blackened and rotting potatoes—a daily scourge with an ever-present stench—produced diseases including scurvy, typhus, and dysentery. The family survived the famine by shearing sheep and selling wool at the local market. Jamie, Elizabeth's robust and hard-working husband, traveled to Scotland twice each year in spring and autumn, where he worked as a farmhand to supplement their paltry income. Elizabeth could still recall in vivid detail the day her husband returned from Scotland in the back of a cart.

Rushing outside to greet her husband of nine years, Elizabeth cried out, "Heavens, what happened ta me sweet Jamie? Is me darling feeling poorly?"

Two men, neighbors of the Ginleys, remained silent as they jumped from their seat high atop the cart to carry Jamie into his home.

"Yer Jamie was kicked in the head by the hoof of a crazed horse."

"But surely himself will be up and about in no time." Deadly silence was their response, and Elizabeth slumped to the floor.

"I'm sorry ta be bearing bad news, but the doctor was not hopeful. Jamie insisted he die in his home with family gathered about."

They gently laid their friend in the bed he shared with Elizabeth and quietly left. Filling a pan of warm water, Elizabeth gathered clean cloths to wipe the blood from Jamie's head.

"Oh Jamie, ye must hang on. We need ye. *I* need ye." With tears streaming down her face, Elizabeth comforted her husband as their children—Brian, Mary, and Patrick—gathered around. Jamie never spoke a word, but his gaze radiated pure love until the light was extinguished from his eyes and replaced by a death stare a few days later. Elizabeth cradled her husband and wept as their children looked on helplessly. When the baby, Kathleen, began to cry, Brian hurried from the room to comfort his baby sister, grateful for the distraction.

With no income from Jamie, Elizabeth appealed to the government for assistance. But politics and greed overshadowed common decency and human compassion in a climate teeming with desperation. Under British rule, Catholics who toiled the earth were considered serfs—prohibited from owning land and prevented from eating their own food because the exportation of victuals was highly profitable for English landlords.

Elizabeth and her children labored from sunrise to sundown tending the remaining sheep on two small farms—their own and her parents' adjacent property. Endless exhaustion became the mainstay, but it enabled the Ginleys to provide scant provisions for all.

Shortly after Jamie's untimely demise, Kathleen, Elizabeth's nine-month-old infant, refused to suckle, and her weight dropped alarmingly. Desperate to save her baby, Elizabeth begged for milk from her neighbors but there was none. Kathleen's constant cries from hunger became whimpers until they silenced altogether. Kathleen was buried next to her father, and in less than a year's time, the Ginley family was reduced to four—all depending on the resilience of one woman.

At times, the weight of her responsibilities generated a deep depression obscuring her normally sunny disposition. Elizabeth fell into an abyss as a black curtain shrouded her, terrified it would devour her soul. But with three small children and aging parents depending on her, Elizabeth would define the strength of Ginley and the subsequent O'Malley women in the face of adversity.

Hearing a soft crying sound brought Elizabeth back to the present, and she rose from her chair to check on her children. They slept soundly from exhaustion after their chores on the farm, several hours before darkness covered the land. Her children looked content in sleep as their dreams assuaged hunger with heavenly feasts in a carefree world. These precious three souls gave her life purpose and became her link to sanity.

Her youngest, Patrick, had kicked off his blanket and shivered in his small bed. Elizabeth gently replaced the blanket and whispered, "Hush, me darling. Go back ta sleep." And with that small act of motherly love, the fog of depression lifted from Elizabeth, and a tiny smile curved her lips.

Overcome with exhaustion, Elizabeth lay next to her daughter, Mary, in the bed she had previously shared with Jamie. She always found comfort in being near her small daughter with the face of an angel and a loving attitude. Before drifting off to sleep, Elizabeth's last waking thoughts were prayers for strength and peace. Tomorrow would come soon enough, bringing a new set of challenges in a world beset with heartache.

It wouldn't be until decades years later when Elizabeth finally acknowledged feelings deeply buried during this difficult time. Without the opportunity to properly analyze memories unconsciously suppressed, Elizabeth allowed the demons of heartache and grief to hold her captive. By opening the rusty door housing portions of her life—akin to missing puzzle pieces—repressed by pain, she was finally able to shed her mantle of guilt. For the first time in her life, true peace allowed Elizabeth the gift of self-assurance and surety God would forever guide all in His care.

ON DAYS when Elizabeth's depression burdened her soul and threatened to interfere with everyday chores, she replaced painful circumstances with happy memories. Not only did this allay her desolation, it also sufficed to ease the tensions of working two farms. Elizabeth took her children to one of many castles in County Mayo occupied by Grace O'Malley, Ireland's infamous pirate queen in the sixteenth century.

After exploring the ruins while listening to Elizabeth's many tales of high adventure by the pirate queen, the boys waged pretend sword fights until their imaginations were overcome by exhaustion and hunger. Providing her brood with a picnic to round out their adventure, Elizabeth placed their meager lunch of bread and cheese on the blanket she'd spread on the ground. As her brothers played, Mary imagined how glorious it would be if she were a descendant of the infamous Grace O'Malley whose lineage inspired songs and poems passed down through the centuries. Playtime and daydreaming on their forays to the castles always had the same result—hunger pangs were assuaged.

2

Patrick, aged four and the youngest of Elizabeth's brood, although scrappy in appearance, managed to fill each day with the enthusiasm of a space explorer ready to conquer new worlds. Elizabeth heard him scream and stopped sheering a recalcitrant sheep, who scampered away, happy to escape. Running toward her son's cries, Elizabeth noticed Patrick's aggressive friend, Damon, had disappeared.

"Patrick, me darling, what is wrong with ye?" She cradled her son gently in her arms as she examined him for wounds. Other than scratches on his knees, Elizabeth couldn't find any major injuries until he attempted to stand.

"Damon knocked me down. Why can't I walk?" Patrick replied in a tremulous voice.

Elizabeth carried her son into their home, where she told Brian and Mary, "Keep yer eyes on the sheep but do not be wandering from the farm. I need ta drive Patrick into town fer the doctor. He fell and is having trouble standing."

Although concerned about their brother, they heeded their mother's directive and headed outside to shepherd the flock, provide them with fresh water, and chase any wayward sheep.

Gently placing Patrick in the cart, Elizabeth covered his legs with a sheepskin throw before they began the journey into town. With each bump in the road, Elizabeth's fears grew as her son's cries intensified. Grabbing the reins tightly, Elizabeth brought their full fury down on the horses to hasten the trip and ease her son's agony. Throughout the interminable odyssey, Elizabeth fervently prayed God would shine His everlasting love on her tiny son and give her the strength to cope with any battles he faced. After forty-five minutes, they arrived at the home of the doctor, and Elizabeth jumped off the wagon to knock on the front door until a nurse answered.

"I need ta see Doctor O'Hannon. 'Tis an emergency," Elizabeth said.

"Y'er in luck. He is in his office and just finished with a patient."

Elizabeth returned to the wagon and gently picked up her son and returned to the front door where the nurse instructed her.

"Come this way, Mrs. Ginley." Elizabeth and Patrick were escorted into an exam room.

Wiping her son's brow, Elizabeth softly said, "Be brave, me darling. 'Twill all be right."

Dr. O'Hannon came in, and Elizabeth explained what happened. He performed a thorough examination. "I am so sorry, Mrs. Ginley. But yer son will never walk again. A sad thing, but 'tis the truth of it."

Overcome with shock and fear, Elizabeth felt unsteady, and the nurse escorted her to a chair next to the examining table where her son lay on his side. As she stroked her young son's back, Elizabeth gasped.

"Doctor, I need ye ta feel me son's spine."

The doctor did as she requested. "I do not feel anything wrong."

Elizabeth pointed to an area of his spine. "Can ye feel anything there, doctor?"

He shook his head. "It feels like a cavity."

Elizabeth instructed him to push on that spot and a displaced vertebra snapped back in place. With assistance, Patrick was placed on the floor, and he immediately began to crawl without any evidence of a prior injury.

"How did ye know, Mrs. Ginley?" asked Dr. O'Hannon in awe.

"When a sheep is born, their spines are not right, and they cannot walk. I have ta feel along their spine fer the hole and press on that area so the lamb can move."

Dr. O'Hannon laughed. "Ye have taught me a new thing and 'tis grateful I am, ta be sure."

Selecting a cherry candy from a large jar, Patrick savored his reward and continued to giggle as Elizabeth carried him back to the wagon. Together they waved to the kindly doctor and his nurse as they headed toward home with joy in their hearts. After whispering a small prayer to thank God for answering her plea, Elizabeth sang a lullaby to her tiny son, soon fast asleep beside her. Elizabeth marveled at the knowledge her humble lifestyle bestowed upon her to cure Patrick. The journey home passed by quickly, and Elizabeth rejoiced at the sight of Brian and Mary running out to greet them. Watching her three children run together with carefree abandon filled Elizabeth's heart with an abundance of love unconsciously spilling onto her cheeks.

3

Each Sunday, the Ginley family dressed in their finest clothes, which were mostly ill-fitting hand-me-downs, and walked to the nearest Catholic Church three miles away. It was a welcome respite from the drudgery of work. Pastor Bryne was a fiery orator who delivered lengthy sermons to spellbound parishioners, with the exception of several members lulled to sleep but awakened when his voice thundered in righteous indignation.

"Ye will not be attending Protestant schools, or yer souls will be damned ta hell. Their lessons will drive ye from the arms of yer Lord and Savior, Jesus Christ, and their heathen ways will be setting ye on the road ta destruction."

On their trek home, the Ginleys thought about the priest's sermon. Knowing the only formal education provided in Ireland was established by the Protestant Church, the Irish would remain uneducated.

"But Ma, how can we be learning without proper schooling?" asked Brian in a perplexed voice.

"Ye have no need of it. Each of ye has common sense and yer share of wisdom. Book learning was not needed by yer ancestors ta work the land."

But hearing those words spoken aloud filled Elizabeth with quiet desperation. Fearful of defying an edict from a priest—considered to be God's earthbound emissary—restricted any options for advancement and guaranteed a life of servitude years after the potato blight resurfaced in 1879. The only path that lay ahead was enslavement to a land filled with the nauseating stench of decomposing crops. During their trek home, their hearts were steeped in a prison of hopeless melancholy. Their long walk was measured in silence until they passed by the O'Leary farm, where a wagon was packed so full, the wheels were bowed outward.

Elizabeth called out in neighborly concern. "Godspeed, Mr. O'Leary. Where would ye be heading?"

"I'll be taking me family ta America where me children can learn proper lessons and there are jobs ta be had."

Mr. O'Leary's proclamation had a profound effect on the Ginleys. The seeds of hope were planted for emigration to a land promising freedom and opportunities. No longer would they be constrained by British tyranny or suffocate in a land plagued by starvation. But the dream of escape reached a critical point when nature's cruelty and indifference was surpassed only by the crisis of victuals that personified downright indolence in their refusal to provide villagers with sustenance. Nature spewed further insult by destroying green, leafy foliage necessary for their flock to survive, thereby eliminating their only source of income.

As the sheep began to die in alarming numbers, the Ginley's only source of income from shearing sheep dwindled. Something had to be done and the thought of emigrating to America, once a beacon of encouragement, was now fundamental to their very survival.

4

The first to flee would be the oldest child, Brian Ginley. In 1901, Brian boarded the *Etruria* steamship of the Cunard Line—boasting a newly installed wireless communication—and entered third-class accommodations. However, the latest technology provided Brian little consolation while crammed into steerage with eight hundred passengers.

When he arrived in Cleveland, Ohio, Brian worked a grueling job hauling ore on the Cleveland docks for twelve hours a day. From his meager salary, Brian managed to save sufficient funds for his only sister to emigrate.

By the time Mary Ginley was scheduled for her voyage, owners of the White Star Line had revamped its third-class quarters from inferior steerage quality to more spacious quarters with simple comforts in deference to their largest source of income—the ever-increasing Celtic immigrants escaping to a better future and a land full of promise.

Mary had grown into a dark-haired beauty with piercing blue eyes and a trim but sturdy build. She carried herself with grace and style, completely unaware of the self-confidence she exuded. In 1903, one week before Mary's departure to America where her brother Brian awaited, she made a solitary last trek to Achill Sound—a lovely bridge connecting County Mayo to the Achill Island, the largest island in Europe bordering the mighty Atlantic. Mary derived strength from the pounding waves lapping the shore, which beckoned to her with a power and potency unlike anything she'd ever known. If she closed her eyes, Mary heard the whispering sound of her ancestors providing comfort in times of uncertainty. Achill Sound had become a landmark in Mary's childhood associated with her love of the sea and a reminder she alone controlled her destiny, much like the water chose to drive in rhythmic waves desperate to reach land.

Once packing was done, Mary's mother and younger brother loaded her trunks onto a wagon borrowed from a neighbor. They traveled to Queenstown Port where Mary would leave her beloved Ireland. Without Mary's knowledge, her mother placed cherished heirlooms into one of Mary's trunks including the family christening gown and good china—along with numerous items passed down for generations.

Holding onto her mother and Patrick, tears spilled onto their shoulders. Mary had been equally frightened and excited about her adventure. Now that she was preparing for her trip, Mary panicked at the realization she was leaving Ireland for the uncertainty of foreign shores. She took one last look and saw the lovely Irish countryside dotted with moss-covered stone walls while breathing deeply the sweet air sprinkled with sunshine. Mary would lock this memory deep in her soul and take comfort from this moment in times of homesickness.

"Perhaps I will wait fer another year or two. Sure, and ye need help on the farms." Mary looked hopefully into her mother's perceptive eyes, which had endured so much tragedy.

Holding her daughter's face in her hands, Elizabeth spoke with an even voice. "Me darling daughter, me heart is breaking at the thought of ye leaving us. But ye need ta do this now while yer young. Ye can join Brian, and with two incomes, save enough money ta pay fer me and Patrick ta join ye. There is nothing fer ye here." Hugging her sobbing daughter, Elizabeth motioned for Patrick to bring Mary's baggage onto the ship. "Now dry yer eyes and imagine the glorious day when we will all be together." Patrick raced up the plank ahead of his mother and sister, eager to explore the ship.

Mary smiled at the thought of their impending reunion. When the whistle sounded for non-traveling passengers to disembark, Mary corralled Patrick before he had a chance to race through the ship. After hugging her mother and brother one last time, Mary bravely boarded the *Cedric*. This ship was considered by many to be luxurious compared to the cramped and steaming confines of steerage experienced by Brian. Although Mary's experience was more comfortable than her brother's, she felt a new and deeply disturbing sensation. Homesickness settled over her like a dark shroud engulfing Mary in fear. For the first time in her life, she felt completely alone despite being surrounded by throngs of passengers. Panic gripped Mary and she questioned if her long-anticipated adventure was a mistake should this new burden remain her constant companion.

5

<hr>

Weary and emotionally spent, she slowly walked to her cabin, each step forward requiring energy sorely lacking. Opening the door, Mary was surprised to see another young lady relaxing on the lower bunk.

"Oh, thank goodness. I was afraid the room would be spent with meself," said the raven-haired young lady. "Me name's Colleen Bunker, and I'm from County Cork." She reached out to Mary, who gratefully accepted the proffered hand.

"Me name's Mary Ginley, and I'm from County Mayo. Would this be yer first trip aboard a fine ship like this?"

"No, 'tis me second trip, so I can show ye a few tricks ta make yer journey more enjoyable."

Mary instantly liked her outgoing roommate and was happy to have a seasoned traveler for a companion.

"First off, dinner is served at six o'clock and ye need ta dress in yer finery. But 'tis a good idea ta be five minutes late before walking into the dining saloon. The men are sure ta notice ye."

Mary was taken aback at such frankness but knowing her travel experience was lacking, replied quietly, "If ye will be going with me."

"Sure, and I will. Now, let us get ye unpacked."

"I am ever so glad fer the help," Mary said with a wan smile and eyes holding back tears.

"Ah, love, 'tis yer family that ye miss, right?"

Mary nodded and fought back the anguish gripping her heart with such intensity, she was certain it would burst.

"Don't worry. We will have a lovely time together, I can promise ye." Her new friend reassured Mary by giving her a much-needed hug. "How would ye like ta explore the ship after we unpack?"

"'Tis a fine idea."

Colleen proved to be an excellent tour guide. She informed Mary third-class passengers were no longer referred to as steerage due to the large number of immigrants, exceeding two thousand—a fact provided by a pamphlet she had received on a prior voyage. Their excursion revealed amenities to third-class passengers, which included a smoking room, dining room, saloon fitted with swing chairs, separate rooms to keep children amused, a recreation room with a piano, and a covered deck suitable for promenading or sports. They noticed men smoked and drank while ladies spent time reading in the lounge chairs. Others took walks along the promenade deck, with ladies using parasols to shield delicate skin or watching the men play sports.

"'Tis so large, I hope meself will not get lost."

"Aye, Mary, I used ta feel that way. But ye can always find signs pointing the way ta various sections of the ship."

Upon returning to their cabin, Collen looked at the clock in their room. "Me goodness, the time has flown by. We need ta prepare fer our first supper. I have some pancake powder ta fix yer face and a bit of lipstick fer yer lips. 'Tis also good fer adding a bit of color ta yer cheeks."

Mary brightened a little at the thought of another task to keep her mind busy. "Aye, 'tis a lovely idea."

Both young ladies selected their best frocks. When Colleen saw Mary's dress was shabby and out-of-date, she selected one of her new gowns and diplomatically stated, "Ye can borrow this dress. See how it matches yer eyes and lovely complexion."

Mary was in awe at the beautiful evening attire and gratefully accepted the offering. After dressing, they fixed each other's hair in the latest updo with special clasps from Colleen, which sparkled and danced in the candlelit room. After donning long white gloves, they made their way down the spiraling staircase toward the main dining room. Their planned delayed arrival was a success based on the admiring glances of men, many staring open-mouthed. Mary thought perhaps the long voyage wouldn't be so bad after all.

6

They retired to the dining hall and selected seats next to an elderly couple. When their meal was complete, they followed signs for the lounge, where they each had a glass of white wine to revel in the magic of their surroundings. Mary and her new friend even joined in songs played by a raucous band of musicians that grew louder as drinks were imbibed.

"Mary, do not look now, but that man ta yer left is staring at ye." Ignoring her friend's advice, Mary whipped her head around to see a handsome man tipping his hat in her direction.

Turning to Colleen, Mary whispered, "I have never been anywhere with a man by meself. Whatever should I do?"

"Ignore him. If truly interested, himself will come over." No sooner had Colleen spoken the words when the stranger approached Mary.

"Would you like to join me in a walk on the deck?"

Feeling flustered, Mary said, "But I do not even know yer name."

"It's Steven." He gallantly tipped his hat. "And yours would be . . ."

"'Tis Mary Ginley from County Mayo."

"Well, Mary Ginley from County Mayo, would you like some fresh air?"

It sounded like a lovely idea, since the smoke and loud off-key singing were irritating, but Mary first looked at her companion, who nodded in approval.

"Steven, I would be happy ta accompany ye on a short walk." Placing a shawl around her shoulders and gloves on her hands, Mary stood to take her first walk alone with a man without one of her brothers in tow. Nervous and quiet, Mary waited for Steven to open the door leading to the promenade. She thanked him and walked slowly outside as uncertainty about conversing with a strange man fed her anguish. Mary's Catholic guilt surfaced, knowing her mother would disapprove.

"Mary, is this the first time away from home?"

"Aye, 'tis me first time."

"Do you have family in America?"

"Me brother, Brian, and cousins."

"You don't say much, do you?"

Steven's reply made Mary question her decision to veer into unchartered acts of independence. "I think I should be heading back inside. 'Tis colder than I thought."

Steven laughed, not unkindly, at Mary's timidity and gently said, "Of course, Mary. Perhaps we can try another night."

"Perhaps," Mary said, noncommittally.

The following evening, Steven was escorting another lovely lady along the promenade, and Mary was crestfallen.

Colleen occupied a chair next to Mary and whispered, "Sure, and men can be fickle."

When the couple returned, they walked over to Mary, who pretended to be engrossed in a book without realizing it was upside down.

"Excuse me, Mary." Steven waited for her to look up. "I'd like to introduce you to my sister. Felicity, this is Mary."

With a sigh of relief as a smile lit up her face, Mary jumped up to shake the woman's hand with a strength she wasn't aware she possessed. "'Tis a pleasure, I am sure."

"Likewise." Felicity massaged her hand. "Now, if you don't mind, I'd like to get back to my husband before he drinks himself into a coma."

"Of course," Mary said, gratefully.

Colleen smiled at the positive events signaling a change in her friend's favor.

Turning to Steven, Mary said, "I am sure a walk on the deck this fine evening would be a welcome sight. 'Tis, if ye like the idea."

Steven smiled and nodded, while Mary pulled on a thicker shawl and gloves. Together they walked the deck and talked for almost two hours. Mary was certain her mother would be proud of this fine gentleman, and she couldn't wait to share her diminishing travel time with Steven. They were scheduled to dock at Ellis Island in three days, and there was a great deal to complete before their journey together ended.

The next evening was a repeat of the night before, and Mary, happier than she thought possible, revealed her travel destination of Cleveland, Ohio. For the first time, Mary felt mature and ready to face her new life, especially if Steven was by her side.

When their final night together approached, Steven said, "Mary, it has been a pleasure to know you. I could listen to you speak all day long—your lilting voice is charming, and you are so beautiful."

Mary looked down and felt heat rising in her cheeks, believing she must have misheard him and wasn't sure how to respond.

Steven continued. "Although we're both going to Cleveland, I'll be joining my wife. We pretty much live separate lives, so it's unlikely she'd ever find out about us. I'd love to continue seeing you."

Steven's confession was a cruel betrayal intentionally withheld until their last night together. But Mary buried her resentment while keeping her dignity intact. With a coldness in her voice surprising even Mary, she politely said, "'Tis a good thing ta know but I have much packin' ta do this evening and must be off."

"Mary, don't be like that," Steven said, as she quickly retreated.

Mary's ire forced her to turn around, eyes blazing. "Do ye really think no one would be hurt? Are ye so blind yer heart cannot see the anguish ye inflict on others?" In response to Steven's puzzled expression, Mary clarified. "Ye cannot build happiness on the pain of another." She continued her journey through the lounge toward the safety of her room. Although Mary refused to bow her head in defeat and pride prevented a breakdown for others to bear witness, Mary's disappointment pushed a solitary tear down her cheek. Mary permitted herself a proper cry when she was in a hallway away from prying eyes.

Entering her room, Colleen saw the distraught expression on Mary's face, noting her red and swollen eyes. Colleen rushed to Mary's side to console her distressed friend.

"I'm guessing Steven 'tis the reason fer yer anguish." When Mary nodded, Colleen gave her a hug, and with the wisdom of one used to heartbreak, said, "With yer natural Irish beauty, 'twill be other men. Do not fret, me dear. We will pack our things and put this trip behind us."

The rest of the night was a flurry of activity, until Mary and Colleen could no longer keep their eyes open. Sleep provided a welcome respite from the frustrations of life, while misery, heartache, and loss disappeared into the void of time.

7

The next day, Mary and Colleen cleared Ellis Island, and after exchanging emotional goodbyes, took separate trains to their final destinations—Mary to Cleveland and Colleen to Maryland. Brian was waiting at the train station, and Mary ran into his arms, happy to be reunited with her brother and feeling secure in the arms of a man who would never hurt her.

Holding his sister at arm's length, Brian said, "Mary, it does me heart good ta see ye. And a lovely lass ye are at that."

Mary smiled and put her head down to cover her discomfort from the unexpected compliment. Together they walked arm-in-arm to a waiting carriage ready to transport Mary to her new life.

When they arrived in downtown Cleveland, Mary was astounded at the cacophony of sounds assaulting her senses. She wavered for a moment when a car honked its horn in anger as she stepped into the street. The paved road was crowded by horse-drawn carriages, motorcars, and bicycles. Pedestrians dodged traffic attempting to safely navigate their way from one side of the street to the other. Mary felt her first misgivings after leaving the quiet beauty and serenity of her homeland, but she buried her feelings for her brother's sake.

Mary was impressed by the accommodations prearranged by Brian and savored the thought of living in her own apartment. Unpacking her trunks, Mary was delighted to discover the surprise of wonderful Irish heirlooms, undoubtedly packed by her mother—items reminding her of home. Of all the items, Mary cherished most the handcrafted baptismal gown and her mother's cherished fine china— a wedding gift to Elizabeth and Jamie from a wealthy friend.

Mary's cousins in Cleveland provided lessons on the finer points of being a domestic worker. Mary's conscientious manner, charming brogue, and quiet deference resulted in being a personal maid to the city's most prestigious families on Millionaire's Row. They included Mayor Tom L. Johnson, where Mary was later promoted to the position of housekeeper; Edwin Prescott, of Prescott, Ball and Turben fame; and Henry Sherwin, of Sherwin Williams paint. Wherever she worked, Mary was provided room and board with one day off each week. Since the gentry had little nighttime entertainment to pass the time, Mary worked many evenings helping to cater expansive dinner parties—an opportunity allowing her to come in contact with Newton D. Baker and John D. Rockefeller.

After working long hours, Mary and Brian took evening courses to learn proper English in addition to citizenship classes. They passionately absorbed every lesson taught by their English teacher.

"Now class, pay attention. When you meet someone, you say, 'How are you?' And, they will say, 'I am fine.'"

Their instructor taught them similar practical phrases over the next hour and recommended they review the examples before their next class. At home, they practiced their lessons as they understood them; only their interpretation included Irish lingo.

Mary would say, "So I says ta him, says meself, 'How are ye?' And he says ta me, says himself, 'I am fine.'"

"Oh Mary. 'Tis wonderful. Ye sound just like teacher." It would take several additional lessons before they fully comprehended their teacher's use of sensible phrases. Once they omitted overlaying Irish idioms incorporated into oft-used expressions, they became proficient in mastering English.

Both Brian and his sister beamed at their cleverness in learning this new language so easily. Living in this land of freedom was becoming a grand adventure.

8

During one of the parties at the Sherwin estate, Mary was carrying a tray of drinks when she accidentally bumped into one of the guests.

"Begging yer pardon, sir."

When the stranger turned around, his annoyance changed to admiration. But his attention made Mary uncomfortable with his overt examination of her like a piece of livestock.

"And who might you be?"

"I am Mary, one of the hired help."

"Well, Mary, my name is Rudolph Weber. I don't suppose I could interest you in leaving early and going out with me?"

"I cannot do that, sir. 'Tis me job."

"What if I talk to your boss? He's a good friend of mine."

"I am not sure 'tis a good idea."

Mary's shocked expression and concern over losing her job to a guest made an impression on Rudolph, who gracefully acknowledged her discomfort.

"Perhaps another time."

"Maybe, sir. But I must go about me tasks." Mary curtsied and left the guest, but she experienced a lingering regret. Mary did find him attractive in a rugged way with wavy, dark hair, dancing eyes the color of an Irish field, cleft chin, and deep-set dimples. When she conceded her honest assessment, Mary chastised herself for having foolish notions.

Over the next two weeks, Mary succeeded in placing the delectable Rudolph out of her mind. While cleaning an upstairs bedroom, Mary was summoned to the parlor by the main housekeeper. It was an unusual command and deeply troubling—possibly a bad omen. Mary attempted to quell her anxiety and calm her demeanor before entering the parlor.

"Ye wished ta see me, Ms. Paulson?"

"Yes, Mary. I understand your family is well-acquainted with the Cleveland Docks."

"'Tis true, ma'am."

"Then I need you to accompany this gentleman to the docks for a short tour. An automobile is waiting outside and will bring you both back this afternoon."

Alarmed at traveling in the confines of a car with a strange man, Mary was frantic to come up with an excuse—conscious any reason might terminate her employment. Fidgeting as a slight sheen of perspiration peppered her brow, Mary was about to speak when the gentleman, sitting in a high-back chair, spun around. It was Rudolph Weber, and Mary's cheeks reddened without realizing her mouth was open in surprise.

Shrewdly, Mrs. Paulson discerned the reason for Mary's surprise and quickly interceded. "Seems as though you two have already met, and I assure you Mr. Weber is a proper gentleman. I trust the task won't be a problem, is that correct, Mary?"

"'Tis fine, ma'am," Mary said in a hushed voice. She removed her full-length apron and followed Rudolph to the car parked out front.

Silence during the short drive became a void roaring in Mary's ears until Rudolph finally spoke.

"Mrs. Paulson was very forthcoming about your family, and I wanted to see you again. When she mentioned your familiarity with the docks, I said it would be wonderful if you could accompany me. I hope you're not disappointed."

Mary didn't want to manifest her excitement or give the impression she was eager, so she remained noncommittal. "'Tis nice ta see ye again."

"I really don't want to see the docks. Instead, I'd like to take you to lunch. Have you ever been to Otto Moser's Restaurant? It caters to famous performers, and the food is delicious."

"I have never been ta any restaurant." Once the words were spoken aloud, Mary was afraid Rudolph would scoff at her inexperience.

"Then we'll have to rectify that."

Wearing a long, dark, maid's uniform, cinched at the waist with a black velvet belt, complemented by lace at the collar and cuffs, Mary said, "But me outfit 'tis not fancy. Sure, and I would be unwelcome in a fine establishment." Bits of curls framed her lovely face, but Mary was ignorant of her natural beauty.

"Nonsense. Don't you realize how beautiful you are?" Rudolph's comment was affirmed by the appreciative glances of male customers as he escorted Mary to an empty table.

The lunch was one of the best meals Mary had ever eaten, and surrounded by the plush atmosphere, she forgot her station in life as domestic help. But when they left the establishment and headed back to the car, reality settled on Mary like an unwanted blanket on a hot summer's night. During the trip to the Sherwin estate, silence thundered in the confines of the automobile.

Sensing Mary's reserved manner was the result of clashing lifestyles, Rudolph asked Mary, "Can I see you again?"

"Ye want ta see me again?" Mary asked incredulously.

"Of course, I do."

"I am but a housemaid. I am sure ye could find someone more refined."

Rudolph grinned, still amazed at Mary's naiveté. "There is no one finer than you."

Mary didn't know how to interpret his remarks. *Sure, and he must be daft.* Although, his demeanor contradicted this assessment.

Coming out of her reverie, Mary heard the last of Rudolph's

question. ". . . accompany me to the Hanna Theater on Sunday afternoon?"

"I suppose me brother could bring me ta the theater."

"But I could pick you up."

"I am not sure 'tis proper. And me brother would insist."

"All right. I'll meet you in the lobby at 1:45 p.m. this Sunday."

"'Tis a lovely idea. Sure, and I would be proud ta go." Mary exited Rudolph's car before he had a chance to open her door and ran into the Sherwin home without a backward glance. Mary thought, *If this is what a dream feels like, I hope I never wake up.*

9

The rest of the week passed quickly, and Mary counted the moments until Sunday finally arrived. Dressed in her Sunday best, she attended St. Patrick's Church in the morning with her brother. "Brian, are ye sure it's not too much trouble ta take me on the subway ta the Hanna?"

"Anything fer me little sister."

Mary didn't notice the gleam in her brother's eye as he plotted the best way to attend the matinee while keeping a close eye on Mary. When they reached the theater, Mary approached her new friend and introduced her brother.

"Rudolph, 'tis me brother, Brian."

"Pleasure ta meet ye." Both men were wary of each other, and their bone-crushing handshakes laid claim to the sanctity of one cherished woman.

"Mary, we're sitting up front, and we should head to our seats."

Turning to her brother, Mary politely said, "Thank ye, Brian, fer escorting me."

With a devilish grin, Brian nodded before making a dash to the box office where he purchased a ticket in the upper balcony. After a few minutes, Brian was able to see his sister and her new friend in the third row. Brian, intent on looking out for Mary, didn't see much of the play and was surprised when everyone stood to clap at the production's conclusion. When Mary got up from her comfortable seat, unlike Brian's tightly packed and confining space, he sprinted into the lobby.

Mary and Rudolph were surprised to see Brian, waiting with his arms folded across his chest. "Me darling sister, are ye ready ta go home?" The two men exchanged glances, and it became clear wherever Mary went, Brian would follow.

Ignorant of the tension between the two men, Mary said, "Oh, Brian, 'tis a lovely surprise. Did ye see the fine play?"

"I did. Now shall we be heading homeward? I am sure Rudolph has other plans."

Taking his cue, Rudolph shook Mary's hand, doffed his hat to Brian, and strode out of the theater.

"Mary, I have a feeling ye may not be hearing from Rudolph again."

"Why?"

"Just a feeling." Brian didn't explain an aristocrat wouldn't stand for this old-fashioned dating custom.

Brian's prophesy was accurate. After a few weeks passed without a word from Rudolph, Mary returned to her routine schedule with a strong conviction her life wasn't meant to be lived in the clouds. It was a painful lesson but necessary to keep her grounded in reality by leaving glamour to women whose station was above her own.

By 1905, after working a total of six years between them, Mary and Brian pooled their funds and arranged passage for their mother, Elizabeth, and remaining sibling, Patrick. Once they purchased the tickets, time dragged onward; each idle minute felt like an hour in the absence of purposeful functions to expedite its passage. The interminable wait was agonizing until the Ginleys were reunited in their new homeland with its promise of freedom.

Elizabeth Ginley managed to sell both farms—her own and the one belonging to her deceased parents. For the first time in her life, she possessed money belonging only to her, which empowered her through financial independence. Although Elizabeth was a widow of over twenty years with graying hair interspersed with wisps of red, her blue eyes remained clear as the Caribbean Sea. Her newfound independence was tested on the journey to America with Patrick. Elizabeth had agreed to shepherd six young boys from their village to be reunited with American relatives in Cleveland. Carrying all the possessions Elizabeth owned in one small wicker basket, she set sail aboard the *Cedric* of the White Star Line in Queenstown on the southern coast of County Cork.

Elizabeth, Patrick, and her young charges gaped at the Statue of

Liberty. Emigrating to the Promised Land in the hope that a release from oppression was within their grasp. Elizabeth reverently informed them, "That lady 'tis named Liberty. She stands fer happiness and giving everyone the chance ta receive education and freedom ta practice their religion."

It took several hours to process the group through Ellis Island before they veered out from the Registry Room toward a wooden column affectionately named The Kissing Post, where new arrivals were greeted by loved ones. Navigating through the hoard of immigrants, Elizabeth and company took the ferry to New York where they boarded a train to Cleveland, Ohio.

Arriving at their destination, Elizabeth was met by relatives of the six boys in her charge. Before releasing them from her custody, Elizabeth was diligent in querying each couple to make certain those who arrived to collect the boys had a legitimate claim.

"What is the name of the boyo ye will be claiming?" After a name and relationship to the child was provided, Elizabeth continued her inquiry. "And who would their parents be, where are they from, and how are ye related?"

One by one, the boys were claimed by family members until Elizabeth and Patrick were left alone to wait for Brian and Mary. Elizabeth clutched her wicker basket tightly to her chest, while she and Patrick nervously waited for the long-anticipated family reunion.

Heading toward the two anxious travelers was a beautiful young lady. She wore a stylish Victorian dress complete with a shorter tartan plaid overskirt covering a floor-length kelly-green gown. It was cinched at the waist, adorned with matching tartan plaid collar and cuffs, and a fashionable bustle in the back. Her hair was fashioned in an updo and topped off with a black hat complemented by flowers surrounding the brim. She was accompanied by a handsome and stately-looking young gentleman wearing a black three-piece suit, which included a long frock coat, gold waistcoat chain, and top hat. At first, Elizabeth thought they were a posh couple, certainly aristocrats, until they got closer.

"Ma and Patrick, we are so excited ta see ye both!" Mary and

Brian cried in unison as they rushed forward to hug their mother and brother.

Holding her children at arm's length with tears in her eyes, Elizabeth said, "I've sorely missed ye two. And a lovely pair ye both make."

Her children beamed at the praise, a rarity for their mother, who believed admiration led to vanity.

The entire Ginley clan was finally together in the United States—and a joyous reunion it was with tears and hugs to celebrate their new life together. Of course, such a momentous occasion would not be complete without a wee bit of whiskey added to the mix, sure to amplify their happiness.

11

———————

Brian had saved sufficient funds, in anticipation of his remaining family's relocation, to rent three side-by-side apartments on West 32nd. Each domicile had a living room, kitchen, two bedrooms, and a bath. Brian and Mary already occupied the end units, while their mother and Patrick would live in the center apartment, the largest of the three units. With the money she brought from the sale of two farms, Elizabeth repaid Brian for her apartment to secure her new station in life as an independent woman of modest means.

While Mary worked in Cleveland's most prestigious estates over the next four years, her siblings established themselves in professions suited to their individual talents. Brian worked on the Cleveland dock, a backbreaking job that required shoveling heavy iron ore. He was happy in his profession, enjoying the vigorous challenge as he worked with friends who respected his work ethic. By 1909, Brian had met Anna Walsh, and they were married at St. Patrick's Church the following year.

Although Brian initiated Patrick into the rigors of working on the Cleveland dock, Patrick preferred a career not so physically demanding. Within two years, he secured a desk job at The East Ohio Gas Company, where he met and fell in love with Trish Masterson.

Just as his brother before, they were married at St. Patrick's Church with Elizabeth and Mary in attendance. Patrick's new bride moved into the apartment Patrick occupied with his mother. Elizabeth welcomed her new daughter-in-law with love and respected their boundaries as newlyweds.

Although Mary rejoiced when her siblings found their soulmates, she longed to find that special someone to share her life. Mary's lack of self-confidence was exacerbated by living in a foreign land bereft of her beloved lush, green fields. Mary remained stoic during her transition to America and remembered the most difficult sickness one could endure was homesickness. Her wistful affection for her childhood home was like a permanent friend—hidden in the background but always at the ready when her new life threatened to overwhelm her. She could easily access her treasure chest of memories by closing her eyes and be instantly transported back to her precious Ireland. Visualizing its luxuriant valleys and rolling hills in the simple Irish countryside, Mary felt renewed as the clamor of city life receded, similar to the waters of Achill Sound rushing toward the shore. Mary's memories provided comfort and serenity but they were also bittersweet childhood reminders of things forever absent.

In time, the pain of nostalgia was balanced by the benefits of living in America—freedom to speak Gaelic, practice her religion, and own a bit of earth, a miracle she never took for granted after living under tyrannical rule.

12

Ironically, Michael O'Malley, born in 1882, grew up in Mulranny, a town bordering Polranny, where Mary Ginley had lived. Despite living in neighboring towns on the West Coast of Ireland, they remained strangers before to leaving their homeland. Prior to meeting his true love, Michael would embark on a diverse and circuitous path in this new land of freedom.

Before Michael left Ireland, he joined his four younger brothers and three sisters in constructing a beautiful, white, brick, colonial home for their parents in nearby Westport, County Mayo. This endeavor taught Michael plumbing and construction—skills he would rely on in the future.

To support their aging parents, they opened up a grocery store, which served as the local gossip mill and a gathering place for local residents.

By the age of twenty-seven, Michael O'Malley was a strapping young man, handsome and sure of his self-worth. Standing at five-feet-ten-inches tall, his robust frame and ruddy complexion were gifts of Mother Nature from working outside. His brown hair, cleft chin, and thick luxurious mustache—groomed daily—were complemented by hazel eyes surrounded by laugh lines. He believed all women were paragons of virtue worthy of respect and admiration.

In the spring of 1907, Michael decided it was time to fulfill his dream of pursuing opportunities in America. Michael's family was aware British soldiers occupied English harbors to conscript Irish men of fighting age into the army before they could flee. Based on their advice, Michael planned his escape via Scotland.

Finally, the day arrived for Michael's grand undertaking. Filled with the excitement of travel and adventure, he packed a small trunk anxious to begin his journey.

But saying his final goodbyes to his parents and siblings proved to be a difficult and agonizing task. Clearing his throat several times helped keep the tears at bay. Michael hugged each member of his family and told his parents, "Ma, Da, I'll make ye proud."

"Ah, go on with ye. We are always pleased with the man ye are," replied his mother, wiping tears on her apron and handing her son a package. "I've packed ye some breads and meats fer yer journey."

While his father shook hands with Michael, he placed something in his palm. It was his father's precious gold pocket watch. Michael was stunned to receive this valuable object, only worn on special occasions and passed down from generation to generation.

"Da, I cannot accept this. I know how much ye love it. Sure, and I don't deserve it."

"Are ye not me oldest child? And has it not always been passed down ta the eldest son? Ye are its rightful owner and besides . . ." his father's eyes twinkled with delight, "sure, and it has mystical powers ta protect ye on yer journey."

Michael was speechless and promised to protect the timepiece from any harm. Facing his family, he barely breathed as his heart skipped a beat. "'Tis with thanks I am fer everything. I love each and every one of youse and hope we will one day meet again."

After many hugs and kisses, Michael made his way to Glasgow where he boarded the *SS Astoria*. His arrival at Ellis Island on March 30, 1907, filled him with optimism when he gazed at America's symbol of a better life—the Statue of Liberty in the New York harbor.

After clearing the nation's busiest immigration port at Ellis Island, Michael was eager to conquer his wanderlust and discover this land of opportunity.

13

Michael traveled to the Yukon, where he joined a group of gold prospectors. Never one to shy away from hard work, Michael put in long hours until they struck gold. Michael couldn't believe their luck and thought, *'Tis true. The streets of America are paved with gold.*

On the morning they were due to leave, Michael awoke with a fever, severe abdominal pain, weakness, and a headache. When he heard his companions packing their belongings and preparing to leave Michael behind, he panicked. "Lads, sure and ye can wait fer me. 'Tis soon I'll be better."

"Sorry, Michael. Can't do it. The longer we wait puts us in danger. We need to get this gold to the next town and cash out."

"And what of me share?" Anger crept into Michael's voice.

"If you want your share, come with us."

"Ye know I can't do that."

"That's the risk you take. We'll leave you a blanket with some food and water. Good luck."

Too exhausted to argue, Michael laid back down overcome with a bout of nausea followed by pernicious and unforgiving vomiting. But Michael was strong of spirit and, after several weeks filled with pain and agony, he gradually improved. He forced himself to walk and exercise until he could start his journey. When Michael was healthy enough, he began the trip into the next town. Halfway there, he came across his former companions—murdered and robbed of the gold they prospected.

Michael gently reached inside his breast pocket and fingered the gold pocket watch while recalling his father's words of its magical powers. He made the sign of the cross and silently thanked his father. Once he corralled the remaining horse, which Michael assumed escaped the marauders but returned to locate its master, he found a shovel inside the saddlebag. After carefully digging a large hole, Michael silently prayed over their joint grave and thanked God for sparing him the same fate. He discovered a life lesson—patience and a strong faith would be his secret to a fulfilling life.

After his complete recovery, Michael moved to Canada where he worked as a streetcar conductor. He then traveled to Bear Creek, Montana, to mine coal after earning his Miners' Examining Board Certificate of Competency on August 11, 1908. Finally, his wanderlust led Michael to Cleveland where he was discouraged by glaring signs warning, "Irish Need Not Apply"—a common sight filling him with helpless rage.

Using knowledge acquired during construction of the family home in Ireland, he opened his own business: O'Malley Plumbing and General Contractor. He would later shorten the name to O'Malley Plumbing when the majority of his projects, except personal endeavors, involved this expertise.

Shortly after his business began to boom, Michael decided it was time to settle down. While walking downtown in 1912, preoccupied with thoughts of his latest job prospect, he accidentally bumped into Mary Ginley, whose vision was compromised by the tower of packages carefully balanced in her arms.

"If ye will please ta be pardon me." Michael spoke softly to avoid startling her. Without realizing it, Mary translated his Irish intonation into what she heard as perfect English.

Mary was speechless when she gazed up at the handsome man standing before her with arresting hazel eyes complemented by laugh lines. When packages tumbled from her arms in response to the unexpected surprise, the stranger gallantly picked them up and placed them in her arms without realizing she was temporarily mute.

"Thank ye kindly fer the help," Mary replied, once she was able to control her speech.

Michael was awestruck by her genteel manner and natural beauty. "Could meself be so bold as ta ask yer name?"

"'Tis Mary Ginley from Polranny, County Mayo. And who might ye be?"

"'Tis Michael O'Malley from Mulranny, County Mayo."

"Sure, and ye must be joking. Saints alive! Ye come from one town over in Ireland?"

"That would be the truth of it. And it only took an ocean fer us ta meet." When Mary laughed, it sounded like the sweetest chimes from a revered cathedral in Europe.

"Now that we have been introduced, could I please help ye with yer packages and walk ye home?"

Mary didn't know how to react since they'd just met. She felt her face growing warm as a bloom of color spotted her checks. She hesitated only for a moment and glanced around to make sure the streets were crowded. The sun brightly lit their way, so she nodded in agreement.

After Michael took Mary's heaviest packages, careful to keep a respectful distance, he waited until they were entering Carroll Avenue, before asking, "If ye are not ta be busy this Saturday, perhaps ye would be inclined ta see meself another time. I don't mean ta be forward, but maybe . . ."

In the presence of this Irish goddess, Michael's words trailed off as any semblance of conscious thought deserted him rendering normal conversation impossible. Convinced Mary would think him a proper eejit—and feeling a fool was completely foreign to Michael's repertoire—his cheeks turned a reddish tinge and to his utter mortification, he began to stammer.

"Do y-ye th-think we could m-meet under th-the lions th-this Saturday? Maybe at h-half past one?" Michael wiped his brow, grateful to finish his query, despite feeling like a moron.

Michael hoped Mary knew he referred to the entrance of

Cleveland's finest downtown landmark where celebrities and politicians graced the lengthy list of honored guests. Flanking the structure's entrance were two impressive statues of lions, a landmark well-known for potential suitors to meet. Mary's response did not disappoint. "I need ta first talk ta me brother, Brian. But I think 'tis a fine idea. If he agrees, I shall see ye there."

On the appointed day, Michael was mesmerized by the beautiful lady heading his way. Mary carried a parasol and wore her favorite, and only, dress made of the finest green and tartan plaid materials in a Victorian style. When Michael finally glanced away from the captivating sight, much to his chagrin, he knew he would not be spending the day alone with this divine creature.

"Michael, 'tis me brother, Brian. He will be spending the day with us."

Although disappointed, Michael was aware of the Irish custom, and the two men shook hands. After bowing to Mary, Michael addressed Brian. "'Tis a pleasure ta meet ye. Mary says we hail from neighboring towns. Ye never know the surprises that await ye from one day ta the next, eh?"

With Michael's easy-going manner and clear deference to his sister, Brian discerned Mary was safe and agreed to walk several steps behind them.

They took a streetcar to a local restaurant, and the trio ate a lovely meal. After taking a walk through a local park and stopping for a soda, they walked home just as the sun began its descent in a dizzying array of blazing red and orange hues. *Surely a fortuitous sign*, thought Mary.

In response to Michael's request to see Mary the following weekend, she looked at her brother who nodded his consent. Mary was pleased with Michael's courteous manner and understanding of Irish customs—characteristics mirrored in Brian's respectful attitude toward Michael.

Come Saturday, Brian decided to follow the couple at a distance. When Michael picked up Mary, Brian was nowhere in sight. For the first several hours, Brian ducked behind trees and pretended to window-shop as he discretely conducted his surveillance. But the task was boring, he became weary, and his feet ached. He determined being the oldest brother was a thankless and exhausting job. Convinced Michael's intentions were honorable, Brian returned home to spend time with his wife.

"Anna, me darling, 'tis yer loving husband back from his brotherly duty." He kissed her on the cheek, and she brought him a cold beer as he sat in his favorite chair.

"And what do you think of Mary's new friend?"

"Did ye know he came from only one town over in Ireland?"

Anna nodded. "How remarkable they didn't meet until he arrived in Cleveland. So, you think he's a good match for Mary?"

"Aye. But I will not be telling himself any time soon." Brian winked and his wife grinned, knowing his devilish ways.

Together they awaited Mary's return and were pleased to hear the enthusiastic summary of time spent alone with Michael. Anna smiled at her husband's inflated ego when he later congratulated himself on his accurate assessment of Michael.

14

Over the next several months, Michael and Mary had a weekly Saturday evening date to explore Cleveland and its surrounding countryside. By July 1913, Michael knew she was the one for him.

"Mary, could I be stopping by early next Saturday so meself and Brian could chat?"

"Me brother?"

"Aye. 'Tis mighty important."

"He will be home Saturday evening at half-five. They leave the docks early on the weekend. Ye can stop after that."

"I shall see him then."

Mary was curious but kept her thoughts to herself. When her brother arrived home, Mary walked over to Brian's apartment and informed him of Michael's impending appointment.

"Are ye sure 'twas me he wanted ta chat with?"

Mary nodded and on the appointed day Mary returned to Brian's apartment to welcome their guest. Mary was greeted by Anna, who would remain with Mary in the kitchen once this potentially fortuitous meeting began.

When Michael arrived at 6:00 p.m., Mary opened the door to a peculiar sight—Michael, normally oozing with confidence, was fidgety and nervous. "Are ye all right, Michael?"

Mary smiled inwardly when she noticed Michael nodded like a bobble-head doll with obvious embarrassment when his normally calm demeanor deserted him.

"I'll be speaking with yer brother now."

Mary hurried into the kitchen, and after exchanging pleasantries with Anna, nervously advised her brother of Michael's arrival.

Brian and Anna were finishing dinner and she had begun to clear away the dishes. Brian dabbed his face and casually sauntered into the living room, relishing the impending inquisition. Anna decided to help keep her sister-in-law's mind occupied.

"Mary, would you help me with the dishes?"

"The what? Oh, of course."

Anna was forced to rewash many items to remove stains missed by a distracted Mary.

When Brian entered the living room, Michael was pacing, unable to sit still. "And ta what do I owe the honor?"

"Brian, ye know Mary and me have been seeing one another fer a while now."

Brian nodded, unwilling to let Michael off the hook, taking a special delight in his discomfort.

"Aye."

"I need ta ask yer permission ta marry yer sister."

"And can ye provide fer her?"

"Business is good. She will want fer nothing."

"And do ye love her?" Brian was enjoying the exchange.

"Are ye daft? 'Course I love her."

"Then we need ta ask Mary fer her thoughts on the matter." Calling to his sister, unaware she was secretly listening in the next room, Mary appeared in the parlor within seconds.

"Mary, darling, Michael would like ta marry ye. Do ye think himself worthy?"

Mary had previously confided in her brother that she was falling in love with Michael and her deep-seated wish for marriage with children was a dream she would love to share with Michael.

Getting down on one knee, Michael held out a beautiful engagement ring. "Mary, I love ye with all me heart. Will ye marry me?"

Brian was concerned, and surprised, when he saw Mary's face lose all color. Thankfully, Mary recovered quickly and smiled at what Brian assumed was relief at achieving her long-awaited desire.

Nodding vigorously with tears of happiness spilling down her cheek, Mary lovingly replied, "Oh, yes, me darling."

They embraced passionately and Brian retreated to the kitchen to give them privacy. While there, he updated Anna, who anxiously paced around the kitchen table awaiting an update of Michael's visit.

Mary called out to Brian and Anna, inviting them to share the good news with the remaining family members. The four of them walked next door to knock on Elizabeth's door.

In anticipation of Michael's potentially significant visit, Elizabeth had invited Patrick and Trish to join her in the living room. When Elizabeth opened the door and invited the party of four into her home, Elizabeth anxiously looked into Mary's eyes. When she saw the reflection of Mary's happiness, Elizabeth hugged her precious daughter. Mary formally announced the good news and basked in the love of her family.

Holding up her engagement ring for everyone to admire, Mary informed her family of Michael's ancestor, the pirate queen. "When ye think about it, the O'Malley castles where we played as children now have a special significance. Why, our family will be related ta royalty!"

Keenly observing Michael at their initial visit, everyone could see the love and contentment shared by the couple. Mary's brothers clapped Michael on the back for his upcoming nuptials and amazing ancestry, while Mary was given hugs and kisses. The family celebrated into the wee hours of the morning to honor Mary's newfound devotion to a prosperous man from the Auld Sod. 'Twas a grand day for all.

For the first time in Michael's life, he was able to lock away his former wanderlust to settle down in one area and spend a lifetime with this incredible woman.

Just as her brothers before, Mary and Michael were married in St. Patrick's Church on Thanksgiving Day, 1913 but celebrated future anniversaries on the holiday, instead of November 27. The ceremony was followed by a modest reception in their recently purchased home at 3104 Carroll Avenue. During the celebration, Elizabeth gave Mary a wonderful surprise.

Clasping Mary's face in her hands, Elizabeth declared, "Me darling daughter, on this wonderous occasion meself will be giving ye a gift ta cherish and enjoy. Yer brothers helped me ta pack it, and 'tis waiting fer ye on the front porch."

Elizabeth escorted Mary onto the porch where an enormous and mysterious package awaited. "Tis a gift from the Auld Sod ta me only daughter."

Intrigued, Mary removed the large green bow and opened the box. She gasped at the most beloved wedding present—her mother's beautiful set of rose-patterned china from Ireland. Mary turned to her mother, moisture leaking from her eyes, and hugged Elizabeth while thanking her profusely.

Mary returned to the parlor and turned to her new husband, excitement evident. "Michael, me love, please join me on the front porch." Curious, Michael complied and, after opening the box, Mary explained its significance. "'Tis me darling mother's fine china that she received as a wedding gift in Ireland."

Now it was Michael's turn to thank his mother-in-law for her generosity and thoughtful gift. That night, with help from Mary's brothers, the box was brought into the home. The following day the dishes were displayed in a place of honor—new glass-leaded cabinets built by Michael. Thrilled to see a reminder of home each time she entered her kitchen always brought a smile to Mary as she began each day.

While Mary began the task of setting up their household, Michael expanded his work force to include neighbors and friends after he secured multiple city contracts. In the evenings, Mary gave her husband basic lessons in the English language. His success enabled him to purchase several homes which he renovated and rented to others. Mary was content in her new role as the wife of a prosperous and loving man from the Auld Sod. Life was surely grand.

15

Michael's business was booming, and Mary's lovely feminine touches in decorating their home were lovingly completed despite morning sickness that began only two weeks after their wedding. Mary knew she was pregnant for her monthly cycle, normally as regular as clockwork, was two weeks late. Before informing Michael, she decided to get a second opinion. Mary visited Mrs. Prendergast, the neighborhood midwife. The moment she observed Mary's radiant glow, present in her pregnant patients, she confirmed Mary's suspicions and agreed to assist with the home birth. Returning home, Mary was anxious to share the news with Michael and alleviate his concerns.

"Me darling, do ye think ye need ta see a doctor? At first, I believed 'twas the excitement from our wedding, but 'tis now several weeks."

"Michael, me darling. Please sit next ta me fer I have something ta tell ye."

Michael's loving expression turned to alarm. "Are ye sick, me love?"

"No, me darling. I'm carrying a precious new life. I know 'tis faster than we planned, but—"

Michael's astonishment was quickly replaced by pure joy. He gently picked Mary up and hugged her until they both cried tears of joy. They settled in to celebrate their first Christmas together as a couple—memorable despite Mary's morning sickness. When she was too weak to get up, Michael or a neighbor brought her trays of food throughout the day. Despite their best efforts, most of the food consumed was recycled into a bucket by her bedside. But on Christmas morning, Mary managed to drag her fatigued body downstairs to discover Michael had set up a Christmas tree in their parlor.

"Oh, Michael, 'tis quite lovely. When did ye find time ta do this?"

"I feel helpless on days when yer too sick ta get out of bed and hid this tree with all the trimmings at a friend's home. I sneaked it into our home early this morning."

Mary responded with tears of joy. "Our first Christmas together before the wee one's arrival and ye have made it so posh."

Michael hugged his wife and gently led her to the love seat. He reached behind his back and deftly placed a small box in Mary's hand. Nervously, she removed the wrapping paper and was astonished to find a beautiful crucifix on a glittering gold chain. Michael carefully placed the cross around Mary's neck and clasped it shut.

With tears anew, Mary said, "But I don't have anything fer ye."

When Michael patted his wife's slightly protruding belly, he softly reminded her, "Ye have the most precious gift growing inside ye. I can't be asking fer a greater present." He gently kissed his wife as they sat together holding hands on the loveseat and admired the most beautiful Christmas tree in the world.

The sickness gradually abated, and Mary was finally able to help Michael complete the nursery for their new addition. Mary informed Michael that Mrs. Prendergast would assist with the home birth when delivery was imminent.

On August 30, 1914, Mary tried to wake her husband at 1:30 a.m. "Michael," she gasped as another contraction gripped her body in pain. "'Tis time fer the midwife."

Still half asleep, Michael asked if she could wait a few hours for a proper night's sleep. Mary thought her husband was crazed to believe their little one would wait until Michael was ready. "Ye need ta go *now!*" Startled awake, for Mary never raised her voice, Michael scrambled out of bed and thrust pants over his nightshirt, slippers on his feet, and a hat skewed at a lopsided angle atop his unkempt hair. If Mary wasn't in so much pain, she would have laughed at the strange sight of her wild-eyed husband intent on this sacred mission.

RACING from the bedroom and out the front door, his fear replaced common sense, he left the door ajar. Michael reached the midwife's house in seconds. Pounding on the front door until lights appeared upstairs, a man leaned out the upstairs window and bellowed, "What's the matter with you? Don't you know it's two-thirty in the morning?"

"Mr. Prendergast, 'tis me wife. The baby's ready. We need yer wife ta help."

The man smiled, for he was accustomed to hearing the words of panic from a first-time father. "Mr. O'Malley, I'll send her straight away."

"Put on a kettle of warm water and grab as many clean bed sheets as you can," said Mrs. Prendergast in a calm voice as she appeared in the window beside her husband.

"I can do that!" Michael sprinted back home, shocked to discover the front door was wide open. Racing to Mary's side, Michael told himself to relax. But seeing his wife agonize when a new contraction seized her body, Michael became paralyzed with fear. Fighting helplessness as he stood aimlessly in the doorway, Michael remembered Mrs. Prendergast's advice which gave him a renewed purpose. With the kettle on the stove, he grabbed a handful of sheets, sweat dripping off his forehead, and entered the bedroom. Michael gently approached his wife, dropping the clean sheets at the foot of the bed. "All will be well, me love. Mrs. Prendergast is on the way."

Mary smiled at her husband and reached up to wipe his drenched brow. "Me poor darling. How difficult this is fer ye."

"I never dreamed 'twould be this hard."

Mary smiled at Michael's words of distress until another contraction drew her back to the task at hand.

Much to Michael's relief, Mrs. Prendergast entered the bedroom and rolled up her sleeves. "You best wait in the other room, Mr. O'Malley. Your wife's in good care." She patted Michael on the back and steered him firmly toward the door. He staggered forward on rubbery legs and relished Mrs. Prendergast's advice, "Perhaps you should have a drink to steady your nerves. It's going to be a long night."

Michael managed to make it to the living room. After many drinks over the next few hours to drown his futility upon hearing his wife's screams, Michael finally fell asleep in the chair. He was awakened by Mrs. Prendergast at 10:00 a.m. to the sweetest words he ever heard.

"Would you like to meet your daughter?"

Shaking his head to clear the confusion and sorely wishing he had limited his liquid courage to only one drink, he was able to reply somewhat coherently as he gazed at the newest O'Malley addition. "Oh me goodness. 'Tis a wee lass." He stared into green eyes sparkling like emeralds and stroked her soft tuft of brown hair. "And what of me darling wife?"

"She's fine and resting soundly. But you can take the baby to her room and wait in the rocking chair until your wife awakens. Mrs. O'Malley put in a long night."

The night was equally long for him but he wisely kept the thought to himself. He slowly navigated the hallway while holding onto his infant daughter with the greatest care for fear she would crumble in his arms. Michael sat in the rocker after he proudly presented their daughter to his drowsy wife, whose smile was brilliant enough to light up the entire street.

"Michael, do ye like the name Margaret?"

"Sure, and 'tis a fine name."

Before long, her name was shortened to Marge and being the first-born, she endured the strictest discipline. Unfortunately for her parents, Marge fought rules and regulations throughout her life and refused to be defined by any pre-set standards.

"Marge, 'tis time fer supper," her parents would call out repeatedly.

But Marge refused to budge as she sat on the bench in the hallway, arms folded across her tiny chest, kicking the bench with greater intensity each time she was called. Her reward for independence often ended in nights without supper, but she reveled in being her own boss.

16

William, or Liam as his father fondly called him, made his appearance on November 5, 1916, and became a welcome respite from Marge's stubbornness. With his emerald-green eyes, dark curly hair, and affable sense of humor, he was quick to please and eager to help. William even had a birthmark the shape of a shamrock on his right ankle, undoubtedly proof-positive he was the quintessential embodiment of a true, Irish-American lad.

The following year, Mayme stormed into the O'Malley home bursting with energy and creative talents. Her tantrums became legendary as she attempted to impress upon the world her own unique impression of events and a deep desire to break into show business. Or the circus. Whichever came first.

Ellen was born on February 7, 1920, and despite her entrance into the world with cries loud enough to deafen anyone within a three-block radius, she was a compassionate soul and similar to her brother —even-tempered and eager to please. Ellen had an independent and adventurous nature that often appeared at inopportune times, including a home haircut styled by Ellen on the eve of her first-grade classroom photo. But Ellen's picture was enchanting with her beautiful smile, despite the uneven bob and missing front tooth. She was blessed with an easy-going manner as she tackled each day's adventures with vigor.

Michael became proficient at his expected duties as a father with each succeeding pregnancy. It was clear to all that his love for Mary grew with each new addition.

With the O'Malley clan's expansion of four children by 1920, Michael made a surprise announcement a few weeks before Christmas. "We need ta have a family portrait taken, and we will go ta a studio in two days' time."

"Oh Michael, 'tis wonderful news." Biting her lower lip, Mary asked tentatively, "Would it be possible ta have me mother in one of the pictures?"

Michael magnanimously agreed to include Elizabeth in the treasured remembrance.

Mary was eager to advise her mother of the special honor awaiting, especially with the time constraints of only two days. She walked to Elizabeth's home while Michael watched the children. When her mother opened the door, Mary blurted out the exciting news. "Ma, we have a surprise fer ye."

"Dearie, ye are out of breath. Come in fer a cuppa tea and share the good news."

Mary's breathing returned to normal, after walking two blocks at a quick pace, as she sipped the delicious tea. "Ma, ye are ta be included in a family picture at a professional studio."

When she heard the news, Elizabeth was overjoyed and took special delight in the thoughtful invitation to include her in their family adventure. "'Tis glorious news ta be sure, and I already know what ta wear."

Mary smiled at her mother's comment and knew Elizabeth's wardrobe was meager but cherished.

The contents of Elizabeth's closet were sparse and limited to old-fashioned clothes. Most outfits dated back to the 1880s. She was oblivious to her outdated fashion sense and possessed only one dress outfit that she saved for special occasions—a blouse with high, puffy sleeves covered with a white bib collar draping her shoulders and chest over a narrow-waisted, floor-length, black skirt. Despite snickers and ridicule from other women on the rare occasions she ventured from home, Elizabeth maintained her dignity and pitied those with nothing better to do than judge others based on their outward appearance.

When the big day arrived, everyone was bursting with excitement although most of the work fell to Mary. As she corralled each of her two older daughters, who jumped up and down in anticipation, Mary managed to dress them in their finest Sunday clothes, combed their hair and placed large bows to the side, polished shoes, and attempted to dispel their restlessness. Mary placed Ellen in her christening gown, passed down many generations in Ireland. Finally, Mary had some time to dress and fix her own hair while Michael, already dressed in his best suit sporting his prized watch fob on a shiny gold chain, dressed William. But Marge and Mayme became fidgety waiting for their mother and decided baby Ellen needed to look more festive. They sneaked into their mother's bedroom and grabbed the rouge from her small makeup container before returning to a cooing Ellen in her bassinet.

"Watch Mayme, I've seen Ma do this a lot." With the greatest of care but uncertain of the amount to use, Marge applied rouge to Ellen's cheeks, lips and since her nose appeared a wee bit pale, applied some there as well. Standing back to look at her handiwork, Marge asked Mayme, with the insight of a three-year-old, if she liked the end result. Mayme nodded vigorously but Mary screamed when she entered the room and saw a baby clown ready for the circus.

"What have ye girls done ta me baby girl?"

Giving Ellen another look, Marge and Mayme realized Ellen's face was a little red and splotchy.

"We're sorry Ma. We just wanted to help."

The girls jumped when their mother entered the room and saw her astonished look. Fearful, they began to cry but Mary quickly intervened knowing reddened, puffy faces wouldn't be very appealing for their family photo. She quietly admonished her daughters and told them if they cleaned Ellen's face, she wouldn't tell their father. Mary had never seen two girls move so swiftly as they remedied their mistake and returned Ellen to her almost-natural color. All the scrubbing gave Ellen's cheeks an even rosier glow and she looked beautiful in her lovely christening gown.

On the way to the studio, their horse-drawn carriage picked up Mary's mother also dressed in her Sunday best—a long, black dress with a large bib collar and a decorative broach in the middle, hair unadorned and tied back in a bun.

When they entered the building, everyone was impressed with the lavish selection of displays for family photographs. They selected one suitable for their family size, and the photographer chose the placement of family members—Michael and Mary sat at opposite ends with Ellen on Mary's lap, Elizabeth, affectionately called Nana by her grandchildren, sat in the center.

When it came to arranging the position of William and Mayme, things went awry. It was decided William should be placed in front of their father and Mayme should sit on a stool between her mother and grandmother. Mayme was not happy with this arrangement and wanted the place of honor in front of her father. When she confirmed this wasn't going to happen, Mayme had one of her world-class temper tantrums. She sprawled out on the rug, and her body stiffened like a rigid board. Intent on getting her way, Mayme was prepared to hold this position until placed in the location she desired. But her mother whispered something in Mayme's ear. She reluctantly took her place on the stool, but her arms were folded on her small chest and a scowl clearly reflected her opinion of this wonderful adventure.

After the picture was taken and they headed back to the carriage, Michael took Mary aside and asked, "What did ye say ta Mayme?"

"I reminded her that God was watching and would not like her behavior." As a good Catholic, Mary understood the power of guilt and used it like a weapon to keep her children in line whenever they strayed from expected behaviors or responses.

Michael smiled at his brilliant wife, took Ellen from her arms, and held her until they reached the carriage. While he held his infant daughter, Ellen delighted in playing with her father's most treasured possession—his shiny, gold pocket watch.

Three weeks later, Michael and Mary received the prints from the photographer and narrowed their selection down to two—one without Mary's mother, which prominently displayed Michael's gold pocket watch and the other with Nana Ginley and Mayme's defiant pose. They laughed out loud as they chose the picture including Nana as the family photograph. When the final print was delivered and framed, it brought a smile to their faces for it was typical Mayme behavior, endearing in its own way.

The next day, Elizabeth was invited over for dinner, and while playing with her grandchildren heard her daughter call out, "Ma, please come here. We have a surprise fer ye."

Elizabeth came into the parlor, where all the O'Malleys gathered to witness her expression.

"And what could be the reason fer summoning me like a hired hand?" Despite the harsh words, Elizabeth grinned as she awaited her surprise.

Mary handed her mother a present covered in the finest foil gift wrap topped with a beautiful bow and streamers. Elizabeth took her time opening the present, careful to preserve the lovely wrappings. Marge, not exactly gifted with patience, started fidgeting and decided some nudging was in order.

"Hurry, Nana. We can't wait!"

"Shush, Marge, and try ta enjoy the moment fer yer Nana."

Sulking, Marge managed to stop squirming for a minute. Just as she was about to open her mouth again, Elizabeth was finally able to see the long-awaited surprise.

"Oh, 'tis beautiful. Me own family portrait and meself with the place of honor in the center. Ye are so thoughtful ta remember me with this treasure." After giving Michael and Mary a hug, she said to Michael, "Would ye be kind enough ta hang it in me room when ye bring me home?"

"'Twould be me honor."

Everyone clapped, including Elizabeth, as her sparkling blue eyes leaked tiny drops of pure happiness. Marge, William, and Mayme rushed to her side and enveloped her in loving hugs and kisses. The day was so special it forged a cherished and enduring memory about rewards of charitable acts doled out to enrich the lives of others.

17

Elizabeth Ginley was a grandmother many times over, now that her children were married and settled in Cleveland. She spent many of her days helping to care for her grandchildren and delighted in pampering the little ones in her care.

When Michael and Mary needed to attend a wake, Elizabeth was delighted to watch Marge, William, Mayme, and Ellen.

"Now ye should be going on yer way. Sure, and yer children will be just fine," Elizabeth said as she gently shooed her reluctant daughter out the front door. It was the first time both Mary and Michael would be away from their children.

With Ellen asleep in her crib, Elizabeth turned to her remaining young charges. With a twinkle in her eye, she asked, "What shall we be doing?"

Giggling, Marge, William, and Mayme decided to play hide and seek with Nana. Elizabeth covered her eyes while Marge snuck behind the curtains with her feet clearly visible. William sat in a chair with a napkin covering his face. He kicked his feet in the air, certain no one could see him. Mayme hid under the coat tree, also naïve about her conspicuous location. Dutifully, Elizabeth counted to twenty before she mimicked an arduous search.

"Now where could those children be? Sure, and I cannot find them." Chuckles could be heard from all three, pleased they selected places their nana would be hard-pressed to find. After pretending to search for ten minutes, Elizabeth said, "Perhaps they have taken it into their heads ta run away from home? Dearie me, whatever will I tell their parents?"

Unfortunately for William, he sneezed and his hiding place was instantly revealed as the napkin flew across the room.

"Bless ye, darling child. I thought ye left the house." William couldn't suppress a belly laugh, convinced he had fooled his wise nana. "Shall we look fer yer sisters together, lad?"

William nodded enthusiastically and ran into the living room, pointing to the feet protruding from the floor-length curtains and under the coat tree. Elizabeth put her finger to pursed lips, and William covered his mouth with chubby hands to prevent squeals of laughter from erupting.

"Dear lad, seems yer sisters're gone. Shall we bake some cookies and wait fer their return?"

William's response was clear when he ran into the kitchen and stood on a chair to help his nana. Selecting ingredients for the batter, Elizabeth was unable to locate one essential ingredient.

"Where could the chocolate be fer the cookies? Sure, and we cannot bake without them."

From behind the curtain, Marge called out, "Above the sink."

Elizabeth calmly replied, "Thank ye, Marge," and went about the task of baking. When the smell was overpowering, and William asked to eat a gazillion cookies—after all, Nana was in charge, and she allowed *anything*—Marge magically appeared to partake in the fun.

"Sweet child, where did ye come from?"

William placed his pudgy hands over his mouth to stifle his laughter.

"I had the best hiding place of all. Behind the curtains," Marge said, pointing to the living room.

"'Tis a grand place. We would never have found ye, is that not right, William?" Elizabeth winked at her grandson, who grinned at their shared secret.

Appearing in the doorway, hands on her hips and pouting, Mayme dramatically announced, "Did you forget about me?"

She became even more incensed when her statement was greeted with laugher.

But cookies had the power to heal any wounds, and the children waited impatiently for the delectable treat to cool. Once ready, each child ate their fill. They helped to clean the mess when Nana reminded them of the possibility she might not be invited back if their parents returned home to a dirty kitchen.

"'Tis a half hour before yer bedtime. What shall we do now?"

"I want to play outside." Marge spoke as she ran to the front door, but Elizabeth raced ahead of her.

"I'm sorry, Marge. But ye cannot open the door. I schwallowed the key." Elizabeth's brogue made certain words difficult to pronounce. Turning to her young charges, she admonished, "Remember, 'tis not something fer a child ta do. 'Tis a dangerous task only grownups can perform. I need each of ye ta promise me."

Elizabeth heard a chorus of "I promise" from each of her grandchildren and nodded in satisfaction.

When their parents arrived ten minutes later, Marge warned her parents, "You can't come in. Nana schwallowed the key." But Elizabeth mysteriously produced the key. "I coughed it up fer yer parents."

AFTER HEARING THE STRANGE CONVERSATION, Michael and Mary walked into their home with puzzled expressions. Once they smelled the freshly baked cookies, still present on their children's faces, hands, and teeth, they just shook their heads. When Nana was in charge, it was always an adventure. One thing was abundantly clear—her grandchildren adored her.

18

The following year proved momentous for the O'Malley clan when Marge turned seven years old. She would be the first O'Malley to receive her First Holy Communion in their new homeland. In second grade at St. Patrick's School, Marge learned basic catechism lessons and practiced for the big day.

One week before any child could receive the Body of Christ, they had to make their First Confession. After gathering children from all three classrooms of second graders, Father Blair instructed them on the process required in the confessional and told them to make a list of sins to confess before absolution could be granted. Each child concentrated on misdeeds they may have committed and, later that afternoon, they were taken to the church. Several priests assisted with the large number of those receiving their first confession. Marge was last in line because she was still compiling her list of transgressions. When her turn finally arrived, she tremulously entered the confessional and knelt down.

As instructed, she spoke words memorized by her class. "Please bless me, Father, for I have sinned. This is my first confession and I've committed the following sins." After twenty minutes passed, Father Blair erupted from his side of the confessional clearly frazzled.

Mary waited with the other second grade mothers in church but started to panic when she alone remained and couldn't see Marge anywhere in the church. Just then, she saw Father Blair running out of the confessional with Marge in hot pursuit of the beleaguered priest.

"But Father, I'm not done yet." Shaking his head, Fr. Blair mumbled, "Child, I'm certain God will forgive all your sins. Just whisper them in your prayers."

Marge complied with Fr. Blair's suggestion and began her penance of ten Hail Mary's as only Marge could. "Hail Mary, full of grapes . . ."

WITH THIS ORDEAL BEHIND HER, Mary took her daughter to the Catholic supply store where Marge selected a First Communion dress and matching veil. Marge selected a dress bedecked with fake pearls and rhinestones to complement a veil of similar appearance. A week earlier, Mary had taken her daughter to the shoe store for patent leather shoes. Marge polished them daily using Vaseline until they shone "like a duck's foot," one of her mother's quaint sayings. Marge tingled with excitement as she counted the days until the big event and barely slept the night before. All second graders were instructed to meet in their respective classrooms at 8:00 a.m. sharp and from there, they would line up for the procession into a church packed with family and friends.

But on Marge's big day, Ellen woke up crying with a slight fever, and the entire household was thrown into a tizzy. Michael and Mary plied her with cold compresses and new-fangled ice pops in her favorite flavor. Nothing seemed to work as precious minutes ticked by and the clock neared 8:00 a.m. with no resolution in sight. Marge anxiously sat by herself, ready for her big day but fearful she would miss the festivities. Finally, at 7:45 a.m., Ellen's fever broke, and she fell asleep. Michael and Mary raced upstairs to freshen up and dress for Marge's big day. William was sent next door to ask the neighbor to watch Ellen, who gladly accepted when William extended an invite to the post-event festivities. Worried they might have ruined Marge's big day, the O'Malleys didn't arrive at St. Patrick's Church until half past eight.

"But I'm late, what if—" began a fearful and upset Marge.

In a firm voice, Mary told her daughter, "Go ta yer classroom. I am certain someone will be there ta help ye." Mary began to pray quietly that her advice would prove accurate.

After sprinting to her classroom, Marge found it empty. A feeling of hopelessness overcame Marge, so she sat on the floor and cried feeling desperate and alone.

"Can I help you?" Sister Mary Mel asked, as she carefully approached Marge.

Marge wiped her tears away with the back of her hand, her voice quavered. "I—I missed my class and now I won't make my First Communion." Hearing those words aloud brought a fresh round of sobbing.

"There, there." Pulling Marge up from the floor, the nun understood Marge's fear for it was quickly approaching 9:00 a.m. when the mass would begin. Sr. Mary Mel had passed the First Communicants organized in the hall and knew the timing for their church grand entrance was tight. She enveloped Marge in a warm caress and reassured her. "Let's go into the main hall and see if we can find your classmates."

Hiccupping, Marge whispered, "Do you think I'll make it?"

"My dear, when God's involved, there's always a chance." Pulling out a handkerchief from her pocket, Sister Mary Mel gently wiped away Marge's tears and readjusted her lopsided veil. "You are beautiful. Shall we search for your friends?"

Hearing the compliment, Marge smiled and felt a glimmer of hope. "Yes, Sister."

Entering the school's main hall together, they found all the children lined up, practically jumping up and down unable to contain their jubilation. Sister Mary Mel approached another nun, explained the problem, and found Marge's place in the queue moments before they paraded into church. As the procession advanced, they passed water fountains covered up to prevent anyone from sipping water, since fluids after midnight prohibited receipt of Communion.

The evening before the big event, Mary had given her daughter a home perm using Silmerine. A neighbor gave a sample to Mary for Marge's big day. It was applied using a toothbrush to spread the cream evenly into Marge's hair before securing bobby pins to assure curly hair. But Marge's hair turned into two fuzz balls—one on either side of her head. When her teacher saw Marge, she quickly approached.

"Marge, would you mind if I comb your hair?"

"Of course not, Sister." But when the comb broke off in Marge's steadfast hairstyle, which the Sister believed would last a millennium, she knew resistance was futile and meekly said, "Marge, your hair is beautiful." Marge glowed from the perception of her beauty because nuns would never lie.

When Michael and Mary saw their beautiful Marge confidently proceed into church beaming so brightly, they sighed in relief. Seated near the back due to their late arrival, the O'Malley family stood when they saw Marge kneeling at the altar with her classmates—William was perched on his father's shoulders and Mary lifted Mayme to witness the splendor. Mary's eyes brimmed with tears as Marge began her sojourn into God's family.

After Mass was over, the children again formed a procession down the main aisle to the *oohs* and *ahhs* of congregants, as the children proudly headed toward the church's main steps. A reception was held at the O'Malley home and Marge was right where she wanted to be— the center of attention. It would be a day she'd remember the rest of her life.

19

By the time Veronica graced the O'Malley family with her arrival, nine-year-old Marge was the only one to notice their mother's weight gain. Despite wearing extra layers to hide her expanding girth for previous pregnancies, none of the children were aware of their mother's pregnancy weight gain.

However, by Easter Sunday in 1923, Marge was more perceptive and noticed her mother was getting plump—even taking into account extra clothes. She'd heard her aunts mention many times it was impolite to ask anyone about their weight. Marge puzzled what it could be. She wouldn't accept the possibility of her mother being sick and decided she was just eating too much. Marge wanted to help her mother lose weight.

"Ma, I don't think you need that extra piece of pie."

Her mother just gave her the oddest look. By July 4, 1923, when her parents hosted a family holiday get-together, her normally trim mother was becoming huge, and she didn't know what to do. And then she had a brilliant, albeit non-too-subtle, idea using her favorite stuffed animal.

"Ma, can we set an extra place for Happy Hippo? He's on a diet and won't eat much."

"Of course, ye can, me darling."

Marge dragged an extra chair, complete with three pillows so Happy could reach the table and set a small plate and spoon in front of him. "Now Happy, remember. You're on a diet, so you only get one pea and one piece of corn." Marge was proud of herself believing she skillfully made her point, but her parents just laughed. Frustrated, Marge continued to carry Happy Hippo at every meal with gentle reminders not to eat so much.

Two months later, on September 23, 1923, the unthinkable happened. Her worst fears were confirmed when a neighbor rushed over to care for her mother. Marge thought her mother must be sick, and her plan to reduce her mother's weight had been a failure. For some unknown reason, her father turned the radio volume up louder than she had ever heard before. *Maybe he's going deaf? I have my work cut out for me.*

Fortunately for their mother, it was a gorgeous day outside with warm sunshine, a slight breeze, and a perfect temperature of 75 degrees.

"Why don't ye all go outside and play with yer friends?"

"But Da, we have to do our chores first or Ma will be upset," said Marge as she thought, *Clearly, he doesn't know the house rules, and I don't want to be punished.*

"Yer Ma gave her permission, this one time, not ta do yer chores before playing. But ye must come inside when I call."

"We will, Da." The children, except Marge, agreed before rushing outside to avoid giving him time to change his mind.

But Marge hung back and fretted. "Da, maybe I should stay inside in case you or Ma need my help." Marge's worried expression deepened as she fought indecision over having fun or duty as the oldest.

She stopped fidgeting when her father responded, "Marge, it would make yer Ma so happy ta know ye helped yer younger siblings."

Relieved to receive her father's permission to play outside, she tried to be sad but couldn't quite carry it off because playing outside sounded like so much fun.

Just as they completed their outdoor missions of conquering new worlds, warding off invaders, and capturing bank robbers, their father called them back inside. Tired out from their hard work, the band of four came into the kitchen looking for their usual treat of hot chocolate. Instead, the neighbor had placed a bundle on the kitchen table. Perhaps it was a fresh batch of chocolate chip cookies or brownies, why the delicious possibilities were endless.

Marge pulled the cover back and saw it was a doll. No wonder they wanted everyone outside. They wanted them to be surprised by a new toy. But then the doll moved! Tiny feet began to kick, and a shrill scream emitted from the tiny bundle.

"It's a *bay*-be." Marge squealed. Three-year-old Ellen stood on tippy-toes and her eyes barely cleared the tabletop to confirm the miraculous new arrival. Marge-in-charge began leading the posse of four toward their mother's room. "Come on, we gotta tell Ma the surprise."

Their father deftly stepped in front of them, blocking the entrance to their mother's bedroom. "Yer Ma already knows the surprise. She's tired and needs ta rest."

William asked his father with lips trembling in anticipation, "Is it a boy baby or girl baby?"

"A girl baby. Her name is Veronica."

William was heartbroken. "You promised the next one would be a boy."

MICHAEL PICKED UP HIS SON, softly rubbed his back, and said, "It's up ta God if it's a boy or girl. Perhaps the next one will be a boy." William's sobs increased until hiccups took his mind off this calamitous event. Through sheer exhaustion, he fell asleep on his father's shoulder and was placed in his bed for a much-needed nap.

Over the next week, neighbors took turns caring for their mother and Veronica. The children were able to visit for thirty minutes each day, provided they were quiet and didn't overexert their mother.

Three days later, their mother was able to eat one meal a day at the kitchen table with her family enjoying food prepared by neighbors.

Marge couldn't believe how much weight her mother lost and was pleased to learn wishes really did come true.

Filled with courage, Marge asked her mother, "How did you lose all that weight so fast?" She secretly hoped her mother would attribute it to Happy Hippo but was astonished at the response.

Her mother blushed and said she was carrying their newest sibling next to her heart. Marge was devastated. *Oh no! Ma ate baby Veronica!* She'd have to be on her best behavior or maybe she'd be eaten, too. Life just got more complicated.

Whenever Marge noticed her mother gaining more than a few pounds, the first thing she did was run around the house to make certain her mother didn't eat any of her siblings. To her relief, everyone was always present and accounted for. It sure was a lot of work being the oldest.

For William, forgiveness was slow in arriving, and it was several weeks before he ventured near life's new disappointment. The day finally arrived when he passed by her bedroom and heard her cooing in her crib. *Guess it couldn't hurt to take a look. I already know I won't like her, so there's no danger.* He cautiously entered the traitor's bedroom and much to his surprise, instantly fell in love with the adorable infant extending her tiny arms up for attention. He picked her up and sat down to gently bounce her up and down on his knee.

Without William's knowledge, his siblings and parents were outside the room watching a miraculous sight appear right before their eyes. With a sigh of relief, everyone quickly dispersed when he carefully set Veronica back in her crib.

William didn't mention his attitude reversal toward the newest addition and attempted to affect nonchalance when she was near. But she kept cooing with her arms raised toward William. He soon realized resistance was futile.

20

Since the early 1900s, engineering advancements propelled the nation into an era of exciting possibilities. Cleveland was no exception; it embraced scientific discoveries by sponsoring the Cleveland Electrical Exposition in 1914. While the event caused a stir among skeptics, it highlighted the versatility of modern miracles. The switch to illuminate East 13th Street on May 20, 1914, was thrown by Thomas Edison at the Exposition. The result was breathtaking—a street brilliantly lit with streetlamps and hanging lights that crossed and dipped in the center from one side of the street to the other. Cleveland became the first city to achieve national acclaim in the field of electricity.

Although power was available in Cleveland, electric streetlights on Carroll Avenue would not be installed until the early 1920s. Prior to that, a city employee would walk down the street every night carrying a stepladder propped against the lamppost to access the gas outlet and ignite the flame. This process would be repeated throughout the neighborhood and reversed at dawn. With the installation of streetlights on Carroll Avenue, the children would gather around this marvelous gift of illumination, proud to have it installed in front of their home.

However, Michael O'Malley did not appreciate the light placed on the tree lawn. The home was so brightly lit it was impossible to sleep and he could no longer sneak a cigarette on the porch swing at night without the entire neighborhood bearing witness. So, he did the only thing he could. He climbed a ladder late one night with a can of black paint and covered half the offending light facing his home. He never had requested this dubious honor.

Michael was quite pleased with himself; but the City of Cleveland was not. They slapped fines on him and replaced the light fixture, which Michael promptly painted the next day. It became a battle of wills until the city finally moved the streetlight to another location.

The O'Malley children, like their counterparts the world over, loved to stay up late playing games of marbles or hide-and-seek. But their exhausted parents insisted on turning out all lamps by 8:30 p.m.

Each night the children whined in unison, "But Da, we can't see."

"Then stick a finger in yer eye, and ye will see starlight."

Michael clearly had issues with technology.

THE HOME at 3014 Carroll Avenue was abuzz each morning as children raced to complete their chores before the O'Malley brood was unleashed on the neighborhood. Once outside, they were transfixed each time they witnessed a car motoring down Carroll Avenue. When the driver saw the gaggle of children, he sounded his horn as a warning. But, to them, it was a clarion call of a magnificent contraption filled with beautifully dressed occupants—why, the ladies even had special hats with scarves tied beneath their chin. Knowing their father's abhorrence of newfangled horseless carriages, the older children considered it their duty to change his mind. And the younger siblings were happy to support this worthy cause, even if they didn't fully understand its importance. As the days passed by, the ever-increasing number of cars driving down Carroll Avenue made them feel as though life's newest mode of transportation was rolling past them—literally. They decided their father needed to enter the modern world and vowed, despite past failures, to convince him otherwise.

"Da, you could get to work quicker if you had a car. Can we *paleese* buy one?" Mayme asked in her most theatrical voice, sure to convince her stubborn father.

"Everyone has one but us." Not even close to the truth, but ten-year-old Marge thought it was a convincing argument.

"Nonsense. Ye do not need one. Ye can easily catch a streetcar at four locations, all close by—Lorain Road, Madison Avenue, West 25th Street, or Fulton Road."

"But Da, we don't have the money."

"Then ye can walk."

"But it's exhausting—with a car, we'd never get tired." Marge knew she was pushing her luck but figured one last try wouldn't hurt.

"If ye get tired, then saddle a cat."

Once again, Michael had an answer for everything.

21

Over the next four years, the O'Malleys were blessed with two additional children. James would follow in 1925 with his gregarious and outgoing temperament, animated hazel eyes, and beautiful, strawberry-blond hair. Thomas would round out the O'Malley children in 1927 with sky-blue eyes, thick, blond hair, ruddy complexion, and a devilish attitude to mix things up.

Each day began the same. In the early morning, Mary O'Malley would climb a stepladder in the kitchen to light a tall gas jet rising to the ceiling. Light and cooking fuel would be provided throughout the day until the process was reversed at day's end. Each night, Mary placed a placard in the front window for the ice man, denoting the next day's need for ice, ranging from twenty-five to one hundred pounds. Milk was delivered weekly, and the cream was scooped off the top for use in their tea—a rare luxury enjoyed by Michael and Mary with immense pleasure.

Mary meticulously cared for the home she dearly loved. The first floor consisted of a parlor—rarely used except for company—the living room, four bedrooms, and the kitchen—the heart of any home. The second story contained two bedrooms set apart from the attic. Michael constructed a full basement by digging under the house to provide storage space. It also contained a coal chute and steps leading to the cellar doors, which opened outward to the backyard. The front porch graced the entire front of the home with steps down the side and a railing to provide support.

The O'Malley home was different from similar residences on Carroll Avenue because it became *the* place for kids to hang out. There was always an air of excitement and gaiety, childish pranks, singing, and absolute joy, which permeated their home.

Dares were commonplace and bravery proven by accepting a challenge. Even the spokes on the front porch railing became a beacon to children as they attempted to prove their fearlessness.

"Betcha can't wiggle through the railing spoke." William taunted his friend.

"I dunno. Looks kinda narrow." Deland was shaking in fear and his voice rose a notch, fully aware what was at stake.

"Well, I did it, but if you're afraid . . ." William left the declaration unfinished to underscore the implied threat.

"No, no, I can do it."

And just like everyone before him, Deland succumbed to peer pressure, and his head was jammed between the spokes. Pure panic threw his test of fortitude and pride out the window. He cried and screamed until Mary ran onto the front porch. By now, he was the fourth victim that Mary had to dislodge from the intrepid railing spokes.

Turning to William and his band of cohorts, she said, "Ye better stop daring boys ta stick their heads between the posts. 'Tis the last time I'll save them. And if there is a next time, ye will all be properly punished." Mary directed her rage at William. "And ye will be washing and drying dishes fer the next week."

Despite William's punishment, and the implied threat for the others, the neighborhood boys giggled as they watched the latest victim freed, clearly forgetting their own terrifying experiences.

ON BEAUTIFUL SUNNY DAYS, the O'Malley children and their counterparts in Ohio City thoroughly enjoyed the playground next to a public grade school on West 41st Street. Racing down the slide, swinging up to the clouds, and navigating the monkey bars with vigor worked up quite an appetite. Best of all, there was a candy store right across the street where they could purchase penny candy and enjoy a respite from their hard work. They took their sweets to the O'Malley front porch to enjoy their delectable treats while sharing jokes and humorous tales as the day wound down.

But, like everything else, all fun had to end. At 8:00 p.m., Michael would clear the porch with a simple proclamation. "'Tis time ta say the rosary." Children flew off the porch and ran home as fast as their tiny legs could carry them, joyous to escape a calamity of magnanimous proportions.

22

All the O'Malley children attended St. Patrick's grade school, where kindness, courtesy, and the absence of swearing were the mainstays of expected behavior. This became a challenge when boys in the playground tried to imitate tough posturing to boost their dominance, a difficult task with the nuns constantly watching their every move. Their dilemma was solved by developing their own lingo.

"Jeffrey, stop pushing me."

"Aw, go to . . ."

A scowling nun towered above him. The threat was completed by adding "heaven and make a U-turn."

But the absolute best "class" at St. Patrick's School was gym— escaping from boring subjects for an hour of playtime. The boys attended gym class on Tuesdays, and the girls were forced to wait until Friday.

One particular Tuesday, after the boys had trooped off to gym, Sr. Victoria decided it was time to teach the young ladies in her class the Christian way to interact with boys, even at a school dance.

"Now girls, remember never to wear patent leather shoes."

"Why not, Sister?" one inquisitive student asked.

"So a boy can't see up your dress."

Her response sent giggles throughout the classroom until Sr. Victoria gave them "the look".

"And don't use a white tablecloth if you invite a boy over for dinner." Seeing the quizzical expressions on her student's faces, she added, "He may think of a bedsheet."

No amusement was generated by this remark. Instead, stunned faces with open-mouthed expressions were directed at Sr. Victoria. Misinterpreting their reaction as amazement at her imparted wisdom gave her the courage to continue her pointed lessons. "When dancing together, make sure your bodies are at least twelve inches apart." Silence greeted Sr. Victoria's lessons, and she thought the message on remaining chaste was better received than she dreamed.

"Who wants to hang out with a bunch of dumb boys anyway?" All the girls nodded, and the dreaded "talk" was over. Sr. Victoria wondered if, next time, she should share her words of wisdom with an older audience.

23

It was unfortunate that every nun at St. Patrick's did not exhibit patience and understanding. When Marge was in the sixth grade, she was in Sr. Gerard's class, a nun well beyond her teaching expiration date. Slightly stooped and resentful of the youth staring back at her—a daily reminder her competence was slowly declining due to early-onset senility—made for some unusual and unpredictable behavior. At times, presumably for self-amusement, she would sing, "I'm a Little Teapot" and perform a childlike dance in front of the glass. Remarkably, no one made fun of her, until she ran out of the classroom.

Unknown to them, Sr. Gerard remained outside the door and listened to all the disparaging comments. Sadly for her students, Sr. Gerard's only fully intact sensory function was her impeccable hearing. She would return to the classroom and give detention to any students who had mocked her. After her first display, the students remained silent when she left the room.

Each fall, the annual candy sale fundraiser for school improvements became a competition between students, with the winner awarded a day off school. To kick off that year's campaign, Sr. Gerard asked the children to sell candy on their lunch hour. Each child agreed except Marge, who had promised her mother to run errands at noon. Sr. Gerard asked Marge to remain behind when the class was dismissed at lunch. Although the nun screamed and ranted at Marge, Marge couldn't hear because her ears were ringing from the open-fisted slap to her face delivered with great force.

She ran home and fortunately her father was taking a rare lunchtime break away from a job site. Michael noticed his daughter's bruised and reddened face bearing the imprint of an adult hand and asked Marge who delivered the blow. He reacted instantly and called the convent.

Michael spoke to Sr. Gerard with a warning, barely containing his fury, his brogue thickened with rage. "This here's Michael O'Malley, and ye slapped me darling Marge. If anyone ever touches me children again, I will be contacting the police and ye will be in jail. If things are not ta be getting better, 'tis certain I will report ye ta Mother Superior fer the harshest punishment she can give ye. Do ye hear me, or do ye need meself ta come down ta the convent fer further discussion?"

Fearful of retribution from Mother Superior, Sr. Gerard relented and apologized to Michael. But the interaction merely served to increase her bitterness toward Marge, treating her with contempt and assigning her chores no one else wanted.

In frustration, Marge sought guidance from Principal Sr. Madie Katherine, well- known for her compassion and wisdom.

"How can I help you, Marge?"

With her head bowed in shame, acutely aware her attempt to seek guidance from her teacher's superior could backfire, Marge stated her case. "Sr. Gerard treats me harshly and refuses a kind word. The tasks I'm expected to complete are difficult, and everyone makes fun of me. It's just not fair."

Marge was unaware Sr. Madie Katherine had previously spoken to Sr. Gerard against the use of corporal punishment and the severe repercussions Sr. Gerard would receive if she defied the principal's edict. She was also cognizant of Sr. Gerard's unjust disciplinary measures doled out to Marge. Sr. Madie Katherine decided this was the perfect teachable moment for a young lady whose legendary beauty garnered favor among students and teachers in spite of her stubborn streak.

"Marge, you never know the suffering that many tackle on a daily basis, especially if their source of misery isn't visible. Feeling helpless in dealing with their own pain, they often take their frustrations out on others through unkind remarks or callous behavior. Sr. Gerard has reached a point in her life where her body doesn't always respond the way she would like, while her mental acuity is declining. Despite this, she has the strength to face young people each day whose bright futures lay ahead of them. This results in making her more aware of her own deficiencies. I'm not excusing her behavior, but in the future try to keep your judgment in perspective by making yourself aware of possible struggles a person may be experiencing. Do you understand?"

"Yes, I do, and I never thought of it like that. Thank you, Sister."

Sr. Madie Katherine decided to teach Marge one more lesson. "There's really only one thing you can count on. Life is unfair. Others may find their path easier with possessions, opportunities, or physical attributes. But once you accept life wasn't meant to be fair and discover your own natural abilities, your path will become less stressful and more productive. Never show weakness if someone is unkind to you, but do as Our Lord taught us—turn the other cheek and replace something bad with something good. Do this and your life will flourish."

From that moment on, Marge treated Sr. Gerard with utmost respect and in time, she became a favorite student of the intractable nun. Marge also shared Sr. Madie Katherine's insights with her classmates who, in turn, responded with kindness toward the elder nun. Later on in life, Marge and Sr. Gerard would become friends and seek comfort in one another's company.

Marge marveled at Sr. Madie Katherine's wisdom and did indeed learn lessons to ease burdens throughout her life.

24

For a toddler, curiosity had no age limits—although the victim of a home-based experiment was usually someone close in age. Veronica and Ellen were three years apart in age but some would say they were of one mind. Both had a fun-loving nature and peaceful manner. They played together and shared invented secrets to elicit nonstop giggles.

But Veronica would prove to be the more spirited of the two. At four years old, she spotted a newly cleaned platter drying on the counter and wondered what would happen if she brought it down on Ellen's head. So, she did and, sure enough, pandemonium followed. Ellen screamed and cried when blood poured down her face and the broken platter fell to the floor.

Hearing Ellen's cries, Veronica attempted to make a fast escape, but her mother caught her dress as she flew by. "And where would ye be off ta, young lady?"

"Me want to—" but words were caught in Veronica's throat as the thought of a spanking from her father brought tears to her eyes. Her screams became louder than her sister's.

"What the devil is going on in this house?" Michael bellowed as his two young daughters wailed—one in pain, the other in fear. Seeing the blood on Ellen's face brought him to an abrupt halt. In spite of her young age, Veronica knew her only hope was to throw herself at her father's feet and beg for mercy.

With the limited vocabulary of a four-year-old, Veronica tried to plead her case. "Da, me try—" but Michael was swift with his paddle and sent little Veronica up to her room for the afternoon. At dinner, a pillow was placed on her seat to dull the pain. After giving her sister a hug and apologizing for hurting her best friend, peace once again reigned in the O'Malley household. Before long, Veronica and Ellen continued their forays into tomfoolery that elicited belly-laughs sure to lift the spirit of anyone within earshot.

But the oldest, Marge, spent her time in more sensible undertakings. In every spare moment, she pursued her love of reading and was rarely seen without a book tucked under her arm. Marge had grown into a beautiful young lady with soft chestnut curls framing her heart-shaped face, twinkling green eyes, and a smile to dazzle even the most downhearted. Fortunately, her beauty was equaled by her intelligence, which was enhanced by her passion for reading.

"Ma, you'll never guess what I got!" Marge waved a card as she entered the house on a lovely summer afternoon.

"Me dear, sure, and they can hear ye on the next block. And fer what reason are ye making all the fuss?"

Marge beamed as she presented her mother with a special pass to sign out books from the adult section—a first-time occurrence and singular honor for a twelve-year-old. Marge's intelligence, combined with a thirst to devour books in the Carnegie West Library, allowed her to zip through the children's section at lightning speed.

"Saints be praised, me darling! What an honor. Yer Da will be so proud."

With the confidence she earned from her love of reading, Marge decided to pursue other interests, which included modeling.

25

While her sister dreamed of contests to showcase her beauty, Ellen was completely clueless about her own natural attributes. But she was discovering a new experience that equally amazed and terrified her. Many dreams, or strong feelings of future events, were coming true. Ellen wondered if she was cursed and discussed it with her mother. Mary reassured Ellen her gift was a blessing known by the Irish as the gift of "fae"—also known as clairvoyance.

"'Tis a beautiful and magical treasure ta be used wisely," Mary advised. Ellen nodded solemnly in agreement.

That night, Ellen had a dream her friend would need assistance the next day during school, and her faith would be tested.

Ellen's new friend from St. Patrick's, Maeve O'Sullivan, possessed beautiful dark hair down to her waist, olive-colored skin, and warm brown eyes. Maeve's parents recently migrated from Ireland and moved into Carroll Avenue. Both families often gathered to share tales of Irish folklore and sing their favorite tunes.

But Ellen soon discovered that Maeve's father had a temper borne from the stress of learning a new language and holding down a job. Ellen tried to help her friend whenever she could to prevent the beating sure to follow if Maeve was late or disobeyed their stringent rules. When their teacher, Sr. Dominica—a kindly but often strict nun —caught Maeve answering a question from another student, she placed both names on the blackboard to deter talking in class.

"Because the two of you didn't pay attention when you were supposed to be quiet, you will stay after class for one hour." Ellen immediately turned toward Maeve who turned whiter than snow and knew her friend was in for a thrashing.

When the children were lined up to return home for lunch, Ellen partnered with her friend and reassured her. "Don't worry Maeve. I'll help you."

"But how? You know what my father will do to me."

"Just keep saying the Hail Mary throughout the day, and I guarantee you'll see a miracle."

"Really?" Maeve asked skeptically, but Ellen's confidence was so strong, she did exactly as her friend suggested.

Together their eyes were glued to the clock as it agonizingly inched its forward movement until their dismissal at 3:30 p.m. Maeve continued to pray silently for the heavenly blessing her friend promised. But by 3:20 p.m., Maeve was beginning to despair until she glanced at Ellen whose nod of assurance and serenity provided comfort. Just then, Sr. Dominica casually erased the day's lessons from the blackboard, including the two student's names assigned detention. Maeve was astonished and looked at her friend. Ellen just smiled and knew her guardian angel watched over her friend. Ellen had prayed since the dire announcement was made earlier. Ellen's childlike faith and growing confidence in her new gift was so strong, she never doubted God would come to her friend's aid. It would be a lesson she would remember when life presented her own challenges.

26

B ut not every home was harmonious—a perfect example lived a few blocks away. Trish Masterson Ginley was livid. Her husband, Patrick, earned a decent wage at The East Ohio Gas Company, and they were without debt. But they still lived with her mother-in-law. Despite Elizabeth's kindness (feelings not reciprocated by Trish, who was consumed with envy), she wanted a home of their own.

Without her knowledge, Patrick had lofty aspirations of purchasing a stately home he admired each day on his bus ride to work. But Patrick was in a dilemma. He believed succumbing to debt resulted in a life of financial regret. Patrick recalled horror stories from his mother about his father's admission to London's Workhouse in his youth. The stigma of being confined to a poorhouse where destitution was punished by grueling work carried an ever-present feeling of shame. Patrick knew workhouses didn't exist in America but the onus of being in debt remained an unconquerable fear.

Patrick's savings were a mere fraction to pay outright for his desired estate. After speaking to his coworkers at the Gas Company, it was the general consensus one particular stock enriched their lives and would greatly improve Patrick's finances. Never one to gamble but anxious to prove his self-worth and stop Trish's constant nagging, Patrick was desperate. He purchased as much of the stock as his savings would permit.

In the beginning, he saw a healthy return. On the day he planned to inform Trish of their good fortune and the fancy home they would soon occupy, the fund crashed . . . and their savings along with it.

When Patrick arrived home that evening, he was fearful of Trish's reaction and uncertain if their marriage would survive. Whatever happiness they shared was usurped by Trish's incessant resentment and jealousy about residing in a home owned by her mother-in-law. When Patrick relayed the devastating news, Trish was apoplectic. But once her rage was spent, she came up with a plan.

Blissfully, Elizabeth was unaware of Trish's discontent or her son's hazardous speculation in the stock exchange. On the evening of their blowup, unaware of the underlying tension, Elizabeth decided to sweep leaves from the front porch. When she sat in a chair near an open window, Elizabeth overheard the painful conversation. She prayed the matter would be peacefully resolved.

"Patrick, you need to tell your mother that we need a home of our own. Since we can no longer afford one thanks to your reckless stock market gamble depleting all our savings, she needs to move out."

"Sure, and ye cannot ask that of me. 'Tis her home."

"If you love me, you'll do the right thing. I will live here with you but not your mother." And Trish withheld her affections until Patrick could no longer bear it and carefully approached his mother.

"Ma, we need ta talk," he began nervously. "Trish feels we should live alone."

Patrick was oblivious his mother had overheard their argument. Crestfallen, Elizabeth whispered to her youngest son, "Are ye asking me ta leave, Patrick?"

"Oh Ma, not me, 'tis Trish."

"I see. I'll ask yer siblings if they will provide me a home."

Patrick trudged back into their shared domicile, ashamed he was evicting his precious mother. To her credit, Elizabeth never complained or resented relinquishing her home but set about the task of finding a new place to live.

Elizabeth first approached her oldest son, Brian. Although he was willing to accommodate his mother, Anna definitely was not. Feeling desperate, Elizabeth approached her daughter, Mary.

"Mary, love, could I live with yer family? Seems Trish wants the apartment fer herself and Patrick. And Brian's wife Anna is feeling the same."

In response to Elizabeth's request, Mary replied automatically, "Of course, Ma. We'd love ta have ye." As she gave her mother a reassuring hug, she planned the best way to approach Michael. Fixing his favorite meal that night and making certain the children were already fed and playing outside, she carefully approached her husband.

"Michael, me darling, ye know how much love I have fer ye."

Michael kissed his wife and sat down to a sumptuous meal. Once he had his fill, Mary broached the delicate subject.

"We need ta have an important talk." Stopping a moment to gather her thoughts, she prayed Michael would be agreeable. "Ye know the difficult life me ma had before she came ta America. Now, she has no place ta live."

"What are ye referring ta? She owns her apartment and even paid cash."

"Trish wants her ta leave so she and Patrick can be alone. Ma asked Brian and although he was thrilled ta help, Anna feels the same as Trish."

"Then where is she . . ." The realization hit home when he glanced at his wife's eyes filling with tears. Michael knew he was defeated. "Then we best make room." Mary hugged her husband and thanked him profusely.

Brian and Patrick were heartbroken to discover they were forcing their mother into a position of homelessness. So, the brothers devised a scheme to help their mother while teaching Trish a lesson in humility. Two days later, when Trish spent the day shopping, a large truck pulled outside Elizabeth's apartment. The brothers loaded their mother's beautiful furniture, bed, linens, dishes, stove, and pump organ, which had buttons, knobs, and an ornate wooden cabinet with an inlaid mirror in the center. After the truck was packed, they brought the treasures back to the O'Malley home.

When Trish arrived home to an empty apartment, she was furious. "What happened to everything?"

Secretly pleased, Patrick said, "Ye threw me ma out, so she took all her things."

"But I wanted to keep her furniture. I was even going to give a few pieces to my sister."

"'Tis too late now. She lives with Mary and is very happy."

"What are we going to do now?"

"Me ma left a mattress in the bedroom. We can sleep there 'til we have money fer proper furniture."

It didn't help when they went over to visit Mary a few days later, and Trish seethed at all the lovely furnishings gracing Mary's home and not hers. And a further insult occurred when Elizabeth plucked out a familiar Irish tune on the pipe organ, and everyone joined the sing-along.

Afterward, Elizabeth sat back and smiled sweetly as she gazed at Trish with compassion. From experience, Elizabeth knew her daughter-in-law would never know serenity until she gave up her selfish ways and embraced harmony in her life.

27

A time-honored axiom that no true coincidences exist would be disputed by the entrance of the Szabos into the O'Malley chronicles. The Szabo family owned the candy store on West 41st Street, an establishment frequented by the children in Ohio City, including the O'Malleys. The business was made prosperous by the Szabos who understood the value of appealing to young customers from the public grade school adjacent to the store.

Regrettably, the cheerful and nurturing atmosphere of the O'Malley home directly contrasted with the life of their only child, Frank. Born on December 21, 1916 in Chicago, his family was true to their gypsy heritage and unhappy to remain in any place too long, Frank's parents—Paul Szabo and his mail-order bride, Emma— reveled in new adventures resulting in a constant upheaval for their only child. Following Frank's birth, the Szabos moved to Cleveland while he was still an infant. Although Paul was fluent in English, he controlled his wife and son by keeping them isolated. They were forbidden to learn English, and communication was limited to Hungarian. Continual abuse by his father with an insular existence forged Frank's personality into a shy and backward child.

Cleveland proved to be a lucrative location and living above the candy store on West 41st Street, the Szabos were able to save money for future endeavors—events that would exacerbate Frank's awkwardness.

"Emma," Paul called out impatiently in their native tongue, "where are you? I have important news."

Emma placed her laundry back in the washtub and dried soapy hands quickly as she raced into the store downstairs. She knew lingering only provoked her husband as she raised her hand to rub a cheek that still bore his handprint.

"Yes, Paul?" Knowing Paul became upset if she didn't look her best, Emma's permanently chapped hands unconsciously tucked recalcitrant wisps of hair behind her ears.

"I just sold the store, and we can finally return home. I've cabled friends in Hungary to begin a search for the largest home on the market. We're returning in style."

"That's wonderful, Paul. When do we leave?"

"Week after next."

"But Paul, that's not enough—"

A loud face slap landed Emma on the floor.

"It's plenty of time. I won't hear another word about it. And can't you keep that child quiet?"

Emma ran back upstairs, reeling from Paul's temper, and consoled her five-year old son, crying from a fall onto already skinned knees. She prayed Frank would calm down before Paul made a trip upstairs. Inspecting Frank's bruised knees, she said softly, "Don't worry, my son. Soon we will leave this tiny apartment and move back to Hungary."

Misunderstanding his mother's statement, and hoping they were not relocating again, Frank innocently replied in Hungarian, "Mama, me not hungry." He enjoyed hearing his mother's laughter—an infrequent delight. Frank's journey would traverse the world as he continued to suffer abuse and neglect at the hands of his father. It would feel like a lifetime before he found happiness, a. concept woven into the fabric of the O'Malley home but absent for young Frank.

28

When the Szabos arrived in Buda, Hungary they were greeted with fanfare by villagers celebrating their former friend who had become rich in the United States.

"Well, lookey who's here! If it isn't the Dollar King."

Word had spread from a letter Paul Szabo sent to his friends advising his upcoming arrival to Hungary. A crowd of friends surrounded Paul while his wife and young son were left to unload the trunks.

"Well, boys," Paul spoke condescendingly, "did you find any large estates for sale? If you're nice to me, I may even allow you to visit."

Guffaws and back-slapping filled the air as Paul basked in the attention, heedless of the burdens his wife and son bore without complaint.

The Szabos settled into the local inn and the following day, Paul and his friends toured the countryside in search of their new home. Emma and Frank were left behind to unpack and establish their life in a new country. When a suitable mansion was found, Paul paid the asking price in cash—an accomplishment that did not go unnoticed and, for many, elicited jealousy.

"If I had that much money, I'd find a prettier wife."

"Not me. I'd have *two* mistresses at my side." Derision-filled exuberance permeated the air as they imagined what they would do with Paul's fortune.

"Did you see his scrawny kid? Good thing his father's rich. I can't see him amounting to much." The gossip, mixed with ridicule borne of envy, continued behind Paul's back from his "friends."

But years later, life intervened to balance the scales when a typhus epidemic swept across Europe.

Frank watched dejectedly from his bedroom window at the funeral procession for the last of his friends expiring from the deadly plague. Despite the rain, Frank was feeling claustrophobic and thought how wonderful it would be to run outside. He knew his parents wouldn't even notice if he left the house. His father rarely acknowledged his presence, and his mother spent most of her time kowtowing to her husband's wishes.

Frank ran through the heavy downpour with careless abandon until he felt himself sliding down a hill into the nearby canal. It would be several hours before Frank could find a proper foothold and escape the raging waters. Shivering with cold, he slowly made his way home. Frank knew his father would beat him for reckless behavior and snuck into his room for dry clothes.

However, within a few days he developed a high fever, and a doctor was summoned. By then, his father discovered Frank's wet clothes and assumed his son was foolish enough to swim in the canal. The thought of his son being in danger from the powerful current of the canal never entered his mind.

"Well, doctor. What do you think?" asked Frank's father, annoyed at the additional medical expense for his son's rash behavior.

"I don't think he'll pull through. You better prepare for the worst." He spoke the harsh words, not unkindly, but with the efficiency of one accustomed to delivering bad news.

"Oh, no, doctor! Not my son. He's all I've got." Frank's mother began sobbing uncontrollably. Filled with despair, Emma felt her only reason for living was disappearing, and she was impotent to stop it.

"It's his fault for wandering around in a storm and swimming in the water. Now stop your blubbering and get supper ready."

Frank's mother, properly chastised, put her head down and began supper preparations. She laid out her husband's meal and retired alone to their bedroom where she could shed tears without invoking her husband's ire.

DISAPPOINTMENT, loneliness, and heartache became mainstays in Frank's life. His lengthy recuperation, involving strict bed rest, lasted almost a year. Despite the slow and tedious process of learning to walk again, Frank's tenacity was indicative of his underlying strength and determination. But this would not be the last time his survival involved learning the basics of mobility and normal activities of daily living.

29

Frank's father became restless and sought another lifestyle change. Emma and Frank had no say in family decisions and were expected to follow Paul's whims. He sold the mansion and purchased a combination farm and flour mill from a Hungarian businessman. It was located in a remote location in Hungary, and the closest neighbor was three miles away. The flour mill was profitable by turning wheat into flour and sold at the market. Everyone wanted white flour, considered to be more refined, and the inferior brown flour was discarded.

Frank's excitement at living on a farm was not diminished by chores that began each day at 5:00 a.m. He watched his mother force-feed their flock of geese until they were large enough to be slaughtered for a sumptuous meal. At first, watching his mother strangle and behead chickens was a shock, especially when the headless animals ran around, bleeding from decapitation until they collapsed. Considering this was an accepted part of farm life, the shock wore off and he became inured to many practices that would never be accepted in civilized society.

But living in the countryside had its drawbacks. When Frank woke up with a blinding pain from a toothache, there was no dentist to ease his suffering. He dealt with the pain by running around the farm until he literally collapsed in exhaustion and fell asleep until the pain roused him. The torture continued until the day when his tooth fell out; he was rewarded with blessed relief.

Frank, eager to learn, was so excited to attend school and finally meet other kids. However, he had to complete his chores prior to his two-mile trek to school, leaving him exhausted before even entering the schoolhouse.

Gradually, his enthusiasm toward school dimmed. The one-room schoolhouse held six different grades taught by a single teacher, and Frank knew he would never receive a proper education. Friendless and living with his abusive father and submissive mother without an outlet or opportunity to improve his mind could have broken other young men. However, Frank's love of books filled the void and became his salvation.

ONE YEAR LATER, Frank was finishing his breakfast when their new life abruptly changed. A stranger showed up at the farm and entered through the front door without even knocking.

"Who are you?" screamed Paul as pieces of toast mixed with spittle spewed forth in shock and anger. "How dare you just walk into my home." Paul yelled as his face reddened with clenched fists preparing to throw the stranger off their property. "You're trespassing, and I'll call the sheriff if you don't leave immediately." Shaking his fist in the air, Paul's intention was clear.

"Me? Who are you? You're living on my farm. My name is Alexander Petrov, and I've lived here with my wife for over ten years. She is staying with her sister until I made sure the home was in good condition."

Both men were equally surprised and upset. They glared at one another, each standing their ground until Alexander broke the silence. "Go ahead, call the sheriff, and we'll settle this once and for all."

Paul reached for the phone and within one hour the lawman arrived to settle the dispute. Smiling, despite feeling righteous anger,

Paul showed his deed to the officer. Crossing his arms across his chest, he turned to Mr. Petrov and smugly boasted, "See? I told you this was my farm and we've been living here more than a year. What proof does this stranger have?"

The sheriff advised the stranger, "This deed seems legitimate. How can you prove ownership? And how do you explain being away for the past year?"

"My deed is registered at the Recorder's Office. Here's proof of my identity." After handing his passport to the investigating officer, he added, "My wife and I have been traveling throughout Europe this past year. As I mentioned to this gentleman . . ." He pointed toward Paul and barely making eye contact with the intruder. "We're staying with my wife's sister temporarily until I was certain our home was fit to occupy."

For the first time, Paul appeared doubtful but maintained his belligerent attitude. "We'll see about that. I'm sure the sheriff will prove we are the proper owners." As he spoke the words aloud, they were tinged with uncertainty.

The sheriff took Paul's deed and Mr. Petrov's passport. "I'll review this information and return tomorrow at 1:00 p.m. with my findings." Turning to Mr. Petrov, he recommended both he and his wife stay the night with his sister-in-law until the matter was settled.

When the sheriff came back the following afternoon to face the two recalcitrant men, he uttered words that left Paul speechless. "Mr. Petrov spoke the truth. He is the true owner of this property and has been for over ten years. Mr. Szabo, we checked into the man who sold you this farm. He's a con man who's been selling bogus deeds to several newcomers in other counties, knowing the owners were away for an extended time."

Paul sputtered. "Where is he now?"

"I'm sorry but we just don't know—he's used several names, but the scheme is always the same. I'm afraid the money you invested is gone forever. If Mr. Petrov is agreeable, perhaps he would allow you one week to pack your belongings."

For the first time in his life, Paul was forced to admit a mistake and apologize for his behavior. Paul fervently desired the true owner would pity him for the unforeseen circumstances and permit them a week's grace period. Sweat covering his brow, Paul could no longer deny the sudden reality—complete bankruptcy with no home or occupation.

Unaccustomed to begging, Paul fidgeted and managed to speak words foreign to his ears. "Mr. Petrov, I'm sorry for the misunderstanding and hope you will allow my wife and son one week to help me pack up our, I mean your, home." Uttering those words from a proud man used to ruling his own domain and those under his control made Paul feel small and unimportant.

In hindsight, Paul wished he hadn't bragged about his wealth to his friends. Now he was forced to endure their ridicule. In the end, Mr. Petrov softened and took pity on Paul and his family, granting them a one-week extension before they were evicted.

Their future bleak, the Szabos were homeless and without funds. Paul took menial jobs to pay passage for his wife and son to return to America. By now, life had become even more difficult for young Frank because the beatings increased as Paul's humiliation grew. It was agreed Emma would secure several jobs in America, and she would send Paul a ticket once they set up temporary housing with Paul's family in Michigan.

FRANK'S SHYNESS, exacerbated by his father's vagabond lifestyle, became a life of misery for their only child. Frank was forced to make friends in a new school several times over with misery underscored by feelings of inadequacy. Frank promised himself that, when he had a family, his children would all attend the same grade school with confidence and security. But until he was self-sufficient and could achieve that goal, Frank would be forced to relocate, bowing to his father's tumultuous urges, while dealing with his growing insecurity.

30

In contrast to Frank's timidity and isolation within his family, William O'Malley was very close to his father and attempted to emulate his hero's every move, sometimes before he should. Fascinated by his father's daily rituals, William was especially mesmerized watching his father shave; it looked so easy, even he could mimic this simple ritual. But first he decided to practice on a willing participant and who better than his sister, Mayme.

"Hey Mayme, want to shave like Da?"

His sister nodded with curls bobbing enthusiastically, proud to be asked by her older brother. William forgot the part about applying shaving cream first and one stroke of the blade down his sister's cheek brought a river of blood pouring down Mayme's face. She wailed so loudly her screams could be heard two blocks away. William, frightened at the sight of blood, and a swift punishment sure to follow, squeezed himself in a nearby cabinet and prayed no one would find him. Ever.

"What the devil is going on here?"

When Michael ran into the bathroom and saw his tiny daughter sitting on the tub's ledge, Mayme was bawling her eyes out as blood dripped onto her clothes. Gasping at the sight, Michael called his wife.

"Mary, come quick. We need yer help. Mayme's had an accident."

He scooped up his daughter and tried to wipe the blood from her face. When Mary entered with a first aid kit, she quickly assessed the situation and told Michael to grab a piece of candy. Mayme's screams quelled as she sucked on the delicious treat while her mother attended to her cut.

"Did William do this, me darling?" asked her father gently.

Mayme nodded and begged for another treat. It would be another six hours before the family finally located William and relief outweighed anger. No one could believe he fit into such a small space, but fear did amazing things. Although William wasn't permitted to play outside for one week, he escaped the dreaded spanking.

Under normal circumstances, logic would have dictated after so many pranks resulting in a bloody mess, the O'Malleys would be inured to the sight of blood. But with the lively brood always up for a new adventure or satisfying curiosities, rational thought would not prevail.

31

Getting off with a light sentence from the shaving fiasco emboldened William as inspiration triggered new antics.

One year later, William and his best friend decided to play catch with Ellen. William stood on the top step of the porch, and his friend planted himself at the bottom. They took turns throwing Ellen up and down the staircase as she giggled, excited to be the center of their wonderful game . . . until one of them missed and Ellen landed on the cement. Her loud screams drew the neighbor's attention as Mary ran toward the source of howling cries. Hearing his mother's approach, William's first impulse was to flee the crime scene—his friend had already sprinted away so quickly he was certainly destined for the Olympics—but William turned around and relented when he saw Ellen in pain and bleeding. William wouldn't leave Ellen's side. Instead, he knelt down next to his sister, attempting to comfort her.

"Aw, Ellen. I'm so sorry. Don't worry, Ma's almost here. You'll be fine in no time."

At that moment, Ellen threw up on her brother. Rushing down the porch steps as she wiped her hands on a rag, Mary panicked at the sight of Ellen bleeding with multiple episodes of vomiting.

"William, fetch Dr. Carns at once." Noticing the vomit on

William's clothing, she quickly added, "Take this rag ta wipe yerself on the way."

William ran at top speed, wiping his top to clean away tangible proof of his shame. Anxiously awaiting the doctor's arrival, Mary carried her daughter into the house and placed her on the couch. Dr. Paul Carns was the neighborhood family doctor and his kind, caring manner to place patients at ease, with a wry sense of humor, made him the favorite of all under his care.

"Marge and Mayme, Ellen's been hurt. Bring me two bowls—one filled with warm water, the other empty—clean rags, glass of water, and a piece of hard candy." Within a few minutes, all requested items were placed next to their mother.

Mary washed away the blood, cleaned up residual vomit, and advised Ellen to rinse her mouth out. Mary gently placed the second bowl next to Ellen. "If ye feel like throwing up, here's a clean bowl."

"Me darling, could ye carefully suck on a piece of candy without getting sick?"

Ellen was weak but nodded, as she managed a small smile at the rare treat. "Yep, but my head hurts."

"Are you okay, Ellen?" Marge inquired, alarmed at the number of bloody rags.

"I feel dizzy and kinda lightheaded."

Hearing the litany of symptoms increasing with each passing minute, Mary began to panic, praying Dr. Carns would arrive quickly. Fortunately, he was in his office. Once William told him of Ellen's symptoms from head trauma after hitting cement, he grabbed his black bag and drove at a perilous speed to the O'Malley home.

Quickly exiting the car, William urged him, "Go right in. My ma's expecting you."

Seeing Dr. Carns, Mary ran to tell him of Ellen's updated symptoms.

Walking over to Ellen with a smile on his face, Dr. Carns said, "I hear you've had a bit of an accident. Your mother's told me about your current symptoms. Mind if I have a look?"

"I guess so. My brain feels like it's in a fog."

He took Ellen's vitals, noting her blood pressure and pulse were slightly elevated as expected. Dr. Carns assessed movement of her extremities, checked pupillary reaction to light, asked if she knew what happened, and tested her ability to speak normal phrases. After examining her head, he located the source of bleeding. Luckily, it wasn't deep despite the notable blood loss. Dr. Carns placed a pressure dressing on Ellen's head to contain the bleeding.

"Gosh, you'd make a great pirate," Marge giggled nervously, but after looking at her mother's serious expression, refrained from further attempts at comedy to alleviate the tension.

Completing his exam, Dr. Carns explained his findings. "Ellen, the reason you've lost so much blood is because blood vessels for the scalp and face are close to the surface. You don't have to be alarmed unless the bleeding increases significantly. You've sustained a concussion, which means your brain bounced against your skull when you hit the ground causing your other symptoms."

Everyone gasped until Dr. Carns continued in his calm and reassuring manner.

"I know that sounds scary, but the good news is that you never lost consciousness and your normal health is excellent. Although it can be potentially serious, we won't know for sure and need to monitor your condition for the next twenty-four to forty-eight hours. Don't hesitate to contact me immediately if your symptoms increase in severity, especially bleeding and confusion." Dr. Carns provided them with a list of items to observe.

Examining the checklist, Mary asked, "Dr. Carns, what else can we do in the meantime?" Her heart was slowing down but the apprehension remained.

"Make sure Ellen doesn't move very much, and if she has to get up, someone must accompany her to prevent another fall due to dizziness. Her head should remain elevated to decrease bleeding. Ellen needs to remain on a liquid diet, such as water, broth, and popsicles as tolerated. Her diet can be increased gradually as her nausea decreases until she's back on a regular diet. She needs to stay awake as long as possible with someone nearby to assess her symptoms. When her condition has stabilized, she should rest as much as possible. Time and rest are the best cures for her brain to heal." Turning to Ellen, he asked her, "Do you have any questions?"

"Am I going to live, Dr. Carns?"

Understanding Ellen's fear, he addressed her concern in a friendly and clear manner. "You certainly will if I have anything to say about it. Just make sure you and your family follow all my directions and you should be back to normal before you know it. I'll return in two days to check up on you, or sooner if you have any problems or concerns. Does that sound all right?"

His response infused Ellen with sorely needed confidence. Nodding slightly to prevent a recurrence of her headache, Ellen had one last question. "Does this mean I can have as many popsicles as I want?"

Laughing, Dr. Carns looked at Mary and said jokingly, "Sounds like she's already on the mend." He said to Ellen, "You can have as many as your family can afford."

Elizabeth, as a mother to three children, was aware of the difficulty to keep a child engaged in any activity, while time ferried along slowly during recovery. She was happy to sit with her grandchild and regale her with stories of past and popular Irish myths, especially tales about her namesake and ancestor, Grace O'Malley. Gradually, Ellen's condition improved slightly. She was thrilled to stay up past her bedtime, eat as many ice pops as she wanted, and be the center of attention—an astonishing feat in a household with seven children vying for their parents' attention. As expected, William's punishment included the paddle, and he was forced to remain standing while eating his meals for the rest of the day.

William was tasked with maintaining extra vigilance in watching Ellen's symptoms, a chore he was happy to perform as penance. By the next morning, other than sporting bruises, Ellen's symptoms decreased. She was permitted to sit on the front porch swing with a pillow behind her head under her mother's watchful eye. When Dr. Carns examined Ellen two days later, he pronounced her symptom-free but cautioned her to take it easy for the next few days, get as much rest as possible, and call him if any problems return.

William's punishment lasted an additional week when he was forced to remain indoors and perform additional chores. Fortunately, he finally learned an important lesson absent from prior escapades—actions can have severe consequences. With this insight, his days of living vicariously through his sisters were, thankfully, at an end.

32

Ohio City, the neighborhood surrounding Carroll Avenue, was the embodiment of America's melting pot consisting of Irish, German, Hungarian, and Italian immigrants. Despite their differences, they lived in mutual respect.

A perfect example was a group of gypsies who occupied a storefront window within Ohio City near the O'Malley home. They were a kind-hearted people who kept mostly to themselves and stored their hard-earned money—what little they had—in mattresses. Although they risked losing everything in a fire, they harbored a deep mistrust of the banking system sufficient to accept the inherent gamble. Poverty-stricken, they grew most of their own food behind the store and used pink sheets to cover storefront windows for privacy.

Similar to her Irish compatriots, Mary O'Malley was particularly sensitive to the needs of other immigrants battling homesickness in a strange land. She understood yearning for loved ones generated a crater of emptiness that, once triggered, threatened to consume their souls if permitted to grow unimpeded. Ellen and her siblings witnessed this compassion espoused by her small community, when intolerance could have threatened their peaceful existence.

When the Gypsy Queen died, Ellen and her siblings watched in awe as her casket, draped with beautiful flowers and rhinestone decorations, was carried well over a mile throughout Ohio City. The entourage of musicians playing familiar, but haunting, renditions of melodies on hand-made violins respectfully walked close behind the casket. All the mourners dressed in brightly colored clothes, and as the procession continued through the neighborhood, people stood mute on their porches as a sign of deference and sympathy for the gypsy clan's loss.

The convoy ended at St. Patrick's Church, a bastion of religious tolerance where all faiths were accepted. Throughout the day, no one judged or criticized them because they were different from their neighbors. Despite the contrary cultures and beliefs of the Irish, Germans, and remaining clans in Ohio City, they accorded one another mutual respect, which surpassed religion, race, or ethnicity. People were accepted for who they were, not defined by skin color, customs, or beliefs.

Ellen took it for granted that people the world over existed in comparable respect and treated one another with decorum. But, as she grew older, events would later prove this was not only inaccurate but naive. It would be her wake-up call that world experiences affected everyone, no matter how far away they occurred from her secure world on Carroll Avenue.

33

After watching the inspiring gypsy funeral, the O'Malley children held their own memorial ceremony with all the pageantry and dignity they just witnessed. Undecided on who the dead person would be, they chose affable five-year-old Veronica.

"Veronica, do you want to be in a parade?"

In response, she nodded with such enthusiasm her vision became blurry, which doubled her pleasure. Everyone found Veronica's smile to be infectious, despite losing her two front teeth, and her personality was sweet as honey. Proud to be the center of attention, Veronica took her role seriously as her siblings put their collective brains together to plan the perfect procession.

Being the oldest, Marge was in charge. "I'll give each of you a task. When you're done, meet me back here in twenty minutes or less."

Without a watch or the understanding of just how long twenty minutes lasted, they interpreted her instructions to mean report back to the front porch as quickly as possible.

"Now, William, go get the wagon."

He took off like a rocket—a man on a mission of utmost importance.

"Mayme, gather together some instruments."

This greatly appealed to her creative side and she, too, ran in search of musical devices worthy of an orchestra.

"Ellen, find some funeral pillows." In response to her quizzical look, Marge added, "Fancy pillows."

Caught up in the fun, Ellen carried out her task with unbridled enthusiasm and delight.

James understood he was being left out and pointed to himself with tears in his eyes. "Me?"

"You can help me gather flowers."

James happily went about his job of gathering pretty flowers—mostly weeds with appealing colors. Thomas, asleep in his bassinet, missed this particular adventure but would hear about it numerous times when he was older, embellished with each retelling.

Within twenty minutes, they reassembled on the front porch, and Marge decided their processional route with the gravity of a five-star general. They carefully placed two funeral pillows (pink and purple cushions from the parlor) in the wagon. Veronica climbed into the wagon and lay down as commanded.

"Now cross your arms across your chest and close your eyes." Marge told Mayme to distribute the musical instruments—a washboard for William, handmade flute for Ellen, a whistle for James, and Mayme used a small pot with a wooden spoon as a makeshift drum. Marge covered Veronica with flowers and stinkweeds that made Veronica giggle. "Hush. Dead people don't laugh." Veronica immediately stopped laughing but couldn't erase the smirk on her face, certain she was the best dead person *ever*.

Marge pulled the wagon while everyone else gathered behind to provide musical accompaniment in what they believed was the most distinguished convoy of all time. The ragtag procession began on Carroll Avenue and headed toward Bridge Avenue. The not-so-melodious sounds attracted the attention of dogs and cats in the neighborhood to add their own sounds to the cacophony assaulting the ears of the entire neighborhood. Their next-door neighbors, the Doublers, joined in the fun—Jerry, a creative and inventive fellow played his handmade kazoo, Diane brought a bell, and Nancy played the harmonica.

Other children within a four-block radius heard the commotion and quickly ran into their homes to gather their own makeshift musical instruments—many selected various pots and pans as drums and cymbals. The participants grew in number as the children's event drew smiles from most adults, although others just placed hands over their ears to drown out the dissonant sounds.

When they reached their eventual destination at St. Patrick's Church, Veronica noticed the beautiful music stopped, but she kept her eyes closed as uncertainty filled her. No one told her what a dead person should do next. When she mustered the courage to cautiously open one eye, two nuns were standing over her with their arms crossed with stern expressions. Veronica jumped up and began to run home but knew her parents would be furious if she didn't return with the funeral pillows. Risking a rebuke from the unhappy sisters, Veronica ran back to the wagon, grabbed the pillows, and continued her trek toward home, trailing flowers and stinkweeds.

As Veronica approached their front porch, the neighborhood children were doubled over in laughter; Veronica couldn't help but join in, even if she didn't understand the joke. The funeral pillows were dusted off and placed back in the parlor as if nothing happened. When the merriment died down, William sprinted back to the scene of the crime to retrieve the wagon, relieved to find the area nun-free.

When William returned home, the kids gave him a standing ovation, and he bowed deeply to acknowledge their accolades. This memory became a wonderful story to share repeatedly, with a few embellishments, by those lucky enough to join the O'Malleys in their latest adventure.

34

The days sped by like the Indianapolis 500 and before the O'Malleys knew it, the delight of winter was upon them.

By December 1928, Thomas was twenty-one months old and enjoying his first real winter and joys of the holiday season. The infectious attitude of joviality filled the air, and he was anxious to join in the fun. The girls helped in the kitchen to make batches of wonderful Christmas cookies as the delectable smells filled the home, while the boys were kept busy shoveling the sidewalk and helping elderly neighbors clear their pathways.

One week before Christmas, the family went to a local tree farm on Lorain Road near their home, and together they picked out a beautiful tree. Mary had already cleaned the family parlor that would house the soon-to-be decorated center of enjoyment.

It was Thomas's first adventure in the snow, and he was determined to make the best of it. He stuck out his tongue and marveled at catching the magical white particles falling from the sky only to have them disappear in mere seconds. Dressed in the warmest possible clothing with a woolen coat, two hats, scarves, and gloves, Thomas managed to wriggle free of his mother's arms and crawled into the forest of Christmas trees on display. With the family engrossed in selecting the best Christmas tree, Mary glanced down and realized in the passage of only five seconds, her baby was no longer at her side.

"Have ye seen Thomas?" she asked her husband in a worried tone, attempting to mask her anxiety.

Michael called out, "Thomas! Thomas, where are ye hiding?"

The older children picked up on their father's alarm and spread out in search of baby Thomas while securely holding onto James and Veronica.

But Thomas was faster than ice cream melting down someone's chin on a hot summer's day. Soon, everyone was calling out Thomas's name and searching the entire lot.

Just as Michael was about to flag down a policeman, someone called out, "Is this your son?"

Sure enough, Thomas's hand was stuffed with pine needles, and he was cheerfully playing with a stray puppy in the tiny shack erected by the lot owner. Michael scooped up his son and hugged him tightly. After placing a gentle kiss on his forehead, he handed the baby over to Mary.

It would be a long time before Thomas would make another escape, much to his chagrin.

Back home, Thomas was content watching his older siblings while the remaining wee folk—namely Veronica and James—were tasked with fixing the tree skirt since they were the perfect height. Although their efforts were uneven and crumpled, the family bestowed high praise on their efforts.

Ellen decided to take a short break, distracted by the mouth-watering smell of fresh-baked cookies. She didn't want them to go to waste—they were her favorite. She walked over to her mother and whispered her question, since she didn't want everyone to hear her great idea. "Ma, can I have some cookies?"

"Of course, me darling. But only a few." Mary walked into the other room to pick up forgotten ornaments to cover bare spots on the tree.

Ellen sat back wondering how many cookies was considered a few. "Marge, how many is a few?"

"A couple."

Another conundrum. How many was a couple? Ellen was tired of asking and decided to answer her own question. Twelve—that's how many cookies were a couple. She proceeded to eat twelve cookies, and just as she began to lick away the evidence from her fingers, her mother walked into the kitchen.

Eyeing the nearly empty platter of chocolate chip cookies, Mary asked, "Oh Ellen, what have ye done?"

Ellen was quite proud of herself, until she heard the shock in her mother's voice. Feeling guilty Ellen didn't identify exactly how many cookies were "a few," her stomach suddenly began a heave-ho until her guilt was on display for all to see. Mary washed Ellen and changed her clothes but took pity on her daughter and decided not to scold her.

"Next time, promise ye will only have two cookies."

Relieved her mother wasn't mad at her, she nodded meekly. "Yes, Ma." Ellen lay down in the parlor, not quite ready to join in the merriment.

Thomas, in search of a new adventure desperately wished to participate in the festivities. Marge and William were creating popcorn strings for the Christmas tree, but they were interrupted at regular intervals by Thomas attempting to eat the delicious treat. Mayme and Ellen crafted wonderful colored paper loops hooked together and strung around the tree. Michael added extra logs to the fireplace, which gave the room a wonderful glow. Christmas carols, many off-key and ad-libbed by the younger children, including their favorite "Away in a Major," added to the Christmas spirit. Michael and Mary hung precious ornaments on the tree, some from Ireland and others just as treasured were handmade decorations created by the older children in school.

Michael had a final and unusual surprise this year. He proudly and with much fanfare brought out four special boxes. Curious, everyone gathered around as he revealed his latest find. Each box contained seven colored lights, which Michael plugged together before fastening them onto the branches. They were the latest invention in Christmas decorations, and Michael was fortunate enough to find them, facilitated by his work in the trades. Although he strayed from any new technology and feared their influence in everyday use would produce laziness, even Michael could surprise himself. To his delight, everyone began to dance around the room—even the wee folk—when he plugged the lights into the wall socket and decorative lights filled the room.

"Oh me darling, however did ye find such delightful wonders?"

With a twinkle in his eye, he said proudly, "I have me ways."

Within an hour, they heard a commotion outside their home. The neighbors had gathered together to admire the unique, mesmerizing sight. Michael hooked his thumbs into his suspenders and puffed out his chest at the hubbub created by the crowd. The final and most important task was performed by Michael, who placed the angel at the top of the tree, which looked down on mere mortals to fill their hearts with love and peace on earth.

The night before Christmas, all the children gathered around to hear the story of Christmas. It was the same one repeated each Christmas Eve but the first time one of their children decided to repeat the story, at least her interpretation.

Five-year-old Veronica bravely spoke up. "God sent His only son as a baby to save everyone. Tomorrow is His birthday."

Michael and Mary beamed in the revelation their daughter grasped the true meaning of Christmas, until Veronica finished her rendition.

"And then . . . and then . . . He grew up to be a statue."

While her parents turned around to hide their amusement, Veronica's older siblings hugged her. In the privacy of their room, laughter erupted at their sister's skewed but unusually accurate insight.

Before going to bed, the children looked out the front window in earnest as Michael pointed up toward the sky.

"Do ye see Santa in his sleigh?"

The elder children smiled but the younger ones nodded vigorously, fearful Santa would pass their home if they didn't acknowledge his presence.

But Mary noticed something was bothering Ellen. Taking her aside, Mary questioned her.

With her head down, Ellen whispered, "My classmates told me that Santa isn't real."

"Ah, me darling. Do not believe all that ye hear. 'Tis a Santa fer every person who believes." Watching her daughter's eyes light up made Mary's heart skip a beat, knowing her young daughter would retain her innocence a little longer.

Michael's booming voice rang out. "'Tis time fer bed or Santa will be sure ta pass our home if he sees children running about."

The children readied themselves for bed quicker than a mouse broke away from the nest to lay claim to a solitary piece of cheese. The older children, worn out by the excitement, were asleep soon after. Now that the house was once again quiet, Michael brought out the children's presents. Together with Mary, they wrapped the presents and attached tiny nametags before they were placed under the tree.

Taking a short break, Michael shyly handed his wife a box. "'Tis a small gift fer ye."

Mary's cheeks flushed as she quickly unwrapped the tiny container. Inside was an Irish Claddagh ring, something Mary secretly wished for her entire life. With tears in her eyes, she clasped Michael's head in her hands and whispered, "'Tis the most beautiful gift in all the world." Kissing Michael passionately, he was breathless when Mary whispered, "Fer me darling husband, I have a gift of me own later tonight."

Michael's face blushed at the thought of shared delights they would soon experience. Just as his children had quickened their pace in preparing for bed, Michael tackled his gift-wrapping with the speed of a gazelle.

The next morning at 5:00 a.m., the children ran into the parlor screeching with delight at the sight of all the presents. Hearing their joyous cries, Michael and Mary joined them as their children waited expectantly for the gifts to be handed out. Within thirty minutes, wrapping paper was strewn across the floor, and sighs of pleasure were heard as they reveled in their gifts and shared them with one another. They quickly dressed in their Sunday best to attend St. Patrick's 6:00 a.m. Mass. The smaller children were allowed a snack and juice but everyone else had abstained from food and drink since midnight to receive Communion.

As usual, the church was crowded on Christmas, and favorite hymns were sung with gusto. Happiness permeated the air and when they exited the church, God surprised them with a crisp white snowfall which added to their joy.

The O'Malleys rushed home to eat breakfast until bellies and sprits were sated. Once the table was cleared and dishes cleaned, the children quickly dressed into winter play clothes to celebrate the enchanting accumulation of snow. Joined by many of their friends, the O'Malleys built a snowman—the best ever, in their humble opinion.

William turned around and was hit in the face with a snowball. Ellen grinned. The fight was on and everyone, including their parents and neighbors, participated in the fun. The snowballs flew like perfectly aimed footballs hitting their targets with amazing accuracy.

Catching snowy particles on her tongue, Veronica asked Mayme, "Where does snow come from?"

"Each flake is a raindrop with a tiny white coat to celebrate the birth of Jesus." Veronica was awed at Mayme's response and later shared it with her friends, who were equally impressed.

The older children shared the sled (one of their Christmas gifts), as their younger siblings used upside-down lids from large pots to slide down a nearby hill, making the day perfect as another Christmas drew to a close.

This would be the last Christmas the O'Malleys could afford gifts or extra treats, except an apple in their stockings and fresh-squeezed orange juice at breakfast. Despite the absence of real presents in the future, the children would be delighted to receive fresh fruit—a rarity when the Great Depression told hold, which signified an ominous destiny affecting the world. But with their continued peaceful and loving family traditions, which sustained the Christmas feeling, their hearts were always warmed by the blessing of being together.

Mary O'Malley knew organized activities were a deterrent to hijinks, and the summer each child reached the age of six, they were enrolled at the Community Center, three short blocks from their home. The Center was a gathering place promoting activities for children of all ages—sewing, crafts, games, sports, and cooking. When Veronica was old enough for the Center, her gentle spirit and shyness around strangers made her reluctant to attend. Marge agreed to accompany Veronica for her Community Center afternoon of activities. Walking into the Center, Veronica was amazed at the bustle of energy but also a little intimidated.

Marge walked up to the sign-in counter and said, "I'll be back at three to pick you up. Okay, Veronica?"

Staring at her older sister, Veronica timidly asked, "Will you stay with me for a few minutes?"

"Why sweetie, of course I will. What would you like to try first?"

Veronica ran over to the crafts table. Talking animatedly to the other children at the table, Veronica didn't even notice when Marge left ten minutes later.

Turning to the girl on her right, Veronica introduced herself and asked, "What's your name?"

"Maria Francesca Rossi."

Veronica was impressed her new friend had two first names. It sounded so wonderful, she decided to make a similar change.

The next day when Marge walked her younger sister over to the Center, Veronica said, "I can tell the nice lady my name. Will you pick me up again at three?" When Marge nodded, Veronica skipped off to give her name to the receptionist.

Returning at 3:00 p.m., Marge walked up to the front desk.

"Hi," Marge said to the woman at the front desk. "I'm here to pick up my sister, Veronica O'Malley."

After checking her records, she replied, "I'm sorry but we don't have anyone by that name."

Marge glanced around the Center and pointed out her sister. "No, her name is Juanita Marie," replied the receptionist.

Surprised and amused by her sister's latest mischief, Marge gently approached her sister. "I understand you have a new name."

Veronica nodded with pride.

"Anything I should know about?"

"I just didn't feel like being Veronica today. Besides, I like having two first names."

"Okay, Juanita Marie, but what should we call you at home?"

After thinking hard for a full minute, Veronica tentatively responded, "Vernita Marie?"

"I don't think Ma and Da would approve of a non-Christian name." When she saw Veronica's crestfallen expression, Marge added, "Perhaps we could call you Juanita Marie for just today. But tomorrow you're Veronica. Deal?"

"It's a deal."

Walking into their home, Marge hurriedly told her mother of their bargain. Once Mary stopped chuckling, she faced her youngest daughter and asked, "Juanita Marie, how did you enjoy the Center today?"

"It was swell."

"Can ye please find Veronica ta help with dinner?"

Veronica giggled. "It's me, Ma. Did I fool you?"

Peering closely at her petite daughter, Mary replied, "Why of course 'tis me darling Veronica. But ye look just like Juanita Marie. 'Tis a miracle."

Veronica was so pleased at the thought of fooling her mother, she skipped into the kitchen to help with dinner preparations. Her desire to become someone else was now a long-forgotten need; after all, if her own mother couldn't tell the difference between Veronica and Juanita Marie, how could anyone else?

36

In addition to the Community Center, Michael and Mary understood the importance for their children to cultivate a supervised exercise regime. Each child was enrolled in Turnverein (pronounced turn-vry'an)—a German American athletic club started in 1849—currently owned by a German proprietor, Mr. Heinz. The atmosphere and routines differed when Hitler came to power in 1933 —Mr. Heinz displayed a large picture of Hitler, with swastika flags flanking both sides.

"Now children, we will start class with a goose-step march around the gym, like me." He demonstrated, and the children were excited to learn a new march. "At the end of each march, we will salute the führer, like this." Without understanding what they were doing, they mimicked Mr. Heinz and felt the same pride exhibited by their teacher, but they were unfamiliar about who the führer was or what he represented.

They continued the marches until 1939, when the führer's picture and German flags were abruptly removed by Mr. Heinz. He was devastated by Hitler's 1939 unprovoked invasion into Poland and terminated all tributes.

The gym consisted of parallel bars (even and uneven), rings

suspended from the ceiling, exercise mats for tumbling and free-form maneuvers, springboard with a hobby horse, and ladder rungs on the wall for climbing. Mayme loved all forms of exercise and excelled at Turnverein, but her siblings merely tolerated the gym classes. It wasn't unusual to enter a room and find Mayme standing on her head. Everyone had to be careful rounding corners or risk knocking Mayme over.

Veronica was never comfortable at Turnverein, especially after she attempted to use the gymnastic rings and managed to twist herself around until she was upside down. The other children said her feet were tongue-tied, and Veronica decided this would be the last torture session she would attend. After making several weekly excuses, her mother wisely decided Veronica could work in her garden for exercise.

37

On May 13, 1929, Mayme awoke with a headache that felt as though her head would explode accompanied by severe nausea which prompted a quick dash to the bathroom just in time to vomit.

"Ma, come quick. Mayme's sick," called out a concerned Ellen.

Mary came running into Mayme's bedroom. "Can ye tell me what yer feeling, dear Mayme?"

"Oh Ma, I have the worst headache and just threw up your delicious stew from last night."

Mary placed a cool washcloth on her daughter's burning forehead and told William to fetch Dr. Carns. "Just ye be resting easy, me darling."

When Dr. Carns arrived, he performed a quick exam but the etiology of her symptoms wasn't readily known. "It could be one of many things. Here's a prescription for the nausea and vomiting. If her headache persists and she can keep food down, you can give her aspirin. I'd like Mayme to see Dr. Ralph at the Cleveland Clinic. I'll contact him with Mayme's symptoms, and you can call him at this number in a few hours to set up an appointment."

Mary thanked Dr. Carns profusely and spent most of the day

sitting next to Mayme's bed to monitor her symptoms. Marge fixed simple meals for the family's lunch and dinner.

Although Mayme's condition improved slightly, Mary decided to keep Mayme's referral appointment to see Dr. Ralph on May 15, 1929. The day began as any other and twelve-year-old Mayme, despite lingering symptoms, looked forward to an adventure with her mother—a rare and treasured occurrence.

As usual, the clinic was teeming with patients, doctors, and nurses. Earlier that day, a steamfitter arrived to repair a leaky pipe located in the clinic's subbasement, where the makeshift storage unit housed the hospital's radiology films, which contained flammable nitrates. When the exposed steam came into contact with the volatile nitrates of the X-ray films, a poisonous gas was released throughout the hospital. As the nitrate gas ignited, two ferocious explosions rocked the hospital. Flames leaped through the air, crumbling structures in its path. Fumes were propelled, via pipe ducts, at a highly pressurized rate, gaining access to every room and floor of the hospital.

Many collapsed where they stood as the vapors filled their lungs. More than 225 people (staff and patients) attempted to escape using the stairways but many were exposed to the deadly gas in varying degrees.

The Cleveland Fire Department arrived to douse the flames without realizing water would increase the deadly fumes when it came in contact with nitrates. Pandemonium ensued and panic erupted as everyone sought a means to escape; many even jumped through windows to their death. Some were rescued by firemen, policeman, or volunteers. But anyone who inhaled the poisonous gas in sufficient amounts would eventually succumb to a painful death, which claimed 150 lives.

Shortly after the tragedy struck, Mayme and her mother disembarked from the streetcar when they reached the Clinic at East 93rd Street and Euclid Avenue. Mayhem and turmoil greeted them as they stared helplessly at the scene of destruction. Mesmerized by the chaotic scene unfolding before her eyes, Mayme overheard a painful exchange.

"Come along, nurse. This one's near death. We must save those who have a chance."

When the doctor hurriedly walked away, Mayme looked with compassion into the haunted expression of the young girl, not much older than she. Despite the pain where fire left its imprint, the girl understood a death sentence had been imposed without a kind word to buffer the shock. Mayme glanced around in desperation, hoping to locate the girl's parents, but there was no adult nearby other than her mother who was helping another victim. Without giving it a second's thought, Mayme knelt beside the girl and took her badly burned hand into her own.

"I'll keep you company until additional help arrives. I promise you won't be alone."

Mayme was rewarded by a slight squeeze of her hand and the attempt to smile despite a face ravaged by flames. Within minutes, the girl was released from her agony and Mayme whispered a prayer for the victim and her family.

Mayme felt her mother's hand on her shoulder as she whispered to her young daughter. "'Twas a beautiful thing ye did, me darling. Now come along. We cannot help these poor people. Best we clear the way fer rescue efforts."

Mayme slowly stood and gazed at the multitude of suffering as far as she could see. Tears streamed unchecked down her face, and she was filled with helplessness. Her legs refused to move, and her body wouldn't respond to her mother's simple request. Mary gently placed her arms around her daughter's shoulders and carefully guided her away from the anguish, choking on the air they breathed.

The streets were mobbed with onlookers in addition to firefighters and policemen responding from surrounding communities. Navigating through the raucous crowd, Mayme and her mother finally caught a streetcar home, where they were greeted by the entire family.

"Mayme, Ma, are ye all right? We heard the news on the radio and were afraid something happened to you."

Marge and her siblings gathered around them and enveloped them in a group hug just as their father burst through the front door. Michael led his wife and daughter to the parlor where they sat with dazed expressions at the sorrow and devastation witnessed an hour before.

"Just sit here and catch yer breaths. Ye are all right now." Michael knelt before them and held their hands until the shaking subsided. When he was certain they were able to walk without losing their balance, Michael and Marge led them to their bedrooms where they could rest after witnessing the catastrophic events. The family completed their chores and waited on their mother and sister throughout the day.

By the time evening arrived, both Mayme and her mother had some color in their cheeks, but their eyes were still haunted by the tragic events. Over the next few days, Mayme's symptoms abated and a follow-up to Dr. Carns determined her temporary illness, never completely identified, had resolved.

38

While Mayme was recovering from her bout of illness, the Szabos were tackling financial problems after discovering their Hungarian farm was swindled. It would take Paul Szabo one year to earn sufficient funds for his wife and son's passage to America where they stayed with relatives. Leaving his father behind, Frank and his mother embarked on a journey to America. Secretly, Frank was thrilled to be away from his abusive father who remained in Hungary. The idea of taking his first railway excursion filled Frank with an excitement that vibrated throughout his body. For the first time, Frank glimpsed how wonderful life could be—after living a life of pain and loneliness, the delights of travel gave him hope for an exciting future.

"Frank!" his mother admonished in Hungarian. "Get your nose away from the window before it's permanently flattened."

Although curbing his movements seemed an impossible task, Frank attempted to obey his mother . . . for all of ten seconds before his face was again glued to the pane. He watched the glorious scenery as they passed through towns and the possibility of additional adventures grew with each passing moment. His mother sighed but didn't correct him further—she knew he couldn't help himself.

When they arrived in Holland, Frank looked up in awe at the

majesty of the stately ocean liner, *S.S. Statendam*, flagship of the Holland-America Line. If he thought a train ride was exhilarating, his first ocean journey was pure magic lasting seven days from July 19, 1929 through July 26, 1929, bound for the land of plenty. Despite traveling third-class, each passenger started the day with a beautifully designed menu card topped with color pictures of the Holland-America Line. Frank was so impressed he kept every menu card as a lovely memory of their adventure.

THEIR JOURNEY ENDED with the awe-inspiring Statute of Liberty in New York Harbor, a symbol of hope and freedom to those in search of a better life. Ellis Island, the entryway for an estimated twelve million immigrants in the sixty-two years it remained open, was a refuge for some and a source of desperation for others. By 1900, an average of five thousand people per day were processed through Ellis Island, and doctors boasted an exam could be completed in six seconds. Questionnaires, filled out by passengers at their origination point, contained legal information and responses to twenty-nine questions. This document was used to cross-examine the new arrivals to assure their veracity and confirm their identity.

Thankfully, Frank and his mother were blissfully ignorant of potential obstacles before arriving at Ellis Island. They were herded with other third-class passengers into a small boat transporting them to Ellis Island. Frank noticed only first-class passengers were taken on a larger boat directly into New York Harbor and bypassed inspection at Ellis Island.

Once their ferry docked at Ellis Island, Frank and Emma were instructed by uniformed officers who spoke with authority as they directed passengers toward the main building. The officers pressed a numbered tag into each person's hand and directed them to pin it onto their clothes. Chaos reigned as people from many different countries attempted to follow directions in a language completely foreign to them. The officers guided them into a daunting and immense red building. They were forced to leave their baggage in a room on the first floor and led upstairs to the Registry Room for medical and legal inspections.

"Hurry up, folks. Get into line. We don't have all day." The man spoke impatiently in English, disregarding the confusion on most passengers' faces.

Without their knowledge, doctors watched the procession of immigrants as they climbed the staircase, looking for any excuse to refuse entrance into America (difficulty breathing, gait deformities, symptoms of disease, and/or abnormal behavior). Once they arrived on the second floor, they were directed to one of twelve long queues, each separated by a long narrow bar.

"Keep moving, people. Stop dragging your feet."

The overall hostile attitude exhibited by those working menial jobs at Ellis Island was evidenced by their abrupt manner and lack of courtesy. Blasé attitudes with a complete lack of concern for others' suffering were job requirements for Ellis Island employees. By exploiting their superiority over immigrants to enhance their own self-worth, they only served to demean their actual worth as merciful human beings.

Frank and his mother were shuffled into one line, bewilderment on their faces. Once they made it to the front of the line, a man dressed in a white coat gave them a cursory exam while reviewing their paperwork. Privacy was noticeably absent with clothes carelessly strewn to expedite the exam. Anxiety_over theft of discarded clothes was intensified by the latest technology—an X-ray machine. Pressed against the strange contraption emitting unusual sounds and lights, cries of terror were disregarded. Ignorance of the possible dangers resulted in the absence of protective clothing for operators and patients.

Hearing a loud cry, Frank turned his head. He witnessed the desolation of a family surrounding a young boy with a "B" chalk mark on his coat. Although Frank couldn't understand their words, it was clear to him that anyone with that distinction was not cleared to enter the United States. This placed the family in a precarious position— the gut-wrenching decision of abandoning the family member denied entry or returning everyone to their point of origin. Ellis Island employees also marked immigrants' outer clothing with a variety of additional chalk letters. Each denoted their disposition ranging from rejection to referral to one of several hospital wards on the island for treatment prior to United States admission.

After Frank and his mother had been medically cleared, they were told to wait for a legal exam. Without understanding, they sat in hard chairs tightly holding onto one another's hand until their names were called. With the aid of an interpreter, Emma was able to correctly respond to the twenty-nine questions completed before their journey.

But passing the medical and legal exams to gain entry to the United States were merely initial steps in the process of assimilation into the land of freedom. Most weren't cognizant the many obstacles awaiting them, including ridicule, prejudice, and difficulty sustaining employment with language barriers.

39

Finally clearing Ellis Island, Frank and his mother took the ferry into New York and boarded a train to Michigan, where relatives would provide temporary housing. They were met at the station in Michigan, and while traveling to their new home on a busy highway, they were involved in a minor fender bender. Frank was so distraught by the bustling metropolis and being jostled from the accident, his initial reaction was to flee. He jumped out of the car and ran across four lanes of expressway traffic. Amazingly, he wasn't hit as cars swerved dangerously close to one another while honking their horns to narrowly miss the trembling youth.

In addition to sensory overload from the hectic American lifestyle, another problem became readily apparent. Neither Frank nor his mother could speak or understand English. In Michigan, Frank was enrolled in kindergarten at age twelve and experienced déjà vu of returning to basics before he could proceed with his new life. He endured the jeers and sneers of classmates as he sat in desks too small for him, painfully aware he was much taller and older than other students. Every few months, Frank would be promoted another grade as his language skills slowly improved.

Shyness and awkwardness in social situations, in addition to his favorite pastime of reading, contributed to a solitary school life. If it were up to him, he would sit quietly in a room and read all day. Education and available resources in America, compared to those in Hungary, were unparalleled. No longer was he stuck in a one-room schoolhouse concentrating on his lessons while ignoring the teacher's instructions to five other grades.

Then Frank discovered baseball—the great American pastime that discounted any prior stigma, and he became one of the gang.

Two months later, when Frank returned home from a game feeling pleased with himself after scoring the winning run, he observed a most unwelcome sight. His mother was boxing up their dishes, and Frank again heard the dreaded words in Hungarian, "Son, you need to pack your things."

Looking up toward her son, Emma's heavy-lidded weary eyes peered from a haggard face. Bits of gray hair escaped from a bun tightly gathered at the nape of her neck. Frank thought she looked like an eighty-year-old instead of only fifty-three.

"But why, Mom?"

"We're moving to Indiana," she said, attempting to place an unruly gray hair back into a bun that never stayed in place.

"I can't go. I just started making friends. The kids no longer make fun of my accent, and we have a *really* important baseball game on Saturday that I can't miss." He begged to, at least, stay with his cousins until baseball season ended. But the more he pleaded his case, the more adamant she became. Neither of Frank's parents understood his difficulty fitting into yet another neighborhood and beginning anew the exhausting task of making friends.

"We're leaving on Friday, and I don't want to hear another word about it. I have two jobs starting next week and we'll stay with friends from the old country. Now start packing."

Once again, Frank's life was being uprooted and he would be forced to find friends in the middle of a school year.

However, once he arrived in South Bend, he was able to watch the fabled Fighting Irish during practice sessions. It almost made the relocation worthwhile.

40

An era of unprecedented wealth and promise peaked in 1929 when the unemployment rate of 3.2 percent was at an all-time low, and stocks were rising until they reached a pinnacle in September 1929. Everyone prospered as money flowed from the affluent economy and luxury items, such as automobiles and expensive vacations. But Michael O'Malley did not trust the stock market and became wary of the current economy. On Saturday, October 26, 1929, Michael told his wife to remove all their money from the bank on Monday.

However, come Monday, utter pandemonium reigned.

Veronica walked into the living room and called out to her mother, "James threw up on Thomas."

Pause.

"Ma, now Thomas threw up on James. Yuk." She relayed the news before joining her other siblings at the breakfast table.

After cleaning up the James/Thomas mess, Mary O'Malley made the beds, washed the breakfast dishes, and began to launder their Sunday clothes using naphtha gasoline, the home version of drying cleaning. When she looked at her watch, it was already noon. She quickly prepared lunch for her children before they returned to St.

Patrick's for recess. This was followed by the lengthy process of feeding and washing up the younger children. By the time she began to gather things for her trip to the bank, it was already 2:15 pm. Mary knew she'd never be able to dress her youngest children and arrive at the bank before the doors closed. She made the decision to postpone the errand until Tuesday.

Mary's unfortunate change in plan would soon prove disastrous when the stock market crashed on Tuesday. A growing panic caused a run on the banks, as people tried to cash out their accounts. When it became apparent there were insufficient reserve funds to meet the overflowing requests for cash, bank doors closed and riots broke out. October 29, 1929, would forever be known as Black Tuesday.

Mary forgot to tell Michael her trip to the bank had been postponed, assuming the delay of one more day would be inconsequential. But when she arrived at the bank with her two youngest children in tow, the doors were closed and angry crowds gathered on the sidewalks.

Mary approached a harassed-looking policeman and fearfully asked, "Officer, could ye please tell me what is going on?"

"Everyone wants to close out their accounts. Banks don't have enough cash reserves, so they closed their doors."

With trepidation, Mary asked, "Do ye think they will be open tomorrow?"

"Based on the angry mob growing with each passing hour, I doubt it."

Mary took out her handkerchief and wiped her forehead, suddenly peppered with sweat despite the cool breeze. Her hand began to shake at the gravity of her situation, and she blanched at the loss of their life savings. More importantly, she agonized about breaking the news to Michael.

By the time Michael arrived home, he'd heard the terrible news on the radio. Walking into their home, something was amiss. The normally wonderful smells from his wife's delectable cooking were absent, and his wife wasn't there to greet him.

"Mary? Where are ye?" Receiving no response, he added, "'Tis yer loving husband." Still nothing, so he walked into the kitchen where his wife was sobbing at the kitchen table. "What is wrong, me love?"

"Oh Michael. Yesterday the wee ones were sick, I had ta do laundry, make lunch fer everyone and . . . and . . ." But Mary couldn't say the unthinkable and began to cry once again.

Although Michael had a sinking feeling their hard-earned money was forever gone, he quickly drew her into his strong arms and told her not to worry because God would take care of them. Michael never made his wife feel guilty or chastised her in any way when fate's cruelty intervened and cast them into poverty.

41

Hopelessness from the Depression resulted in a rising crime rate of unprecedented heights as the seeds of discontent festered. A dark period in the Ohio City area ushered in shortly after the Depression involved two separate kidnappings of young boys grabbed off the street never to be found. The area was abuzz with anxiety and alarm for their children's safety. Parents started walking their children to school—a destination where their offspring would spend the day in a location considered a safe haven.

In 1930 at the age of fourteen, William experienced a frightening episode when a strange man came to his classroom.

"Class, please take out your English books and turn to page—"

"Excuse me, Sister," the stranger politely murmured as he knocked on the classroom door and interrupted the teacher. "But Mr. O'Malley asked me to bring William home right away. Here's a note from Mr. O'Malley about a family emergency."

With no further thought or questions to determine his veracity, Sr. Joanna told William to go with the stranger.

He drove William around town continually plying him with questions.

"Can you confirm your address? I'm not sure I remember it."

William provided the information, happy to help his father's friend.

"Is there any money in your home?"

"Does your mom have any jewelry?"

"Is there ever a time when the house is empty?"

William obligingly answered all the man's questions, since he was a friend of his father. William was certain his parents would be proud, completely unaware of potential danger.

As the car whizzed past Carroll Avenue, William pointed out, "But, sir, my home is back that way."

"We're just taking a shortcut."

Something about the stranger's attitude sparked fear in young William. Perhaps he really wasn't a friend of his father and that thought, combined with recent kidnappings, sent a jolt of alarm coursing through William. He began to look for a way out but knew he had to remain calm.

"But Mister, don't you know you could end up in jail?"

"Quit your sassing, or you'll be sorry."

"Look, there's a policeman. You could just drop me off, and I won't say a word."

As William was attempting to negotiate, the kidnapper delivered a sharp slap across William's face for his temerity in speaking out.

AT THE SAME time of William's ordeal, his siblings began to arrive home.

"Where's yer brother?" asked a concerned Mary.

"I dunno. Someone said he was called to the principal's office. We haven't seen him since. He must be in a lot of trouble."

Mary calmly called the principal. "Sister, I am looking fer me son, William O'Malley. He's in Sr. Joanna's class."

"Let me check with his teacher."

Several minutes passed before a distressed-sounding principal picked up the phone to deliver a shocking statement. "He was sent home with your husband's friend for a family emergency."

"I do not know what y'er talking about." Mary's voice began to rise in panic, and her face lost all color. Mary's thunderous heart pounded in her ears, and she sat quickly, feeling faint and unsteady. Fortunately, Michael entered their home at that precise moment in search of a forgotten tool. One look at Mary told him that tragedy darkened their happy abode. Mary thrust the phone at her husband and began to weep as she recalled the recent kidnapping of boys around William's age.

Shaking in fear and anger, Michael said, "What is the meaning o' this? Me wife is pale and crying." Once he heard the nun's reply, a series of expletives never heard by Mary or their children were spewed into the receiver. His brogue growing thicker with every spoken word, the O'Malleys sensed danger touched their lives.

"What do ye mean? Ye sent me darling Liam off wit' a total stranger and dinna see any identification? If me son 'tis not home by tonight, 'tis me ye'll be dealin' wit' and I kinna' guarantee meself will be in control." Michael slammed down the receiver.

Michael's palpable fear threatened to choke him. Seeing their father so upset, the children began to cry and rushed to their mother for comfort. Mary held them all close and prayed for the safe return of her beautiful boy.

Gaining control of his rage, Michael picked up the phone and called the police. "This here is Michael O'Malley and me boy, William, has been abducted from school."

"Mr. O'Malley, my name is Sergeant Ralph Dunn. If you give me your address, we'll send a squad car over."

There was a knock at the door fifteen minutes later.

"Oh, praise be ta God. If ye would please ta be comin' in." Michael nervously ushered the officers into the parlor and explained the day's events. Turning to his children, Michael told them to play in the backyard and stay there until they were told to return inside.

Once the children were out of earshot, the policeman introduced himself. "My name is Lt. Rich Connolly." After shaking hands as Michael and Mary introduced themselves, he continued. "Yours is not the first case we've encountered. Times are hard and people are desperate. Do you have a recent picture of William?"

They provided William's current school photo to the officer.

"Do you know of anyone who might wish you or your family any harm?"

"No, sir. We can think of no one."

"It's best if you remain home in case someone tries to contact you. We'll take the case from here."

"But Sergeant, surely I can—"

The officer patted him on the back. "Mr. O'Malley, we've done this before. It's best if we take it from here."

But Michael couldn't sit still once the officers left. "I'm goin' out ta look fer him. Mary, wait by the phone fer any news."

Michael had the easier chore, for his task was purposeful, but his wife remained house-bound, filled with despair.

While Michael was out searching, Mary called her siblings to inform them of William's kidnapping. Each offered to search their respective neighborhoods and help organize search parties. Mary gratefully accepted their help.

After combing the neighborhood until he could no longer walk, Michael returned home dejected and alone. That evening, the O'Malleys received phone calls from family members who reported similar results from their neighborhood-organized explorations. Still awake despite the late hour, the family gathered in prayer for a safe return of their beloved William. Tomorrow, at first light, Mary's siblings and neighbors would meet at their home to continue the search.

42

When Ellen was finally able to sleep after the long and exhausting day, she had a strange dream. From infancy, Ellen was taught her guardian angel was a heavenly messenger, often the spirit of a deceased relative or friend, to protect and watch over her. Ellen believed her intuitive ability was the work of her angel, a constant companion in whom she secretly confided and was often rewarded with tidbits of events to come.

But on the night her brother was kidnapped, Ellen's dream reflected events in real time. She envisioned her brother in a dark place, similar to their basement, with his hands and feet bound, a rag stuffed in his mouth. William was asleep beside two other boys, similarly bound. However, next to him was a vaguely familiar sight. It was a box with writing on it partially obscured but she was able to make out. Cl—nd-Clif—

Ellen immediately awoke and ran into her parent's room, knowing they'd still be awake.

"Ma, Da, I had a dream about William."

Her entire family knew of Ellen's cognitive abilities.

"Tell us, lovey, whatever did ye see?"

Ellen explained the dream and wrote the letters on a piece of paper, hoping they could figure out the puzzle.

Michael's eyes lit up when he recognized the missing letters. "Why Mary 'tis Cleveland-Cliffs, the iron ore company used by most contractors."

"Oh Michael, 'tis good news, but what does it mean?"

"I do not know but we best be letting the police know."

Michael phoned the police, but despite his exuberance at providing a clue to his son's location, the policeman remained skeptical.

"You say this is based on your daughter's dream? We don't put much stock in dreams and stick to just the facts."

"But me child has never been wrong. Do ye not understand?"

The officer treated Michael with a patronizing attitude, which infuriated Michael, but he managed to keep his temper under control. After several attempts, Michael was unable to convince the officer of the valuable information to update his report. Despite Michael's desire to express his rage at the condescending officer, he remained calm and gently replaced the receiver, resisting his desire to slam it down.

"Mary, 'tis up ta us now."

"Where will we start?"

"I'll call yer brother since he works at the iron docks. Maybe he can help."

A call was placed to Brian Ginley at 2:00 a.m. After several rings, a sleepy voice answered, "Hallo? Is this Michael? Have they found William?"

"No, Brian, not yet. But me child, Ellen, had a dream. William was in a basement next ta a box marked Cleveland-Cliffs. Can ye help us ta figure out what it means?"

"Well, 'tis a common sight in mining operations with hundreds of boxes down at the docks alone. I will go into work early and see if I can find any clues ta William's whereabouts."

"Ah, we'd be thanking ye kindly fer yer help."

Michael relayed the conversation to Mary and Ellen, but his earlier elation had dampened at Brian's noncommittal response.

"Ellen, me darling, go back ta sleep. Yer Ma and I will use yer sign and take it from there."

"Are you sure I can't help?"

"No, sweet child. Ye have already helped us, and we love ye more than ye can know."

Her parents kissed her on the forehead, and Ellen trudged back to her bedroom, defeated. After tossing and turning, sleep finally claimed her.

43

Ellen lapsed into a deep sleep where she found herself back in the basement with her brother. She could see a plate of hardly touched food next to William and his two unfortunate companions. Their faces were streaked with tears, and they shivered in the cold. A rag had fallen out of William's mouth, and he mumbled in his sleep, "Don't hit me again. I promise I'll be good."

Ellen saw her brother thrashing around before a stranger picked him up and threw him next to the other boys. The image was so real, Ellen began to shake and she could feel her brother's terror as if she was in the same room. In spite of the darkness, Ellen could see water seeping into the basement of what was once a brightly painted red house, now in serious disrepair. In the distance, she could hear boats on the water sounding their horns to signal the bridge needed to be raised for safe passage.

Ellen awoke abruptly, now certain her brother was near the Cuyahoga River in the Cleveland Flats where many ore ships were docked until their cargo was unloaded. Growing up, Ellen and her siblings had played near the docks and the High Level Bridge spanning the area, careful to stay away from the treacherous Irish Ghetto. She headed toward her parents' room but remembered how disappointed they were when the police didn't believe her. With a childlike certainty and false bravado, Ellen was convinced she and her older siblings could find their brother and woke up Marge and Mayme.

"Come on. Get dressed. I think we can find William. Won't Da and Ma be proud of us?"

Wiping sleep from their eyes, her sisters quickly donned their clothes as Ellen explained her plan.

"Did you have another dream?" Marge asked.

Ellen nodded. "Remember, you need to wear boots and a coat."

Her sisters complied and the trio quietly headed out the back door after grabbing a flashlight. Ellen knew they had to act quickly. The basement where William and the other two boys were held captive would soon be filled with water. William's life depended on their actions carried out with speed and cunning. Grabbing their bikes, the three warriors set off on a mission to save their brother.

4 4

Feeling trapped, William looked around for a way out as he attempted to quell his growing fear. The two other boys whimpered as they curled up in the corner.

William shook his head to loosen the scarf covering his mouth.

"Hi," William spoke with a confidence he didn't feel as he turned to his companions. "I'm William. What are your names?" Both boys noticed William's calm and reassuring manner. They attempted to mimic his bravery, and after several minutes, the first boy responded, "I'm Brad."

"And I'm Arthur."

Turning to Brad, William asked, "How long have you been here?"

"They brought me here after Arthur, so I'd guess about a week. I was walking home from school on a Tuesday . . ." Brad began to cry at the difficult recollection before fear paralyzed his vocal cords.

"They nabbed me on my way to the grocery store . . ." Arthur attempted to speak further, but words were stuck in this throat. Since Arthur was smaller, and probably younger than Brad, William guessed he was unable to maintain a brave façade and tried to refocus their attention on facts.

"Why did they take us?"

"They use us for cheap labor down at the docks. We help load some of the ore into baskets and run errands."

"Is there any way out?" William asked hopefully, knowing the answer was a last-ditch effort to assuage his anxiety.

"We've searched every inch of this basement. It's part of a run-down house near the Cleveland Flats. Sometimes we hear noises upstairs late in the day, and ships are not too far off. They bring us some food each morning and again at night."

"Do they ever untie your hands?"

"No. We have to eat like dogs, and there's a bucket in the other corner as a bathroom." Just as Arthur finished his sentence, he emitted a small cry. Water began pouring through many of the cracks in the basement walls.

"Has water leaked into the basement before?" William asked as both boys, clearly frightened, shook their heads. All three boys crowded into the highest point in the basement but, with little room to move, they were trapped.

"Have you tried calling for help?"

"We each did that on the first night we arrived, but the beating we received discouraged any further noise."

With no hope or options, William prayed for a quick and safe rescue as the water level continued to rise.

45

Ellen and her sisters took a shortcut to the Flats and abandoned their bikes when they could no longer manage the rough terrain. They continued their rescue mission by carefully climbing over rocks and navigating the muddy landscape. Mayme began to slide down a rocky hill before Marge managed to pull her up.

"Mayme, you have to be careful. Why don't you lead the way with the flashlight, and we'll place a hand on the shoulder of the person before us?"

Eager not to lose one another in the dark night, they readily complied with Ellen's suggestion. Reaching the base of the hill that entered the Flats District, they glanced around.

"Now where do we go, Ellen?" In the darkness, Marge was able to hide from her sisters a growing unease as she realized their vulnerability. The Flats, especially the Irish Ghetto where immigrants with little or no money congregated, were well-known for unscrupulous behavior and desperate people who would do anything for a bite of food or a place to sleep.

"We need to look for a broken-down house with peeling red paint near the Cuyahoga River."

Hearing voices nearby, the sisters crowded behind a stack of lumbar until the men passed near them. Luckily, they were able to overhear part of their conversation.

"Having those three boys sure makes work easier. The boss had a great idea, so we'll pick up a few more kids next week. Plus, the last kid we picked up told me about where his parents and neighbors keep their valuables. Perhaps we could start our own side business." They chuckled among themselves at the ease of obtaining free help and a potentially lucrative source of income.

"Is it safe to keep them all in one place? That's a pretty old house, and the basement's starting to fall apart."

"Who cares? If something happens, there's plenty more where they came from." His companions shrugged and trudged over the muddy terrain.

"Did you hear that?" Mayme asked. "They're holding three boys, just like Ellen dreamed."

Confirmation of Ellen's dream gave them increased strength of purpose as the sisters carefully looked around the ramshackle homes until one looked familiar. "Look! That's the one from my dream."

The sisters crept up behind the house and knelt down beside the basement, where they heard whispering and crying.

Leaning in close to a crack in the wall, Marge quietly whispered, "William, is that you?"

William heard a voice but kept quiet. Perhaps the kidnappers were tricking him into eliciting a response so they could deliver a beating.

"William, if you're in there and don't respond immediately, you're in big trouble."

"It's me, Marge," William whispered, acknowledging his forceful older sibling. "There are three of us. You need to hurry up because this place is filling with water."

"Any suggestions, Ellen?" asked a hopeful Mayme.

"William, how do they feed you?"

"They bring us small plates of food through the cellar doors on the other side of the house. But they're kept locked all day."

"Well, it'll be daylight soon. Don't worry, William. Tell your friends that your sisters have a plan, and we'll have all of you out in no time," replied Ellen with a surety that reassured the unfortunate prisoners.

Ellen motioned her sisters over to the other side of the house, where a storage shed provided a temporary refuge. Once inside, they inventoried its contents and hatched a plan while waiting tensely for daylight to appear on the bleak horizon.

46

Once they heard voices nearing the cellar doors, the three young, but very determined, girls each grabbed a weapon from inside the tool shed and waited until the doors to the dilapidated house were unlocked. They snuck up behind the burly man and struck him with shovels and spades until the man lost his balance and fell down the cellar stairs. During his temporary loss of consciousness, the O'Malley girls each untied one of captives and together they quickly began their ascent to freedom.

Ellen, the last to emerge, was abruptly stopped by a hand that grabbed her ankle.

"Get back here now, you little brat. I'll beat you black and blue—"

But he never finished his sentence because Ellen reeled around and hit him in the head with all her might wielding the shovel as a lethal weapon. Freed from his grasp, she ran outside breathless.

"Are you okay, Ellen?" asked a frightened Marge.

With a lopsided grin and false courage, Ellen replied, "I am, but I'm not sure about the other guy. Come on, let's get out of here fast."

Each sister helped a kidnapped boy, weak from hunger and overwork, as they retraced their path out of the Flats. Hearing angry, resentful shouts from the kidnappers when they discovered their junior work force was gone, the escapees and their rescuers broke into a run. Ignoring the fear and forging ahead, the six children headed toward the High Level Bridge. Exhausted but intent on making their way home as quickly as possible, each of the boys were ecstatic at the thought of soon being reunited with their families.

As they neared the halfway point across the bridge, William and his sisters saw a miraculous sight, convinced their tired eyes were deceiving them. Their father was running across the bridge toward them! They were so happy to see their beloved da, they ran into his arms, safe in his strong, muscular grip.

By this time, the sun was beginning to wake up and light their way home. Happily, they all walked into the O'Malley home for a joyous reunion.

"Liam, me dear boy, we prayed fer yer safe return. And hear ye are." Mary cried as she wiped the tears coursing down her cheeks onto her sleeve. She hugged William tightly. Finally releasing her son, she said, "Run upstairs, so ye can tell the others."

Marge, Mayme, and Ellen entered behind their father. Her daughters were covered in mud and bruises but the smiles on their faces exuded pure happiness from their successful adventure. Two additional boys shyly entered the home and cowered in the corner.

"Girls, ye have some explaining ta do. And who are the young lads?"

The girls began to speak at once until Mary held up her hand. "Marge, tell me what happened."

Marge relayed the events in vivid detail as their mother's face turned pale. "Ye three were in the Irish Ghetto in the dark of night?"

Their mother's concern underscored just how dangerous their journey had been. They were so focused on a successful mission, Ellen and Mayme's prior joy turned to fright, and they trembled at the reality of a potential horrifying outcome. Marge was aware of the danger but didn't want to deter her sisters from rescuing William. Mary quickly took her three daughters into her loving embrace and kissed them on tear-stained cheeks. "Promise me ta never do that again." The sisters nodded vigorously, relieved to escape punishment. "Up the stairs with ye ta wash and put on clean clothes." They raced each other upstairs and later emerged clean and happy.

Michael asked William for details on their capture. William explained the ordeal of the three young lads, all forced into labor near the docks. Michael immediately called the police, then phoned the parents of Brad and Arthur. Word spread throughout the neighborhood as neighbors congregated around the O'Malley home just as the police cars pulled up front. The grateful parents of Brad and Arthur raced into the O'Malley home, where a joyful reunion lifted the hearts of everyone.

"Mary, I know ye would like ta go with William ta the precinct, but the children are all wound up and filled with excitement. They probably need ta unwind, so I will go ta the station."

"Of course, Michael. A hearty breakfast will be ready fer ye." Mary kissed her husband's cheek and gave William one more hug, thrilled he was home safe once again.

Ellen relayed a forgotten detail to her father. "We left our bikes in the Flats. Hopefully they're still there."

"Don't ye worry," said her father. "Tell us where and we will bring them home with help from the police."

Ellen was relieved she didn't have to return to the crime scene; her adrenaline was rapidly depleting as the gravity of their adventure fully registered.

The three boys, with their parents, were taken down to the precinct, where they were interrogated. After statements were taken and composite sketches of the kidnappers from combined details provided by the three lads, a car was dispatched to the location where the boys were held. But the house had been cleared of all occupants and any potential evidence. Fearing the kidnappers might return to their home after William revealed their address, the police reassured them.

"The criminals are long gone since they left behind witnesses capable of giving us their descriptions. From the boy's observations, we were able to draw composite sketches that we'll share with other precincts. Abductions in other cities ended when their hideouts were discovered, so I wouldn't worry."

Fortunately, just as the police predicted, the kidnappings stopped in Ohio City once their scheme was revealed. The O'Malleys' fear lessened with each passing day until life returned to normal.

Mary knew sometimes everything had to go wrong before fully appreciating the love of those held dear, as the restoration of life's balance brings a person back from a precipitous event.

When William and his father returned home with the girls' bikes, William was surrounded by his loving family, and for a fourteen-year-old boy escaping near-death, it was the perfect place to be. To make the occasion even more special, his mother made his favorite dessert.

"But how did you know where to look?" asked a curious William.

"Ellen had a dream and with yer sisters followed the clues in her vision."

William absorbed this wondrous revelation and sought out Ellen.

"I understand you're responsible for my rescue."

Humbly, Ellen responded, "It wasn't me. My guardian angel gave me signs about your location."

Kissing his sister on her check, William whispered, "You're my own sweet guardian angel, now and always."

Ellen was touched by William's words, and they remained in her heart. After the fuss over William, he began to think maybe being kidnapped wasn't so bad after all, until he recalled the fates of prior victims and his own recent brush with death. He thanked God for his safe return home, and William gained a new respect for his sisters who gladly placed themselves in harm's way to save him from evil strangers. William heard the expression "every cloud has a silver lining," but never understood what it meant until now. Certainly, that was true when three boys, strangers mired in deplorable circumstances, forged a life-long friendship.

47

Trying to make the best of their recent move to South Bend, Indiana, Frank Szabo discovered three magical words forever changing his life—Tippecanoe Place Library. The first time he walked up the steps into the ornate library, Frank thought he was in heaven. When he discovered he could check out several books to read at home, he was certain of it. Frank's new refuge at the library was a godsend. Books transported him to new places and fed his imagination as he became a swashbuckling pirate one minute or a space explorer the next.

Friendless and alone, Frank's happiness was found in reading, but joy was routinely interrupted to perform chores or errands.

"Frank, you need to get milk from the corner store," said his mother.

Frank took his time as he tore himself away from the latest adventure, which consumed and sustained his solitary existence.

"Coming, Mama."

Frank ran to the store and attempted to hightail it back to his room. He almost made it, but his mother wasn't finished with her list of chores. After he swept the floors and washed the dishes, Frank made a beeline back to his room and began an exciting novel about a crime-solving detective. Frank was so engrossed in his latest novel, he gazed dreamily out his bedroom window and imagined himself as a detective when he was older.

The next year, between wages earned by Paul in Hungary and Emma's two jobs in America, Paul was able to rejoin his family who relocated back from Indiana to Cleveland, Ohio. Although Frank wasn't thrilled to have his abusive father back in his life, he knew it was only a temporary situation until he was old enough to support himself. He just needed to hang on and stick to his goals.

Now that Frank was in Cleveland, his parents enrolled him in St. Patrick's Commercial High and Grade School. At least one dream had come true—his desire to remain in one locale to complete his education. His father's prior wanderlust was quelled with his last humbling experience at the hands of the Hungarian thief.

Frank's parents went to bed by 7:00 p.m. every evening, worn out from daily hardships and an underlying bitterness borne of life's cruelties. When they retired for the day, all lights were turned off despite Frank's timid requests to leave just one lamp lit.

He learned at an early age that imploring any favor from his father only resulted in a beating and additional chores. Frank's solution was to sneak out of the house after his parents were asleep to read his prized possessions under the nearest streetlamp. There was something special about reading under the stars that made the stories come alive, and if he closed his eyes, Frank could visualize swashbuckling pirates brandishing their swords. He hoped life's wondrous possibilities and unfulfilled aspirations would one day be a part of his life. Frank had read knowledge was power, and he was determined to attain that goal by absorbing wisdom from each book.

48

Following her latest venture to help save the lives of three young boys, including her own brother, Marge O'Malley's imagination rose to new heights. Uncertain what her next challenge would be, Marge recalled her dream as a twelve-year-old of possibly becoming a model. But it remained an elusive pipe dream without proper knowledge to enter this exotic world.

By the time she was sixteen, Marge found an answer to her enigma. She entered Kresge's Drugstore and there was a sign for the Janet Gaynor look-alike contest with a prize of twenty-five dollars and a crown! This was her entry to fame and would surely lead to modeling. Next to the sign was a display for the latest in hair care products—Brylcreem—guaranteed to make anyone's hair shine with a strong hold to keep any hairstyle looking great all day. This wonderous hair care product, purported to be a favorite of British models, convinced Marge that it was a necessary item for any aspiring model like herself. She immediately signed up for the contest and for extra luck, purchased a tube of Brylcreem.

The day before the contest, Marge washed and ironed her favorite black dress and located her red belt with a gold buckle. She washed her hair in the sink, towel dried it, and sat in the sunshine to make certain it was dry. She set her hair in pin curls overnight and, when she brushed it out the next morning, Marge had soft curls gently framing her face. Sleeping on crisscrossed bobby pins was painful but Marge was living proof of the saying, "It hurts to be beautiful."

Ellen helped Marge on her big day and watched her older sibling as she began her beauty regimen. Marge followed the Brylcreem instructions and worked the hair gel through her curls.

"Ellen, what do you think?"

"Your hair is so shiny." Reading the tube's directions, Ellen asked, "It says your hair will keep the curls in place all day. But what happens if you shake your head?"

Marge did and not a curl moved. "This stuff is amazing. I'm sure to win with this new product. What could possibly go wrong?" Marge put on her favorite dress and the mirror reflected how much her outfit accentuated her slim figure.

"Ellen, could you please cut a rose from the garden to match my red belt?"

"Sure thing, Marge. You seem so calm. I'd be a nervous wreck."

"That's because I'm confident I'll win."

Ellen shook her head in amazement and ran outside in search of the perfect rose to enhance her sister's chances. She returned with a rose in perfect bloom and handed it to her sister just as Marge was reaching for the face powder. Their hands collided and the container of powder flew into the air. Marge could see the slow-motion catastrophe moving toward her like an unstoppable bullet heading toward its target. She put her hands in the air hoping to stop the calamitous trajectory of the powder toward her dress. Instead, she merely diverted its path onto her head and hands. At least it missed her black dress, so all was not lost.

But looking in the mirror, Marge was shocked to see the powder encased her hair resulting in a perfectly styled snow-covered hairdo. Without thinking, and purely out of habit, she shook her head to eliminate the reflection of someone with a case of world-class dandruff. Unfortunately, as the powder escaped her Brylcreem-bound head, it entered her nasal passages and Marge sneezed. Reflexively, she reached her hands up to cover her nose, which expelled powder from her hands onto her face and dress. Formerly pristine, her frock now expelled a fluffy cloud of white powder with each movement.

"Oh Ellen, I can't believe I did that. What can I do? Maybe I should just cancel."

"No, you won't. We'll work together and fix it."

Ellen helped Marge remove her dress, then ran for a towel and robe. Marge carefully put on the robe, and Ellen held the towel in front of Marge. She advised Marge to shake her head into the towel until all the powder was expelled and her hair was back to its lustrous brown color, curls still intact. Ellen guided her sister into the bathroom, making sure her hands were raised to prevent further damage, then used a washcloth to clean Marge's face and hands. Ellen called out, "Mayme, come here. We need you."

"Be right there." When Mayme arrived, she was told to take Marge's dress outside and clean it. Mayme hung it over the clothesline in the backyard and used a broom to remove the offending powder until the dress was restored to its original color. Returning to the bedroom, Mayme hung the dress on a hook, and all three sisters agreed it would be the last thing Marge would put on.

With utmost care, Marge carefully applied a small amount of face powder followed by lipstick applied first to her cheeks and gently rubbed in for the desired cheek color, then her lips. Marge placed the rose in her hair to complete her beauty routine. She gently put the newly cleaned dress on and adjusted her belt.

"Marge, you look beautiful." A sentiment echoed simultaneously by both her sisters.

"Thanks to you two, I feel beautiful. I need to be there by two but it doesn't start until three. I hope you both will be there."

"Are you kidding? The whole family wouldn't miss this for the world. But aren't you forgetting something?" Ellen pointed down and Marge realized she wasn't wearing any shoes. With that omission remedied, Marge hurried out.

"But Marge—"

"Sorry, I'm running late. You can tell me at the pageant."

Like a flash, Marge was hurrying toward her destiny. Regrettably, with each step, a cloud of powder ejected backward. On the outside, her shoes were cleaned but they didn't realize most of the powder from Marge's head landed inside her shoes and blended into its white interior lining.

Ellen and Mayme ran onto the front porch and couldn't help but giggle as the small white tornado walked several blocks toward Kresge's. They tried calling out to her, but she was too far away. At least the white puffs were decreasing in size with each step and by the time she'd arrive at the drugstore, the problem would probably be resolved. The sisters quickly went upstairs to clean up the upheaval before anyone questioned what happened.

The family arrived at 2:45 p.m. and saw a group of twenty-five contestants lined up on stage. An entire section of the store was cordoned off and chairs set up. The O'Malleys and friends took up two full rows with a clear line of sight to their precious Marge. The judging panel consisted of three employees varying in ages. The O'Malley clan agreed Marge was clearly the winner with her Janet Gaynor-likeness. They waved to Marge, and she discretely returned the greeting.

Finally, after what seemed like time was standing still, the oldest judge used a megaphone to make the long-awaited announcement. "The winner of the Janet Gaynor look-alike contest is . . ." He paused to build up tension. "Marge O'Malley."

The O'Malleys jumped up to cheer the prettiest contestant, and Marge waved to her fans. The older judge presented Marge with her $25 prize, and the youngest judge carried the crown over to Marge.

"My name's Judy. Can you please bend over so I can place the crown?"

"Of course, I will." Marge was thrilled to comply.

Judy encountered a mass of goo making crown placement a job more suited to a fisherman attempting to remove a slippery fish from its hook. After working hard for several minutes, sweat pouring down her cheeks, the crown was placed crookedly on Marge's head. When Judy stepped back and examined her hands, sticky and covered with a strange white powder, she scowled before rushing to remove the gooey mess in the nearest bathroom.

But the crown didn't stay in place and fell onto the stage. When

Marge bent over to pick it up, a cloud of white mist scattered into the audience. Anyone in the front row with their mouths open, began to cough as a white residue sprinkled into their oral cavity. To expel the unknown substance, audience members were clapped on their backs until the raucous sounds of choking subsided. It was the strangest ending to a beauty pageant and one that would be remembered by all who attended.

But one lesson was learned—never sit in the front row of a beauty competition.

Marge's attempt to replace the crown was a feat of pure determination. She, too, was unable to place it straight on her head and finally gave up, just happy it rested somewhere on her head. Blushing furiously and attempting to make a fast exit, the oldest judge wasn't done with the pageant or his brief moment of fame.

"Marge, please tell us everything. What's your secret for winning the contest?"

"Brylcreem," Marge replied through gritted teeth. Despite Marge's glorious and unforgettable win, all she wanted now was to run home and hide.

The O'Malleys, confused but still proud of Marge, replaced their clapping with open-mouthed expressions of disbelief as the contest winner hastily walked out of the store trailing a strange white powder and a crooked crown fastidiously held in place.

Michael looked at his wife and she shrugged, completely in the dark. The dinner conversation would certainly be lively. The moment Marge arrived home, she rushed upstairs to throw out the tube of hair superglue which kept its promise to maintain a hairstyle no matter what happened—and it did, to Marge's dismay. Despite her innate beauty, this was the last beauty contest Marge ever entered. She would never have guessed her path to fame was littered with humiliation, hair epoxy, and a trail of white powder.

49

More than a thousand miles from Cleveland, Ohio, another family was struggling with adversities doled out by fate. Harry DuChez was a God-fearing man who raised his children with love and a deeply rooted faith. He firmly believed God would watch over his family no matter what afflictions they would face. Harry moved his family to Denver when his wife, Nina, first contracted consumption (tuberculosis), and the cool Colorado air was recommended by her physician. While there, Harry joined the Loyal Order of Moose—a fraternal service organization started in the 1800s, well-known for its humanitarian efforts in addition to community service projects, family activities, and sports programs. There were numerous moose lodges across the United States, but the main headquarters was in Mooseheart, Illinois, where an entire city, aptly named Child City and funded by membership dues, was constructed to accommodate children in need.

Many would say Harry's decision to join the Moose Order was an act of divine providence because he expired one month later in 1920 from the Spanish Flu pandemic. Following the death of her husband, Nina and their four children (Dorothy, Louis, Harry, Jr., and Gertrude) moved to Mooseheart, Illinois, where Nina died from consumption. Thanks to Harry's foresight, despite being a member only one month prior to his death, his four children were eligible to live and prosper in Mooseheart Child City. Although many couples came forward at various times to adopt one of the four children, they refused to be separated and grew up in close proximity to one another.

Child City was a town with amenities catering to children with separate dormitories (boys, girls, and infants), church, medical clinic, schoolhouse, cafeteria, post office, auditorium, laundry facilities, and vocational structures. The siblings took comfort in seeing one another daily and gravitated toward interests that suited each one's unique talents.

Dorothy, the oldest child, controlled major decisions for her siblings. She agreed they would all join the Catholic faith and forgo their Protestant upbringing, when encouraged by the priests at Mooseheart. Although Louis, the second oldest, was happy to grow up near his siblings, he dreamed of adventures outside the confines of Child City. He excelled in woodshop and loved playing football. When Louis was on the field, he ran with unbridled joy as he scrambled for the ball with the intensity of a man on fire.

The years passed quickly and happily.

When any child reached the age of eighteen in Child City, they were given a generous stipend of $25 and a bus ticket. When Dorothy matured on her eighteenth birthday, she promptly returned the generous remuneration in exchange for an office job to resume her role of a surrogate mother to her siblings.

However, when Louis turned eighteen in 1930, he was forced to make a difficult decision—work at Child City with his siblings or pursue his lifelong ambition of travel and adventure. Shortly before his birthday, Louis met with his family and presented his conflict. Understanding his longing for an independent life, his brother and sisters agreed he should follow his passion. It was understood that, when Louis could finance their relocation, he would reunite the family at his ultimate destination.

After a tearful goodbye, Louis exchanged his bus ticket, combined with the extra cash he had earned, to purchase a one-way ride as far as the funds would take him. He landed in Cleveland, Ohio, to begin his new life.

50

When Louis stepped off the bus near the center of downtown Cleveland, he wasn't sure what to do or where to go. Completely alone, the only thing Louis knew for certain was that his destiny would be aligned with this bustling city. His confidence was brimming like a coffee cup overflowing with its delectable beverage. His excitement propelled him forward, and Louis walked for over an hour to explore his new hometown.

Feeling the heat of August, he stopped at a local store on Lorain Avenue for a soda. It was difficult to part with his paltry fortune, now reduced to jingling coins in his pocket. As he wiped the sweat from his brow, Louis glanced around and saw a highly competitive football game in progress. As he neared the field, he saw the school's name of St. Ignatius College above one of the building's entrances on Carroll Avenue.

Standing near the endzone, the ball whizzed by his head, and he automatically reached up to make an incredible catch with apparent ease before throwing it back with razor-sharp precision. The coach gave him a strange look and walked up to Louis.

"Where'd you learn to throw like that? Or make that unbelievable catch?" the coach asked, scrutinizing the relatively short powerhouse standing in front of him.

"I played some ball during school in Illinois."

"Think you could do it again?"

"Sure. Can I join the game?"

The coach was dubious since Louis was short, but he decided to give him a shot. "Sure, give it a try." Clearly, he wasn't expecting much from the new kid.

Louis jumped into the game, ignoring the derision about his stature from team players towering over him. But Louis was confident of his self-worth, and when his speed and agility were combined with a deadly accurate throwing arm, he brought his team to a quick victory. Stunned at their new player's innate skills, team members surrounded Louis, peppering him with questions.

The coach asked to see Louis in his office once the scrimmage ended. After getting directions from one of the players, Louis knocked gently on his door.

"Come on in. It's not locked."

Louis stepped inside, and the coach motioned for him to sit on the only remaining chair in the room.

"You wanted to see me, Coach?" For inexplicable reasons, Louis had a nervous feeling this meeting could define his future. Sweat dripped down his back, and he unsuccessfully attempted to hide his fear. Louis clutched his suitcase to his chest but couldn't stop his right leg from shaking.

"What's your name, son?"

"Louis DuChez, sir."

"Where are your parents?"

"They died. I've been living in an orphanage with my siblings."

The coach glanced up from his paperwork and his features softened. "Tough break, kid." Louis became self-conscious when he noticed the coach looking closely at his shabby clothes and shoes held together with tape. "How'd you like to attend John Carroll University? You can be the JCU equipment manager to pay your way. If you make the cut, you can even join the Blue Streaks. Would you like that?"

"Oh yes, sir. I really would. I'd work so hard and do anything you needed. I never thought I'd be able to attend college. Why it's like a dream come true—"

The coach smiled at the apprehensive young man and interrupted his nervous ramblings. "That's fine, Louis. Meet me on the field tomorrow, and we'll get started."

"Thank you, sir. But, I . . . I . . ." Louis wasn't sure how to solve his dilemma or ask a complete stranger for help.

Louis clutched his suitcase closely, intensely aware he didn't know how to ask the coach for help finding free lodgings. Fortunately, the coach came to his rescue. "There's a boarding house up the street on Carroll Avenue run by Aunt Annie. Tell her that I sent you, and she'll put you up with the rest of the boys on the team. Here, take this." The coach handed a piece of paper to Louis with an address and a brief note to Aunt Annie introducing her newest boarder.

"Gosh, I don't know what to say except thank you. I'll make you proud."

"I have a feeling you will," said the coach as he shook Louis's hand and watched the young man exit his office.

Once he settled into Aunt Annie's, he immediately penned a note to his siblings, advising them of his good fortune and noting life in Cleveland was swell. He told them that when he saved enough money, he would pay their bus fare to see him in action. When Louis's head hit the pillow, he was asleep in minutes dreaming of the fame and glory awaiting him.

51

As expected, Louis easily made the JCU Blue Streaks, and he thanked God for giving him the incredible opportunity of a college education. During the time that Louis DuChez attended John Carroll University (JCU) from 1930–1934, it was located between Lorain and Carroll Avenues, occupying the bottom two floors of what is now the current site of St. Ignatius High School in Cleveland.

The JCU graduating class of 1934 included future Hall of Fame Coach, Louis DuChez. He was only five-feet ten-inches but possessed an athlete's build, warm brown eyes, chiseled features with a cleft chin, and dark hair with a twist that furled over his forehead giving him a dashing air.

Aunt Annie's Boarding House (located on the same side of the street as JCU) remained Louis's residence while he was a varsity letterman from 1930–1933 and team captain from 1933–1934. Aunt Annie's was also located across from the O'Malley household. When Louis, called Lou by his friends, was a sophomore in 1932, he caught his first glimpse of Marge and was captivated by her rare beauty. Louis knew their fates were aligned before he ever opened his mouth to ask for a date.

When he saw her on the front porch, Lou casually crossed the street. Uncertain what he would say or how to address this goddess, he decided a direct approach was the answer.

"Hi, my name's Lou DuChez and I attend John Carroll University. I've seen you many times and wanted to meet you, but your family was always around." Lou knew he rambled but couldn't help himself. If he didn't get it all out, he might never have the courage again.

"I'm Marge O'Malley. I've noticed you around the neighborhood, too. After your practices, you look so hot and tired. Would you like to come over one afternoon for a glass of lemonade?" Marge asked with her eyes downcast, fearful of rejection—foreign and unsettling feelings normally absent around high school boys her age.

"Gee Marge, that would be keen. Perhaps tomorrow afternoon?"

"Sure. I'll see you around four if that works."

Practically speechless at his good fortune, all he could manage was, "See you then." His pulse accelerated and Lou became concerned it might never return to normal. As he began a countdown of the hours until he could see Marge, he began to panic. He didn't know what he would say or what they should do.

When he arrived at JCU practice, he decided to get his teammates' ideas for conversation topics and what to do on his first date—items sorely missing from his skillset. After they hooted and hollered the usual locker room banter, a general consensus was reached: a movie followed by an ice cream cone as he walked her home was the courting routine of choice. It sounded good to him.

With the security of a plan in place, Louie was impatient for the next day's arrival. After practice, he ran home for a quick shower and change before arriving at the O'Malley residence. Marge, waiting for him with a cool pitcher of lemonade on the front porch, was surrounded by her siblings. He realized this was going to be more difficult than he thought.

"Hi Marge. I see the whole gang is here to welcome me."

"Sorry, I tried to get them to stay inside or play anywhere else, but they insisted this was an experience they wouldn't miss for the world."

Lou smiled as Marge rolled her eyes. Marge and Lou had a glass of lemonade. The remaining children were too keyed up to drink, their thirst quenched by intense examination of their sister's new friend. As Lou emptied his glass, he contemplated the best way to appease the eager young gang facing him. "Okay, then. How about I teach everyone a few basics about football in the backyard?"

The kids were ready for a new challenge; even four-year-old Thomas scrambled behind his siblings, trying to keep up.

Diplomatically, Lou said, "Thomas, would you like to keep score?"

Everyone stifled a laugh—Thomas could barely count and needed to take off his shoes and socks when he got to eleventeen. But Thomas took his new-found duty seriously and tried his best.

Lou taught them basic tackles, offensive maneuvers, and defensive postures. He organized them into teams—Marge, Ellen, and himself on one team while Mayme, William, James, and Veronica composed the opposing side. After an hour, everyone was covered in grass stains, slipping and sliding on the grass, as the boys laughed uproariously. The girls' hair, wild and sticking out in every direction, had nature's decorations consisting of dandelions and assorted twigs. Of course, it didn't occur to the boys that their appearance was equally unruly.

When Mary O'Malley went into the backyard and saw what a wonderful time her children were having with Marge's new friend, she invited Lou to dinner. Their meal was simple—noodles, vegetables from Veronica's garden, spices, and a homemade sauce. Lou's first bite confirmed the mouth-watering meal was incomparable to anything served at Aunt Annie's, and sitting next to Marge added to his enjoyment.

Weekly football games in the O'Malley backyard became a highlight of the week, and Marge's sisters were secretly envious of Marge's new beau. Lou quickly became ensconced in the fabric of the O'Malley household, although her parents kept a strict eye on him since their lovely Marge had recently turned seventeen. Michael made it clear to Lou that their darling Marge would not be wed before she was twenty-one. To Lou and Marge, this seemed an eternity, but they agreed to respect his wishes.

52

No matter what occurred outside James's sphere of influence, to an impatient seven-year-old, listening to his favorite radio program took precedence in his hierarchy of needs.

"Are you guys ready yet? We'll be late if you don't get in here." James was attempting to gather everyone together for the next installment of *The Detective Story* narrated by the Shadow. Despite his youth, James knew the important things in life—like staking out a centerstage seat in front of the radio and making sure late-comers didn't disturb his favorite show.

The Shadow was someone he could relate to—a superhero with psychic powers. He considered them practically brothers! With James's many inventions, all in various stages of assembly or disarray, they could easily be completed after tapping into the Shadow's psychic powers. He knew they'd make an unbeatable team.

"We're here. Don't go bananas, James, for Pete's sake."

His sisters, ages nine to eighteen, tolerated the broadcast although they wouldn't admit they thought the narrative's voice was so hypnotic they didn't even mind the commercial interruptions.

"Wait for me, gang." Thomas, age five, rushed into the room, anxious to be part of the action. "Will he be invisible?"

"Of course. His magic powers to cloud the minds of his enemies will make him invisible. He's a solid hero who always overpowers the no-goodniks. The bad guys don't know doodley-squat," James replied impatiently, impressed with his newly acquired slang. He reached for the volume control to drown out the comments of his siblings.

Although William was one of the first to arrive, he sat back quietly and smiled at his younger brother's exasperation, content to watch his siblings' interactions.

As the show came to its exciting conclusion, with the requisite cliffhanger to ensure audiences would tune into future installments, James decided it was time for him to discover his own superpowers. He raced upstairs and donned a long bath towel as his cape, tied it under his chin, outstretched his arms, and flew down the stairs. Or, rather, he flew for two seconds then tumbled, stumbled, and fell the rest of the way. Hearing the racket, his siblings ran toward the commotion to find James at the bottom of the stairs wrapped in a towel and shaking his head.

"Are you okay, James?" Marge asked in concern.

Still in a daze and feeling the effects of a bruised ego, James shrugged. "Flying ain't what it used to be."

Silencing their laughter, everyone backed away slowly to alleviate their brother's embarrassment and loss of confidence.

But giggling could no longer be held at bay when their brother mumbled, "Maybe next time I'll try super-hearing instead. The worst that could happen is listening to my dumb sisters talk about some dreamy boy."

53

Protecting their children from the hardships of the Depression was of paramount importance to Michael and Mary as they kept daily routines status quo. Elizabeth was acquainted with the void of despair created by unfulfilled cravings. Each day, she forged ahead and utilized tools in her finely tuned arsenal—an abundant supply of tales to inspire everyone's imagination, music, and laughter—anything to stave off hunger pain. Her stories covered a variety of events, including her job as a teenager to provide food to soldiers fighting in assorted conflicts.

"Food was scarce and many workers in the large kitchens would sneak food under their shawls as they walked home with heads bowed in shame."

"Nana, did you ever take any food? After all, you were hungry, too," said an inquisitive, and sometimes pragmatic, Mayme.

"No, me darling. 'Twould not be right. Stealing food from soldiers risking their lives in battle would surely have been dishonest. I made certain ta wrap me shawl tightly around meself ta show the guards I'd never be stealing."

This statement had a profound effect on her spellbound audience as a valuable lesson was imparted and morality imbued upon youths eager to emulate their nana.

THE ENTIRE FAMILY continued normal nighttime routines, assisted by the older children, as everyone worked in concert to prepare the youngest for bed. Prayers were said, and the children were tucked in followed by kisses from their parents. The older siblings were permitted to stay up until 9:00 p.m., using the extra time to read, write in their diaries, or share neighborhood gossip.

The normal routine worked well until Veronica woke up screaming. She saw a spider crawling on the wall and continued wailing until her mother ran into her room.

"What is wrong, me darling?" her mother asked.

Shaking, Veronica pointed to the multilegged creature beginning to spin a web in the corner of her bedroom.

"Hush now," her mother said calmly. "Do not be afraid. Did ye not know 'twas spiders ta save Jesus as a baby?"

The waterworks stopped instantly, replaced by an expression of awe. Mary continued, "When the Holy Family escaped the fury of King Herod, they sought refuge in a cave. Tired from a day of hard travel, they soon fell into a deep sleep. They did not know King Herod's men were close by and sure ta find them. Outside the cave, 'twas a large group of spiders spending the night weaving a web so thick the soldiers were not able ta break the strong barrier. They gave up and thought surely the cave was empty fer no one could gain entry. By the next morning, the webs came apart as easily as butter melts on a hot roll. They continued the journey home without further problems."

"Oh Ma, that's a beautiful story. Perhaps I should keep the spider as a good luck charm."

"No, me love. Some creatures are meant ta be free ta work their magic. Now return ta sleep and be sure ta take comfort as the spider spins a web ta hide bad dreams fer the night."

"Gee, Ma, you know everything."

Mary smiled at her young daughter's naiveté and recalled her own sweet mother's view of education.

"I have forgotten more than ye will ever learn."

After the excitement died down, Mary tucked Veronica under the covers. Smiling contentedly, Mary sang her favorite lullaby, "Too-ra-loo-ra-loo-ral". The tune worked its magic by drawing comfort into her daughter's heart followed by sleep to chase away nighttime fears.

VERONICA SOON FELL into a deep sleep and never again feared the sight of spiders. She shared her mother's story with other children to help them overcome panic when encountering multi-legged creatures. The O'Malley home became a safe haven for spiders—but only after they were gently escorted outside.

54

After losing their savings, Michael's business began a steady decline. With no money coming in, the bank still expected monthly payments from Michael for his four rental properties. As ironic as it was sad, those living in Michael's renovated homes were exempt from paying rent although he was still expected to make mortgage payments. When this became impossible, Michael's rental properties reverted back to the bank.

The Great Depression, a global event, became the Great Equalizer as an overnight culture of heartache and emptiness emerged. With the exception of the very few born into privilege, the majority were humbled by the economic tsunami. The former distinction of rich and poor blurred as each man's plight morphed into the same fate of others, thereby leveling the playing field. A common sight of someone surrendering to his new reality included an unkempt presence defined by hair that never met a comb with rumpled clothes that appeared to hang lifeless and disinterested. A man's physical girth and stamina were halved, leaving him in a perpetual state of exhaustion, devoid of emotion. Those more fortunate would look with derision upon the newly bankrupt, treating them with mockery and disdain. But their taunts were ignored, as each man, consumed with meeting his family's needs, continued his never-ending sojourn toward survival.

During the Depression, the unemployment rate reached 25 percent, and hard times fell on everyone, including the O'Malleys. Jobs were scarce and even menial positions, such as newspaper routes, were only offered to grown men with families to support. Department stores, reduced to one clerk per floor, felt like ghost towns. Finally, both Taylor Company and Bailey's Department stores closed their doors for good—harbingers of the economic downturn.

But Ellen's first recollection of the Depression came rolling down Carroll Avenue one sunny afternoon. "Ma, what's that man doing?"

Glancing out the front window, she saw a man without legs peddling down the street on a homemade cart powered by his powerful arms.

"Will sharpen any knife for only a nickel!" the man called out loudly as he propelled himself down the street.

"Ma, why's that man on a rolling board using his arms?"

"Ellen, he lost his legs in the war. Go, fetch me purse."

Mary O'Malley removed a dime from her purse and handed it to Ellen with two knives. "Give these ta the man and bring the sharpened knives back."

"But Ma, these knives are sharp enough." Ellen knew they were short on funds and didn't understand the needless expense.

"He needs the money more than we do. If we help one another, God helps us all. Now off with ye." Always cognizant of other's misfortunes, Mary reached out to help those less fortunate, even if it meant she would go without.

The O'Malley children contributed to the family's coffers during lean times. William worked as a "shake boy" in a speakeasy located at the back of Cubars barbershop on Columbus Road in "Duck City," a name used by bootleggers from "ducking" into this locale during Prohibition raids. This establishment was next to Ohio City and William's job entailed shaking mixed drinks 100 times per concoction to save the bartenders from developing sore muscles. Marge, Mayme, and Ellen made butterflies out of clothespins and tissue paper wings gilded with gold sprinkles. They took the streetcar to affluent neighborhoods on the East Side of Cleveland to sell their treasures for ten cents each. It was a good day if they sold two or three, but their small efforts were heralded with applause and fanfare when they arrived home. All endeavors by the children instilled pride for their efforts to feed the family while keeping creditors at bay.

55

In addition to Elizabeth's small financial contributions from her savings in Feighan's Bank to the O'Malley household during the Depression, Mary would further supplement their income by taking in wash from prosperous communities. Veronica, happiest working in her garden, applied her love of the earth to augment nature's vegetables, as she grew items supplying nutritious staples to their diet. Many evening meals consisted solely of a loaf of bread, a beefsteak tomato, and homemade mayonnaise. The children were blissfully unaware of their family's precarious financial situation. But they knew some families didn't even have the luxury of tomato sandwiches. Meals from the garden, combined with family love and shared happiness, turned their simple fare into feasts.

Their father was able to procure small plumbing jobs and managed to keep busy each day. Before the Depression, O'Malley Plumbing had employed every able-bodied man on Carroll Avenue. But as the Depression dragged on, he was forced to lay off men one at a time—people who were not just employees but neighbors and friends. Michael deeply regretted the lack of business to keep his friends employed but did the best he could under the circumstances.

On a sunny Tuesday afternoon, William begged his father to let him help with the family business. After purchasing a new toilet at the local plumbing supply store, William asked, "Da, how are we going to get this to the neighbor's house?"

"We will take the streetcar," replied Michael.

William accepted his father's solution, without questioning logistical problems because he trusted his father implicitly. But when they boarded the streetcar, it was filled.

William asked in a whispered voice, "What do we do now?"

"The only thing we can do." Michael plunked the toilet in the center aisle of the streetcar and perched himself upon his throne as riotous laughter and snickering broke out.

"Y'er looking a wee bit flushed, Michael," commented the conductor, a fellow Irishman from the neighborhood.

With this remark, even the most sedate passengers were unable to suppress chuckling. Michael had a wicked sense of humor, even in difficult times.

In addition to employment as a plumber, Michael was gifted as a carpenter and general contractor from days in his youth constructing his parents' home in Ireland. Searching for ways to further augment their income, Michael built a separate apartment behind their kitchen. It rented for $15 per month and consisted of three furnished rooms—kitchen, bedroom, and bathroom. But they learned, the hard way, even honest folk confronted with desperate times resorted to deception.

One day, Michael knocked on the front door to the apartment, as he had each month for the past year, saying, "Mr. O'Toole, I'm here ta collect the rent."

The door opened slowly as his tenant grimaced in pain. "Me money's in the back room. Can ye gimee the receipt now so I don't have ta make two trips? Me leg's botherin' me today."

As Michael handed over the receipt, Mr. O'Toole jumped up and down in elation. "Don't need ta pay ye now. I got proof with this here receipt."

From then on, someone always accompanied Michael as a witness for rent collections, and Mr. O'Toole was evicted at the month's end. The price of Michael's innocence was only fifteen dollars.

56

Fortunately for families struggling to survive, St. Patrick's school did not require uniforms, but hand-me-down clothes were the norm. Mary made all her children's clothes from material on sale or left over from other projects like tablecloths and curtains. Even flour factories began to package their goods in printed material for customers to make homemade garments. The girls didn't mind wearing pink floral dresses, but her sons drew the line at ruffles and barnyard animals—after all, a fella's gotta have standards.

At noon, all the children dashed out of school to race home for a quick lunch before they rushed back for recess. While dishing out the food, their mother quizzed them about lessons they learned.

"And what did ye learn today, Ellen?"

"At least Sr. Rosario didn't get mad when I explained why I couldn't sit back in my seat."

"And why could ye not do this?"

"Because I'd crush my angel's wings. Boy, sometimes it sure is a lot of work looking out for her," Ellen replied, shaking her head.

Mary turned around so her daughter didn't witness her soft laughter.

Continuing her inquisition, Mary asked Mayme, "And what did ye learn today?"

"Our teacher taught us about erosion. It's when portions of land are destroyed by natural processes like water or wind."

"Ah, I see. And William what about ye?"

"We learned about some guy, Newton."

"And who might himself be?"

"Why don't I show you?"

"All right, me dear."

William promptly demonstrated by tossing his lunch plate into the air. When it came crashing down, an exasperated Mary asked her son, while cleaning up the mess, "And what is the purpose of this lesson?"

"He discovered gravity. What goes up must come down."

"I see. Next time if ye would please just recite yer lesson, I would be much happier. No need fer further demonstrations."

Although Mary was upset at William's display, her children didn't realize their mother wasn't asking out of idle curiosity but an intense hunger of the formal knowledge denied in her own childhood. Although Mary O'Malley's children were convinced that she was the smartest woman in the world, it would have surprised them to learn how much she envied their education. Mary was not book-smart, but she possessed a rare combination of common sense, an aura of self-confidence, and an intuitive compassion to address any problem that arose. Had Mary known those innate gifts were more precious than a diploma or any type of formal schooling, she may not have felt compelled to continue her education by osmosis.

57

During the Great Depression, the O'Malley clan was able to weather the Depression with love and shared memories. Mary had her hands full caring not only for her rambunctious brood and running a household but also tending to the needs of her own mother.

With foresight and luck, Elizabeth contributed to the O'Malley family's diminishing funds during the Depression from money deposited into Feighan's Bank, the only institution to remain open during the Great Depression.

Elizabeth loved to sit in a rocking chair by the fireside as she smoked her corn cob pipe, filling the air with sweet-smelling cherry tobacco. Her clear blue eyes sparkled despite life's harsh tragedies that would cripple others. But Elizabeth would not allow them to define her life or dictate her actions. She wore her long, gray hair with wisps of red—a solitary reminder of her youth—in a braid wrapped around her head.

When Elizabeth was surrounded by her seven grandchildren, nothing else mattered as she plied her rapt audience with tales of her favorite subject—Ireland and its grand history filled with adventure and excitement.

She proudly regaled them with memories of days long ago while growing up in Ireland, lovingly referred to as the Auld Sod. Elizabeth vividly recounted the lush green fields, thatch-roofed cottages, and sheep roaming the countryside—memories to fill the hearts and souls of anyone blessed to be immersed in Elizabeth's colorful accounts. Her daughter, Mary, remained in the background as her eyes misted over when her mother's words ignited her own recollections of the land she left behind.

But the most exciting tales, that filled the O'Malley children with a longing to visit their ancestral home, involved stories of the famous pirate queen—Grace O'Malley (*Granuaile or Ghrainne Ní Mhaille* in Gaelic). In spite of Irish law prohibiting Grace from becoming the official chieftain of the O'Malley clan in the male-dominated society, she was awarded the unofficial title of Ireland's Pirate Queen through her successful and highly profitable exploits. Elizabeth's stories included her own childhood explorations of the O'Malley castles, many commandeered by Grace's successful battles with rival clans throughout county Mayo on Ireland's western seaboard.

Elizabeth enthralled her grandchildren with tales of Grace's fierce battles and pillaging that carved out her sixteenth century motto, "Powerful by Land and Sea." Legends and folklore documented her grit and the sheer force of her prowess, which endeared Grace to hundreds of men under her command. Considering the age of her audience, Elizabeth withheld tales of Grace's alleged sexual exploits— a woman who transcended societal norms by using lovers for their ability to aid her exploits when her own spouse proved to be a weak and ineffectual leader. Grace was able to rebuild the sagging fortunes of the O'Malley clan, depleted by her husband's ineptitude, in addition to fighting against Great Britain's tyranny.

With Grace's enviable leadership skills, she attracted fighters skilled in all manner of sword fighting. Her army grew in numbers and strength beyond the borders of Ireland to include Scottish Highlanders, Celts from Western Europe, and Vikings. By joining forces with Grace, her army was assured of their seafaring adventures ransacking British ships to relieve them of precious jewels and treasures that promised great wealth.

Elizabeth took great pride in regaling stories of the relationship between Grace and Queen Elizabeth I, reveling in her grandchildren's incredulity. Despite Grace's successful naval battles against British ships to commandeer their precious cargo, Queen Elizabeth I admired the young leader's tenacity and accomplishments on behalf of her impoverished nation.

"Did the two women ever meet, Nana?" inquired William, practically salivating at the spectacular sword fights he imagined occurred on the high seas between rival nations.

"Aye!" Elizabeth's eyes twinkled with exhilaration as she relayed one of her favorite stories. "Grace considered herself a queen and equal ta Britain's sovereign. Legend has it that Grace's arrival in England ta the customary port at Howth was a complete disaster. Lord Howth was dining and refused Grace and her crew entry ta the castle. They were forced ta remain outside Howth's locked castle gates, and the custom of providing a meal ta seafaring visitors was ignored. His rude and disrespectful behavior toward Grace's entourage was too great ta be overlooked. Furious, she abducted the son of Lord Howth and went back ta Ireland with him in tow."

"Was the son returned unharmed?" asked Mayme, with hope-filled eyes for a happy conclusion.

"Aye. Lord Howth's initial offer of a ransom fer his son was scoffed by Grace. Instead, her simple demands were the implementation fer expected decorum of the day. She gave his son safe passage once Lord Howth agreed ta meet two simple requests: a promise ta keep the gates open ta anyone seeking hospitality, and assure a place setting in the dining hall would always be maintained in anticipation of future guests."

"And did he keep his promise?"

"Aye, he was so relieved when Grace returned his son, that Grace's demands are said ta exist ta this very day."

"Did she meet Queen Elizabeth I at that time?" asked Ellen softly.

"No, legend notes Grace did not meet the Queen until 1593 when Grace was sixty-three years old. 'Twas a high honor, and though no record of their conversation exists, it is believed the Queen was in awe of Grace's achievements given she was a woman without the formal support of a country, government, or established armed forces. Letters from the Queen document she aided Grace in her personal and political struggles, including those of her family. But can ye picture the amazing energy present when these two powerful women from widely diverse backgrounds finally met on equal footing?"

Her grandchildren shook their heads in unison, and Elizabeth noted each child sat up a little straighter in response to her query. Elizabeth was in awe of the courage and bravery exhibited by Grace O'Malley, feelings she hoped were conveyed to the pirate queen's seven direct descendants sitting at her feet.

"In the end, Grace even defied the natural laws of life expectancy in the sixteenth century—averaged at thirty-five years. Yet she lived from 1530 ta 1603 and died at the robust age of seventy-three."

Without an abundance of food, stories from their nana fed their passion for adventure once again and assuaged hunger pangs until they became a distant memory. Just as the traveling Storytellers from long ago in the Auld Sod, the O'Malley children shared their nana's stories of exciting escapades with pride throughout the neighborhood. Imaginations were ignited in the O'Malley neighborhood as they engaged in spirited recreations of sword fights with garbage can lids as shields.

Without realizing it, their actions were a repetition of centuries-long escapades by Irish children, including the Ginleys in their youth. During forays to the O'Malley castles throughout County Mayo, determination rallied their passion while standing in the presence of historical greatness. Reenactments of epic battles were carried out with fervor using wooden sabers as they clashed one another in homage to the infamous pirate queen confronting the British. Transcending space and time—whether County Mayo or Cleveland —one predictable outcome was certain. Hungry bellies were temporarily replaced by the glory of battle and high adventure.

FOR ELLEN, her nana's stories about Grace O'Malley became a source of immense pride, and she developed a surety her path was destinated for greatness. Her middle name of Grace practically demanded it, and Ellen was determined to live up to her legacy.

58

As Thomas grew older, his sense of adventure grew. The neighborhood children returned to the O'Malley front porch with the understanding that joining in the antics of the O'Malley children was not for the fainthearted.

"Bring the bag with you and we'll meet in front of St. Patrick's at seven o'clock tonight." Thomas was in full command mode as his cohorts looked up to him. The neighborhood kids admired his devil-may-care attitude and thick, blond hair that cascaded over one eye.

"Think we'll get in trouble?" asked Deland, the youngest in their band of pranksters.

"Nah, it'll be quick and smooth. Just be sure to keep your trap shut afterward." Thomas spoke the last sentence with just the right amount of menace to ensure a clean getaway.

At the assigned time, Thomas emptied the bag of goldfish into the holy water font. The next day was Sunday, and there was literally holy hell to pay. Mrs. Peebles fainted and later claimed she felt the Holy Spirit touch her hand as she reached into the holy water to bless herself.

Father Blair investigated the source of commotion by asking,

"Who's responsible for the goldfish?" Obviously, he was not amused by their little escapade.

When thoughts of hellfire and damnation were implied, Deland screamed out, "The devil made us do it." All eyes were immediately on Thomas. Busted, again, and grounded for sure.

Two weeks later, Thomas and his friends were outside playing when the irresistible smell of freshly baked apple pie wafted overhead. Everyone knew LaTressa Thompson made the best pies on the street, and this one was cooling in her front window, begging to be tasted.

"I think we should make sure the pie tastes good." No one disagreed with Thomas as they wiped drool from their chins. As anyone would expect, they dug their hands into the center and yanked out sections of the fluffy pie.

"Ummm. Tastes even better than it looks." Licking each sticky finger, they heard Mrs. Thompson's approach and scurried away amidst her shrill expletives about the neighborhood going downhill.

But their best caper, one certain to become legendary in the kid's hall of fame, was the rescue of Molly's pups. A lovely Irish Setter, Molly was a neighborhood fixture who belonged to no one in particular but stole the hearts of the Irish community. All except for mean old Miss Stitch—a curmudgeon. Molly was fed scraps supplied by the children, who noticed she was getting a really round belly. What a surprise when she delivered five pups just a couple of weeks later!

When Miss Stitch found out, she immediately contacted the Cleveland Animal Protective League, an organization dreaded by kids since its inception in 1913. When the kids saw the horse-drawn wagon with the APL logo two blocks away, Thomas ran inside. He quickly devised a plan to thwart the dreaded Miss Stitch and brought out four water balloons.

"Timmy, Danny, Neil, and Louie. Each of you take one of these and wait on the four corners along Carroll Avenue. When I say, 'Woof,' launch them at the driver." He then ran around back and placed a box in the alley behind his home.

At the prescribed moment, Thomas gave the signal and water balloons went sailing toward the driver each time he attempted to exit his perch from atop the truck. Determined not to be outdone by a bunch of children, the dogcatcher drove around the block and waited a long time—thirty minutes at least. Without finding the culprits, the driver approached the box of sleeping pups, covered with a small blanket, from the back alley and chuckled at the thought of outwitting their neighborhood protectors. However, when the dogcatcher arrived back at the APL, he discovered the box contained an assorted selection of old stuffed animals.

At the same moment, five kids each took a pup home to their mothers. One tiny puppy, was promptly named Viv after a family friend. With tears in their eyes, a pleading tone in their voices, promises to care for the puppy, and (best of all) a firm pledge to eat all their vegetables, the puppies were saved.

Thomas carried one pup into the O'Malley household and handed it to Mayme, whose theatrical performance would have earned her a role on Broadway. The family pet, a gorgeous Irish setter with a sweet temperament, was promptly named McTavish. Although Michael and Mary O'Malley had reservations about fostering the new pup, they believed this would be a much better lesson in responsibility than their last pets.

The year before, they were given four goldfish and selected wonderful Catholic names—Matthew, Mark, Luke, and John. Each child believed the fish belonged to them and fed them accordingly. By the time the bowl was cleaned a week later, all four were belly-up and quite rotund. On that particular night, the younger children exhibited unusual speed in preparing for bed. Their deep-felt piety, with a small amount of trepidation, could be heard in their voices during their nightly prayers. They hoped God would forgive them for annihilating the four Gospel authors in less than a week. Maybe God had a similar pet experience? If so, surely He would understand.

59

At the start of a sweltering summer day in 1933 when it felt like running barefoot would melt the soles right off your feet, the O'Malley siblings decided a trip to the local swimming pool was the perfect solution. Ellen immediately ran across the street to 3105 Carroll Avenue in search of her best friend since birth, Aileen Himmelspach. Being only one year apart, Aileen was born in 1919. She never let Ellen forget she was the oldest in her sweet, good-natured way. She was included in most O'Malley activities during Ellen's childhood.

"Hey Aileen, wanna go swimming with us?"

"Boy, would I! In this heat, that sounds heavenly. Be right out." Five minutes later, Aileen reappeared with her curly auburn locks dancing, green eyes sparkling, and adorable dimples framing her cherubic face. Racing across the street, Aileen joined Ellen as they rushed ahead to catch up with the O'Malley clan. They wore their swimsuits under their clothes and carried a bag with swim caps, towels, and fresh underwear. Arriving at the pool, it was fairly crowded but sure to be jam-packed by the afternoon. In addition to being close by, this pool had the advantage of two diving boards.

Aileen and Ellen raced each other in the pool as their legs slogged in turtle-slow speed, attempting to be the first to reach the opposite side. Aileen, being taller, was usually the winner, but sometimes she took pity on her friend and congratulated her when she "won."

"Betcha you can't dive off the high board." William taunted Ellen.

Aileen was clearly nervous for her friend. "As your elder . . ." Ellen rolled her eyes. "Don't do it. Looks dangerous." But when Aileen saw Ellen's determined expression, she knew from experience any further appeals would be ignored.

Although this would be an endeavor Ellen never attempted, she responded to the dare with a nonchalance she didn't feel, "Sure, why not?" After climbing halfway up the stairs, the high board seemed to reach up to the sky. Gulping, she constantly reassured herself. *You can do this.*

Finally reaching Mount Olympus, also known as the high board, Ellen attempted to conquer her apprehension by glimpsing her siblings and Aileen, but they were no larger than sticks of carrots. Ellen reminded herself she was an excellent diver on the lower board, so she'd simply apply the same technique and ignore the altitude.

Calmly walking to the edge of the board, she assumed her diving stance, took a deep breath, and said a quick prayer she'd survive before jumping through what she imagined were clouds, given her current height. Despite her perfect form, her second-hand swimsuit chose that very moment to fail her.

The right strap of her bathing suit broke mid-dive. Exposed on one side, Ellen was unable to fix the problem halfway through her dive or risk a very painful belly flop.

A simultaneous loud overhead noise occurred at that very moment, as everyone looked up to witness Ellen's mortifying clothing failure. "*Ahhhh*," Ellen screeched, and her eyes opened as wide as a gecko.

When she hit the water, Ellen stayed underwater so long her companions thought she drowned.

"She's been under too long. We need to do something." Aileen and Ellen's sisters huddled together and came up with a plan to save Ellen.

"Ellen, we're on the way!" Marge shouted as her sisters and Aileen jumped into the pool with two large towels kept above the water. They circled around Ellen to cover her offensive and tattered swimsuit. "Come on, Ellen, we'll walk with you to the bathhouse so you can get changed."

"I can't get out. Everyone saw me. I'll just stay here forever."

"No, Ellen, your fingers will get all shriveled up like a prune."

"Better than dying of shame."

"What'll happen when it snows?"

"I'll become an ice statue."

"I'll make you a deal," Mayme said. "No one saw your face. They were too astounded to see your disintegrating swimsuit."

"Thanks, that's reassuring."

"Wait, let me finish. Aileen and Marge can hold the two towels around you and I that will shield us as we switch bathing suits before getting out of the pool. Then I'll drape the towels around myself, and we'll all walk into the bathhouse. That way everyone will think it was me on the high board. How does that sound?"

"You'd really do that for me, Mayme?"

"Of course, that's what sisters are for."

"But won't you be embarrassed?"

"Nah, someday I'm going to be an actress, and I'll have to handle wardrobe mishaps. Might just as well gain some experience now."

"Okay then, let's do it."

They changed in the pool, then exited together, heads held high. Mayme endured the jeers and gawking stares with the dignity befitting a Broadway star. Once they were all dry and appropriately clothed, they headed toward home, but William kept a dozen feet behind them pretending he'd never seen them before. When they got home, the first thing they did was reinforce all swimwear.

"I bet no one will ever experience a wardrobe mishap as embarrassing as mine," said Ellen.

IRONICALLY, the journey of Ellen and Aileen's friendship had an unusual path with a circuitous ending. After graduating from West

High School, they lost touch in their pursuit of different careers, dating, marrying, and moving away.

Two decades later, Aileen Kerns had two wonderful children, each born in the same year as one of Ellen O'Malley Szabo's children. Marlene Kerns would become Eileen Marie Szabo's best friend, while Paul Kerns would befriend Mary Frances Szabo.

By the 1960s, despite both families living in the same neighborhood only a few blocks apart, Ellen and Aileen never reconnected. But how magical it was for a childhood friendship from one generation to transcend through their children, creating something akin to a filial bond between the two families. Without knowing their mothers knew one another, the connection of their mothers' friendship was made when Paul and Mary Frances discovered their mothers (so close in age with similar temperaments and living across from one another on Carroll Avenue), were undoubtedly friends. Finally, the secret of Ellen's best childhood friend (beside her siblings) was revealed during the writing of this novel. But this story does have a happy conclusion. Now that Ellen and Aileen are both in heaven, they have finally rekindled their friendship for eternity.

60

Ellen was too shy to return to the swimming pool after the recent bathing suit fiasco. As summer dragged on, there was no respite from its unrelenting heat. It became an equalizer among the young and old, refusing to be quenched by an occasional ice cream cone or hand-held fan. On one of the hottest days, a memorable event took place on Carroll to extinguish the rising temperatures and infuse the day with an exciting adventure.

William called out to his siblings from the living room. "You guys better get out here before you miss all the action."

They raced to the front window and saw a red fire truck with a round smokestack in the middle pulled down the street by two white horses. With excitement brimming, they quickly ran out front chasing the red truck as their imaginations soared with anticipation.

Luckily, the fire on Carroll Avenue was small and quickly extinguished before any major damage or casualties. But afterwards the volunteer fire department opened up the fire hydrant and all the neighbors ran into the cool water gushing high into the sky. Even the normally reserved adults got into the action, tired of the exhausting heat, which drained their energy. On that afternoon, everyone on Carroll Avenue released their inhibitions, giddy as they drenched themselves in the cool bliss of the hydrant geyser. Even McTavish frolicked in the geyser of delight, barking to his friends about the biggest faucet they'd ever seen as they, too, played games and romped in the gushing water.

In anticipation of scorching Sundays, after attending early mass each week, Michael and Mary would take their children on the streetcar down to Edgewater Park. Fortunately, Michael knew the streetcar conductors and they permitted McTavish to tag along for the ride. The O'Malleys left home as quickly as possible to secure a picnic table and eat the lunch prepared by Mary. After playing with McTavish for an hour to fulfill the required fast before swimming, the children swam in Lake Erie while their parents waded in the cool refreshing water. Veronica took her sibling's good-natured ribbing in stride as they oft repeated her initial impression of the lake, "Look at the big bathtub."

With McTavish's love of water, he relished their forays to the lake. Everyone giggled at his antics and his favorite game, fetching a stick or ball, would keep him happy for hours.

But on days when the humidity was high, poor McTavish's thick furry coat completely zapped his energy. He remained on the front porch with his tongue hanging out and his large sad eyes begging for relief. His water bowl was constantly filled, but some days it just wasn't enough.

"How can we help poor McTavish?" asked James of his siblings, after filling the water bowl for the fourth time, knowing it would be empty in less than fifteen minutes.

"Let's sneak him into the theater this Saturday. We could put a towel over him. No one would guess he's a dog," said Thomas enthusiastically. He couldn't understand why everyone laughed.

To all the neighborhood kids, going to the theater was nirvana on a hot Saturday. They gladly performed odd jobs during the week to earn a precious five cents—their ticket for one day in the delightful, cool air while being entertained with movies, cartoons, and newsreels. And, when that happened, everything in their small world was jake.

61

All but the wealthy were afflicted by the Depression, but the resulting oppressions affected families differently, depending on their station in life and strength of spirit. For Frank's mother, Emma Szabo, the Depression was especially difficult. She withstood the brunt of Paul's anger and misery when his job offers decreased. He experienced incapacitating pain from a foot ulcer limiting his mobility.

Frank did not escape his father's frustrations, and beatings became a daily occurrence. But Frank took solace being in a grade with near-contemporaneous students at St. Patrick's, despite being four years older. Once again, sports helped him assimilate with classmates, and books became his link to sanity. Shortly after Frank entered the tenth grade, Assistant Principal Sister Abigail called Frank into her office.

Filled with apprehension, Frank entered Sister Abigail's office. *Uh-oh. What did I do wrong?*

"Sit down Frank. I'd like to speak with you. I've been keeping an eye on you. Despite your difficulties in learning the language and customs of a new country, your diligence and dedication are most impressive."

Whew! Maybe I'm not in trouble after all.

"Thank you, Sister."

"I know your financial status is limited," she said kindly and with great diplomacy. "I've spoken with the principal at St. Ignatius High School, and they agreed to accept you into their freshman class. As long as you keep your grades up, your four-year tuition will be covered. Would you like that?"

Frank was breathless at the possibilities he had just been presented. He was about to accept the generous offer when he realized the dream would never become a reality.

Swallowing a lump forming in his throat, Frank voiced the unthinkable and erased his newfound dream. "Thank you, Sister, for your kind offer. But, without funds for book fees or proper clothes, I have to turn it down."

After shaking hands with the assistant principal, Frank walked dejectedly out of the office, realizing he had no one to share this incredible opportunity offered to him, a humble youth struggling for acceptance.

On June 1, 1933, Frank graduated from St. Patrick's yet, once again, his parents were not in attendance.

62

President Roosevelt helped improve the mental health of the nation's workforce by enacting the New Deal in 1933—federally funded programs to provide employment and renewed self-esteem for the staggering twenty-five percent of men reduced to joblessness by the Depression. Michael O'Malley earned several city plumbing contracts, which provided a financial security absent for many years. The family, along with the entire neighborhood, breathed a collective sigh of relief knowing Michael's good fortune would result in jobs for others.

Michael was painfully aware of other's plight and tried to lend a helping hand wherever possible. When he walked by a stranger with only one leg visible, holding out a tin cup as he sat on a Y-shaped abutment from a large downtown building, Michael took pity on the man and placed a coin in his cup.

"Good luck ta ye," Michael said feeling pleased with himself and walked away whistling a merry tune.

"Hey Mack. What'd you do that for? I just bought this here cuppa coffee on my lunch break." The man jumped up from where he sat, one leg tucked under him, and began to run after the man who had plunked money into his freshly brewed coffee. Michael sprinted away amidst the sounds of laughter from other workers. For the rest of his career, Michael would be teased when someone bought a cup of coffee by asking if the taste was rich enough.

Fortunately, Michael's expertise was well-known, and in 1934, he was awarded a plumbing contract by the City of Rocky River at the prestigious Westlake Hotel. Four years after becoming a city, the western suburb of Cleveland was considered by many as an overgrown garden suitable and an unlikely location for a hotel. In spite of this, Rocky River had a unique reputation of catering to famous pilots passing through Cleveland-Hopkins International Airport, the nation's first municipally owned airport. In essence, the Westlake Hotel was built with foresight to provide the only lodgings for out-of-towners using the airport.

When his father proudly told the family about the new project, all James heard was the word "aviator," and he jumped up and down with unbridled excitement.

"Can I go with you to the hotel, Da? I promise not to get in your way." James pleaded with his most engaging grin, and his father relented.

"We'll try it fer one day. Just don't ye be bothering anyone."

WHILE WAITING for his father to complete his work, James roamed the halls of the spacious hotel. As he rounded a corner, James nearly collided with his two heroes—Amelia Earhart and Charles Lindbergh! Believing karma smiled on him, James stood taller, prepared to heap praise on his gods of aviation. That is, until he noticed it was merely a life-size poster of the duo from their special appearance the day before.

James couldn't believe the passage of one day prevented him from impressing them with his substantial knowledge of flight. The fact he'd never even been in an airplane didn't factor into his personal assessment of aviation comprehension. Lamentably, missing this momentous event also meant he missed the chance to obtain their autographs, a memento he could have cherished forever.

Gazing at the picture of Amelia Earhart, taken several years earlier during the 1929 Cleveland Air Race, James whispered, "Golly, she's even prettier in person."

Images of flying surged to the forefront, and his dream of one day becoming an ace in the sky, while breaking speed records, of course, was once again rekindled. And, if he couldn't fly a plane, at least he could take it apart, which would involve a million pieces. *Pure heaven,* he thought. For the rest of the day, James walked the halls in a daze with a goofy grin on his face.

"James," his father called to him as he gathered his tools.

No response. Passersby looked on curiously as Michael's numerous attempts to get the young man's attention—growing louder with each utterance—failed to elicit a response from the boy.

James finally heard someone shout his name. Moving in a trance, his mind occupied by the recent presence of his adored Amelia, James turned toward the source and replied in a distant voice, "Yes, Amelia, dear?"

"Amelia? No son, 'tis yer father." Michael felt his son's forehead to rule out a fevered response, but it was cool to the touch. He took his son's hand and guided him out of the hotel toward the streetcar. That same silly grin was still there when James arrived home. Walking inside, James turned to his mother and said, "Thank you, Amelia."

On some level, James was aware his parents exchanged strange glances, but it was inconsequential. James was in his own private world and what a marvelous place it was!

63

After working at the swanky Westlake Hotel with its entourage of custom vehicles in the parking lot, Michael still considered a car to be an unnecessary luxury. But Michael tried to make amends by purchasing an RCA Victrola as a special treat. He made a flamboyant presentation as the family watched in disbelief. Was their father actually embracing technology?

"Oh Da, it's keen!" Marge exclaimed, as she reverently touched this marvelous invention. It contained a fourteen-inch nickel-plated cone horn with the ends shaped like a large bell flower connected to a turntable.

"Can we listen to it?" asked James, as he quietly walked around the device mentally taking it apart—his favorite hobby. To his dismay, he usually wasn't able to reassemble items back into their original format. His projects normally ended up looking like science projects from another planet. A small price, he would always say, to become an important inventor.

"It came with a free disk fer us ta listen. I think the salesman called it a *record*." The thin black record, labeled 78 rpm, was ten inches in diameter and capable of containing up to three recorded minutes. The demo disk, however, was much shorter.

After winding up the crank, Michael placed the record on the turntable and set the needle carefully on the record.

A German voice loudly proclaimed with much authority, "Da vind blew da shudders off da side of mine house."

Pure magic! They listened to it over and over until their parents couldn't stand it any longer.

"We need another *re*cord," exclaimed Mary O'Malley, who covered her forehead to offset the beginning of a headache.

"Oh yes, lots," said Ellen.

"At least fifty. Maybe some boogie-woogie records," said Marge in earnest.

"We could sure cut a rug with that! I think we need more like a hundred," chipped in William, trying to sound cool.

Michael shook his head and instantly regretted his good deed. And now he'd need to purchase a dictionary to keep up with his kids' slang. Michael believed this new age of inventions would get the better of him; unbeknownst to Michael, his troubles with technology were just beginning.

64

There was no doubt Thomas was a climber who accepted any dare and never displayed any sign of apprehension, not even when it involved revisions to a major department store that encompassed ten floors.

"Betcha won't climb the steel girders of the Higbee building," dared his neighborhood pals.

They never thought Thomas would take the challenge and started to walk away, confident their friend would shrug off their taunt. But Thomas's steely blue eyes sparkled in defiance.

Fearless, he climbed up the girders and reached the fifth floor when a terrified crowd gathered below. The police were quick to arrive, along with his mother, and a bullhorn was thrust into her hands.

"Please, Thomas. We can work this out, me darling. Just come down. Be stepping careful now, Thomas." The sound of his mother's quiet voice booming throughout the neighborhood left him shell-shocked, and he began to slip during his slow descent. A cry arose from the crowd below, but he managed to right himself. Being the center of attention, Thomas felt a surge of adrenaline from his daredevil stunt. It was a feeling well worth the spanking he would receive that night.

But it was just Thomas's luck that he pulled this spectacular feat on a Friday—a day mixed with joy (end of another school week) and trepidation. Every Friday night, the O'Malley children lined up, oldest to youngest, and received a tablespoon of castor oil. Its slimy consistency tasted like water from Lake Erie powerful enough to make the evening meal do a little heave-ho dance in the stomach. Fortunately, they received a piece of sweet candy as a reward before anyone got a glimpse of recycled food.

"Aw, Ma. Why do we have to take castor oil? It tastes awful." Every Friday night this complaint was followed by the same response.

"'Twill keep ye regular," replied Mary O'Malley sagely.

"Then why don't you and Da take it?" Marge said defiantly. Silence enveloped the room. No one contradicted their parents—ever.

"Ye can be sure we are not ta be needin' it at our age," their father replied in a no-nonsense tone. Whenever their father's brogue became more pronounced, his kids knew he was serious and any further discussion was moot, if not outright dangerous.

However, after all the children received their treats, Michael and Mary O'Malley each stuck their finger in the bottle cap to taste the dreaded medicine. Luckily, their children weren't around to see their disgust when their faces turned a lovely shade of green. Following this, the Friday night torture sessions continued, but each child now received two treats as a reward.

6 5

For Ellen, being one of the younger girls in the O'Malley clan had its advantages. Boundaries were broken by her older sisters, making restrictions and punishments less strict. But one downside was limited funds to purchase new clothes, and her wardrobe consisted of hand-me-downs from two older sisters. By the time Ellen wore her sister's clothes, they required well-placed stitches and safety pins to prevent her prior bathing suit catastrophe.

Marge attempted to provide her younger sibling with outfits in vogue with current fashion, but her sewing skills were haphazard. Marge managed to create a cotton skirt using a tartan plaid material. Ellen was enthralled with the simple but fashionable skirt wrapped around her sister's waist and held together with ties.

"Marge, your skirt is beautiful. Will you make me one?"

Delighted at her sister's admiration and proud of her creation, Marge replied, "I'd be happy to. Would you like one in plaid?"

"Oh yes, that would be lovely."

Within two days, Marge purchased the material and presented Ellen with the finished product.

"Why, it's as beautiful as yours."

Ellen was ecstatic and decided to wear it to Mass on Sunday. On her way to church, Ellen received many compliments from friends and family members. "Marge made it for me," Ellen said with pride.

Walking into St. Patrick's Church, late as usual, Ellen felt a slight breeze and heard several giggles with several people pointing at her. *They must love my new skirt. Bet they're jealous.* She took the attention in stride and walked to the pew occupied by her family.

Sitting next to her sister, Mayme whispered, "Ellen, what are you doing?"

"Huh? What are you talking about?"

"Where's your skirt?"

Ellen peered down and was mortified to see that she was only wearing a slip. Without rising up, she looked backward and saw her wayward skirt wrapped around the church doors. "Uh, Mayme, could you please fetch my skirt? It's on the church door."

Mayme made her way to the back of the church and attempted, as discreetly as possible, to grab the garment and walk to the front amidst laughter. She quickly gave the skirt to Ellen who retied it around her waist. When it came time to kneel, Ellen's heel caught on her skirt. When she tried to stand up, she felt a familiar breeze. *Uh-oh, it happened again. This was going to be a really long Mass.*

When Ellen got in line for Communion, the offending garment started another downward slide, but Mayme reached forward and pulled it up before another embarrassing episode.

"For heaven's sake, Ellen, could you please keep track of your clothes?"

Ellen smiled and said, "Why do you think it's called a wraparound skirt? It wraps around a door, my waist, my heel, and my hips."

Mayme rolled her eyes.

After Mass, Marge heard about Ellen's problems with her new wardrobe item and tried to make amends by teaching her sister how to knit. Ellen tackled the new hobby with gusto. However, without knowing how to cast-off knitting stitches to finish her scarf, Ellen's simple scarf had grown to twenty feet long. Ellen considered donating it to the Cleveland Metroparks Zoo, thinking possibly an elephant was in need of some styling. But Ellen stopped asking Marge for help when it became clear Marge's domestic skills were sorely lacking.

66

To anyone Irish, or even remotely close, St. Patrick's Day was the highlight of the year. The O'Malley children awoke every March 17 to their mother's lilting Irish accent and melodious voice calling up to them.

"Top of the mornin' ta ye. And what would ye be wantin' fer breakfast this fine mornin'?"

Her children chuckled at the question spoken with an exaggerated brogue, for they always had the same breakfast on St. Patrick's Day.

"Why, oatmeal and Irish soda bread, if ye please," they called down, positively giddy to start the day's events.

The soda bread, hot from the oven, was light in texture and filled with sweet raisins. The butter melted on top almost as quickly as the bread disappeared from the table. They ate so much, the boys' belts were loosened one notch and when they stood, it felt as though their stomachs remained seated.

As usual, everyone wore green, but Ellen decided to liven up the day's festivities in a special way. Unfortunately for Ellen, her big surprise didn't go exactly as planned. She rinsed her hair in the bathroom sink using her mother's green food coloring and couldn't wait to see everyone's reaction.

Confident she'd set a styling trend, Ellen towel-dried her hair. When she looked in the mirror, Ellen panicked at the nightmare staring back. Her reflection was a brownish-green, frizzy-haired monster with green rivulets staining her cheeks. She panicked but, after much thought, came up with a brilliant idea. Ellen went in search of her watercolor set and left-over material from her mother's sewing basket.

When she came down to the breakfast table, pretending everything was status quo, her entire family stopped what they were doing as they stared open-mouthed at the stranger in their midst. Her brothers chuckled, while their mother swatted the back of their heads. Ellen's sisters tried to think of something complimentary to say about her new appearance.

After several minutes passed, Mayme said diplomatically, "Why, Ellen, how colorful, but what are you supposed to be?"

Her face was painted with swirls of green and brown and she draped a long dark cloth around her uniform. "One of the snakes that St. Patrick banished from Ireland. Since they made him famous, shouldn't someone remember them, too?"

Although her sisters couldn't fault her logic, her mother marched Ellen promptly into the bathroom and made her stay in the tub until her skin was almost back to normal. Her hair, however, remained a shade of bilious green and she obtained special permission from the principal to wear one of her mother's hats to hide most of the damage. Ellen and her mother missed the St. Patrick's Day Mass that year, but her daughter looked so *clean* when she arrived at school the following day.

The next year, Ellen learned her lesson and wore a green bow in her hair. After breakfast, the family attended early Mass at St. Patrick's. Ellen and her sisters were members of the choir and sang their hymns in Latin with great enthusiasm. All were welcome to join, even off-key singers.

The children were dismissed from classes early to attend the St. Patrick's' Day Parade in Downtown Cleveland. It was an event not to be missed with decorated floats, marching bands, and a special treat— their father was given the select honor as flag bearer for the West Side

Irish-American Club. They could barely contain their excitement and stood proudly on the sidewalk watching their father carry his banner with the precision of a drill sergeant. On that day, everyone claimed to be Irish—why even the Plotniks referred to themselves as the O'Plotniks.

67

After St. Patrick's Day, the school year dragged on. But soon spring would roll into summer, and then utopia was within their grasp.

On the last day of school, each child brought a pail and scrub brush to school. The teacher supplied abrasive cleanser to scrub away ink stains from their desks.

"Once everyone's desk is clean and all personal belongings packed up, you will be dismissed. If anyone's desk isn't spotless, I expect others to help them. The quicker this is done, the sooner you can begin your summer vacation."

The mention of three glorious months without school and the absence of dreaded homework assignments produced deafening cheers from an invigorated class to complete their last task at a feverish pace. All children worked together to expedite those whose desks were seemingly unredeemable. Thanks to teamwork, all students were sent home by noon to enjoy freedom and release from captivity to focus on what was really important—playtime.

Arriving home, the O'Malley children were released to wreak bedlam on the neighborhood after they completed their assigned chores. In mid-July, with her chores incomplete, Ellen glanced longingly out the window and saw girls pretending to be members of rich and famous high society while boys played baseball, dodging a motorcar or occasional horse-drawn carriage. Ellen didn't feel like doing her chores, so she fabricated a marvelous excuse.

"Ma, I'm sorry but I don't think I can make my bed or wash the dishes today."

Mary O'Malley glanced at her child, curious to discover the invented excuse. "I see. And what would be the reason fer that?"

"I'm too little to do any chores and should be outside playing all day."

"All right, me darling," Mary replied sweetly as she glanced at Ellen's dumbstruck expression. "I didn't realize ye were still a baby, so run along outside."

And out to play she went but, somehow, her mother's words took the joy out of playtime, and she never used the excuse again.

Feeling dejected that evening when playtime left her feeling unfulfilled, Ellen asked her mother what she believed was a simple question. "Ma, what is true happiness?"

At first taken aback at the magnitude of the simple query, Mary asked her daughter a question of her own.

"Me darling, can ye think of one thing that gives ye great joy?"

"Oh yes. Chocolate." Just conjuring the word made Ellen's mouth water.

"Shall we try a wee experiment?"

Ellen nodded vigorously.

"Do ye think if ye would eat only chocolate fer one week that would be making ye happy?"

This time, Ellen squealed with delight—the only response needed.

"We can start tomorrow if ye like."

Ellen couldn't believe it. Not only could she eat her favorite food for an entire week, but she'd also finally understand the meaning of happiness. Let the experiment begin!

After two days, Ellen's siblings began to complain.

"Hey," said Thomas indignantly, "how come Ellen gets to eat chocolate all day and we're stuck with these?" All the children, except Ellen, made a face as Thomas pointed to peas.

But after eating nothing but chocolate for seven days, just the sight of it produced a queasy feeling, increased by its smell. The idea of eating it was repulsive. Her siblings were no longer jealous as they noticed their sister's complexion turn a pale shade of green when offered a chocolate bar.

Mary took pity on Ellen and decided to end her suffering. "Do ye now understand what makes ye truly happy?"

Forlornly, Ellen could only shake her head. "I still don't have an answer."

"'Tis easy, me darling. Happiness comes from within. The true test of happiness is finding someone or something that fills yer soul with pleasure and will always bring ye joy, despite the passage of time."

It would be years before Ellen understood her mother's wisdom, but when she did, her mother's sage advice became her mantra.

6 8

As the world was gradually digging itself from the pall of the Depression, children reared in loving homes prevailed in their resiliency, capable of discovering new adventures in the smallest of ventures. All they had to do was look. And that's exactly what Thomas did. He heard the neighbor's cat bore a litter of kittens, so he ran over and asked if he could play with them. An Irish woman, readily acquainted with Michael and Mary, quickly gave permission for not only Thomas but his siblings as well. Thomas ran home to spread the good news.

"Hey guys, have I got a surprise for you!"

Like a clarion call, kids appeared from all corners of the house.

"What is it, Thomas?" inquired Ellen.

He explained their new adventure, and the whole gang stopped whatever they were doing. After they received their mother's permission, they raced one another to reach the neighbor's home. Surprising herself, despite being severely out of breath, Ellen arrived first to see the box of tiny mewling kittens. She heard it said a person does not select a kitten—the feline chooses the person. Sure enough, one of the tiny creatures crawled over the others in search of Ellen's touch. Her fur was reddish in color and soft brown eyes, opened the day before, were just in time for Ellen's arrival. She picked up the tiny creature, fitting in her palm, and lovingly stroked it.

Her siblings played with the remaining six kittens until the sky began its nighttime ritual.

"Uh-oh, we need to get home now before Da tans our hides."

They carefully replaced the kittens in the box and thanked their neighbor profusely. Ellen reluctantly stayed behind to hold her newfound friend a little longer before she returned it to the box. Ellen fervently wished she could take it with her but knew her Da wasn't fond of cats.

They raced home to get washed up and seated at the kitchen table before Michael doled out punishment for breaking the steadfast rule "home before dark." Everyone at the table salivated at the bowl of their mother's famous Irish stew. After giving thanks to God for blessing them with the delectable meal, they were stopped midbite by their mother's question.

"And where might Ellen be at this hour?"

They glanced at one another with collective guilt, wondering what happened to their sister.

"Where did ye see her last?"

"She was petting a cute red kitten at the Thompson's home," said Thomas.

Mary and Michael exchanged worried glances. Everyone arose from the table as they ran toward the neighbor's home. Ellen was found propped up by a tree two houses down, panting heavily and completely out of breath. Michael carried his daughter home and gently placed her on the couch.

"Can ye eat, me child?"

"Yes, Da. I think being a teenager is harder than I thought. It was probably the excitement of holding that adorable kitten. I'm sure a good night's rest is all I need."

Her parents attempted to contact Dr. Carns, but he was out of town. His replacement was tending to a difficult birth and promised to stop first thing in the morning. He urged Ellen's parents to check on her throughout the night, and if her condition worsened, take her to the hospital.

Although Ellen slept through the night and never awoke during her parents' frequent bed checks, Ellen's symptoms increased by the following morning. She awoke with a sore throat (the second in as many weeks) and became short of breath with minimal exertion. Ellen developed a rash on her arms in addition to her joints becoming swollen and painful. Michael debated staying home but Mary convinced him to return at lunch after the doctor assessed their daughter's condition. "No sense losing a whole day's pay if her condition is minor." Michael agreed with his wife's sage advice.

After Michael left, Mary entered Ellen's room, keeping her outward appearance cheerful to hide any alarm. "Rest in bed, me darling. The doctor will be here soon Can ye eat some toast, me darling?" Ellen nodded and her mother hurried to the kitchen, glad to have a chore occupying her thoughts while waiting for the doctor. An hour after Ellen consumed toast and weak tea, the doorbell rang.

Mary escorted the on-call physician, who brought with him an assortment of placards for contagious diseases tacked on the front door placing a home under quarantine.

After preliminary introductions followed by an exam and a brief explanation of symptoms, the doctor said, "Ellen, you need to stay in bed for several months and avoid any activity. You rest while I speak with your mother in the hall."

Now Mary O'Malley was truly concerned. "What is it, Doctor?" she asked in a small voice.

The doctor found it best to first explain the curable malady or instructions would be forgotten once the more serious problem was mentioned. "Ellen's tonsils are swollen, and she has red dots on her throat typically seen in a strep throat infection. I recommend gargling with saltwater and voice rest. Be careful to keep family members at a distance because it's highly contagious and spreads through droplets." Pausing for a moment before delivering the distressing diagnosis, the doctor continued, "Ellen also has rheumatic heart fever, usually found in patients with repeat strep throat infections. This is a very serious condition."

Mary's face drained of all color as she inquired in a soft voice, "Doctor, what can we do?"

"The only treatment for rheumatic fever is aspirin and strict bed rest for six months to a year. If she regains strength, she will be on limited activities for the rest of her life. Ellen will be lucky to see her twentieth birthday. I'm sorry," added the beleaguered physician. He briskly walked out and nailed a STREP THROAT placard to the front door warning visitors they risked exposure upon entering the home.

After the doctor departed, Mary's legs sagged until she collapsed into the nearest chair and sobbed at the enormity of Ellen's condition. She didn't know how to tell her daughter, or her husband, the doctor's assessment of Ellen's condition was her premature demise.

After she composed herself, Mary brought a tray of soup and crackers to Ellen's room. "Me darling, ye need ta keep up yer strength." As her daughter began to eat, Mary reached into the pocket of her apron and pulled out a shiny object. "Dearest, I'd like ye ta hold onto yer father's pocket watch ta keep it safe. Sure, and 'twill bring ye good luck." Her mother gently thrust her husband's most prized passion into her child's hands. Ellen was filled with pride to be chosen as the custodian of this precious heirloom. Since she was a little girl, Ellen had admired her father's shiny gold pocket watch, giving him a dashing look of elegance. She turned it over in her hands, inspecting it, promising her mother to guard it with her life.

69

After working a half day, Michael returned home for news of Ellen's condition. Noticing the placard in the window gave Michael hope, for he knew many with strep throat, normally a nonfatal condition. Walking into the kitchen, he found his wife with her head down on the table, weeping inconsolably. Michael gently lifted his wife into his arms and comforted her, patiently waiting until she could speak the words impossible for any parent to digest.

"Our darling Ellen has rheumatic heart fever and . . . ." Tears choked any further speech.

Composing himself in response to Mary's words, he gently asked the unthinkable, "Will Ellen live?"

Mary's initial response of a nod was encouraging until she delivered the prognosis to pierce a loved one's heart. "The doctor said she'd be lucky if she made it ta age twenty."

Michael's legs started to buckle but he tapped into a well of untapped inner strength to sustain his upright stance and support Mary. Michael escorted his wife to the couch, where they held onto one another until tears were spent.

"Michael, I gave Ellen yer watch ta hold until she's feeling better. I hope 'twas all right."

"Of course, me love. But I feel so helpless, is there anything else we can do?"

"Thomas mentioned a tiny red kitten at the Thompson's home that gave Ellen so much happiness. I know ye are not fond of cats, but perhaps—"

Michael nodded his head before she could complete the sentence. "I'll go right now and hope, God willing, 'tis still available."

With a purpose at hand to dispel his feeling of impotence, Michael sprinted to the neighbor's home. Mrs. Thompson graciously ushered Michael into her home and became distraught hearing about Ellen's condition. She recalled which kitten captured Ellen's attention and gently handed her to Michael. After thanking Mrs. Thompson profusely, Michael returned home carrying the tiny bundle of hope. Mary and Michael said a prayer before knocking on Ellen's bedroom door.

"Yes?" called a weak Ellen.

"Yer Da and I have a surprise fer ye. May we enter?"

"Of course," responded a voice strengthened by the promise of a treat, in addition to seeing her father in the middle of the day.

Placing the warm ball of fur in Ellen's hands might have been the best medicine possible. Ellen's eyes, previously downcast, now brightened with happiness. For the briefest moment, she seemed her normal healthy self.

"Thank you, thank you. Oh, how much I love her. Wishes really do come true," Ellen exclaimed with undisguised joy.

That afternoon, Michael traveled to the drugstore for cat supplies. In the evening, they called a family meeting to advise Ellen's siblings of her serious condition. They were incapable of uttering the terminal nature of her illness but asked them to spend extra time with Ellen to overcome the alienation of being bedridden for an extended period of time. They all quickly agreed and were happy to hear she had a lovable kitten to keep her company. To the relief of all, time proved McTavish, their beloved pup, and the new addition would become fast friends.

Michael was delighted to see Ellen's outward improvement to the warm bundle of love that redirected prior despair into optimism and happiness. Ellen named the kitten Celtic Thunder (later shortened to Celtic)—Michael assumed the name was based on the feline's possessiveness of anyone who attempted to separate them. Seeing Ellen cuddle her new friend, who remained by her side and slept at the foot of her bed, brought Michael joy and helped lift his own anguish. He was relieved to note Celtic took the sting out of Ellen's solitude, especially when she couldn't play outside and attend school with her friends.

While Ellen napped—unfortunately for Michael—Celtic only had eyes, and claws for him. Any amount of cajoling, tiptoeing, or avoidance maneuvers were unsuccessful, as Celtic jumped out from nowhere, sailing through the air like a guided missile, claws bared.

Michael considered "losing" the cat but knew his sickly daughter would be devastated. They began a long sojourn of cautiously moving about the home in a series of moves and countermoves similar to a hunter stalking its prey. They finally came to a compromise. Michael carried a pocketful of treats doled out to Celtic before her claws found their target. But when he left the house, a tsunami of cats pestered Michael as he walked to work, an experience best described as the Eleventh Plague—a continuation of pestilence from the biblical plagues. It would be days before he realized why the neighborhood cats constantly pestered him, and he changed his morning routine. Before leaving the house, Michael turned his pockets inside-out to rid himself of any crumbs to discourage further enticements from his new feline fan club.

APPROXIMATELY TEN MONTHS after the doctor proclaimed her death sentence, Ellen was ecstatic when her strength gradually improved, and she was allowed to sit on the front porch with Celtic on her lap. Ellen reveled in feeling the cool breeze on her face and breathing fresh air despite the cold weather. She was sufficiently bundled in winter clothes and a cozy, floor-length robe. Looking in the mirror, Ellen saw her rosy cheeks and healthy glow, surely a sign she was on the mend.

Fortunately, Ellen remained in bed less than a year. Her outside forays beyond Carroll Avenue were limited and reserved for special occasions until she was assessed as cured by her doctor.

When the physician proclaimed Ellen's bedridden exile no longer necessary, unless she had a relapse, Ellen's lack of any exercise forced her to completely relearn the basics—crawling, standing, and walking—while increasing her stamina, just as Frank Szabo—her future spouse—had experienced as a youngster. Ellen was sad to miss an entire year of school but grateful to be outside once again and returning to a somewhat normal life.

Ellen's doctor wrote a note to the principal, permitting access to the school elevator to avoid climbing stairs. But, without realizing it, Ellen had a secret weapon against this dreaded disease. She was always late. For everything. She ran to school and instead of waiting for the elevator, flew up several flights of stairs to her classrooms. She knew running was contrary to her doctor's advice, but it was her only way of compensating for tardiness. When Ellen was reprimanded for running, she walked at a brisk pace and pretty much did the opposite of what her doctors advised. Much to everyone's surprise, her exercise regimen improved her symptoms until it became apparent Ellen was fully recovered and showed no signs of relapse.

"Ellen, me darling, now that ye are feeling much better, I can hold onto yer father's pocket watch fer safekeeping."

"Sure, Ma. Whatever you think is best." Ellen was honored to be its custodian (no matter the length of time), for it absolutely had miraculous powers to heal her heart.

It wasn't until Ellen was an adult when she realized this act of kindness was only intended to be a temporary consolation prize while she was battling a deadly disease. Each Sunday after her illness when her father wore his pocket watch, Ellen would be reminded of the brief time she was selected to be the guardian of her father's beloved possession, and it never failed to fill her with immense satisfaction.

But Ellen did learn two important lessons from this episode in her life. First, tardiness saved her life. It also became a lifelong habit she was unable to break. By running to school and avoiding the school elevator, she was forced to increase her exercise, which accelerated the healing process. And second, experts do not always have the correct answers. When in doubt, she would conduct her own research tempered with common sense.

It has since been proven that the clinical course of children with rheumatic diseases can be improved by certain exercises under a doctor's supervision. The result is an overall improvement of cardiovascular health which, in turn, reduces swelling, pain, and helps to alleviate depression from chronic pain.

Ellen was far ahead of her time.

70

With Ellen's return to normal activities, her need for Celtic's constant presence was no longer essential. Celtic became restless and began to explore the world outside 3104 Carroll Avenue. Ellen wasn't worried because Celtic always returned home each night —until the evening she didn't. After checking the entire house and the yard, Ellen couldn't find her beloved friend.

"Ma, have you seen Celtic?"

"'No, me darling. If she doesn't return home by tomorrow, the family will search the neighborhood. Does that sound all right?"

"Sure."

When Celtic failed to return home the next day, fortunately a Saturday, a search posse was formed by the O'Malleys to track down the recalcitrant creature. Ellen found her beloved friend three blocks away. She was sitting on the lap of a young girl confined to a wheelchair. Approaching the child, Ellen asked gently if she could hold her beautiful cat.

After she acquiesced, Ellen held Celtic in her arms for the last time and whispered, "I see you've found a new purpose in life. I know you will help her just as you were there for me. You are a special treasure, and together you will forge a healing bond. I love you, but the time has come for you to comfort this child." Ellen kissed the top of her head and was rewarded with a lick on her face and one last snuggle. Ellen returned her former guardian to the girl and told her, "What a special cat you have. I had one just like her and loved her so much."

"What was her name? Did she die?"

"Her full name was Celtic Thunder, but it was shortened to Celtic. No, she didn't die. She decided to console someone else who needed her. Now she has a new loving home."

The little girl examined her new pet and before giving her a hug, said, "I christen you, Celtic."

Ellen was certain Celtic loved her new role, fulfilling her gift of helping those in need. Before Ellen left, she took one last look at Celtic smiling at her new owner.

Surprisingly, Ellen wasn't heartbroken and found peace at the thought of Celtic's loving heart. Ellen called off the search party, and the O'Malleys returned home, rejoicing in Celtic's path to comfort another young child afflicted by life's cruelty.

But, of all the O'Malleys, Michael was happiest to hear Celtic had a new home. When Ellen noticed her father's reaction, she thought, *How sweet, he really loved Celtic.*

ELLEN NEVER LEARNED the real reason behind her father's apparent glee, and Michael was pleased to keep this secret to himself.

71

During the summer months, many children enjoyed sleeping late. But Ellen arose at 6:00 a.m. to quickly dress and accompany her mother to 6:30 Mass at St. Patrick's. As a reward, her mother purchased two cream-filled chocolate cupcakes from the neighborhood bakery for Ellen to munch on before arriving home.

When they walked in the front door, they were greeted by an excited James for today his da was teaching him to ride a two-wheeler bike. Despite Michael's best advice, his son couldn't grasp the idea of using his brakes.

"Son, ye need ta keep yer balance before I let go," Michael said breathlessly as he ran behind James's bike.

When he finally grasped the concept of navigating the bike on his own, everyone clapped and cheered his progress. The only problem left was how to stop. Before James found out how to conquer this feat, he used stop signs, buildings, and even a parked car with two teenagers kissing, who were greatly annoyed at the interruption despite James's giggling apology.

EVERY YEAR, on the first mild day of summer, it became a neighborhood tradition for the annual bike parade. Each child woke early and grabbed a bucket full of soapy water, rags, and a scrub brush. They would clean and polish their bikes until they could see their own reflection. Once the work was done, the fun began. They would beg their mothers for scraps of material, broken jewelry, bits of paper, crayons, clothespins, and unused playing cards before heading outside. Decorating their bikes became a feat unrivaled by any other summer activity. Attaching colorful pieces of leftover cloths to their handlebars, affixing playing cards with clothespins, or weaving other scraps around the spokes became a test of creativity as each child tried to outdo the other.

When satisfied with their colorfully decorated bikes, they would meet at the O'Malley home where the judging began. The oldest child in the neighborhood, not a contestant to assure lack of bias, would act as the moderator to select the winner. The victor wore a paper crown and was given a bike horn (to use until the near year's contestant winner) and led the bike parade throughout the neighborhood. Any adults outside, familiar with the annual kids' tradition, would clap their hands or tip their hat as the children tooted their horns in undisguised satisfaction. The younger children were unaware but, by the time they were selected as the moderator, every contestant over the years would earn the grandiose title of bike king before passing the mantle onto next year's winner. It was understood, without ever verbalizing, that fair play was essential to the annual event, and everyone deserved the title of champion.

When Veronica earned the coveted paper crown decorated with streamers and stickers, she ran home to show her mother.

"Ma, come outside. I won the bike contest this year."

"Well, me darling, let me have a look." Mary called out to her mother. "Ma, come see what Veronica won."

Mary and Elizabeth went outside to see the beautiful decorations proudly displaying her Irish heritage, including a large green cutout of a shamrock placed in the middle of her handlebars.

"Well, St. Patrick himself would be pleased." Elizabeth beamed at her granddaughter's creativity.

Examining her daughter's hard work, Mary said, "My goodness, yer bike shines like a duck's foot."

Veronica's face radiated pure joy at the hard-won praise, and after thanking her mother and grandmother profusely, she ran upstairs to place the cherished crown on her dresser.

ON RAINY DAYS, kids from the neighborhood gathered together on the O'Malley front porch with a copy of yesterday's newspaper grabbed from the trash before it became covered in food scraps. Each child would tear an ad from the newspaper, making certain to eliminate the product's name, for others to guess which product was being promoted.

"Okay," said Marge, "who can guess what this is?"

"That's easy," said Alicia, "it's an ad for Coca Cola."

Everyone was immediately thirsty and collectively ran to the kitchen for a quick drink of water.

Returning to the porch, Michele held up a different ad, hoping no one would guess. "What's this?"

The boys didn't have a clue, but Kaleena proudly guessed it was a Raggedy Ann doll. All the girls stopped for a moment to admire the photo and dreamed of being its proud owner.

William produced an ad sure to please the boys.

"That's a Cadillac pedal car. Wow, it cost a whopping ten dollars and ninety-five cents," replied Kaleena's brother, Mattie.

Soon each boy was in their own world as they imagined pedaling around the neighborhood in their fancy Cadillac.

The afternoon passed pleasantly with pictures of Betty Boop, Babe Ruth candy bars, teddy bears, and Crayola crayons submitted for the guessing game. Until Thomas, true to his rambunctious nature and quick to display a devilish sense of humor, produced an ad guaranteed to get everyone's attention.

"And who can guess what this is?"

The girls squealed immediately as they attempted to grab the paper from Thomas as he ran around with the picture of a ladies' corset held high above their heads, until Marge wrangled it from his closed fist. The boys were rolling around the porch, holding their sides as laughter filled the air.

Each day was a challenge to pass the hours until it became dark and then, like magic, everyone was filled with ideas of new and exciting adventures.

72

The O'Malley household attended Mass at St. Patrick's Church every Sunday morning, but it was a hectic time as family members vied for the solitary bathroom before donning their Sunday best. The children walked the short distance to St. Patrick's Church in single file ahead of their parents, who hoped mischief would be kept to minimum.

But on the short trek to Mass, giggles and jokes were never far away as amusing stories and playing telephone—whispering a short story down the line until the last person's rendition, told out loud, was gibberish but still humorous. Throughout the service, Mass was said in Latin and the priest had his back to the congregation, except for the Homily and Communion.

On especially hot days, many heads were bobbing, especially if the sermon was lengthy. By the time Mass was finally concluded, the backs of many children's legs, if they wore shorts or a dress, were stuck to the wooden pews, and they walked home with indentation reminders of keeping their Sunday obligation.

But Sundays became even more special when Thomas entered the second grade and was selected for the coveted honor of becoming an altar boy. After taking lessons for four weeks, Thomas could hardly believe his "performance" would soon become a reality.

With stringent restrictions placed on parishioners before receiving Communion, members had to fast and refrain from drinking any liquids after midnight the night before. It was fortunate for Thomas that he would serve his first mass at 6:00 a.m. Michael's alarm clock was set for 5:00 a.m. but the battery died, and everyone overslept. When he awoke at 5:30 a.am., Michael ran through the house rousting everyone from sleep. Abruptly awakened from deep sleep, everyone stumbled around to wash and dress despite tripping over one another. The comical moments would be shared later: clothes being tossed around like a beach ball and James (still half asleep) putting on a dress while Veronica grabbed William's shoes and almost tripped. Setting a new record despite using their solitary bathroom, it was a miraculous achievement when the entire family showed up on time to watch Thomas serve his inaugural mass.

In spite of Thomas arriving a few minutes before Mass, he was the last altar boy to arrive and, consequently, was forced to wear the only remaining altar vestment—a floor-length Roman-style garment of black silk (known as a cassock) with a white collar and large black bow. It was too long and more suited to a fifteen-year-old boy than a lad eight years younger.

Gathering the extra folds above his shoes, Thomas succeeded in walking with minimal problems during his official first Mass and thought, *This is a piece of cake.* But he forgot the challenge presented when Communion was distributed—a feat he practiced with ease when he wore normal clothes. The altar boys walked down the steps backward to face the altar in veneration to the Eucharist. At this point, Thomas's coordination and dignity disappeared when his feet became tangled in the long cassock. He did a graceful head-over-heels somersault and somehow landed on his feet. To his mortification, Thomas faced the wrong direction when he stuck his landing. His automatic response to a successful touchdown was to raise his hands to the heavens—until Thomas remembered he was in church.

Thomas attempted to see his family's reaction, but his head was spinning so hard, his eyes rolled around. Once his head and vision cleared, Thomas tried to gather his robes as gracefully as possible, while attempting to ignore the embarrassment reflected on his bright-red face. He heard snickers from the congregation that, before long, became outright laughter. Being a good sport, Thomas joined in the merriment until the priest have him "the look." Thomas learned an important lesson and was never again late to Mass during his tenure as an altar boy.

In spite of his unusual performance, Thomas's family was proud of him and toasted him (with water, of course) at Sunday dinner.

73

For those without a specific skill in demand, the Depression affected many of Michael's customers. In lieu of paying his fee, Michael received goods for service. But one memorable cash-poor customer, unable to pay Michael's plumbing bill for extensive repairs, presented him with an old Model T. Ironically, after years of complaining to his family that a car was an unnecessary expense, he was now in possession of a dreaded automobile.

Sitting behind the large steering wheel, Michael pulled the ghastly contraption into the parking lot of the Motor Vehicle Department. Without revealing his difficulty in maneuvering the machine and barely missing turns as people quickly scattered away from the vehicle swerving frantically down side streets, Michael was stunned to discover it would cost him money for an operator's license and new license plates.

"'Tis the devil's machine costing me hard-earned money," Michael muttered as he paid $7.25 to the clerk—$0.25 for the license and $7.00 to purchase plates.

After leaving the motor vehicle department, Michael once again grabbed the steering wheel until his knuckles were white and began his trek home in a herky-jerky set of attempts to control the car's speed while maneuvering the gearshift. By the time Michael pulled the car, crookedly, in front of their modest home, he quickly wiped sweat from his brow and took a deep breath to portray a calm he didn't feel. He stepped outside with his arms crossed in a gesture of nonchalance leaning casually next to the car as he waited for his family's reaction.

Within sixty seconds, everyone ran out and danced around the car, clapping their hands. The O'Malleys had finally arrived!

But perhaps the most excited person was James. With his supreme confidence, James was just the person to take it for a test drive, after he took it apart and rebuilt it, of course. To James's chagrin, he looked much younger than his ten years, with his short stature and unruly blond hair that would not bow to any comb. It gave him the childish appearance of an unkempt lad. Even his winning smile couldn't overcome it.

Everyone piled into the car and admired the interior.

"Keen. It even has plush seats," marveled Mayme.

"And the beautiful wooden dashboard. Why, it's gleaming as though someone just polished it," Marge exclaimed, as she ran her hands over the sleek panel.

"There's even a circle here. Who knows? Maybe one day cars will have a working clock. Or maybe even a radio." William was mesmerized as he stared in wonder. Everyone's imagination went into overdrive at the opportunities presented by their newest possession.

"Ye must be touched in the head. No car would ever have a clock or a radio," Michael said, shaking his head at the absurd notions.

"Da, when can I drive it?" inquired James.

"Are ye daft? Y'er too young."

"But I know how it works."

"Ye cannot drive until ye get a driving license," Michael replied. Believing the matter was settled, he marched proudly into their home.

But James would not be deterred and asked his father for the car keys the following morning. Recalling the prior evening's conversation, James produced his father's license. No amount of reasoning by his father would convince James otherwise, until his mother produced an article from the newspaper about a toddler in

New Jersey who caused a multicar pileup and a dozen people were hurt.

"Ye see, James, 'tis a complex and potentially dangerous machine. That's why ye have ta be older fer so much responsibility," his mother gently explained.

JAMES WAS crestfallen and returned his father's license. To ease his bruised ego, Mary took James out for an ice cream cone. Temporarily appeased, James smiled. But he promised himself one day . . .

74

All the O'Malley children attended St. Patrick's School, but its curriculum would transition with the passage of time. Marge, William, and Mayme attended St. Patrick's Commercial High and Grade School, which covered grades one through ten. Of all the children, William was the only one who elected to end his formal education in the tenth grade at St. Patrick's. This allowed him to apprentice with his father and earn money for the family.

Michael was forced to make a difficult decision regarding his two oldest daughters. He wanted his lovely daughters to attend a Catholic high school, but they'd be forced to repeat grades nine and ten. However, the appeal of West High Public School assured a transfer of credits from St. Patrick's and a high school diploma in only two years. Michael relented, after much pleading and cajoling from Marge and Mayme, and allowed them to attend West High.

By the time Ellen and her younger siblings attended grammar school, the school's name had been changed to St. Patrick's Parochial School, in line with current trends offering education from grades one through eight. With proof of adequate learning by his older children in the public school system, Michael decided to send all his children to West High School. Although he still had reservations of classes containing teenagers of mixed genders—a problem avoided by parochial institutions—Michael encouraged his children to watch over one another.

ELLEN DESPERATELY WANTED to graduate St. Patrick's with her grade school friends so they could attend high school together. She made an appointment with the principal and said a brief prayer he would find a solution to her dilemma.

After knocking on his door, with verbal permission to enter, Ellen sat down and inquired, "Excuse me, sir, but I have a very important question."

"Certainly, Ellen, how can I help you?" The principal was aware of Ellen's situation and although she beat the odds of dying as a youngster, she remained one grade behind.

"As you know, I lost a year of school. But I'd like to graduate with my grade school friends. Is that possible?"

"Well, let's review your file." After retrieving her information, the principal said, "You've maintained excellent grades."

Ellen nodded, hoping her hard work would lay the foundation for the dream she craved.

"If you continue to keep your grades up, attend summer school, and complete extracurricular assignments, I'm sure you can achieve your goal."

"Oh, thank you, sir. I'll do whatever it takes."

"I'm sure you will. Best of luck to you, Ellen."

They shook hands, and Ellen left his office feeling like St. Patrick had reached out to make her dream come true.

Ellen kept her promise to excel in grade school and graduated St. Patrick's with her childhood friends on June 9, 1935. Following in her sibling's footsteps, Ellen attended West High and graduated in 1939 with her friends. For someone who was supposed to be dead before the age of twenty, Ellen was exceedingly proud to prove the medical community wrong.

CONTRARY TO MICHAEL'S belief that exposure to West High Public School would steal his daughters' virtue, they remained innocent and, unknown to them, managed to steal the hearts of all the neighboring boys. It was understood that, if a guy went out with one of the O'Malley girls, you were one hep cat!

75

W hile playing outside on a warm day in 1935, William saw a stranger handing out flyers. Curious, he ran up to the man. "Whatcha got, Mister?"

"Flyers about the Great Lakes Exposition. It's like a World's Fair but right here in Cleveland next summer. Give this flyer to your parents."

Grabbing the piece of paper, William looked at the fascinating pictures of the Expo and ran into his home. "Ma, Ma, come quick."

Her hands covered in flour, Mary quickly washed and dried them before entering the living room. "Dearie, what is it?"

"Ma, you won't believe this." William thrust the flyer into his mother's hands. The flyer stated a celebration of Cleveland's Centennial—known as the Great Lakes Exposition—would be held in the summer months of 1936 and 1937. The event was sponsored by civic leaders to celebrate world events and provide free entertainment to all in attendance.

Looking at the circular, Mary replied, "'Tis a wonderful thing. We'll show yer da tonight."

She returned the flyer to her son, who ran upstairs to inform his siblings. By the time Michael arrived home, he was greeted by eight eager and excited people grinning at the prospect of a new adventure.

"Ye missed me that much?" Michael grinned at his loving family.

"Look at this, Da." William waved the handout in his father's face before he even had a chance to put his toolbox down or change from his work clothes.

"Give yer da a minute ta get settled." Mary knew her husband would be more receptive to any new ideas if he was clean and comfortable.

William carefully held onto the revered flyer until his father had washed up and was sitting in his favorite chair. Without realizing it, everyone held their collective breath waiting for Michael's proclamation, "Now what have ye got ta show me?"

Resisting the urge to wave it again in his father's face, William carefully approached and said, "Cleveland is going to have a World's Fair that's free for everyone. Here's the information." William gently placed the leaflet in his father's lap.

Rumors about the upcoming Exposition spread through Cleveland but, with multiple failures and unfulfilled promises arising from the recent Depression, most people refused to believe it until it was a reality. They were accustomed to disappointment and would not raise their hopes in what could easily turn into a pipe dream.

Although Michael had bid for the plumbing contract for the Exposition, his competitor with political connections secured the job. Michael never told his family about his disappointment at losing the lucrative contract. Luckily, Michael had other government contracts to fill his schedule and keep his neighbors employed.

Michael hid his inner turmoil as he pretended to review the document and with a false bravado, said, "Well, 'tis going ta be a wonderful summer adventure that we can all enjoy."

Everyone cheered and hugged at the prospect of the thrilling escapades the following year would bring.

76

Frank Szabo accepted his fate and attended West High Public School instead of the prestigious St. Ignatius High School. By the time Frank entered high school, his father was no longer able to work, and the family's coffers were near depletion. Financial responsibilities would fall to their only child.

Battling alienation of being older than his classmates exacerbated Frank's innate shyness. He worked in the school cafeteria, bussing tables during the day to the jeers of his classmates. He learned to keep his head down and ignore the taunts because his weekly income of six dollars paid the family's rent.

Instead of gratitude for his son's assistance, Paul's resentment increased. Frank endeavored to stay far away from his father's punches, which became easier when his mobility severely decreased. Whenever possible, his mother attempted to intervene; but she, too, could not escape her husband's ire and was struck with fists meant for Frank.

In Frank's early years at West High, he experienced difficulty making friends—few understood his strange accent or the reason he was older than his classmates. Frank concentrated on his studies, especially English, and even won the local spelling contest. Still, he never heard a compliment or even an encouraging word from either of his parents.

With time and hard work, Frank became the captain of the basketball team and won several medals in track. For the first time in his life, Frank was graced with a wide array of friends and surrounded by a bevy of girls. But to Frank's dismay, his shyness prevented him from taking advantage of his newfound popularity.

"Oh Frank, would you like to get a soda after school? I know this wonderful place two blocks from here," asked a coquettish young blonde with her hair tied in a ponytail, wearing a distracting amount of makeup that accentuated full lips and captivating gray-blue eyes.

She began to bat her eyelashes so rapidly, Frank wondered if she had something in her eyes.

The mere suggestion of being with a girl sent Frank into full-panic mode. Unsure what they would talk about, Frank was terrified of making a mistake. Just being near a girl intensified his anxiety, and his hands began to shake. To prevent a nightmare scenario of tripping over spilled soda, he dumped the beverage just purchased into the nearest trash can. With insecurity roiling throughout his brain, Frank decided to make a plausible excuse that wouldn't offend her.

"Normally I would, but I promised to run errands for my parents right after school." Relieved at his plausible, if inaccurate, response, Frank smiled to soften the blow.

The young lady walked off in a huff and immediately approached Frank's teammate with the same offer. He leaped at the chance to accompany the gorgeous young lady and, when her back was turned, looked at Frank as though he was an idiot for passing up the opportunity to date a gorgeous classmate.

Frank resolved his paralyzing shyness by pouring his frustrations into exercising and excelling in sports until he was too exhausted to think about his solitary existence or endure yet another lonely walk home.

77

As usual, Frank's parents never deigned to consider his activities or pursuits worthy of their time. In the fall of 1936, Frank experienced a phenomenal occurrence in his athletic career. As a member of the West High School track team, he participated in an event at the Cleveland Public Auditorium. The moment he entered the auditorium, Frank was in awe of the grand location seated in the epicenter of downtown Cleveland with a capacity of ten thousand seats.

Determined to ignore his intimidating surroundings, Frank entered the arena and took his mark for the 400-yard dash. Surprising even himself, considering the stiff competition from elite private schools, Frank took first place. Immediately after his race, he made a dash toward the bathroom where the combination of adrenalin from competing and the anxiety of performing before the massive audience resulted in nausea. He splashed water on his face, now a lovely bilious color, and was surprised to feel a hand on his shoulder.

"Don't feel bad, son, that's happened to me hundreds of times." Frank looked up and was astonished to see the infamous Jesse Owens, whose four gold medals for track and field during the Summer 1936 Berlin Olympics were legendary.

In awe of his hero, Frank was temporarily speechless but finally managed to cobble together a humble, "Thank you, sir."

"It's my pleasure. You ran a fine race. And now it's my turn."

He shook Frank's hand before entering the auditorium for his race against horses. Frank couldn't believe one of the world's greatest athletes, upon his return to America after the Olympics, was never given the accolades or respect for his athletic prowess. Instead, Jesse was forced to race against animals, cars, or anything else relating to speed—except other humans.

To supplement his meager wages while supporting his wife and three-year-old daughter, Jesse took any menial job as his fame and accomplishments were dismissed because of his skin color. For the first time, Frank understood the existence of racial discrimination and knew, despite his own poverty, Frank's life was richer in opportunities and advantages because he was Caucasian. Frank tried to reconcile the basis for any inequality he witnessed throughout his life—to no avail.

Frank experienced another source of consternation—one closer to home. He yearned for his father's approval in his achievements—especially the prestigious meeting with his hero. Despite Frank's mother attempting to be supportive of their only child, his father spoke with his fists. Frank's desire to hear a kind word from his father would remain an unfulfilled wish. He was treated as nothing more than a paycheck supporting his family—yet this contribution was unappreciated and unrecognized by his father.

In the end, despite the abuse and emotional neglect from his father, Frank completed his filial responsibilities and provided care for his parents until their deaths.

78

When each of the O'Malley children reached the age of sixteen, they were expected to secure jobs. William helped his father while learning the tradecraft of plumbing, Marge worked as a governess, and Veronica became an elevator operator at Higbee's Department Store. Ellen and Mayme worked at the A&P grocery store—Mayme bagged potatoes on Saturdays for one dollar per day while Ellen worked as a clerk. Grocery stores were not self-service—the counter was placed in the front of the store close to the entrance and all grocery items would be retrieved by the store clerk.

Ellen was grateful for organized customers who provided her with a handwritten list of groceries. Being intimately familiar with the organization of store items, she was able to race through the store and complete their list in a timely fashion. For those less organized, Ellen received a verbal list which required several hours of brisk walking to retrieve items piecemeal. In the days before prepackaged foods, additional time was required to count, weigh, and parcel individual items.

By the end of the workday, Ellen felt like a marathon runner before trudging home and collapsing into a chair, just in time to complete her homework. Being a full-fledged teenager was more difficult than she would have imagined. She couldn't wait until she was a grown-up, certain her life would be easier.

By the time she was an adult, Ellen fondly reminisced about her time as a teenager and wished she could return to events in her youth. But the emotional appeal of time travel was usually perceived through gauze-filtered nostalgia restricted to favorable memories. Had she realized this, her longing for the "good-old-days" would have lost much of its charm. But Ellen knew the instinct to block out difficult memories was a compensatory measure to prevent sensory overload. Without it, she could not have effectively dealt with current problems that, at times, threatened to dominate her.

On Saturdays, Ellen, her sisters, and girlfriends liked to go into town to gaze at the wonderful window displays. At the beginning of their journey, they each purchased a nickel bag of peppermint patties, which sustained them during their long walk over the High Level Bridge connecting Ohio City to Downtown Cleveland.

The strenuous stroll up and down the lengthy bridge sometimes left Ellen breathless, similar to the sensation experienced after working long hours at the A&P. All of Ellen's friends had streetcar passes but chose to walk so Ellen wouldn't feel left out. One week, Ellen timidly asked her father if she could borrow his streetcar pass—good for the upcoming week. She knew her friends preferred the streetcar and wanted to repay their kind gesture by avoiding the long walk for their usual trek downtown. Michael graciously loaned it to her, but on the way home Ellen discovered a hole in her pocket and the wayward pass was forever gone.

Fearful her father would be angry or disappointed in her, Ellen approached him, head down to avoid her shameful confession. "Da, I've searched everywhere but can't find your streetcar pass. It must have fallen out of my pocket."

Much to Ellen's relief, her father calmly replied, "Do not worry, Ellen. I know ye would never do this on purpose."

Michael never mentioned he would be forced to walk everywhere for the rest of the week.

Once Ellen's relief passed, the love and respect toward her father grew to immense proportions, and a lesson of forgiveness was well-learned.

As the O'Malleys waited for the upcoming World's Fair in Cleveland, Lou's mind was on something more important. He waited four years for his love to reach the magical age of twenty-one. On the day after Marge's twenty-first birthday, Lou approached Michael O'Malley with a great deal of anxiety and not a small amount of fear to ask for his daughter's hand in marriage.

Lou greatly admired Michael's ability to provide for his family throughout difficult times and hoped to emulate his example. In turn, Michael's high regard for this young man, with his traumatic childhood and willingness to tackle the unknown completely alone, grew in proportion to the respect he'd shown the O'Malleys. Michael had a great fondness for Lou and promptly gave his blessing for the young man, who possessed academic and athletic accomplishments in addition to a future in football coaching.

During the past four years, Lou had given much thought to his remaining siblings in Mooseheart, Illinois.

Carefully approaching Marge, Lou remarked in a soft voice, "I've been thinking about our marriage and my family in Mooseheart."

"Will they attend our wedding in Cleveland?"

"That's what I need to talk to you about." In response to Marge's quizzical expression, he forged ahead. "Sometimes I feel like I've abandoned them, and it would mean so much if they could witness our marriage."

"I don't understand. Can't they afford to make the trip?"

"That's only part of the problem. Perhaps they could afford for one of my siblings to attend, but not all of them."

"But I'm certain my family would help financially to pay travel expenses for the rest of your family," Marge responded, clearly not understanding Lou's predicament.

"I'm the first of my siblings to get married, and I'd like to have the ceremony where I grew up. I haven't seen them since I left Mooseheart, and it would make them feel special to host our nuptials. Also, there's a priest who always guided me with wisdom, and I'd love for him to marry us."

Marge was taken aback because Lou was normally quiet and rarely spoke in such detail. This only served to underscore the importance of his unspoken question. Placing her arms around his neck, Marge replied, "If it means that much to you, I think it's a fine idea. Now we just have to convince my parents."

When Marge noticed Lou blanch at the enormity of his request, she reassured him. "Don't worry, we'll ask them together. How about tomorrow at six p.m.?"

Lou nodded but Marge noticed worry etched on his face.

The following day, Lou arrived at 3104 Carroll Avenue at 5:45 p.m., pale and reserved at the task ahead. At Marge's request, the O'Malleys ate an early dinner and were just cleaning up when Lou knocked on the front door.

"I'll get it. It's probably Lou to discuss our marriage plans," Marge stated with a small amount of anxiety.

Opening the front door, Marge hugged Lou and whispered, "Don't worry. Everything will work out." Holding hands, Marge called out to her parents, "Da and Ma, could you please come into the parlor?"

This request in itself was unusual and heightened her parents' uneasiness.

When Michael and Mary sat in a loveseat across from the couple,

Marge stated their request as simply as possible. She assumed being upfront was the best approach.

"Da and Ma, we would like to be married at Mooseheart in Illinois so Lou's family could attend. It means a great deal to Lou, so it's important to me as well."

Lou's sharp intake of breath at the bluntness of Marge's approach filled the deafening silence.

Marge knew her father to be a kind and fair person but wondered if he would accommodate the enormity of their request. Clearing his throat, Michael calmly said, "We want all of our children ta be married at St. Patrick's Church. Especially ye, Marge, since y'er the first. We wanted ta have the reception at home fer family and friends. We've been planning this fer years." Turning to Lou, he continued sympathetically, "I am so sorry, young man. Ye know how much we admire all yer hard work, but I don't see how this could possibly work."

Lou's heartfelt response was endearing to all. "After our parents died, we were very young and the oldest, Dorothy, was only fourteen years old. Yet she accepted total responsibility for decisions and care of her three younger siblings at Mooseheart. When she reached the age of eighteen, Dorothy was given a choice to leave Mooseheart and live her own life. She declined their generous offer of twenty-five dollars and a bus ticket to a new life.

"Dorothy took her role as our mother very seriously. She sacrificed her life to make certain our family remained together by giving up her own dreams. When I turned eighteen, with the approval of my siblings, I left Mooseheart to make my own way in the world. I promised to return one day, and I would like that day to be when I marry your beautiful daughter." Seeing the dampness on his cheek, Marge brushed away a tear. She understood the difficulty of his request and its deep significance.

Marge pleaded her fiancé's case. "I've always been fortunate to be surrounded by a wonderful family and stable home, never forced to make the painful decision of leaving my home and family to follow an uncertain future alone. We would like you both to discuss this tonight and tomorrow you can give us your answer. I know you will decide what's best for Lou and me." Marge took Lou's hand, and they went outside for some fresh air and a quick trip to St. Patrick's to pray for an amiable outcome. When they returned, Michael asked them to come into the kitchen.

"I have a few questions. First, how will ye obtain a marriage license in another state?"

"I contacted Fr. Laffey, one of the Catholic priests at Mooseheart. He became my spiritual confident and guidance counselor. He advised me, when I turned eighteen, to follow my heart, which led me to Cleveland and my true love." Lou kissed Marge gently on the forehead. "Fr. Laffey said he could help us obtain the marriage license once we provide a date."

"What date did ye plan ta be married?"

"Marge and I discussed a wedding this fall but we'd only have one month of guaranteed good weather. Chicago's weather in the fall can be unpredictable and brutal, and we wouldn't have much time to plan. We thought it prudent to be wait until next year on Saturday, May 7."

"Will ye be married in a Catholic Church by a priest?"

"There's a special Catholic chapel reserved for weddings in Mooseheart and Fr. Laffey promised to perform the ceremony. There's also a hall for the reception afterward."

"I assume yer brother will be yer best man?"

"Yes, sir."

Michael turned to Marge. "And who will be your maid of honor?"

"I'd like to ask Mayme once the details with Mooseheart are finalized. She would drive up with us to Mooseheart."

"Yer Ma and I have come ta a decision." Michael held Mary's hand to deliver their resolution—personally difficult but morally correct. "Ye have our permission ta be married at Mooseheart. Unfortunately, I am unable ta travel due ta work. Me wife and I discussed this and believe the reunion with yer family, after so many years, should be shared with yer siblings. One day we will meet them and welcome all into our family. In the meantime, ye must promise us one thing."

"Anything, sir. Just name it."

"Ye must be taking many pictures ta share yer momentous event."

Laughing with delight, Lou and Marge readily agreed to take a gazillion pictures. Michael and Mary called a family meeting to announce the good news. Marge and Lou were glowing amidst the overall happiness, group hugs, and congratulations. Mary offered her wedding gown to Marge, who readily accepted the generous offer.

"Mayme, would you come into the other room, please?"

Closing the kitchen door to give them privacy, Mayme hugged her sister and asked, "What do you need Marge?"

Marge gently held her sister's hands and said, "Mayme, I'd like you to come with us to Chicago as my maid of honor next year on May 7."

"I'd be honored and so proud to be a part of your special day." She hugged her sister and said, "In the upcoming seven months, we'll certainly have plenty of time to finalize our plans. How is Lou handling all this?"

"He'd like to be married tomorrow!"

Both sisters giggled at Lou's eagerness.

"He's already checking bus schedules and confirming the date with the Mooseheart church. I'm wearing Ma's gown and called the dressmaker to prepare your gown. You can select the color and style. We will send money to Lou's family for our bouquets and boutonnieres for the men. They will also arrange food for the reception. Oh Mayme, I can't believe it's finally coming together." The sisters hugged and Mayme's large expressive blue eyes sparkled with anticipation.

THE NEXT SEVERAL months passed quickly until May 1936 finally arrived, and the trio traveled to Illinois where Marge and Mayme met Lou's siblings. Despite Marge and Lou's nervousness, the ceremony was flawless. It was followed by a small reception, where the room was decorated by Lou's family with white bows, streamers, and a "Just Married" banner—the perfect touch to an already memorable day. Lou held their marriage certificate in the air as everyone cheered the newlyweds. He wanted the whole world to bear witness that wishes really do come true.

Once the reception ended, Lou gathered his family together. He assured them the O'Malley family were hard at work arranging jobs and housing in Cleveland for Lou's older sister and two younger siblings. The joyous news was celebrated by a group hug, tears of happiness, and excitement at the adventure awaiting them. Keeping his promise, Lou made certain pictures were taken throughout the day to share with the O'Malleys.

When Lou and Marge returned to Cleveland, they resided in the back apartment of Carroll Avenue to save money for his siblings' relocation.

80

In the months before Marge and Lou DuChez's wedding, the O'Malleys worked diligently to make the dream of relocating Lou's siblings to Cleveland a reality. Each family member tapped into their considerable array of friends for assistance and guidance in housing and jobs. During this time, Lou's siblings made plans for the eventual transition.

In less than six months after their wedding, the DuChez family was once again reunited—a glorious day for all! Lou knew his mother and father were smiling down on them for the strides and teamwork to ensure the family reunification was successful.

Now that Lou's family was nearby, he and Marge saved money for their own home. It was purchased just in time for the arrival of their son the following year—Louis Jr., nicknamed Buddy. Marge started a new tradition—childbirth in the old Fairview Hospital located just around the corner from Carroll Avenue. Marge received a general anesthetic and delivered her son without any pain. She was confined for a week, allowing her to rest and receive proper instruction for her new baby. Based on the rave reviews to her sisters about her confinement, they would follow suit when it came time for their own deliveries.

Dr. Christopher Hooker, the physician who delivered Buddy, was just beginning a new practice and lacked funds to purchase medical tools for his physician bag. He agreed to make house calls at a discount rate.

When Buddy was only six months old, he spiked a fever and cried nonstop. In the middle of the night, during a vicious storm, Dr. Hooker responded quickly and saved Buddy's life, certainly the best three dollars ever spent by the DuChez family.

As time passed, Lou DuChez's future shone brightly, surprising even the O'Malleys' expectations and within four years of their marriage, they had sufficient funds to build a home in North Olmsted, Ohio. Lou would achieve four Hall of Fame titles emanating from his basketball and football coaching skills, which spanned more than four decades at Westlake High School in Westlake, Ohio, a western suburb of Cleveland. His accomplishments were honored by the high school when they named the new sports complex, which included football, soccer, and track stadiums, as the Lou DuChez Field.

While Marge's college man certainly made his mark on the world, she increased their family size with the birth of three additional sons —Danny, Neil, and Timothy.

81

When spring 1937 arrived, all the O'Malley siblings, and the newlyweds, walked down to their favorite theater, the Hippodrome. After the main feature, *Lost Horizon*—a drama involving fantasy and adventure—cartoons were followed by news of the day. One newsreel featured German airships that captured the world while promoting luxurious air travel. They had a maximum speed of eighty-four mph, capacity for seventy-one passengers, sumptuous meals served, and spectacular scenic views displayed during their transatlantic voyages between Europe and the United States.

"Cool," whispered James. "A lot of people think a Zeppelin could land on top of a skyscraper. But they can't."

"Why not?" asked Thomas.

If anyone knew the answer, it would be James. He was passionate about anything that flew, even paper airplanes.

"Because it can't dock safely. Remember seeing that airship land at the Great Lakes Exposition? It takes real skill, good weather, sufficient space, and a seasoned ground crew."

James was anxious to see footage involving the *Hindenburg*, certain they would be treated to the wonders of airships. But the newsreel featured the May 6, 1937, *Hindenburg* catastrophe unfolding on the large screen, forever dashing James's hopes of traveling on a German Zeppelin. The news feature began innocently as the Zeppelin took off from Frankfurt on May 3, 1937, with a return trip to England by mid-May 1937 for King George VI's coronation. When adverse weather prevented the ship's anticipated route, it detoured over New York, causing a spectacle as people rushed out into the streets to see the astonishing sight. From there, the dirigible attempted to land at the Lakehurst Naval Air Station in Lakehurst, NJ, when the weather cleared on May 6, 1937.

A series of events proved fatal when the airship attempted to dock. The ground crew wasn't fully prepared for the extensive procedures, the mooring ropes were dragged through muddy water, attempts to brake the ship failed, and wind shifts caused the airship to dock unevenly. Spectators stared in shock as they saw portions of fabric flailing in the wind, and blue electrical discharges ignited the highly flammable hydrogen gas. This resulted in flames that quickly spread throughout the ship, engulfing the Nazi Swastika-painted fins. Screams could be heard as the *Hindenburg*, now a ball of fire, quickly descended toward the ground killing thirty-five passengers and crew with one fatality on the ground. Those lucky enough to survive jumped from the airship, risking broken limbs over death by fire.

Events were reported by Herbert Morrison in a live radio broadcast, and when events spiraled downward, he was overcome with emotion at the tragedy unfolding before his eyes. The newsreel footage and radio broadcast, although recorded separately at different speeds, were later combined, and the audio was accelerated to match the images, producing a powerful documentary that crippled future airship travel.

Although William reveled in world events brought to his doorstep through modern technology, watching them on the big screen had a profound effect. William could almost feel the airship's heat, which consumed everything in its path, and he felt helpless to dispel the agony. William realized progress afforded them opportunities to experience events first-hand, but it had the deleterious effect of bringing death and destruction up close and personal. It often resulted in nightmares for his younger siblings, although William knew they could not exist in a protected shell forever. But he would certainly try his best to protect them from the harsh realities of life until they were older.

After graduating from West High School in 1937 at the age of twenty, Frank Szabo continued to support his family through a part-time job building roads sponsored by the Works Progress Administration (WPA), one of the many programs established through President Roosevelt's New Deal.

Although he was grateful for the income through the WPA, Frank knew he was destined for better things and worked hard to achieve that goal. For the first time in his life, Frank received assistance from one of his parents to help advance his career.

His mother, Emma, worked as a housekeeper for Mrs. Selbert, head of the Personnel Department at National Acme—one of the country's largest tool manufacturers. Mrs. Selbert was impressed with Emma's dedicated work ethic and, at Emma's suggestion, hired Frank in the summer of 1939, where he was employed as a machinist at the East Side plant located on East 131st Street. Frank did well with his on-the-job training and was eager to make friends, a novelty for him. He befriended a group of young men, who turned out to be a corrupting influence on young Frank.

"Hey, Frank, want to take a trip to Norfolk, Virginia?"

"Sure, but I don't have any money."

The gang laughed and said, "Neither do we."

Excited at the prospect of an adventure, they traveled in an old Ford Model A convertible. With the wind in their hair and the luxury of traveling in a roadster with the top down—a first-time experience for Frank—they laid their heads back and admired the clouds as the scenery whisked by in a blur. Frank was thrilled to share an escapade with friends and wanted to hold onto this feeling forever. But time seemed to pass more quickly than the Model A could travel. Until their escapade came to an abrupt halt when the gas gauge was on "E." Spending money on gas wasn't an option, so they pushed the car up an incline and jumped in before racing downhill.

"Okay guys, I see lunch ahead."

"Where?" Frank asked innocently, looking for a restaurant or grocery store. He knew they had no money.

His friend pointed at a farm. Without funds for groceries, they sneaked onto farms and stole fruits, especially watermelons during their expedition—oftentimes hightailing it out of town as farmers chased them down the road.

Frank reveled into his first foray of sharing escapades with friends, and his normally excellent work ethic was sullied by imitating his new friends' behaviors.

With quitting time set at 5:00 p.m., they left exactly on time even if they were in the middle of a job, disparaging those who still remained on the job. But Frank's lackluster attitude did not escape Mrs. Selbert's attention, and she called Frank into her office.

"Frank, I gave you this job as a courtesy to your mother. But I see you're not up to the task. Leaving at five is unacceptable if your job is not complete. Today is your last day."

Frank was stunned, but certain he could easily get another job. After two weeks of searching in vain, and without a wide range of skills to draw upon, Frank became desperate and sought help from his former employer, head down, hat in hand.

"Mrs. Selbert, I . . . I'm so sorry for the way I acted. If you'll give me another chance, I promise to work as hard as possible and will never leave a job unfinished, even if I have to work late into the night and on weekends."

"Well Frank, we can try again and reevaluate in two weeks. But there won't be a third chance."

During that time, Frank worked long after his shift ended and never again disappointed his employer. By the time Frank left the plant with a wonderful letter of recommendation from Mrs. Selbert, his work ethic was fully internalized.

Years later, Frank discovered National Acme increased wartime production to seven days a week, twenty-four hours a day, and the president of National Acme met with President Roosevelt weekly to discuss the status of war machine production. Learning of his former employer's prestige in their overall wartime contribution, Frank was proud of his prior affiliation.

83

After waiting an interminable amount of time for the Cleveland Exposition, everyone was excited to attend the much-hyped Expo in the summer of 1937. Despite Elizabeth's advanced years, she was normally spry and eager to join the fun. Unfortunately, she usually developed cold symptoms with any change in the outside temperature and was forced to keep her activities to a minimum.

On that particular day, the weather dipped ten degrees to a balmy seventy-five. When Mary heard her mother sneeze first thing in the morning, she knew Elizabeth would not be able to withstand a day of walking. To complicate matters, temps at the Expo, closer to the lake, would be even cooler than inland.

"Ma, we can do this another day when ye are feeling better." When the younger children began to groan, Mary gave them "the look."

Elizabeth glanced at her young grandchildren, primed for the day's excursion, and didn't want to postpone their escapade.

"Ah, sure and 'tis a slight cold. Nothing ta worry about. Me neighbor will be here ta play cards, so I won't be alone. Now off with ye and be sure ta bring back souvenirs."

Surrounded by hugs and kisses from her family with promises to bring reminders of their day's events, Elizabeth waved and relaxed in her favorite rocking chair.

Mary made a quick stop next door to make certain the neighbor would keep her mother company until they returned. Finally, the O'Malleys, DuChez family, and friends marched over to the Midway at East 9th Street in downtown Cleveland close to Lake Erie. Everyone was dressed in their most fashionable outfits, including hats and white gloves for the ladies and suits and hats for the men. The entrance to their long-anticipated adventure was greeted with a golden banner overhead proudly asserting the Expo was a centennial celebration of Cleveland's incorporation as a city. The entrance was an ostentatious portal surrounded by a dozen columns, each three stories high and painted a dazzling white with three black stripes at the top. Flags from many different countries, catching a breeze from Lake Erie, flapped in the brisk wind and welcomed all who entered. Flying overhead was the Goodyear Blimp, and the skies were awash with planes that whooshed in synchronized aerial displays. Crowds gathered in wonderment as spectacular sights filled their vision with achievements and possibilities.

Entering the gateway, each person was given a souvenir map, provided by Standard Oil of Ohio, founded by Cleveland's own John D. Rockefeller. The map promised something for everyone. Many local businesses promoted their products, including a large replica of the Higbee Company Department store within an impressive tower. Many men and young boys were drawn to The Romance of Steel exhibit, which promoted the modern advances made possible through steel. Participants could even enter the Goodyear Blimp Field cordoned off for spectators to watch the landing and takeoff of an airship. Teams of men waited patiently, one holding a windsock to test the wind's direction as others raced ahead to pull the dragging lines anchored into place followed by manually guiding the Zeppelin's base to a stop.

The Streets of the World fairway was divided by a wide green concourse running down the middle, which ended in the Coca Cola structure that promised to quench the thirst of weary visitors. Each country was represented by a building synonymous with local color, forestry, gardens, pageantry, and ethnic-related activities complete with delicacies and sumptuous meals. There was hearty German beer, Irish whiskey, palm trees sashaying in the breeze, penguins to delight children in their tuxedoed performances, Belgian wooden shoe dancers in native costumes, and the ever-popular Ripley's Believe It or Not display. Anyone in pursuit of serenity was drawn to the Japanese gardens known for their miniaturized beauty and cascading waterfalls with brightly painted bridges. In the cool summer nights, stone lanterns lit the path with a soft glow as the heady smell of lotus blossoms filled the air.

Each of the O'Malley children clambered over one another trying to glimpse the map and decide which exhibits best suited their interests. Marge, Lou, and their baby, Buddy, decided to follow their own path.

"I want to go to the Romance of Steel, then the Goodyear Blimp," proclaimed James.

"Me, too," nine-year old Thomas agreed.

William signaled his approval and the brothers felt like pirates ready to discover new treasures on the shores of Lake Erie.

Mayme chimed in, "I'd like to visit the Higbee Company tower." Her sisters nodded in mutual accord, fascinated with the latest fashion. Her brothers groaned, not understanding why their sisters would choose shopping over the wonders of technology.

Mary timidly said, "I should like ta see the Streets o' the World, if we could find the time."

With so many selections and the wide array of interests, Michael made a command decision. "Ye can go ta yer own areas on this here map." He stopped while everyone cheered before he gave them strict instructions. "However, ye must never go alone and be sure ta go in groups of two or more. There are maps inside so ye do not get lost. And ye will meet at this spot precisely at four p.m., not one minute later. Look around. There are large clocks inside the park, so ye best be sure and keep track of the time. Does everyone understand?"

Everyone nodded vigorously.

"Yer Ma and me will be heading over ta the Streets o' the World. Remember, four p.m."

"Yes Da, we promise," they replied in unison and took off like jet-propelled rockets in different directions, grinning so wide an entire watermelon could fit in their mouths—almost.

Michael and Mary made their way to the Streets of the World, where they discovered artistic fountains created for aesthetic beauty. Along the wide sidewalks on each side of the fairway, separated by lovely topiary amidst green gardens, benches were generously placed to accommodate the throngs of guests.

"Oh Michael, 'tis wonderful," Mary replied, as she grabbed her husband's arm and gave it a loving squeeze.

Michael beamed at his beautiful wife and kissed her brow. "Aye, 'tis lovely."

The sun shone brightly overhead, and they purchased a nickel bag of candy and sat contentedly on a nearby bench as they watched throngs of people eager to escape their mundane lives.

WILLIAM, James, and Thomas made their way in single file toward the Romance of Steel when William stopped midstride in front of a special attraction on Lake Erie's shore.

James and Thomas plowed into him in exasperation as James said, "Watch where you're going. No need for us all to get hurt while you—"

James's speech was stifled as he gazed up at the embodiment of their nautical adventure come to life. A gargantuan ship labeled *Submarine S-49* was sitting in the water just waiting for them to board. The brothers gaped open-mouthed as the site reeled them in like powerful magnets.

"What do you say, boys? Shall we start here?" William asked James and Thomas.

They were tongue-tied with excitement and nodded as they practically ran toward their adventure on the high seas. Luckily, the line was short, and they were inside the cramped quarters quickly. William and Thomas listened intently to the tour guide as he explained the inner workings of life on a sub. But James eyed the levers and gauges, mentally taking them apart to see how they worked. It wasn't long before James lagged behind and sneaked into a strange room filled with cylindrical tubes and numerous buttons. He almost swooned at the multitude of screens, as he attempted to repress the urge to push at least one of the buttons. James rationalized pushing just one button surely wouldn't do any harm, so he did. He immediately covered his ears when ear-piercing alarms sounded throughout the ship. James was certain he blew up the sub and panicked. He attempted to run away but an overhead pipe clocked him on the head, and he dropped to the floor.

After several minutes passed, James awoke with a powerful headache as his brothers surrounded him in concern.

"Are you all right, James?" William held a cold washcloth over his brother's forehead. Just as he was about to grin, James noticed an angry captain towering above them with arms folded over his chest, glaring down.

"Well, son, what do you have to say for yourself?"

Thinking quickly, James offered an explanation, one he'd heard before, with all the innocence he could muster. "I couldn't help myself, the sub was practically calling to me." Thinking of his younger brother, James added, "The devil made me do it."

His brothers turned away to hide their grins; clearly the captain didn't appreciate the levity.

Eager to impress the young lad with the gravity of his actions, the captain walked with an exaggerated strut and solemnly responded, "Fortunately, we removed all live torpedoes before allowing civilians aboard. But if the crew missed even one bomb, you could have blown up everyone at this exhibition and several neighborhoods beyond."

Hearing this, James's face turned a bright shade of green at his foolish and potentially fatal mistake.

"I'm sorry, Captain. Is there anything I can do to make it up to you?"

"As a matter of fact, there is. Since you and your brothers find this episode so amusing, you can all swab each deck from two to three this afternoon."

James grinned in excitement as his brothers groaned at the chore just for being in the wrong place. Feeling justified as he doled out the harsh punishment, he stared peculiarly as James grinned in excitement. The captain just shook his head at the boy's strange reaction.

FOR THEATER ENTHUSIASTS, the Old Globe Theater was built as a replica of the original structure located on the Bankside London in 1599. Tourists were permitted to step back in time and relive Shakespearean dramas to the fullest. Despite their plans to view the Higbee's Department Store exhibit, Mayme cajoled her sisters into entering the theater so she could give the performance of a lifetime. They examined the schedule and noticed the next show wasn't slated for two hours. Sneaking into the theater proved easier than they thought, and Mayme confidently strolled onto the stage where she delivered what she believed to be a magnificent rendition of a soliloquy from Hamlet—the only speech she knew.

Using her arms in sweeping gestures and throwing her voice to a pretend audience at the rear of the theater, Mayme began, "To be or not to be, that is the question. Whether 'tis nobler in the mind to suffer—"

Mayme's flamboyant entrance to life as an actress was abruptly stopped when a solitary actor clapped off stage.

"And where did you learn your theatrical skill?" asked the stranger with a booming voice.

"I'm self-taught," Mayme said with pride and certainty the man was impressed with her considerable talent.

"Well," the man said, "I suggest you find another teacher."

Red-faced with embarrassment, Mayme stormed off the stage as her giggling siblings followed her out the front door. They didn't know this experience would propel Mayme into improving her craft until the day arrived when her professional career was launched.

In the meantime, they headed over to Higbee's department store to see the latest fashions.

When the family reunited at four o'clock, their parents were eager to hear of their children's adventures.

"So, boys, what was yer favorite exhibit?"

Thomas quickly replied, "The submarine. It was a blast."

James and William stifled guffaws.

Frowning, uncertain of his son's strange reply, Michael cautiously inquired about his daughters' adventures. "How about ye ladies?"

Mayme proudly stated, "I learned the value of education."

Her mother hugged Mayme until Veronica blurted out, "Mayme really learned being self-taught isn't worth her time."

She and her sisters burst out laughing as Mayme haughtily trudged off toward a concert being given in Municipal Stadium. Her puzzled parents followed her as they attempted to understand their children's antics.

After the music ended, the family attended a show at the Aquacade, where several daily performances demonstrated choreographed water ballet and diving extravaganzas.

"Oh, I want to see the Goodyear Blimp. It's set to land any minute according to the sign in the field."

The family knew how important air flight was to James, and they eagerly paraded over to the field where they were just in time to see the airship dock. James was awestruck at the wondrous event he witnessed and clapped so hard his hands were numb.

Attendees gaped in wonder at the inspiring sites, which instilled pride in Clevelanders for their hometown. Knowing that people from all over the country and many foreigners graced their humble community served to increase their community spirit. To commemorate their adventure, each person signed *The Golden Book*, rumored to be the largest book in the world. With over a half-million signatures, it was the size of a queen bed and weighed more than two tons. In addition, each person was given a small golden book with a Native American gracing the cover and within was a personalized message from President Franklin D. Roosevelt. Each recipient could fill in their name and date of attendance in the book. The back cover contained the official *Golden Book* registration seal.

As the O'Malleys walked home carrying packages, Elizabeth and her friend were listening to their favorite radio program. Michael gave their neighbor a gift from the Expo, and she thanked the O'Malleys before returning home. Once she left, the children were eager to share their treasures with their nana, especially *Golden Book* souvenirs.

Elizabeth's eyes filled with delight. Mary was pleased her mother was feeling better. Michael gave Elizabeth assorted postcards purchased from the Expo detailing the wonderful events and sights they experienced.

"Why I feel as if meself traveled by yer side." Elizabeth chuckled and admired the colorful pictures of the lavish World's Fair.

After sharing their thrilling adventures, followed by an evening snack, everyone was ready for bed, signaling the end of a perfect day.

The next evening, Michael hung the postcards near Elizabeth's bed. To her delight, they were the first thing she saw to begin her day and the last thing each night, which exhilarated her dreams filled with wonderous adventures.

84

The remainder of the summer months passed uneventfully, occupied by swimming, outdoor games, and homemade activities during inclement weather. Elizabeth was always the first one up and eager to play with her younger grandchildren. Her boundless energy was an inspiration to all, but Elizabeth was reluctant to slow down, even when she started to feel sick.

In October 1937, Elizabeth played outside with her grandson for ten minutes, despite the forecast for decreasing temperatures.

"Thomas, playing with ye makes me feel younger." But when she started to cough, she excused herself.

Mary kept an eye on her mother. "I heard ye cough, Ma. Are ye all right?" Mary asked worriedly.

"I was having too much fun with Thomas, I didn't want ta stop."

Overnight, the weather turned unseasonably cold. Mary checked on her mother throughout the night to make certain she hadn't fallen ill.

The following morning, Mary became concerned when her mother hadn't come down to breakfast by 7:00 a.m. With each tick of the clock, Mary's heart hammered with worry, but she knew her mother was tired from playing with her grandson the day before.

Hoping her mother was merely exhausted, Mary gently knocked on her mother's door with an icy feeling of dread. There was no answer. When Mary entered Elizabeth's room, a loud cry escaped her lips. Elizabeth's breathing was shallow.

Elizabeth was eighty-three years old, and her skin had taken on a bluish hue. Her grandchildren gathered around her bedside after a doctor confirmed she was near death. Mary immediately called her siblings, and all family members were present when their mother/nana exhaled her last breath. The shared grief of family members was expressed by saying the rosary aloud for this incredible woman as she made her journey home. Immediately after this, Mary and her siblings began the Irish death rituals. They placed pennies on their mother's eyelids to cover the death stare, held a mirror in front of her face to confirm no respirations clouded the glass, and covered all mirrors in the home with black cloths to prevent Elizabeth's spirit from becoming confused, thereby missing her entry into heaven.

After her siblings returned to their homes, Mary sat down on the sofa, exhausted from her chores and dealing with grief. Her mind traveled back to her beloved childhood in Ireland and the powerful homesickness she experienced in America—anguish that diminished as the remaining members of her family emigrated piecemeal. With the arrival of the most important person—her dear sweet mother—Mary finally felt at peace in her new homeland. Deep into her reverie, she barely heard William's quiet and respectful voice, which carried an intensity powerful enough to return her to the present.

Although he was aware of his mother's recent loss, William was unable to quell his concern brought about by the death of his nana. He queried in a timid, quivering voice, "Ma, what is heaven like?"

Initially taken aback, Mary realized William's question carried a child's fear of death hoping for solace. "Me darling, 'tis different fer each person. Fer me, 'tis a beautiful cottage deep in a forest with God's glorious array of foliage welcoming all who enter. Outside, horses are patiently waiting fer an afternoon ride. Inside, 'tis filled with sunshine and gleaming surfaces, bookshelves stocked with rare finds difficult ta put down once opened. Delectable scents fill the air, enough ta make yer mouth water, and apple pie is cooling in the window. A candlelit table 'tis set with the finest china and an appetizing feast is cooking on the stove ta welcome God fer an afternoon visit. With frequent appearances from loved ones residing in God's loving arms, 'tis forever a welcoming place filled with happiness and peace."

William gave his mother the biggest hug. "Your heaven sounds wonderful, Ma. I can't wait to go there."

Returning the hug and smiling as she cupped her son's face in her hands, Mary softly said, "Hopefully not fer a very long time."

William smiled, kissed his mother's cheek, and ran to tell his siblings the wonders of heaven.

A customary black wreath was hung on the front door to signify a death in the family. Elizabeth would be waked in the family parlor. However, the evening before, Ellen and her siblings—joined by Marge while Lou took care of their infant in the back apartment—quietly sneaked into the parlor to get a glimpse of their first dead body.

"Do you think she'll sit up if we jiggle her?" asked Mayme in a whisper.

"Are you daft? Of course not. We need to scare her first so she'll wake up," James said with confidence.

Getting caught up in the adventure, Marge touched her nana's hand. "Oooh, her skin is so cold. Maybe she'd like a cup of hot tea."

When she realized how foolish she—a married woman of twenty-three—sounded, Marge laughed self-consciously. If she'd known her parents were at the top of the stairs listening, grateful for their children's antics to offset the sadness of Mary losing her best friend, Marge would've been mortified.

"What happens when you die? Why can't we see her soul?" asked the youngest, and ever-inquisitive, Thomas.

Ellen walked over to a dish containing shelled peanuts and held one in her hand. "What's the best part of this—the hard shell or the peanuts inside?"

"Peanuts," they said, nodding in unison.

"Well, the hard outer shell is like our bodies. When it's intact, you can't see the best part inside—your soul." She broke open the shell and gave the peanuts to her brother. "Once your soul goes up to heaven, the shell is all that's left. And that's what remains behind to be buried."

Proud of her explanation, Ellen turned to go upstairs.

"Then, why doesn't Nana look like Mr. Peanut?" wisecracked William with his emerald-green eyes dancing in amusement at the comical image of the cute top-hat icon for Planters Nuts.

Ellen just shook her head as she ascended the stairs. "I may never eat another peanut again."

85

The wake for Elizabeth Ginley lasted an entire week as relatives from Ireland who had relocated to America paraded through the O'Malley parlor to pay their respects to a wonderful and loving matriarch. Tears were shed by all who felt kinship to the remarkable woman who overcame adversity and hardship in her long life. With drinks freely flowing, the compliments became more effusive as alcohol intake increased. The grandchildren watched these events and secretly vowed when it was their turn, they would set up a full bar near their coffins to assure others would loudly sing their praises.

Despite the unseasonable ice storm that blanketed the city, the crowds were nonstop. On the second day, a mysterious long, black limousine easily navigated the icy roads before stopping in front of the O'Malley home.

High-beam headlights temporarily lit the parlor. Peering from behind the curtains in the parlor, William exclaimed, "There's a fancy car outside. Think they're here for Nana?"

Before anyone could respond, two men with flashlights exited the vehicle and glanced in all directions before opening the back door of the limo. A well-dressed, distinguished man stepped from the car and together with his two bodyguards entered the O'Malley home.

Gasps were heard throughout the crowd as one exclaimed, "That's Shimmy Patton. He owns the Harvard Club, a speakeasy and gambling casino." Gossip was rampant as someone else added, "Eliot Ness raided his club and is still looking for him."

Another person added smugly, "I'm from Chicago and Ness had a band of loyal crime-fighters nicknamed 'Untouchables.' Shimmy's considered to be Cleveland's Untouchable 'cuz Ness can't catch him."

Everyone knew he was Elizabeth's favorite cousin, but no one thought he would dare to make the potentially dangerous trip. However, love and admiration trumped risk as he endeavored to see his beloved cousin for the final time. After saying a brief prayer with a tear escaping down his cheek, hastily brushed away before anyone could see, he once again exited the O'Malley home behind his bodyguards. Waiting on the porch until his guards cased the neighborhood with flashlights blazing, Shimmy waited until the all-clear sign was given before he was safely ensconced in his limo. The silence at this unexpected exchange left everyone speechless until nervous laughter broke through the stillness, and alcohol was once again consumed.

However, more surprises were in store for the O'Malley family. Six strong, middle-aged strangers entered the parlor and politely asked, "Excuse us, but is this the wake fer Elizabeth Ginley?"

"Yes," Marge replied quietly.

The strangers paid their respects and before exiting, asked if they could speak with Mary Ginley O'Malley.

She stepped forward with her head held high and asked, "How can I help ye?"

The oldest man stepped forward and respectfully kissed Mary's hand. "Did yer mother ever tell ye the story of her journey ta America?"

"Aye, sir. She came with her youngest son and brought six young lads who were met with relatives in New York."

"That's correct Mrs. O'Malley. And we would be those six boys. We wanted ta thank her one last time fer bringing us ta the land of freedom. If ye wouldn't mind, we would be honored ta be pallbearers."

"'Tis a grand gesture, and I believe she would be very proud," Mary replied, as her eyes overflowed with tears at the kindness exemplified by her mother's acts of compassion.

By the end of the week, Mary O'Malley and her family were finally able to place Elizabeth Ginley to rest. The funeral was held at St. Patrick's Church filled to capacity with family and friends as they bid farewell to an extraordinary woman whose gentle ways touched the lives of so many.

The O'Malley children would learn that death is a part of life marching ahead without regard for anyone's pain. But given time and space, the heartbreak of losing their beloved nana was replaced by wonderful memories. They also learned that death visits everyone, sometimes in unexpected ways. For example, Elizabeth's oldest son, Brian Ginley, died after he was struck by a truck while walking home down an unlit street. The truck driver never saw him and continued along his route, blissfully unsuspecting his vehicle had just taken a life. Despite the sadness of mortality, it reinforced for the O'Malleys how precious life was and its bountiful gifts should be enjoyed daily to the fullest.

B y 1939, the O'Malleys believed their family was replete with new gadgetry currently available. They had electricity, a car, telephone, Victrola, and radio. But new and amazing technological advances were ushered in and demonstrated at the 1939 New York World's Fair. They boasted the magic eye of television, provided by the MGM Studio and the National Broadcasting Company, which first premiered on April 30, 1939. To verify events being televised were live and not pre-recorded, cameras were installed to film visitors who watched themselves on TV as they exited the pavilion, and each participant was given a special card stating they were televised. The O'Malleys witnessed these astonishing events on newsreels at the movie theater.

Mayme shook her head marveling at the potential. "Imagine that. Watching a movie on a television set in your own living room. Will wonders never cease."

Thomas said, "Who knows? Maybe they will invent a remote control so kids won't have to get up and down to change the channel."

William admonished, "Are you touched in the head?"

James kept quiet as he mentally embraced the possibility. He still had leftover pieces from a couple of clocks and even a toaster that he would, one day, reassemble, as soon as he could find the time. But in the meantime, perhaps he could use the parts to build a remote. James was up for the challenge. But then he realized TV sets weren't available to the public. Undeterred, he was willing to wait.

But when Ellen applied the current profound strides through engineering advances (cars, automobiles, television, etc.) against the limited resources of yesteryear, she realized viewing time through the lens of progress was an enigma. Its forward momentum was a comforting reality, while memories were a gift to make time stand still. Ellen's intuition told her the world was entering a new era where the fragile barrier separating reality from perception would be set on a collision course.

She recalled two specific newsreels regarding the New Germany. The first took place in November 1938, *Kristallnacht* (Night of Broken Glass). Two days when Nazi soldiers broke the glass of Jewish-owned businesses and synagogues while beating Jewish citizens—horrific actions unimpeded by the police. The second, in direct contrast, involved the February 20, 1939 Nazi rally in New York's Madison Square Garden sponsored by the German-American Bund. Despite the Bund rallies set in a picnic setting of bonhomie with American and Nazi flags prominently displayed side by side, Ellen was unable to shake a foreboding sensation of a malignant power directly infecting America.

Presented with stark presentations of Germany, Ellen discussed her misgivings with Helen Lerner, a young Jewish neighbor with relatives trapped in Germany. In response to Ellen's questions, Helen confirmed they were unable to maintain any contact with German relatives, until finally mail and packages were returned unopened. She heard stories of camps where Jews were transported, but Helen didn't have proof or understand what occurred in the camps.

After Helen confirmed her suspicions, Ellen was concerned about the cancerous growth in her homeland. She felt a hostile undercurrent would emerge affecting millions around the world and families in their small community of Ohio City, including the O'Malleys. But, for the time being, Ellen hoped her instincts were merely an overactive imagination.

87

Mayme auditioned for many local plays in Cleveland and was happiest performing in front of a packed house. She landed bigger roles as her expertise grew, and she even performed at The Palace Theater. Located in the Cleveland's downtown theater district, it was a premiere facility with its opulent entrance and capacity to seat over three thousand patrons. Her family attended all opening night performances. Each was filled with an air of contagious excitement. However, as her career blossomed, Mayme began to think she was better than her siblings. She felt household chores were beneath her star-studded status and relegated them to others.

Mary encouraged Mayme to pursue acting, for she believed the noble profession enlightened the soul and brought joy to many through expression of the arts. But Mary could not foresee or accept her daughter's self-aggrandizement and condescension toward others in her pursuit of excellence. She knew Mayme was losing perspective in other aspects of her life and needed to be taught a lesson. She sat Mayme down one Saturday afternoon at the kitchen table and placed a large piece of paper, with two columns, and a pen in front of her.

"Ma, what are these for?"

"Ye need ta make a list fer me."

"Sure, Ma. Grocery or what?"

"I want ye ta complete each column in the privacy of yer room. When ye finish, bring it ta me." The sheet contained a header on top of each column.

Things I Do fer My Family
Things My Family Do fer Me

MAYME GLANCED at her assignment and thought she'd be done in fifteen minutes. However, three hours later a stunned Mayme emerged from her room. She handed her mother the list. The left column, The Things I Do fer My Family, was limited to one item while the right column was completely filled and extended onto another page.

"I'm sorry, Ma. I didn't realize my career was more important than family and pretty much everything else. I promise to do better."

"Of course ye will, me dear. I expect nothing less."

Mary was pleased with Mayme's transition, noting she became more attuned to other's needs. Mayme learned fame alone, as a rewarding challenge, was insufficient if the scales of contributing to the well-being of others were not balanced in kind. By accepting responsibilities to her fellow thespians, she was rewarded by increasing her skill set until she became a seasoned actor. And on the home front, she no longer shirked her chores and showed appreciation for the sacrifices made by her family to attend performances. Once again, Mayme marveled at her mother's wisdom and insight.

As Mayme matured, she grew into a beautiful young lady whose beauty was noticed by all when she walked down the street with her long, dark locks, expansive blue eyes, elfin mannerisms, and bewitching smile.

But in November 1939, Mayme experienced a potentially life-changing event. All the O'Malleys, including Marge and Lou DuChez, attended the new blockbuster movie, *The Wizard of Oz.* Although it had premiered three months earlier, the theater was still packed with stunned audiences and much fanfare as they witnessed the first movie in brilliant technicolor, a welcome relief from black-and-white films. Mayme was enthralled with the larger-than-life potential and imagined herself up on the big screen. By the time the movie ended, she was certain her destiny lay in Hollywood or Broadway. Mayme began her life-long sojourn to meet that goal, and by aiming for excellence, further improved her craft.

88

Although 1939 would be a year filled with promising achievements, it was offset by the beginning of turbulent events in Europe. Global unrest spread throughout Europe like a fire feeding on itself until reduced to ashes leaving survivors shell-shocked into a new reality.

In response to a fear of being drawn into the conflict, the United States resurrected the World War I program of America First. This policy of isolationism aimed at protecting only American interests allowed dictators unfettered access to commit atrocities in foreign lands without interference by the United States. This concept was espoused with great enthusiasm by the wildly popular aviator, Charles Lindbergh, an avid admirer of Hitler.

But for sixteen-year-old Veronica, ensconced in typical teenage angst in 1939, her days were populated by highs and lows. Fortunately, she was popular among her classmates, and her good days outnumbered difficult ones. She possessed a natural beauty with soft, brown, wavy hair and hazel eyes adorned by specks of gold. But her favorite days at West High School were field trips, meant to be educational. However, Veronica viewed them as a wonderful time to bond with friends and the added advantage of being away from the classroom.

Her sophomore class went on a field trip to a farm twenty miles south of Cleveland. Two school buses were reserved for their outing with girls on one bus and boys on the other. Veronica sat beside her best friend, Alexis, who lived a few houses away. Since they first met at St. Patrick's, they began a bond of friendship for life.

"Do you know where the farm is?" asked Veronica.

"All I know is that it's in Amish Country."

"Is that where they have no electricity, use buggies, and women wear long, plain-color dresses and white caps?"

"Yep. I was there once with my parents, and they have the most delicious food you'll ever eat, especially tasty pies and cakes."

"Gosh, I sure hope we can stop for some dessert. Do you have any idea who owns the farm?"

"I know it's wealthy relatives of a St. Patrick's parishioner, but I don't know their name. They share their farm one day each year with the sophomore class at West High. When my brother went two years ago, he said there were horses, woods to explore, a swimming pool, and a lovely lake."

"I can't wait!" Veronica exclaimed, hardly able to contain her enthusiasm for what would be an unforgettable adventure.

The moment the buses stopped, the explosion of kids, like the propulsion from a rocket launcher, fanned out in groups heading toward different activities. Some explored the woods while those less adventurous played games over the next few hours, including potato sack races, horseshoe toss, Red Rover, and dodge ball. By 1:00 p.m., everyone was tired and congregated under shade trees to eat their packed lunches. Many brought larger lunches to share with classmates whose families were less fortunate. Relaxing for thirty minutes while digesting their food, everyone looked for their next adventure.

Veronica and Alexis decided to try something they couldn't do in the city—horseback riding. It didn't seem like a difficult undertaking, but their combined knowledge of horses could fill a thimble and still have room leftover. The equestrian horse manager selected gentle, elderly mares—Moonlight for Alexis and Serenity for Veronica. They petted their horses carefully and with some reticence. The manager gave each girl a carrot to feed their horse, which created an instant connection and boosted the girls' confidence. They used step-stools to climb onto the saddle, and both mares calmly accepted their latest riders. Veronica, brimming with confidence, held onto the reins lightly because Serenity moved at the pace of a centipede wearing 100 pairs of shoes backwards. But Veronica's poise in learning a new skill ended swiftly.

To her detriment, Veronica's knowledge of horses was limited to the cinema. Serenity was half-blind and filled with an abundance of gas. With every step they took, a plume of smoke evacuated behind Serenity. When the wind shifted, Veronica's eyes watered from the noxious fumes. It was really hard to sit tall and proud when mounted above an animal constantly tooting an off-key melody, followed by a malodorous and lingering smell.

"Veronica, phew! What did you eat for lunch?" Classmates teased as they passed her as quickly as possible to avoid the stench.

"Oh Veronica, maybe you should exchange your horse for another. Or perhaps go on a different path far away from others," Alexis suggested helpfully.

"I would if I knew how to steer this gasbag," lamented Veronica. She would have been happy to end this adventure, but her limited knowledge of dismounting meant she was stuck with the horse's slow-moving trajectory. She'd seen enough Western movies to know gently squeezing her legs into the horse's sides helped spur the animal forward. To her horror, Serenity responded with a series of cataclysmic events. She began to gallop, and in Veronica's surprise-filled panic, the reins were dropped and she held onto Serenity's mane for dear life.

This is the moment Serenity's vision became Veronica's next handicap to overcome. She was headed directly into the lake.

"Nooooo!" screamed Veronica. She passed all her friends, who were helpless to assist her since this was also their inaugural attempt at riding a horse.

Her classmates watched in horror as Veronica's first venture in horseback-riding was rapidly turning into a potential disaster. Alexis, a natural athlete, jumped off her horse and ran for the equestrian's help, but she was delivering a foal in a breech position and unable to leave.

Serenity traveled so quickly into the water that she was deep into the lake before realizing she was no longer on solid ground. Still holding onto the horse's mane, while half-riding and half-swimming, Veronica prayed the ride from hell would end quickly. She made a life-saving discovery when she saw the reins flapping in the water and courageously let go of the horse's mane to grab onto them. Out of sheer panic, Veronica again recalled Western movies where experienced cowboys used the reins to control the horse's direction, so she gently steered the mare toward solid ground. As Serenity finally walked out of the water, everyone surrounded a bedraggled Veronica.

"Are you okay? We were so worried about you." Alexis voiced concern expressed by her classmates.

"I'll be fine once I get down and catch my breath."

By now, the upset equestrian arrived to help Veronica dismount. "My dear, are you all right?"

Surrounded by concerned friends, she said sarcastically, "Oh sure, I always wanted to be dragged into a lake by a half-blind, gas-filled horse. You should all try it. It's quite an experience." Everyone started to chuckle, even Veronica. But when she stopped shaking, Veronica promised herself never to ride another horse.

Alexis helped Veronica locate the restroom where Veronica was able to dry off and change into clean clothes. She now understood why everyone was cautioned to bring a change of clothes and realized her inability to exercise with panache, present since she was younger, still plagued her.

"Thanks for your help, Alexis. Clearly, I'm a city girl and would never make it on a farm."

"It could've been worse," said Alexis.

"I can't imagine how."

"The horse could've run into the deep end of the pool."

Veronica groaned as she relived the experience of her mare running amok. Fortunately, along with her siblings, she shared the ability to laugh at herself. But the culmination of her tortuous and embarrassing misadventure tested that gift to its limits.

89

With each movie that Mayme saw at the Hippodrome, her conviction for achieving celebrity status grew exponentially. Her latest on-screen adventure, *The Philadelphia Story*, merely served to augment her confidence. In June 1941, Mayme auditioned for *Macbeth* at Cain Park Theater, which premiered on July 9, 1941. She knew her supporting role was the beginning of long-awaited fame, and performing in the outdoor amphitheater under the cover of darkness was the very essence of live theater.

"Are you nervous, Mayme?" Veronica asked.

"A little bit, but that means I'm more aware of my surroundings, and it will improve my performance." Mayme wouldn't admit it, but her stomach was doing flip-flops, and at times, her hands trembled. But as darkness descended and the stage lights were turned on, Mayme's sights were focused on impressing the audience with her talent as a steppingstone to fame. A wonderful calm descended over her, and Mayme knew performing on stage would shape her future. She delighted in watching the spellbound audience while the stars glistened above, and the moon provided nature's answer to augment outdoor lighting. The show proceeded flawlessly, and time flew by. At the play's conclusion, Mayme was proud to stand in a row with the entire cast bowing to multiple curtain calls.

Mayme was thrilled her entire family attended this particular opening night, for it was certainly her best. After exchanging hugs and congratulations, Thomas was the last to approach. His demeanor, suddenly shy with eyes downcast, rendered him temporarily dumbstruck at being so close to a celebrity.

"Here," was the only word passing his lips as he presented his sister with a bouquet of garden flowers thrust into Mayme's hands. Thomas's wonderment returned him to an unprecedented state of muteness.

Mayme was touched by her youngest sibling's reaction, and she gave him the biggest hug of all. Her simple gesture returned Thomas to his normal, gregarious self, shrugging off his recent feeling of fascination. The O'Malleys smiled at the siblings' tender interaction and to Mayme it signaled her affirmation of the excitement awaiting her.

Mayme hugged her fellow actors, and by the time the successful run ended, she experienced a sense of loss most thespians feel at the final performance. Her feeling of emptiness was soon dispelled when the cast discussed auditions for a new production beginning the following week. Hope filled the air with the possibility of new friendships and reconnecting with current friends.

Mayme was grateful to perform at the Cleveland Playhouse, where she knew many of theater's giants received their first big break at this infamous theater. Mayme memorized their names including Joel Gray, Margaret Hamilton, who was terrific as The Wicked Witch of the West in *The Wizard of Oz*, and Paul Newman. Mayme was certain her name would one day join their illustrious ranks. Under the artistic direction of Frederic McConnell, the theater flourished and in 1941, she landed a role in *Invitation to a Murder*.

Mayme received a leading role and during the production, met a fellow Cleveland actor, Wilbur Staab, who was the epitome of the cliché—tall, dark, and handsome. He carried himself with grace and style, as the female members of the cast vied for his attention.

But Wilbur's attention was focused only on Mayme, and he

approached her with a terrific opening line. "Since we'll be working together, I wanted to introduce myself. I'm Wilbur Staab and, from what I've seen, I'm in the presence of someone destined for greatness."

With a line like that, she couldn't resist. They began dating and before she knew what was happening, Mayme constantly daydreamed about Wilbur, and her heart tingled when he was near. Although Mayme had never been in love before, the feeling she experienced was without a doubt the cat's pajamas.

90

As Wilbur Staab captured Mayme's complete attention, soon another man (to rival Lou DuChez's tremendous athletic prowess) would intersect with the O'Malley family, especially the lovely Veronica.

Edward Collins was on a path toward athletic stardom. Eddie, as his friends and family called him, was tall, handsome with blond hair, and was expressive with his blue eyes flecked with gray. He walked with the easy grace and confidence of a young man who knew his own self-worth. Living on West 81st Street in Cleveland, Eddie took the Bridge Avenue streetcar to attend West High School on West 30th Street. He acquired a letter jacket for his enthusiastic performance on the baseball team, earning the prized position of second base. With his batting average of 476, he would be scouted by two prestigious teams.

Unknown to Eddie, Alva Bradley (president of the Cleveland Indians) heard about the wunderkind and attended a game in Eddie's senior year, where he hit the winning home run against their rival team. Impressed by the young man's skillfulness and agility, Mr. Bradley signed Eddie to the Cleveland Indians in 1935. As a rookie player at a contracted salary of $60 per month, Eddie needed several winning seasons before he would be eligible for the unbelievable salary of $5,000. Unfortunately, Eddie was forced to quit the Cleveland Indians just before the season even began. He needed to support his mother, unemployed father, and three siblings—$60 a month wouldn't suffice, and he needed to work a fulltime job.

To assuage the pain of giving up his dream job, Eddie played for minor league teams in his spare time. From 1935 to 1941, Eddie played for Chicks Blue Ribbon Grill where his quick-handed second baseman's skill came to the attention of Branch Rickey of the St. Louis Cardinals. He was considered the "father" of the league farm system, where minor league players perfected their abilities until they were accepted into major league teams.

Branch Rickey was fully aware of star athletes in the minor leagues and would later make his then-controversial decision to hire Jackie Robinson. (Both Branch Rickey and Jackie Robinson would be inducted into the Baseball Hall of Fame.)

On February 8, 1941, Eddie trudged home after an exhausting day at work. Gathering the mail, consisting mostly of bills, his hands shook in anticipation when he saw a letter from the St. Louis National Baseball Club. It included an invitation to attend the Cardinals spring camp in Albany, Georgia, on Monday, March 14, 1941. All travel expenses would be paid by the ballclub, and if they deemed his ability worthy of the Cardinals, he would be offered a contract. The letter was signed by Albert L. Finch for the Cardinal System. The only thing required of Eddie was to accept their offer and complete a standard form outlining his employment and athletic statistics.

It was a fantasy Eddie never thought would come true. His long-awaited trophy was finally in his grasp. But his elation didn't last when his economic concerns reared their tormented head. Eddie was again forced to abandon his personal happiness and rejected their wonderful offer. Relinquishing his dream transformed Eddie's normally optimistic outlook into melancholy. His conscious moments were filled with an ephemeral feeling similar to the whispering remnants of a forgotten dream upon awakening. Eddie's filial responsibilities compelled him to reject his beloved career path into the majors, despite numerous offers from Branch Rickey over the next few years.

However, Eddie was about to meet his true love—Veronica O'Malley.

Like her sisters before her, Veronica had the natural beauty of the "Black Irish". Her petite frame was accentuated by a peaches-n-cream complexion surrounded by naturally wavy, soft brown hair. Her easy-going manner and infectious laughter catapulted her into the esteemed position as president of their high school sorority—the Moran Club, named after Father Moran. During their monthly meetings, they proudly wore specially made red sweaters with a large "M" embroidered across each garment.

Although Eddie and Veronica attended West High School, Eddie was eight years older. Their chance meeting took place two months after his tumultuous decision not to join the Cardinals.

"Come on, Eddie. A walk will do you some good. We can even stop for an ice cream cone. How does that sound?"

Although Eddie was fighting the doldrums, he was never able to resist an invitation from his sister, Rita, only one year his junior.

"All right, Rita. But I won't enjoy it."

Rita laughed as her brother's lips curved into a slow smile. The surprise she had in mind was sure to take his mind off his current dilemma.

"Let's stroll over to Bridge Avenue and make a stop on Carroll Avenue. There's someone there I promised to meet."

Eddie moaned at the thought of walking over forty blocks on his only day off when he had better things to do, like sit home wallowing in the unfairness meted out by fate. But being around Rita always cheered him up, so he quickly acquiesced as they made small talk, and her humorous stories actually made him laugh.

Rita stopped at 3104 Carroll Avenue and forced Eddie up the front porch steps. As prearranged, Veronica answered Rita's knock. Eddie was in awe of the gorgeous female standing before him. His eyes sparkled, and his prior predicament melted away like an ice cube placed on a hot sidewalk.

"Eddie, I'd like you to meet my friend, Veronica O'Malley."

With his jaw hanging down just shy of dislocating, his limbs felt stiff. For the first time in his life, Eddie was speechless. Rita nudged him, and Eddie realized he must look like a schoolboy drooling over his first chocolate bar.

"Uh, pleasure to meet you. My name's Veronica. No wait, that's not right. My name's Eddie."

He shook Veronica's outstretched hand with all his might until Veronica's curls bounced up and down, almost touching the ceiling. Veronica managed to politely remove her hand before Eddie crushed her fingers.

With a gracious smile, Veronica quietly replied, "Pleasure to meet you, Eddie."

Words escaped Eddie's lips before he realized his voice was on autopilot. "Would you like to see a movie on Saturday night?" Noticing her slight reluctance—after all, they had just met—Eddie added quickly, "We can double with Rita and her beau, Johnny Patton."

"That sounds lovely."

With Eddie's whimsical daydreaming, he didn't notice the two girls wink at each other. Their mission was accomplished.

When Saturday night approached, Veronica must have tried on at least ten different outfits. "Ellen, which one do you like?"

With a small amount of amusement and a knowing smile, Ellen responded, "Actually, I liked the very first outfit best."

Veronica groaned but thoroughly enjoyed her sister's teasing.

The doorbell rang downstairs, and Veronica shrieked when she noticed the time. "Ellen, he's fifteen minutes early. What do I do?" Veronica's face immediately turned pale, "He'll be stuck with Da. You know how he can be."

"Don't worry. Put on your first outfit, and I'll help with your makeup. Your hair is beautiful just the way it is, so you'll be ready in no time."

Veronica gave her sister a hug and dug through the pile of clothes until she located her original outfit.

Downstairs, Michael O'Malley was anxiously waiting for the Grand Inquisition to begin—a part he greatly relished. "So, are ye here ta take me darling Veronica on a date?"

Nervously, Eddie nodded his head. "We're going to the movies with my sister and her boyfriend."

"And what movie are ye seeing?"

"*Here Comes Mr. Jordan.*"

"'Tis a fine film. Or so I hear." Michael rocked back and forth, thoroughly enjoying his role as interrogator.

Fidgety and feeling slightly unhinged, Eddie blurted out, "Your daughter is so beautiful. I've looked forward to this all week." Feeling his cheeks fill with color, Eddie quickly added, "I guarantee I'll be a perfect gentleman."

Michael knew he had the young man just where he wanted him and didn't say a word. Eddie glanced anywhere but at the intrepid Mr. O'Malley, hoping anyone or anything in the universe would miraculously come to his aid.

"It's nice weather we're having, sir."

"'Tis, if ye like cold weather."

Feeling perspiration gather around his collar despite the cool breeze from the open front door, Eddie came close to bolting and calling off the entire night, when Veronica appeared at the top of the stairs. Dressed in a crushed-velvet black dress cinched at the waist with a large red bow, Eddie felt the tension flow from his body like a rowboat carried down a lazy-flowing stream.

As the vision approached him, Eddie whispered, "You're gorgeous."

Now it was Veronica's turn to blush, and she kissed her father good night.

"Ye will have me darling Veronica home by eleven o'clock or ye will be dealing with me once again."

"Yes, Sir," Eddie answered as he escorted Veronica to the front door.

They both felt an intense excitement, floating into a journey neither could have foreseen.

After leaving the Granada Theater, the two couples ate at Diney's Drive-in on West 117th Street, where carhops on roller skates brought their food to the car, accustomed to the loud music emanating from all the cars in the parking lot. Eddie ordered his favorite meal—fried bologna sandwiches with cherry pop—and everyone decided to try the unusual combination. Fun-loving camaraderie completed the perfect date before Veronica was taken home at 10:59 p.m. Eddie was just about to give Veronica a kiss when the front porch light illuminated the entire street (Michael insisted on using the highest wattage for occasions like this), and Eddie's only recourse was to shake her hand.

When Eddie returned to the car, frustrated and embarrassed at the denied good-night kiss, he told Rita and Johnny, "Take a good look at that home 'cuz I won't be coming back here."

Rita never said a word but just smiled.

91

Frank Szabo discovered the best part of attending West High School, despite the age difference, was meeting Ellen O'Malley in 1937, just before he graduated. Frank was barely sleeping and couldn't get the thought of Ellen out of his mind. Frank knew asking Ellen on a date would be a perfect solution to sleepless nights filled with images of her.

But Frank's innate shyness and the intersection of making friends at Acme National delayed his fateful decision to pursue the beautiful Ellen. After leaving Acme, where he learned the advantage of a stellar work ethic, Frank pursued his ultimate goal of joining the Cleveland Police Department. Frequent nighttime trips to the Cleveland Public Library increased his knowledge of police procedures and his bilingual skills of both Hungarian and English catapulted Frank into his childhood dream of becoming a detective. Despite being a successful sleuth, Frank was uncertain how to approach Ellen.

Fortunately, Frank was given a free ticket for a show at the Palace Theater. Glancing at the program, he was stunned to discover Mayme O'Malley was a member of the cast. After he saw a show, he stopped by the stage door and decided to ask Mayme about Ellen, hoping she was still single.

"Hi, Mayme. I don't know if you remember me, but we went to West High together. That was a terrific performance. Gosh, I wish I had even a small amount of your talent, but I'd probably be mute from stage fright." Frank stopped when he realized rambling was probably not the best way to ask about her sister.

"I vaguely remember you, but weren't you a couple years behind me in school?"

Emboldened by her response of recognition, Frank said, "That's right, you graduated two years before I did. My education was delayed because my family emigrated from Hungary, and I didn't speak any English."

"Well, it's nice to see you again, Frank, and I'm certainly glad you enjoyed the show." Mayme started to walk away, and Frank knew he couldn't let the opportunity pass. "Mayme, I met your sister, Ellen, during my senior year and I wondered how she's doing."

Mayme could see Frank's anxiety and discerned his interest in her sister. "Ellen's doing fine, working at Lampl's, and still single. She did mention how impressed she was when she met you."

Frank reddened at Mayme's ability to read him so easily.

"Why don't you give her a call? I can give you the number, if you'd like."

"I'd really like that. Thank you so much." Mayme wrote down the home phone number and handed it to Frank, adding "Good luck to you."

Mayme relayed Frank's conversation to Ellen, and Ellen felt a familiar spark of excitement as she anxiously awaited his call. However, Frank didn't need Ellen's phone number. Two weeks later in the fall of 1941, Frank bumped into Ellen on the streetcar. Working up his courage, Frank asked Ellen on a date to see the box office smash, *Gone with the Wind*.

Thrilled and shocked, Ellen did her best to casually accept the invitation. "I don't have any plans this Saturday, if—"

Before she finished her sentence, Frank said, "That would be perfect, and if the weather isn't too cold, we can start with a walk around your neighborhood before we leave for the show."

Frank's ruddy complexion turned a brighter shade of red when he realized he had cut Ellen off mid-sentence and didn't allow her the courtesy of completing her response.

Ellen realized his discomfort and decided to overlook it. "All right, Frank. Would you be able to pick me up at six o'clock?"

Frank nodded, and with plans now made, he spent his free time thinking about Ellen and preparing for their date. Fortunately, after working eleven-hour shifts at the Cleveland Police Department, his remaining time was limited, which suppressed his nervousness. He selected what he hoped was an appropriate outfit of black slacks, white shirt, and a gabardine jacket ribbed at the waist. The rest of the time was spent waxing his car until he could see his reflection.

On the big day, Frank forced himself to relax. By this time, he was experienced in dating lovely ladies, but Frank was didn't understand why Ellen made him so nervous. She should've been like any other twenty-one-year-old, so what made her so different? Despite attempts to build up his confidence, Frank stumbled throughout his routine in a daze as he prepared for his date. Before leaving the house, he wore his favorite black fedora. It had a beige satin band and a red feather tucked into the band. The crown was pinched forward and the brim tilted at a rakish angle. Frank admired his appearance in the mirror before exiting.

His trusted jalopy, gleaming like polished silver, didn't start until the fifth try.

When he arrived at the O'Malley residence, Ellen came out of the house, and her sibling, Veronica, followed close behind. In true Irish fashion, Ellen's mother was overly protective and made certain someone tagged along if one of her daughters went for a walk with a young man—a strict rule imposed on all the O'Malley girls who ventured out with a boy. And it usually worked. After one date, the potential suitor gave up. Anyone willing to withstand this amount of scrutiny deserved a second chance.

But Frank would not be deterred. "Ellen, I'd almost forgotten how stunning you are." He kept sneaking glances at this vision before him, sporting a stylish below-the-knee Scotch plaid skirt, short-sleeve white button-down shirt with matching epaulets, and a tricornered hat surrounded by her curls. Frank hoped his future would include many dates with this dreamboat.

"Thank you, Frank for the lovely compliment. It's kind of you to say that, even if it isn't true," Ellen said with a hint of sadness.

Frank gaped open-mouthed at Ellen's statement. He detected no guile on her part and was amazed she truly believed herself to be plain. All he could see was a slender woman with twinkling hazel eyes, wavy brown hair, translucent skin, and a smile so brilliant it reduced a star-studded night to shame.

With the weather turning chilly, they cut their stroll short as Frank devised a plan to lose their slighter younger chaperone. "Veronica, you're shivering. Why don't I take you home?"

"Th-th-thank you, but I th-think I'm supposed to go with you to the s-show," she said through chattering teeth.

Frank escorted Veronica to their front door and diplomatically said, "Wouldn't you be more comfortable inside your nice, warm home?" Sensing Veronica was still reluctant, Frank decided bribery was the perfect solution. "If you go inside, I promise to give you a ride in my patrol car."

Torn between her mother's directive but eager to capitalize on a situation when she had the upper hand, Veronica added, "Can we use the lights and siren?"

Frank laughed and readily agreed.

With one dollar to spend on their long-awaited date, he recalculated their expenditures to now include carfare when his car refused to start—fifty cents for two movie tickets, thirty cents for the streetcar, and twenty cents for ice cream sundaes to cap off their first night on the town.

When Ellen gazed into Frank's eyes, she completely forgot her planned religious vocation. Ever since she was a little girl, Ellen assumed she would become a nun, believing herself to be unattractive and therefore would never marry. Although Ellen fully intended to tell Frank about her pending religious vocation, the words never passed her lips. Instead, she focused on her date.

"Frank, why did you become a detective?"

"As an only child born to older parents set in their ways, I sought refuge at the Carnegie West Public Library. Books transported me to new places and fed my imagination, as I became a swashbuckling pirate one minute or a space explorer the next. But my favorite books involved detective stories, and I decided to pursue an exciting career of solving mysteries. After I applied to the Cleveland Police Department in 1940, I continued research on my own time and discovered the CPD was one of the most progressive local law enforcement agencies under the Eliot Ness's direction. He earned his popularity in Chicago waging a war against organized crime, and his force became known as the Untouchables."

"I think I've heard the term 'untouchable,' but can't recall when. Who were they?"

"The Chicago Underworld bought many city officials through wealthy bribes. But the men in Ness's unit refused bribes, so they were untouchable. He was hired as the safety director in 1935 and completely reorganized the CPD to increase efficiency and reduce traffic mortalities. He has the backing of Cleveland's 'Secret Six'—an anonymous group of prominent businessmen—in response to escalating crime. In 1936, he organized a raid on the Harvard Club but was unable to capture Shimmy Patton."

Frank stopped his narration when Ellen gasped. "Is something wrong? Your face is so pale. Do you need some water?"

Ellen was shaking but managed to reply, "No thank you, Frank. I just remembered where I heard the term Untouchable. Shimmy Patton attended my grandmother's wake in 1937 under guard and great secrecy. Apparently, she was one of his favorite relatives, and he risked everything to say goodbye. I never saw or heard from him again."

Frank was stunned at the revelation and ended any further discussion of an obviously painful subject. "I'm sorry, I get carried away."

Ellen recovered from her shock at the mention of Shimmy Patton at her nana's wake and managed a smile in appreciation of Frank's sensitivity. "It's okay. I enjoy your enthusiasm." Together they easily transitioned to a neutral subject, and Ellen felt so comfortable with Frank. It was something she could easily become accustomed to.

The following Saturday, they decided to double-date with Marge and Lou DuChez. Frank drove his jalopy over to the O'Malley home, once again displacing a polished sheen after another day of waxing.

But this time, Michael answered the door. "Me daughter's not quite ready. I would like ta have a little chat with ye. Shall we sit in the parlor and talk?"

Instantly, Frank's hands felt clammy and a thin layer of sweat beaded his forehead.

"Feeling a tiny bit hot, young man?" Once again, Michael savored this inquisition with the added benefit of watching the young man's discomfort increase under his steady gaze.

"I, um, well . . . no sir. I mean, maybe a little." Sounding like a babbling idiot as his voice squeaked, he managed to say with more than a little desperation in his voice, "Any idea when your daughter will be ready?"

"Me darling Ellen's known fer being late. But the good news is we can spend more time talking so I can get ta know ye better."

Unfortunately for Michael, his daughter came running down the stairs as she ran to rescue Frank from her father's legendary enquiries. At the same time, Marge and Lou left the rear apartment and walked around to the front door of 3104 Carroll Avenue.

After brief exchanges, Frank escorted Ellen, Marge, and Lou out to his car, but it was sitting at a lopsided angle. A quick inspection revealed a flat tire that was soon good-naturedly replaced by Frank and Lou as the ladies waited inside. Once they were on their way, they stopped for mugs of hot chocolate and toured the countryside as they loudly sang the most popular tunes of the day.

However, as they drove home, a light flurry began, which turned into a snowstorm. By the time Frank pulled into Carroll Avenue, the streets and sidewalks were heavily laden with snow. Ellen glanced at the dreary weather and wanted to prevent Frank's car from getting stuck if he parked.

"Thank you, Frank, for the lovely evening." She shook his hand and said, "With the snow so deep, there's no need for you to get wet. I can walk myself to the door with Marge and Lou, but I *really* had a wonderful time."

Frank sat in a stupor as his date gave him the brush-off, his long anticipated good-night kiss now a distant memory.

FOR ELLEN, weeks turned into months before she knew with certainty a second date with Frank remained a foolish dream. She couldn't figure out why Frank didn't contact her. She'd gone out of her way to be considerate, but at least Ellen had a backup plan, since she pictured herself as a nun since childhood.

Meanwhile, Frank decided there were other women in the neighborhood. He called a Swedish girl from his graduating class, and they went out on a few dates. However, he soon realized she did not compare to Ellen's quick wit, kindness, vivacious spirit, and natural beauty.

92

December 7, 1941, began as any other Sunday. The O'Malleys went to St. Patrick's Church, and the family gathered at 3104 Carroll Avenue for Sunday dinner, conversation, and laughter. By the time dinner ended and dishes were washed at 1:30 p.m., they were oblivious about the simultaneous suffering that occurred more than forty-four hundred miles away in the Pacific Ocean.

That evening, the O'Malleys were joined by the DuChez family from the rear apartment as they entertained their gregarious grandchild, Buddy. They tuned into Eleanor Roosevelt's Sunday evening radio program, *Over Our Coffee Cups*, on the NBC Blue network. It was a fifteen-minute program airing at 6:45 p.m., first broadcast on September 28, 1941, and featured important topics of the day—rising costs of living and other newsworthy subjects.

However, on that particular evening, fear was broadcast around the nation when Mrs. Roosevelt mentioned the attack on Pearl Harbor. She indicated the Cabinet and members of Congress, with appropriate government and military departments, were meeting to discuss a plan of action that would be announced the next day to address this crisis. This would be the only time a First Lady delivered news of such import before the President.

Mary sank back into her chair with trepidation, certain the outcome would deeply impact her family, especially her draft-age oldest son.

She looked at William, and her fears materialized when he jumped up and shouted with his fists pumped into the air. "We'll toss out those Japs in no time." James and Thomas were caught up in the moment and danced around the room without understanding the gravity imposed on the nation.

Mary held back her tears until she was alone with Michael, who shared her foreboding. Together they prayed for William's safety and a quick resolution to the conflict.

On December 8, 1941, *The Cleveland Plain Dealer* headlined the probable intention of President Roosevelt to declare war on the Japanese Empire subject to Congress's approval. Articles confirmed America's lost innocence and decreased invulnerability, events previously unthinkable. Every family read the morning edition cover-to-cover, which noted the President would speak to Congress and the nation later that day.

In the afternoon, every household gathered around the radio to hear President Roosevelt's "Day of Infamy Speech." When the President announced the United States would be victorious, members of Congress cheered in wild abandon. Within an hour after his stirring call to action, Congress overwhelmingly approved the Declaration of War against the Japanese Empire (with the exception of one female member, a pacifist, the only holdout).

After the broadcast was over, William asked a poignant question. "But what about Hitler?"

Everyone was stunned and silent at William's astute query, but no one had a response. It was widely accepted that Congress would never approve a declaration of war against Germany without an act of aggression against the United States. The answer presented itself in a most unusual way when Hitler declared war on the United States. Now America was fighting war on two fronts.

The O'Malleys, similar to their counterparts across the nation, were eager for any news and updates. When the evening paper, *The Cleveland Press*, was delivered, they raced outside—hungry for any sign of hope to dispel news of world hostilities touching their lives. The O'Malleys breathlessly read the President's full address to Congress and confirmed their swift approval to declare war against Japan. They learned multiple nations joined the United States in declaring war against Japan, including Great Britain, France and many others. Hearing the contingent of allied nations joining their fight encouraged the O'Malleys in their belief the war would end before their precious William would enter the fighting. But headlines the following day noted Hitler declared war against the United States— any sign of reassurance was quickly dashed.

Newspapers also carried heartbreaking eyewitness accounts of the attack. Heartrending recollections of the day's events, affecting military personnel and civilians alike, painted a horrendous picture of an enemy without honor. Their unprovoked aggression by air rained destruction on warships, planes, and innocent occupants of the former island known for its serenity and tranquility. December 7, 1941, began as a routine day in paradise heralded by warm island breezes and surrounded by perfection. The peaceful atmosphere was obliterated shortly after early morning Sunday services with the deafening approach of Japanese airplanes clouding the skies leaving destruction in their wake.

But one of the most surprising newspaper accounts concerned the Japanese ambassador who arrived two hours and fifty-three minutes late for his appointment with the Secretary of State under the auspices of continuing peace negotiations. He delivered an unread document containing Japan's Declaration of War but claimed ignorance of its contents. Secretary of State Cordell Hull soundly berated him for his country's cowardly attack on the unsuspecting military and civilian inhabitants of Pearl Harbor. The Ambassador left in disgrace and, until that moment, was ignorant of the betrayal perpetrated by his beloved Japan. Experts chimed in on the war coverage and determined the reason behind the attack stemmed from America's oil embargo against the Japanese Empire. Quickly running out of this precious commodity to continue their war efforts, Japan required access to the Pacific Rim—a trade route blocked by the heavily fortified bases on the Hawaiian Islands. To circumvent this obstacle, the attack on Pearl Harbor was deemed the best solution, especially after Japanese spies in America relayed the current sentiment of "America First" and their refusal to engage in a global conflict.

Although the Japanese gained access to oil, their Admiral Isoroku Yamamoto would utter a prophetic, albeit slightly underestimated, quote three months before Pearl Harbor.

"For a while, we'll have everything our own way, stretching out in every direction like an octopus spreading its tentacles. But it'll last for a year and a half at the most."

Experts postulated that President Roosevelt had a difficult task to ready the nation for war. A peacetime draft had not been initiated and the enlisted number was less than 400,000. The naval fleet, composed of antiquated tankers, was compounded by sorely lacking trained personnel in all branches of services, and equipment never updated or replaced since World War I.

But the American people, and the O'Malleys in particular, were unaware of the precarious military status. Their knowledge was limited to the elimination of "America First," as patriots were confident of their participation in America's retribution. Recruiting offices for all branches of service quickly filled as all able-bodied men in Cleveland and throughout the United States responded to the moving call to arms. Men enlisted in defense of their country with the added bonus of seeing the world and the chance to experience exciting adventures otherwise unattainable.

93

Both Brian and Patrick Ginley worked at the Cleveland docks—a career for Brian but a gateway to employment at the East Ohio Gas Company for Patrick. Regardless of their respective time spent working the docks, both brothers established life-long friendships from those who lived nearby. The Cleveland docs were rife with politics and illegal activity. Although the brothers didn't partake in either, they were the beneficiaries of secrets and back-stories of the underworld few were privy to.

Shortly after Pearl Harbor, Brian and Patrick were invited to gamble at the Harvard Club by dockworkers. At first reluctant, the new experience sounded too exciting to ignore. As they walked into the spacious main room, the brothers were assaulted by the sounds of joy and despair from customers testing their luck against slot machines, poker tables, roulette, and craps tables. Uncertain where to go, Brian spotted a fully-stacked bar and motioned for his brother to join him.

Sipping on his beer and looking around the club run by Shimmy Patton, Brian recalled their mother's wake four years earlier. "Remember how astonished we were when the sleek limousine pulled up and mysterious bodyguards appeared in Mary's living room fer Ma's wake?"

Patrick laughed added, "I still can't believe our sweet ma knew Shimmy Patton, and he risked everything to say goodbye. 'Tis a small world."

They clinked beers at the mention of their mother, oblivious others were listening to their conversation.

A stranger tapped Brian on the shoulder and inquired, "Yer ma knew Shimmy Patton? She must've been a real special lady."

"Aye, she was."

"Did she live on Carroll Avenue?"

"Aye. And who might ye be?"

"Me name is Shamus and I was one of the bodyguards that night. I remember Shimmy was sad and told us she was one of his favorite people. She never judged his lifestyle but was always proud of Shimmy."

"That sounds like Ma."

All three men clinked glasses and, without spoken words, a shared bond developed.

Over the next few months, Brian and Patrick would meet their new friend, Shamus, at the Harvard Club. They discussed Elizabeth and the Auld Sod, especially Shamus's birthplace of County Mayo near Achill Isle where the brothers and Mary played as youngsters. The conversation was easy-flowing and routine until the night Shamus ingested too many drinks and told them fascinating tales about President Roosevelt and his "Day of Infamy speech."

"Did ye know President Roosevelt is a cripple?"

"That's not possible," replied Patrick. "He's never needed any help walking."

"Hah! Ye have never seen him walk now, have ye?"

The brothers shook their heads, and their facial expressions reflected doubt at the veracity of Shamus's statement.

After a minute, Brian replied first. "Come ta think of it, no we haven't. Now why is that and how do ye know?"

"Roosevelt had polio in his late thirties and became a paraplegic. He needed heavy steel braces on each leg from foot ta hip, locking his knee. He also required tons of therapy fer upper body strength. The press corps made a deal with Roosevelt—he'd give them free access ta interviews if they wouldn't photograph his difficulty getting around. And I know 'cuz I got friends in the Mafia. Also know congressmen—they're not as lily-white as they appear—but they got real interesting stories."

Brian and Patrick glanced at one another in shock. Patrick was the first to recover.

"Oh yeah, what kind of stories did ye hear from Congressmen?"

"President Roosevelt would never have made his infamous 'Day of Infamy' speech without help from the Mafia."

"Very funny. I doubt the President needed assistance from gangsters."

Initially, Shamus's face darkened, and the brothers became afraid they'd pushed their new friend too far.

Readying themselves for a fast exit, Shamus calmly replied, "Guess again. Before he could make the most important speech of his life, he needed ta arrive before Congress in one piece, right?"

The brothers nodded, clearly intrigued as they leaned in to hear Shamus's fantastic tale.

"His office contacted the boss of bosses and asked ta borrow their bullet-proof car fer the ride ta Congress. Word quickly spread through the ranks that the Mafia helped the President on the most important day of his life. They dropped him off at the Capital doors."

"That's amazing," replied a breathless Brian. "But wait. If he's a cripple, how did he get to the podium?"

"A friend in Congress told meself that Roosevelt normally used a backstage entrance so he'd only have ta walk a few steps and people wouldn't see his hobbling walk. Over the years, he worked continuously ta increase his upper body strength needed fer even these short walks ta give the impression he ambulated on his own. But fer something this important when America needed ta see their commander strong, he took the biggest gamble of his life. 'Twas a feat of sheer strength, and likely tremendous fear, that he would trip and fall—an act sure ta undermine America's resolve. He wore his bilateral steel leg braces and used a cane while holding onto his son's arm. Roosevelt's halting gait involved moving his hips from side-ta-side and swinging one leg forward at a time. Ye could see each step produced agonizing pain, but he was motivated ta make the long walk up ta the Congressional podium. When he finally arrived, sweat pouring down his face, Joint Sessions of Congress gave him a standing ovation. It only took an hour after his wonderful speech fer Congress ta pass his Declaration of War against Japan."

After relaying these tidbits, the brothers could see that Shamus became fidgety and wondered if he regretted sharing these stories. Once Shamus downed two shots of whiskey and a beer in quick succession, he continued to amaze them. "Would ye believe that Americans fired the first shot at Pearl Harbor?"

The brother's expressions of incredulity were enhanced by their excessive beer consumption. "Ye must be joking!" cried Patrick.

"I have it on the highest authority from a friend aboard the *USS Ward* that a radio message was sent ta naval command at 6:00 a.m., more than ninety minutes before the Japs bombed Pearl Harbor. They advised the War Department that they sank a Japanese sub off the Harbor's coast. Watching the crippled sub nose-dive into the sea, everyone believed 'twas an off-course enemy vessel. They had no idea this was part of the Japs' invasion."

"Wait. How come we never heard this?" asked Brian incredulously.

"Are ye joking? Can ye imagine how embarrassing this information would be if it ever got out that we knew Japs were near Pearl Harbor just before their attack?"

"Aye. That makes sense."

"This information is highly sensitive and classified, so ye best not tell anyone." The menace in Shamus's statement was clearly understood and the brothers promised not to repeat this story.

"Ye are a wealth of information," said Patrick, "But can we share with others the story about the Mafia helping Roosevelt?" asked Patrick.

"Aye. Sure, people need ta know the Mafia helped the President. Sometimes gangsters get a raw deal from the papers. Some good press is sure ta do us good."

"Consider it done." Brian said confidently and compensated their new friend for his entertaining stories by covering Shamus's bar tab—a worthwhile expense for the ability to relay an astonishing story.

THE SIBLINGS COULDN'T WAIT to tell their newly discovered fascinating stories to all who would listen, each time embellishing the details to keep their audiences spellbound. The Ginley brothers were especially proud of their friendship with Shimmy Patton's bodyguards, the source of their stories. And they reminded everyone that their very own ma was one of Shimmy Patton's favorite relatives. Their sense of self-importance grew with each retelling.

94

Before Pearl Harbor, William O'Malley worked at O'Malley Plumbing. William and his best friend, Bill "Goosie" McGovern, decided to enlist together, hoping they would be recruited into the same branch of service.

To discuss their plans further, William knocked on Goosie's door just as fate intervened. William's pulse galloped furiously at the sight of Peggy McGovern, Goosie's little sister. His last recollection was a pesky little tomboy decked out in pigtails and rolled-up dungarees. But on that particular day, all William saw was a petite and gorgeous young lady with her red hair curled around her face and dimples that accentuated a smile sure to raise the pulse of any red-blooded male.

With color rising in his cheeks, William stammered, "Um, is Bill in? I mean, is Goosie home? I mean, aw heck, I can't remember."

Peggy seemed to thoroughly enjoy William's unease but chose to ignore it by changing the subject. "He's here. Care to come in?"

After his embarrassment of fumbling with a language suddenly foreign to his lips in front of this knockout, William just nodded. Peggy yelled for her brother and smiled when William almost tripped as he entered their home. William panicked at the thought he might be having a stroke affecting his speech and legs.

Goosie came racing down the stairs. If he noticed an unusual electricity in the air, he wisely kept his thoughts to himself as he caught the glances between his sister and best friend.

"William, let's go in the kitchen and discuss our trip downtown to register."

But their planned trip would be postponed for two months as the force of a cyclone would collide between two young lovers with a passion surprising them both. William and Goosie planned to enlist over the next six weeks based on a desire to enter a war before it ended. Many believed with America's entrance into the battle, it would surely be over by December. However, no one factored in the power of romance. With the young couple's hearts filled with love, William was compelled, as were many young lovers, to decide between personal happiness or the inspiring call to support his country, making him duty-bound to enlist. William and Peggy decided to make the difficult decision to marry just prior to his enlistment. With only two weeks to prepare, they had a relatively small ceremony at St. Patrick's Church followed by a weekend honeymoon in Akron, Ohio.

Since the DuChez family resided in their new home, the spare apartment in the back of 3104 Carroll Avenue was empty and rent-free for the newlyweds. Although William only resided in the apartment for a few nights, Peggy remained while her new husband was overseas. Peggy was thrilled to be so close to William's family, who welcomed her with open arms as the newest O'Malley.

Although William hated to leave his new bride, he joined Goosie the following Monday and together they reported to the recruitment office. Despite their pleas to remain together, the recruitment officer ignored their request; William was inducted into the army while Goosie was shipped off to the navy. Both families placed a blue star in their windows, signifying pride that a family member enlisted in defense of their country. Unknown to William and Goosie, their fight would be against a drug-fueled army who liberally used Pervitin, also known as crystal meth, thereby cheating in their goal for world domination.

William discovered one advantage of his induction into the armed forces was an honorary diploma from West High School.

While William fought the Germans, Goosie's battles were against the Japanese. Despite distance, both experienced similar terrors and a longing to return to their loved ones.

95

By 1942, the O'Malleys had become survivors and victims of The Greats—from the Great Potato Famines, Great Depression, and the Great Wars—I and II. They didn't complain and concentrated their efforts on the best way to help. Each O'Malley child was assigned a specific task to aid the war effort. The result was a steadfast pride, and certainty their contributions would bring William home faster. Veronica maintained a victory garden to supplement fruits and vegetables. She worked closely with Mayme to plan family meals for the upcoming week, using the monthly publication *Health-For-Victory-Club Meal Planning Guide*—a valuable tool for only fifteen cents. Ellen was given the arduous task of juggling ration points—prior to expiration—against available supplies at the local grocery store. Marge helped when she could, but her own growing family kept her busy.

James and Thomas were responsible for ensuring the viability of leftover summer fruits and vegetables for the upcoming winter. They became proficient in canning and dehydration involving heat, pickling salts, and drying fruits with sulfur. However, they first had to overcome the stigma that working in the kitchen was silly women's work. Their mother decided to teach them a lesson.

"Girls, I want ye ta leave the kitchen as I teach yer two brothers ta bake a pie," said Mary O'Malley confidently.

Her daughters were certain they heard wrong. *James and Thomas baking*? They'd have to find a good hiding spot for what was sure to be a highlight of their lives!

"James and Thomas, would ye come into the kitchen?"

They raced forward practically tripping over one another, believing a new treat or dessert would be their reward. When they heard their mother's plans and tried to escape, she grabbed each by the collar and warned them not to leave or they'd each have two doses of castor oil come Friday.

"Aw Ma, why don't the girls bake a pie? That's their job." James would learn to regret those words.

"Then I apologize," their mother replied contritely. As her sons were walking away with smirks on their faces, Mary added, "But I thought ye were smarter than yer sisters. But 'tis not the case, so ye should be going about yer business."

They came to an abrupt halt to face their mother's dare— something no guy could resist.

"Well, Ma, I suppose we could try," said Thomas bravely.

"And James, how about ye?"

"If the girls can do it, so can we," he said with a confidence he didn't feel.

Their mother fixed bandannas on their heads, to keep unwanted hair from falling into the food, and adjusted full-length aprons to protect their clothes. They soon learned resistance was pointless. Tentatively, they set about to work and after four hours, finally took slightly smashed and uneven pies out of the oven.

Mary O'Malley whispered something into Veronica's ear, and she ran upstairs to fetch their Brownie camera. Mary took a picture of each son, still wearing bandannas and aprons, with their misshapen works of creation. The family gathered around and hesitantly tasted the pies. Surprisingly, they were pretty good. Mary kept the pictures at the ready whenever her sons complained about women's work and threatened to show the embarrassing photos to their friends. Mortified, the boys never again complained about their kitchen duty and before long, even managed to enjoy kitchen patrol.

96

In the summer of 1942, Frank and Ellen became reacquainted—once again on a fortuitous streetcar.

"Ellen O'Malley?"

Turning her head at a familiar voice, Ellen laughed as she nodded. "Where are you going, Frank?"

Frank smiled in response to Ellen's laughter. "I have several stops to make. How about you?"

"I have a few errands downtown."

Frank was afraid to mention his real destination and risk exiting the streetcar before Ellen, so he kept his options open.

Although Frank's destination was uptown, he blurted out, "I'm heading in the same direction." He knew when Ellen smiled that his response was correct. "Ellen, would you care to trip the lights fantastic?" Frank secretly hoped Ellen was impressed by his use of the current vernacular for dancing to popular tunes.

"You mean on the streetcar? Can't say I've ever tried it."

Her dazzling smile reiterated the wonderful sense of humor he missed.

"Well, I thought perhaps we could attend the Hotel Statler Ballroom next Saturday. Sound like a plan?"

She responded with the colloquial expression, "UBBI, baby."

Frank smiled since, "You better believe it, baby" was the perfect response.

"Frank, I thought you'd never ask."

Once again, Michael O'Malley waited for Frank's knock on the door and answered with a devilish grin. "So, Frank, what have ye been up to?"

Luckily, Frank fared better than his initial meeting with Ellen's father.

When Ellen appeared in a classic, form-fitting, kelly-green dress belted at the waist and wearing a cocktail hat dipped low over one eye, he blurted out, "Wow, you're spectacular." After those three words, he was incapable of further speech and his feet refused to move. This time, Michael took pity on the young man and guided them out the front door.

The evening sparkled with magic and adventure as they danced until the stars came out, and the night whispered a lovely tune meant for young lovers.

As the end of their enchanted evening approached, Frank became nervous. He wasn't sure if he should kiss Ellen, shake her hand, or pat her on the back. The suspense grew as they neared her front door, but when the time came, he knew the right answer. He hugged Ellen and tilted her chin upward to kiss her softly on the lips, while they lingered in a world filled with moonbeams. Their hearts raced in anticipation. They reveled in a kiss unlike anything either of them had experienced before they pulled away, breathless and filled with euphoria.

After Frank said good night, he got into his car and drove home. When he arrived in his driveway, he wondered how he had gotten there. He still felt the softness of Ellen's lips and sat transfixed in his car, unable to move. He stared out the window, reliving the enchanted moments from the unforgettable night.

❦ ❧ ❦ ❧ ❦

SEEING Frank again reminded Ellen of his gorgeous blue eyes, now filled with admiration each time he sneaked a glance in her direction. His wavy, blond hair blew in the breeze during their conversation and once again, she was smitten with this handsome man. She could feel a flush creep into her cheeks and hoped Frank didn't notice. Ellen was also impressed Frank understood the vernacular uses of UBBI and dancing as they tripped to the lights fantastic.

At the conclusion of their date, no matter how hard she tried, Ellen couldn't keep a silly grin off her face. She floated on a cloud, and her entire body tingled, coming alive. In a daze, Ellen entered the house, oblivious to her siblings witnessing this event from their post at the living room window with noses pressed against the pane. She didn't notice they were out of breath from trying to imitate the prolonged kiss. And it didn't faze her when they dished out teasing remarks until Ellen was safely ensconced behind her closed bedroom door. Her lips still tingled from the kiss, and her heart raced at a pace quick enough to win the Kentucky Derby. She never dreamed a kiss could result in unbridled passion, but Frank's gentle touch was pure magic.

97

When Frank enlisted in 1942, he was assigned to the army and already bound for boot camp when he heard his name called. He was escorted off the bus and advised the doctor exempted him from service after finding a hernia. Although greatly disappointed, Frank could turn to Ellen for comfort and continue to help others in his role as a detective at the Cleveland Police Department.

Each time Frank picked up Ellen for their standing Saturday night date, James O'Malley, now a budding teenager, would admire Frank's car with undisguised appreciation. One Saturday evening, Frank stayed inside to enjoy a meal with Ellen's parents. All remaining siblings were fed earlier and told, in the strictest terms possible, to play outside until after Frank and Ellen left. They could see Ellen was becoming infatuated with the handsome young detective and wanted to decide for themselves if he was worthy of their precious child.

On that fateful Saturday night, James decided he would take Frank's car for a spin. *How hard can it be for someone as mechanically inclined as me?* Although James was short for his age, he placed a large book on the driver's side and was able to see over the dashboard. *Hah, always knew books were good for something.* He moved the seat forward so he could reach the brake and gas pedals—barely. *Even a baby can do this, so why all the fuss?* After sneaking back inside, he grabbed Frank's keys off the parlor table and made sure to close the front door, normally kept ajar, to muffle any noise from the engine. James assumed, once everyone saw his mastery of driving, they would no longer deny his rightful place as a capable driver. That was his first mistake.

He placed the key in the ignition, and it started right away. *Wow, a good omen right from the beginning.* James's excitement was palpable, and he could feel the beginning of a new chapter in his life; unfortunately, this episode was better suited to a horror story.

As the car gained speed, James noticed a third pedal on the floor. *Uh-oh, what is that? And why is there a second handle just behind the steering wheel?* James, confident in his mechanical abilities, was sure he'd solve these mysteries by improvising. That would be his second mistake.

As he neared the end of the block, he saw his family running in the street behind him. He believed they were cheering him on and applauding his efforts. James puffed up with pride and sat up a little straighter as he waved to pedestrians on the street, no doubt gazing at him in wonder. But through everyone's cheers, he was unable to make out individual words, until it was too late. A stop sign was coming up, and the car was making funny noises while gaining speed. When he depressed the brake pedal, nothing happened! Now he was getting a little afraid and sweat was dripping down his back. He kept pressing the brakes as he neared the busy intersection, but nothing happened. James was also beginning to slip off the book and the dashboard loomed large in his now-limited field of vision. *Think, James, think,* his brain screamed. By now, he could decipher the cacophony of sounds were clearly not cheers but screams and warnings.

Then, it hit him. He tried pressing the third pedal, and the car began to slow down. The engine still made funny noises, and he was experiencing difficulty controlling the steering wheel, which seemed to have a mind of its own. With the intersection quickly approaching, James had to think fast as he continued to lose control of the car. Up ahead, he saw a miracle in the making. The garbage truck stopped just before the street's end and contained lots of soft stuff to buttress a quick stop. As he headed toward the truck with its rear portion piled high with smelly garbage, he could hear Frank's voice above all others. "Nooooooo."

James's head hit the steering wheel on impact and, although he didn't sustain any major injuries, he was momentarily semi-conscious. His parents ran up to him, filled with concern, always a good sign when a child is in trouble. James kept his eyes closed a few moments longer to soak up the attention before the yelling started. And, even then, it was worth it.

Frank just stood there with a dejected expression as he envisioned his world falling apart. His beautiful jalopy smelled like a garbage truck.

"Well, Frank," said Michael O'Malley, "what do ye think should happen ta young Master James?"

Frank was too distraught to realize Michael's question was a test of future parental wisdom.

"After James empties my car of all the trash, vacuums the carpet, then scrubs the interior and exterior thoroughly with soap and water, he should come over to my house once a week and cut the grass for the rest of the summer."

The more he thought about it, the better he liked the idea. And it relieved him of a weekly chore he personally detested.

Everyone agreed with Frank's wise decision except James, but he couldn't object after the mess he created.

Boy, the price a kid has to pay growing up just isn't fair, James mused as he picked pieces of garbage out of his hair.

98

In April 1943, Peggy moved from the O'Malley apartment into William's old room. Her belongings were meager, and with the help of James and Thomas, it took less than an hour. Peggy didn't need an entire apartment for just herself and loved being surrounded by William's belongings and family. She could easily pretend he was just out of town and would return home soon. She knew it was just a silly game, but sometimes that's exactly what she needed to get through an ordeal of undetermined length or guaranteed outcome.

After Peggy settled into William's childhood bedroom, she walked around his room and admired his school ribbons and awards for spelling bees and classroom competitions. Lying down on William's bed, Peggy felt a lump that wouldn't go away no matter how much she repositioned herself. She got down on her hands and knees and discovered a two-inch, uneven bulge. Peggy removed a bundle tied together with a ribbon. Flipping through them, she was surprised to discover they were letters all addressed to her. There must have been seventy-five pieces of mail, dated but never mailed.

Peggy began to read the earliest correspondence, clearly predating their marriage, with the following note attached:

<u>TO BE OPENED AFTER
GOOSIE & I SHIP OUT</u>

My soon-to-be darling wife,

Although I haven't even proposed yet, I feel deep in my soul that we are fated to be together. I already consider you as my wife because you make my heart sing with joy. I don't know when we will be together again and have a feeling I won't be able to write very often when I'm overseas. To remedy that, I decided to write you a letter as often as possible until your brother and I are deployed.

I want you to know that you are the first and last person that I think of each and every day. Your beautiful smile fills me with happiness, and it's impossible to be gloomy when you are near. I thank God each day that He led me to you and pray you keep in good spirits until Goosie and I return home.

Although I have the best family in the world, for the past few years, it felt as though something was missing in my life. But the moment I met you, the hole in my heart was filled to overflowing with peace and love. I knew then that you were the one for me.

I'm not usually good at writing letters, but it feels like I'm talking to my best friend, and the words just pour out of my heart onto this page. I want you to know you are a gift from God, and I will spend the rest of my life proving my love to you.

All my love,

William

After Peggy closed the letter, she smiled at the thought of her precious William struggling to compose each letter. And after all the time he spent on his letter-writing project, William forgot to present her with his special gift. She wiped a tear away from the corner of her eye and appreciated, yet again, what an endearing man she had married despite his absent-mindedness. The rest of the afternoon was happily spent reading William's letters, which filled her aching heart with love and soothed the pain of his absence.

99

P eggy hungered for more letters to fill the void of William's absence. She raced each day to the mailbox for a letter from her beloved. His intermittent communications were usually brief because mail was censored to remove exact destinations or detailed battle information.

One postcard, sent in September 1942, contained a picture of the naval aircraft carrier where William had been assigned—the *USS Hornet*. Once again, he couldn't provide details about his mission, but his prior letters made his travels seem so exciting that Peggy and the O'Malleys deluded themselves into believing he enjoyed the time spent in foreign lands. He didn't get hurt, was able to see the world, and everyone was certain the war would soon be over now that America was involved. It wouldn't be until several years later that he would disclose the truth about the destruction he saw and the horrors witnessed.

On October 30, 1942, after retrieving the mail, Peggy ran into the kitchen. She was sobbing hysterically and unable to speak. Instead, she thrust the newspaper into Michael O'Malley's hand. The headlines stated the *USS Hornet* was destroyed by a Japanese sub three days earlier; the loss of William was almost more than they could bear. After hanging a black wreath on the front door and a gold star in their window signifying the death of a service member, the entire family made several trips to St. Patrick's Church to pray for a miracle.

The family waited for a Western Union telegram from The Adjutant General to inform them of William's condition or probable demise. On the second day, Ellen approached her mother, grateful that Peggy was in William's room.

"Ma, I had a dream last night about William." She hesitated. *What if I'm wrong?*

"Me darling, ye need ta tell what ye saw."

"He's alive, Ma. I don't know how, but he is. And he said to tell you that he's fine."

Mary bowed her head and prayed aloud in thanks to a merciful God who spared her family the burden and heartache of a tragic loss. "Ah me darling Ellen," Mary began, but paused when her voice was overcome with emotion. "Ye have been blessed by God with a rare gift. 'Tis like a jewel shining brightly through the mist, guiding us toward the truth." She stopped to wipe her eyes and stem the flow of tears. "Now, be a good girl and call the entire family together to share the good news."

"But Ma, what if I'm wrong? Everyone, especially Peggy, will be even more heartbroken."

Mary gently placed her hands on her troubled daughter's cheeks. "Ellen, yer eyes are a mirror into yer soul. The reflection of goodness and purity is so profound, 'tis the angels speaking through ye ta provide comfort fer the rest of us. Whenever ye have doubts, listen ta yer heart and ye will find the truth. Now, call yer family."

Ellen did as she was told and no one, including Peggy who knew of Ellen's visions, questioned her revelation. They hollered and cheered at the restoration of hope. The wreath was removed from the front door and the star from the window as they waited for confirmation of the prediction now accepted as fact.

Just as Ellen was beginning to despair that she had raised false hopes concerning her brother, Peggy received a letter one week later from William, dated one day before the *Hornet* left port. William stated he was assigned to another carrier at the last minute, where he was reunited with friends from the neighborhood. He was blissfully ignorant this strange turn of events permitted him to escape the fate of those aboard the *Hornet*. The family once again wept with joy but, for Ellen, it was the sweetest affirmation her guardian angel was still hanging around.

100

Six months had passed after Veronica's first date with Eddie Collins, and although she was attracted to him, Veronica was disappointed a second date wasn't forthcoming. Undeterred, Veronica knew in her heart their fates were aligned but wished kismet would hurry up and get its act together. But fortune was smiling on the star-struck lovers.

RITA COLLINS once again came to their rescue. She knew Eddie was depressed since his last and only date with Veronica. Rita knew her brother needed help, so Rita called Barbara, a friend from West High who also knew Veronica.

"Hi Barbara, it sure has been a long time since we spoke. How are you?"

"How lovely of you to call. And it certainly has been a while. I'm starting a new job next week at the A&P, and I'm really nervous. I've never worked in a grocery store before."

"Don't worry, my friend's two sisters worked there, and all the employees were helpful and friendly."

"That's a relief, thanks. Now, what can I do for you?"

"We're going to play matchmaker along with your neighbor, Bob, only he doesn't know it yet."

"I'm in," laughed Barbara. "But I need a few details before I can work this magical feat." Rita provided specifics, and Barbara agreed to elicit Bob's help. "See you both on Sunday."

"I look forward to it." Rita's reply was tinged with excitement at the thought of reacquainting Eddie and Veronica.

On Wednesday, Barbara called Veronica and invited her on Sunday for the 10:00 a.m. Mass at St. Colman's Church. Veronica missed her friend and readily accepted.

"Have you ever been to St. Colman's before?" Barbara inquired.

"Sure, I went once with my mother. It's on Lorain Road and West 65th Street, right?"

"Yep. I'm pretty sure the Lorain Road bus has a stop right outside the church. I'll even reimburse you for the return carfare."

"Gee, thanks, Barbara. That's really sweet. I can't wait to see you on Sunday."

"Same here," Barbara said.

BEFORE BARBARA HUNG UP, Veronica heard something in her friend's voice that she couldn't discern. Her curiosity grew with each passing day, and Veronica decided to wear her favorite dress and placed a flower in her hair on the fateful day.

When Veronica arrived at St. Colman's, Barbara was waiting by herself outside the church. Veronica was happy to see her friend, but disappointed there was no big surprise.

After Mass, Barbara walked Veronica outside. For the ruse to work, Barbara included her younger sister, Paula. As prearranged, Paula was out of breath when she frantically approached Barbara. "Mom's looking for you. She needs your help now. It's an emergency."

"Thanks, Paula. I'll come right away." Turning to Veronica, she said, "I'm so sorry, but I have to leave. The bus should arrive soon, and I'll call you during the week." Giving her friend a hug, she rushed off with her sister.

Veronica waited at the bus stop, more than a little frustrated, and checked her purse but thanks to Barbara's unfulfilled offer to pay, she had no money. Veronica panicked until she saw two men walking out of St. Colman's, stunned at what must be a mirage.

"Eddie, is that you?"

"Why Veronica, what are you doing here?"

"Meeting my friend, Barbara, for Mass but she had to rush home for some type of emergency."

Turning to the gentleman standing next to him, Eddie introduced him as Bob. "That's strange, Bob begged me to come to this Mass today, I usually go to the 11:00 a.m."

In response to Bob's huge grin, Eddie smiled just as broadly.

Glancing from one grinning man to the other, Veronica could see Rita's handiwork. She was grateful for Rita's friendship and pleased she followed her instincts to look her best.

"Can we walk you home? It's a lovely day, and we could use the exercise."

"I think that would be delightful. Do you remember where I live?" Veronica asked so sweetly, Eddie didn't realize it was a lighthearted reminder she still lived on Carroll Avenue since their last date.

"Of course, I remember. It's right by St. Patrick's church." Veronica nodded and beamed when Eddie admitted he hadn't forgotten her despite the passage of time

Right on cue, as planned by Rita, Bob said, "Sorry, Eddie, but I already have plans. I have a feeling you and Veronica will be just fine." Bob kissed Veronica's hand and bowed before exiting.

What a gentleman.

Veronica and Eddie had an amiable walk home conversing like old friends and Veronica agreed to a second date the following week. They went to a hockey game at the Arena on E. 40th and Euclid Avenue. At that time, Eddie was working at General Motors Diesel Plant during the war, and they paid his tuition for night classes in business education at Case Western Reserve University. Despite his hectic schedule, Eddie visited Veronica once a week and thus began a romance to last a lifetime.

They normally double-dated with Ellen and Frank, singing popular songs loud enough to scare the birds while driving in the countryside. They also loved to see live plays at Cain Park on the East Side of Cleveland, especially if Mayme was in the cast. Within six months, Eddie and Veronica were engaged, and Eddie declared his wish was to marry Veronica the following spring.

"But Eddie, I can't marry you before Ellen gets married. It's against tradition. The oldest always marries first, and my parents would be furious."

"What about Mayme? She's not married yet. Do I have to wait for her, too, before we can get married?"

"Mayme is dating a fellow actor, Wilbur Staab. She told my parents that she's willing to wait for him and shouldn't be concerned if her younger siblings wed first."

"But Veronica, honey, Frank is moving too slow, and I don't want to wait."

Sure enough, Michael and Mary were upset that Veronica would be married before Ellen, but Ellen came to her sister's rescue.

Calmly addressing her parents with a voice of reason, Ellen stated, "Perhaps seeing Veronica married will spur Frank into popping the question." Although she would never admit this to anyone, she, too, was anxious to marry Frank and begin their life together. Eventually, Michael and Mary saw the wisdom in Ellen's statement and gave their blessing.

In May 1943, Veronica and Eddie were married at St. Patrick's Church—Ellen was her maid-of-honor and Frank was in the wedding party. Several years later, Veronica asked her husband if he ever regretted not joining his dream team in St. Louis. Eddie smiled and said if he did, he'd never have met Veronica and the happiest time of his life would have been an unfulfilled dream.

Veronica teased him, "I thought baseball was your first love."

"I guess now it's my second love," Eddie said, and sealed his statement with a kiss.

The back apartment had been a godsend to each newlywed

couple. First, Marge and Lou DuChez, later William and Peggy. It was now Veronica and Eddie Collins's turn to occupy it, furnished and rent-free, contributing to their future financial endeavors.

FRANK DIDN'T REALIZE IT, but his single days would soon be numbered.

101

Despite the country at war, love prevailed. Or perhaps it was because of the war. Those left behind saw the fleeting moments of life and death, which made them more determined to make the most of whatever time they had before their lives were forever changed.

It had been two years since Frank's first date with Ellen, and he knew they were meant for each other, but he wasn't quite ready to make a commitment. But after witnessing the beautiful wedding of Veronica and Eddie Collins and the happiness they shared, Frank knew it was time to step up and begin the next stage of his life.

On his lunch hour, Frank made many trips to different jewelers, hoping to find that special ring to signify his love and fit into his limited budget. Almost ready to give up, Frank found the perfect, solitaire, diamond ring in a plain gold setting with tiny baguettes on either side. But now he had another problem. How would he propose?

One night, sitting in his unmarked car during a stakeout, Frank's mind wandered as he wrestled with various scenarios about the perfect proposal.

I could rent a small boat and take her out on Lake Erie and pop the question. No, I'd probably get seasick. Perhaps we could go up the Observation Deck of the

Terminal Tower in downtown Cleveland. Nah, heights make me kinda dizzy and I might pass out. We could go for a long drive and . . . my poor old car would probably break down.

While still musing, Frank came up with a unique plan, and at 4:30 p.m. that night, gathered together his courage and called Ellen.

"Ellen, I'm running a little behind. Could you catch a streetcar down to the station?"

"Sure Frank. When would you like me to leave?"

"How about thirty minutes? That way, it'll still be light outside."

"All right. See you in a little while."

Unsuspecting, Ellen left her home in a half hour and caught the streetcar heading toward the Second District. The car was crowded during rush hour, and she didn't notice someone quietly approaching the seat behind her. Glancing around, Ellen was startled to see Frank.

"Frank, what are you going here? I thought you were working late." But Ellen could see that Frank was nervous and barely able to contain his excitement. Curious, she asked, "Are you all right, Frank?"

"Oh, sure. Sorry to tell you a little fib. I actually called you from home. I had special plans for tonight."

"Oh? Care to fill me in?"

"All in good time, my dear." Luckily there was a recently vacated seat next to Ellen, and Frank joined his soon-to-be intended.

"Did I ever tell you that the first time we became reacquainted on the streetcar, I was traveling in the opposite direction?"

"Really?"

"I just wanted to spend more time with you. Not sure why I waited so long to tell you. I think I was embarrassed."

"Well, I think it's very sweet." Ellen gave Frank a peck on the cheek as she squeezed his hand.

Somehow Frank managed to continue a normal conversation as his hand periodically checked his pocket. The ride proceeded without incident until they came to a stop near one of Cleveland's finest restaurants. The Theatrical Grill catered to celebrities and provided the best jazz music around. As a special attraction, tonight they were featuring a new singer, Dean Martin.

Before exiting the streetcar, as prearranged with the conductor to wait a few minutes at this particular stop, Frank got down on one knee, and pulling the ring from his pocket, nervously recited his rehearsed speech.

"Ellen, you're the love of my life, and I can't imagine my world without you. For the past two years, I've been unable to think of anything else but spending the rest of my life with you. Will you marry me?"

As Ellen hugged Frank with tears of joy streaming down her face, she said, "Oh, Frank. You know I will."

The passengers stood and applauded. Frank's idea went according to plan. And this time, they were both going in the right direction.

102

Taking a break from Ellen's upcoming wedding preparations, the O'Malleys attended a screening of the latest box office sensation, *Casablanca,* at the Hippodrome. In between the ten-minute Paramount Newsreel and the main attraction were assorted cartoons and a special documentary titled *December 7th.*

The movie short was a thirty-four-minute profile focusing on pre-war Pearl Harbor and the devastation caused by the infamous attack. Created by the U.S. War Department, with legendary director John Ford at the helm, Hollywood film crews arrived at Pearl Harbor a week before the attack. Their aim was to film a propaganda movie highlighting safety plans and high-tech radar in place to thwart an attack. Instead, they captured the once peaceful island with real-time footage of smoldering planes. The wreckage of ships were a fresh reminder of the destruction by the Japanese. The film short won an academy award in 1943 for best short subject.

"Do you think we'll see William?" asked a wide-eyed Mayme before the feature began.

Marge rolled her eyes. "Of course not. He was never in Pearl Harbor." Although she secretly hoped his face would magically appear on the big screen because his contribution to the war effort was certainly massive.

As the documentary unfolded, tears were freely flowing in the theater. Men pretended to cough as they blew their nose while dabbing their eyes. Anger abounded at an attack perpetuated on a Sunday, following church services, and solidified the malevolence before them.

As they watched images of ships ablaze and blackened skies from thick plumes of smoke, they imagined the suffering and terror as unsuspecting soldiers and civilians attempted to outrun death raining down. They knew the bloodbath on the islands would be repeated throughout the Pacific and in Europe, but this time it included their fathers, husbands, brothers, and sons in defense of their country. The air was filled with a quiet desperation in the hope their loved ones would remain intact throughout the war—both in body and spirit. The original film, eighty-two minutes in length, wasn't released in theaters. Given the correctly anticipated audience reaction to the shortened adaptation, the full documentary may have been more than the viewers could tolerate.

103

Since 1939, Ellen worked at Lampl's Clothing Store where she obtained the latest fashions at a discount price. She worked diligently and was awarded a promotion from secretary to accounts payable. Ellen was so proud of her advancement at Lampl's, which included a secretary and a glass-enclosed office with her name painted in gold on her office door. Ellen consumed at least eight glasses of water each day and was delighted to have a Belleek crystal pitcher of water with matching glasses on a silver tray prominently displayed on her desk. To Ellen, the ability to offer visiting clients and staff a beverage represented the epitome of success and elegance. Sometimes it's the small things that give us the most pleasure.

Two weeks before her wedding, Ellen gave notice at Lampl's—a chore that delighted and saddened her. Despite her pride at the strides made in the workforce during the past four years, being a wife and mother had always been her ultimate goal.

Approaching Mr. Lampl's office, Ellen knocked on his door and entered after he gave permission. "Mr. Lampl, there's something I need to give you." Ellen was overwhelmed at the array of feelings she experienced as she handed her resignation letter to Mr. Lampl.

After reading Ellen's resignation letter, his expression was momentarily saddened which surprised Ellen. She knew he was not the type to display emotions. "I'm truly sorry to lose you. Your work is exemplary, and your sunny disposition will be sorely missed."

Ellen wiped away a small tear and said, "I'd also like you to have this.' She handed him a wedding invitation.

He quickly scanned the invite. "I'd be honored to attend. Frank is a lucky fellow."

Ellen felt the heat rise in her cheeks as she thanked her boss, a man who intimidated many but was someone Ellen found to be kind and conscientious. "Thank you so much for the opportunity to work for you and the promotions that you approved."

"You deserved it, Ellen. I wish all my workers had your work ethic."

He shook Ellen's hand, and upon leaving his office, Ellen headed to the washroom to fix her makeup where she encountered a fellow worker, Betty. Ellen noticed Betty was angry and in a foul mood.

"That Mr. Lampl, he's the meanest and stingiest boss that I've ever had."

"What happened?"

"I told him that I've been here over two years and it was time for a raise."

"What did he say?"

"Not only did he say no, but he also said it's because I was late today and two other times this month."

"How late were you?"

"Only fifteen minutes, so it's no big deal."

"I've always found Mr. Lampl to be fair, caring, and generous. Did you have a good excuse each time?"

"I overslept. It's so hard for me to get up early."

"I've been here four years and haven't been late, unless I had a doctor appointment and brought a note explaining my absence. I have a feeling Mr. Lampl will be happy to give you a raise if you're consistently on time. He's a fair-minded boss, and I'm sorry that I'm leaving. I don't think I'll ever find a supervisor as wonderful as Mr. Lampl. Try not to judge him harshly. He can be intimidating but underneath he's swell."

"Thanks for the advice, Ellen. I could sure use the extra cash, so I'll keep that in mind."

They hugged and when Ellen exited, she almost bumped into Mr. Lampl leaving the men's room.

"Excuse me." Ellen laughed as she wondered if he had overheard their conversation. With poor building construction post-Depression and lacking improvements from wartime rations, the bathroom walls were paper-thin—it was understood any speech above a whisper was likely to be eavesdropped.

"No problem," said Mr. Lampl as he smiled at Ellen before returning to his office.

Ellen knew leaving a company she loved would be difficult, but her last day was proving quite a challenge despite her bright future.

104

Several months before their wedding, Frank purchased a home on West 110th in Cleveland. In the interim, Frank and Ellen scoured the city for estate sales and discount stores to fill their home with essentials. The night before Frank gave up his bachelorhood, he hosted a gathering with his groomsmen in the home of the soon-to-be newlyweds.

Similarly, Ellen and her sisters celebrated the eve of her wedding with a small party at the family homestead. This would be the fourth marriage in the family. Marge married Louis DuChez in 1936; William and Peggy wed just before his deployment in 1942, and Veronica married Eddie Collins in May 1943. Six months after Veronica's wedding, it was now Ellen's turn to be the bride, and she was ecstatic. The siblings shared in good-hearted teasing as they bantered back and forth on the night before Ellen's big day.

Instead of making the short journey from the back apartment by cutting through 3104 Carroll Avenue, Marge circled to the front. Standing on the front porch, she called out, "Ellen, can you come outside for a minute? And, Ma, could you please join Ellen?"

The happiness of Ellen's sisters was overflowing, for they knew the surprise ahead, while curiosity piqued for Ellen and her mother.

"We'll be right out," said Ellen, escorting her mother and trailed by her giggling siblings. On the front porch was a large and heavy box, with a lovely plaid bow on top.

"What is it?" she asked her sisters.

"Guess you'll have to open it up and find out for yourself."

Opening the box, Ellen discovered her sisters had given her a full set of the exact rose-patterned china proudly displayed in Carroll Avenue. They heard Mary's sharp intake at the memory of her own mother's generosity in gifting her a similar present thirty years ago. Surrounded by her daughters, Mary was hugged and kissed without reservation at the tender reminder of her dearly departed mother.

Brushing away tears of joy, Ellen deflected the emotionally charged moment by asking, "How will I ever get this box to our home?"

"Lou and Wilbur moved the box here." Marge said.

"And they'll help move it to your home, they just don't know it yet," laughed Mayme.

Turning to her sisters, Ellen rejoiced in their thoughtfulness. "You know how much this cherished gift means to me and, just like Ma, they will be placed in a location of honor."

Mother and daughter walked arm-in-arm back into Carroll Avenue; Ellen and her sisters retired upstairs to help their sister prepare for tomorrow's festivities.

Ellen's younger sister, twenty-year-old Veronica, perused magazines until she found something to contribute. "Sis, this article describes a new facial mask to make your skin shine. Wanna try it?"

"Sure, I need all the help I can get."

While her sisters vehemently disagreed, Ellen burst out laughing and a pillow fight ensued. When the merriment died down, she read the article. "Sounds good, Veronica. Let's try it."

Veronica ran down to the kitchen and brought up a jar of pickled beets with a bowl. She drained the juice into the container and gently spread it over Ellen's face. After waiting one hour, Ellen washed her face and felt a tingling glow. Looking in the mirror, she was amazed at the beautiful reflection staring back.

Finally, the big day arrived. When Ellen awoke, she rushed into the bathroom, expecting to see her glowing complexion. But the sight reflected back turned Ellen's expression to horror. Her face was covered in red blotchy stains. Panicked, she sought help from her sisters.

"Marge, can you—"

"Sorry, Ellen but I'm busy putting on makeup."

Running down the hall into Veronica's room, she pleaded, "Can you help—"

"No, my gown is wrinkled, and I need to touch it up."

"Mayme, I need—"

"Oh, Ellen, my hair is a disaster. It will take me *forever* to get it right."

Rebuffed by all three sisters and even her own mother, who was helping her husband with his bowtie and cummerbund, the bride was on her own. After much powder, and the right amount of rouge to blend in with her new coloring, she glowed. Ellen gently stepped into her satin gown with rhinestones around the neckline and a fifteen-foot train. Bursting with excitement, Ellen could've run to the church. But she didn't want to risk tripping on her long train or soiling it on gravel stones.

Her sisters wore long taffeta gowns, cinched at the waist, in a rainbow array of colors and complementary flowers in their hair. Mary's handmade dress of light paisley with a matching hat complimented her Irish complexion.

SITTING IN ST. Patrick's Church, Mary sparkled with delight as her two youngest, James and Thomas, escorted her to the second pew. Ellen's father, in tux and tails, proudly walked her down the aisle as everyone watched the alluring vision in flowing white satin with a fifteen-foot train.

Fr. McNally presided over the wedding Mass and Frank was standing at the altar surrounded by his groomsmen. Ellen beamed at her tall, handsome, soon-to-be husband. Frank looked at her with an overflowing expression of love in his eyes, and Ellen blushed through her beet-juice facial. But, somehow, her facial no longer mattered.

As dictated by the times, they held a wedding breakfast instead of an evening reception. Most frowned on nighttime galas when so many men were suffering in foreign lands. Ellen believed a festive party at night would dishonor sacrifices made by William and others fighting for their survival in far-away countries.

A recurring thought, particularly on her special day, was that Ellen's most memorable event occurred while William was enduring the deprivations of war. Ellen greatly missed William and secretly dedicated their wedding Mass to her brother's safe and speedy return home into his family's loving arms.

En route to the wedding breakfast, Frank's clunker stalled on a streetcar track. Everyone in the waiting railway car hooted and hollered as Frank and his groomsmen, dressed in tux and tails, pushed the car off the tracks while Ellen laughed at the attention. After their feat of strength, Frank and his wedding party bowed to the patient riders and received a rousing burst of applause.

105

Frank and Ellen's wedding breakfast was held at Kaase's Restaurant in Lakewood, Ohio, a western suburb of Cleveland. The decorations were a combination of Thanksgiving and marital bliss. Each table was adorned with white tablecloths and a cornucopia filled with fruit, grain, and colorful flowers complementing the bridesmaids' gowns. Hanging above the bridal party table was a congratulatory banner wishing the newlyweds happiness and continued love, trimmed with balloons and streamers. The food was delicious and plentiful, served family-style, to make sure no one left the restaurant hungry.

Frank was in awe of his lovely bride. "I can't believe we're finally married. I love you so much, Mrs. Szabo."

"And I love you more, Mr. Szabo."

Members of the wedding party started clinking their glasses with a knife, and the remainder of the guests joined in. They stopped when Frank and Ellen rose and exchanged a fierce and steamy kiss sure to trigger smoke alarms if they were available.

Once Frank was able to catch his breath, he held Ellen in his arms and they gazed into one another's eyes with love and tenderness. There would be multiple episodes of glasses clinking, and each one was a memorable testament to the cherished vows exchanged hours earlier. When the newlyweds rose to cut the cake, Frank took Ellen in his arms and dipped her to the side as they exchanged a sensual kiss leaving them breathless and lightheaded.

The breakfast continued until the early afternoon allowing the newlyweds time to visit each table and express their thanks for attending.

Frank jovially commented to his groomsmen, "It's a good thing the food has been cleared away. If I eat any more, the tux will rip at the seams and I won't be able to return it."

The wedding party laughed at the accurate statement. After four hours, the party was nearing its end and Frank signaled the waiter to ask for the check. Although Michael O'Malley offered to pay for the reception, Frank was grateful for his most important gift of Ellen. Plus, he was proud that months of saving gave him a feeling of independence and maturity.

When the waiter returned, he had a puzzled facial expression.

"What's wrong?" Frank asked.

"There's no bill. I mean, there is a bill but it's already been paid."

"Who paid the bill?"

Ellen overheard Mr. Lampl's name and was initially in the dark when Frank asked why her former boss paid the expensive tab. Then she recalled the last time she saw Mr. Lampl and was convinced he overheard her conversation with Betty extolling Mr. Lampl's virtues. She quickly explained this to Frank, and together they walked hand-in-hand over to Mr. Lampl's table to personally thank him.

"Mr. Lampl, when we stopped at your table earlier to thank you for attending, we had no idea of your thoughtful gesture and generosity. As newlyweds, the money you've saved us will be of great assistance."

Ellen gave him a kiss on his cheek, and the two men shook hands as Frank thanked Mr. Lampl.

"I thought perhaps you could put the money toward something more pleasurable, like the honeymoon." Mr. Lampl grinned when both Frank and Ellen's faces blossomed with a scarlet tinge.

Ellen smiled as she thanked her former boss once again before they headed back to their table. After thanking their guests as they exited, the newlyweds gathered their belongings then walked to Frank's car where Ellen was enveloped in a tight embrace as she placed her head on Frank's shoulder. Ellen said a quick prayer of thanks for their good fortune and was grateful for life's unexpected blessings.

They honeymooned at the Commodore Perry Hotel in Toledo, Ohio, for five nights. The total bill of $24.95 included several long-distance calls to Cleveland, made by Ellen, of course. Frank and Ellen didn't see too many sights in Toledo, although the city boasted many fine tourist attractions. Their cozy room contained everything they needed—love and each other.

On the drive home, with Ellen safely snuggled beside her husband, they hit a bumpy patch of road and the tire blew out, as it had on most of their prior dates. At least, this time, it wasn't in front of a streetcar and memories of their honeymoon kept them warm and content as the affectionate newlyweds began their new life together.

Years later, when Ellen admired her wedding photos, she once again felt the intense guilt of her joyous wedding while William suffered in Europe. His journey would be fraught with danger and inflamed by an unexpected conclusion.

106

Mayme was getting impatient. Her three sisters and one brother were already married. Life was flitting by without giving her another thought. Wilbur procrastinated in popping the one question every girl dreamed about. Now it was her turn, but she wondered how she could make Wilbur propose, while believing it was his idea all along. After dating for two years, Mayme couldn't imagine a life without him, yet there wasn't even a hint of marriage in the near future.

Similar to Frank Szabo, Wilbur also tried to enlist in the army, but failed the physical when they discovered a history of ear infections affecting his balance. Deeply disappointed, Wilbur took comfort in Mayme. But she didn't want to remain just a girlfriend. Mayme learned several tricks from acting, and now was the time to make every effort to achieve her goal.

While rehearsing for *Hadrian* at the Cleveland Play House in 1943, Mayme approached a fellow actor who had previously flirted with her. She pretended to trip in front of him and was caught in his arms. Of course, she knew Wilbur was in the wings waiting to rehearse his scene. Mayme fluttered her long eyelashes and thanked him profusely while gently touching his arm. Out of the corner of her eye, she saw Wilbur fuming. Success. Now onto step two.

After rehearsal, Wilbur said matter-of-factly, "Mayme, I'll pick you up at seven Saturday night, and we'll catch a movie." It was their standard Saturday night date, and he fully expected her to enthusiastically accept his offer, as usual.

"Oh, Wilbur. Didn't I tell you? I'm going out with William's friend. He's home on leave this weekend. William previously warned me that he's a real ladies' man, and I'd need to be careful if we ever went out. But maybe we'll try another weekend, okay?" Mayme walked away, thoroughly pleased with herself.

Being Wilbur's girlfriend for so long, she knew exactly what he was thinking—as one of the most handsome men in the production, every girl wanted to be his date. She laughed inwardly but kept her outward façade neutral as Wilbur stomped off the stage.

Success again. Now to the coup de grace.

Mayme overheard the play's leading actor, Albert, would soon be celebrating his thirtieth birthday. Being a suave man with the ability to send each female member of the cast swooning in his presence, she would initiate the final step in her "Get Wilbur Plan." Mayme slipped into the production office to find out his exact birth date and was pleased to discover it was next week.

On the following Tuesday, Mayme brought a large box into the Green Room where all the actors were assembled prior to the day's rehearsal.

"Could I have everyone's attention?" Mayme called out and waited until the room was silent. "On behalf of the entire cast, we would all like to wish the happiest of birthdays to Albert."

Everyone cheered and clapped him on the back.

"And, as a special treat," Mayme said, "I've made double-fudge brownies in his honor."

Glancing sideways, Mayme took great delight in Wilbur's dumbfounded expression and astonishment that she made his favorite dessert for another man.

The cast crowded around Mayme and praised her wonderful baking skills, while Albert gave her a smooch right on the kisser.

"Uh, Mayme. Could I see you a minute?" Wilbur asked, somewhat nervously.

"Could it wait, Wilbur? We're right in the middle of a lovely party."

"No, it can't wait." Wilbur's voice actually squeaked as he choked out the last word.

Mayme gave Wilbur a noncommittal response. "All right I'll be right there as soon as I finish handing out these brownies."

Wilbur seethed at her nerve for making him wait. When she finally joined Wilbur, he asked angrily, "What do you think you're doing? Doesn't everyone know you're *my* girl? And what'll they think after we're married?" *Now where did that come from?*

"Why, Wilbur. Are you asking me to marry you?" Mayme said in a rather loud voice, her doe-eyed expression complementing a feigned look of surprise. By this time, a crowd had gathered, excited about the prospect of attending another party. Defeated, Wilbur got down on one knee and immediately asked for Mayme's hand in marriage.

Before the next year's end, they were married at St. Patrick's Church. In keeping with family tradition, her siblings were all in the wedding party. They purchased a home on Valleyview Drive in West Park and Mayme temporarily gave up her acting career to raise three wonderful children—Kenneth, William, and Jean Marie. As her children grew, Mayme resumed her career as she joined Wilbur to star as a real-life married couple on the stage.

Sergeant William O'Malley's tour of duty navigated him throughout Europe, where he valiantly fought German troops. Confrontations were long and bitter, with days spent in trenches no more than dirt hovels. Homesickness and fear abounded, as time crawled by until the next skirmish, when thoughts of home became a luxury replaced by the goal of survival.

In May 1944, William was assigned to the *USS Indianapolis* and noted this in his postcard home with only a generic location in the Pacific Islands. The O'Malleys were anxious to learn all they could about the vessel that carried their precious William. They went to the library and were filled with pride to discover he served on a premier flagship, which transported presidents and other dignitaries during peacetime activities. They hoped a ship that important would be invincible.

The men on the ship were taken to the staging area at Weymouth where they crossed the English Channel. After several days of inactivity, the tension on board the *Indianapolis* was palpable. It wasn't until the ships were away from port that their true mission was relayed. Shouts and cheers at striking a serious blow to an unscrupulous enemy and payback for lives lost filled the men with hope.

Looking across the water on June 5, 1944, William was awed by the massive armada consisting of 5,000 ships spanning miles of water and bearing 160,000 troops toward their destiny. Glancing up to the heavens, the skies were filled with airplanes and gliders from a combined Allied offensive involving American, British, and Canadian troops. As they made their way toward the heavily fortified beaches of Normandy, France, the sheer magnitude of this historic mission filled William with pride. Logic dictated this massive undertaking required an inordinate amount of time to plan, but only high-ranking members of the Allied forces knew it required years of preparation. For the next twenty-four hours, anxiety and apprehension increased as Operation Overlord, dubbed D-Day. invigorated the men primed for a fight against the German war machine.

With heavy storms predicted for the week of June 5, 1944, Nazi hierarchy made the incorrect and costly assumption that no invasion would be on the horizon. General Field Marshal Erwin Rommel, also known as the Desert Fox for his cunning victories as the Afrika Korps Commander, left France to see Hitler about reinforcements for the upcoming Allied invasion. His personal plans included attending his wife's fiftieth birthday celebration.

Both Rommel and Hitler knew the invasion would occur at one of two French locations—Port de Calais or Normandy. Unknown to the Germans, a lengthy deceptive campaign dubbed Operation Fortitude involved the use of inflated trucks, tanks, and planes covered with camo nets placed along the Port de Calais coastline. From overhead reconnaissance, it appeared an entire armada was poised to attack Germans from this location, and it was logically assumed this was the invasion site. Just prior to the invasion at Normandy, members of the French Resistance were instructed in coded dispatches to destroy bridges, railroads, and all lines of communications, including phone and cable lines.

Unknown to Allied command, Germany's elite twenty-first panzer divisions were just miles away from the real planned invasion site. Placed close to Normandy in Caen, France, they had instructions to remain on standby until countermanded by Hitler. But the Führer's habit of staying up late and arising mid-morning would prove detrimental. Leaving strict orders not to be disturbed left his generals in limbo, fearing retribution if Hitler's command was ignored.

By the time he awoke, the battle was well underway, and his precious panzer divisions were hampered by bridges that no longer existed, as they attempted to navigate the muddy terrain.

Sitting on the deck of the *USS Indianapolis* across from William was a former neighbor on Carroll Avenue, a lad two years his junior, by the name of Isaac Soto.

"Isaac, is that you? It's William O'Malley from Carroll Avenue."

The young man stared back with vacant eyes. But the reference to Carroll Avenue finally registered and a small smile appeared on his face. "Of all places to meet. Hiya, William. You ready for this next round of fun?" Although he tried to sound blasé, his voice cracked and the bags under his eyes told a different story.

"Oh sure, Isaac. Can't wait. Have you seen much action?"

Isaac was silent as a cloud passed over his face. "Only one battle, but even that was too much. People dying all around me, blood spurting in all directions, and watching friends die in my arms. It's just too much. I'm tired and don't know how much more I can take."

Concerned, William reached out to his friend. "Just take it one day at a time. And I'll be right beside you. Can't ask for anything better than that, can you?"

Isaac just smiled glumly and faced forward waiting for his next battle to begin.

When dawn approached on Tuesday, June 6, 1944, soldiers were lined up and herded onto small landing crafts that would take them ashore to one of five Normandy beaches. William's Third US Army Corps were assigned to land at Omaha Beach, the largest landing site at six miles. The first wave deployed at Omaha suffered a ninety-percent casualty rate, and many drowned without life vests in steep, icy waters. Ramps were later rebuilt following a heavy storm but not in time to save the first troop surges. Those who didn't drown were hampered by carrying their rifles overhead covered in plastic, making them easy prey for decimation by Nazi firepower from hidden bunkers on hilltops.

With waves pounding over the troop carriers, men were required to use their helmets as they scooped water out of the small boats. Before the front of the landing craft dropped down, everyone on board feared the danger awaiting them. Many prayed for a quick death before diving into the cold and unforgiving water.

When the signal for William's craft was given to exit the landing craft, each man fought back the fear clawing at his throat, leaving each man gasping for air. Ordered into chest-high water facing overwhelming horror, William plodded forward, watching helplessly as friends were shot down on either side of him. He strained to navigate around the floating dead as he fought back the feeling of overpowering revulsion. If the troops landing on this beach knew the treacherous and deadly trek ahead, many would never have left the safety of their boats.

"Move it! Move it! Move it!" Sergeant O'Malley screamed as the troops bravely made their way onto the beach laden with dead and dying soldiers. "You can't remain still, or you'll die."

When they finally stepped onto the beach, many were shell-shocked as the desperation of their mission hit them, and they froze in terror. But their sergeant's harsh orders catapulted men into forward motion—anything to carry them away from the death and destruction as many trudged toward their own demise.

As soon as he landed, William ran a zigzag course on the beach. He noticed several men bent over, hands clasping onto their helmets, with inertia taking hold from a paralyzing fear.

"Get up now. Stagger your lines. Staying still just makes you a target," William commanded his colleagues while attempting to master his own fear. He saw Isaac, and many others frozen in shock, and William shook each one to physically propel them forward.

William made it to the beach despite rounds whizzing close to his head. Continuing his haphazard trek, he was finally able to plant himself on firm ground and open fire in the direction of the bunkers. He kept up this routine of crisscrossing maneuvers interspersed by firing into the vicinity of enemy fire. Guided by instinct, he stumbled across a place of refuge behind a large rock.

Joined by his friend, Isaac, William saw the fervor in his eyes as he said, "All I want to do is survive."

William nodded in agreement. Isaac's breathing was irregular as his heart raced, and he braced himself for the daunting battle ahead. William and Isaac were unlike some soldiers who took pleasure in killing and viewed annihilation, sometimes with post-mortem mutilation, as their God-given right to settle a score. In Isaac's nervousness, he screamed at the enemy and fired shots into the air.

"Take it easy, Isaac. You'll run out of ammo and become an easy target for the Nazis. I know you're still new to this, but trust me. Staying alive is key, so pace yourself." But William saw the wild expression in Isaac's eyes as adrenaline coursed through his veins and knew his advice was ignored.

When Isaac saw a group of Nazi soldiers pinned down behind a log on the beach, Isaac stood and ran toward the enemy without concern for his safety. He continued to fire until bullets ripped through his body and he fell backward, forever silenced. William dragged his friend to a safe position, crossed himself, closed his friend's eyes, and said a prayer for Isaac and himself.

Wave after wave of men left the safety of their boats as they forged ahead to continue the attack on beaches against overwhelming odds of survival. Many fortunate enough to reach land were cut down by booby traps in the form of underground mines and railroad ties crisscrossed over the beach.

William and others lucky enough to escape injury in the water and make it to the beachhead, continued their staggered course across Omaha beach. They gingerly moved forward while Germans pummeled them with heavy gunfire from a well-fortified bunker located high above the beach on a hillside. This site was impenetrable until soldiers could scale the hill and destroy the fortification.

Of all five landing beaches along Normandy, Omaha Beach proved to be the deadliest with approximately 2,500 troops dead, missing, or injured. Despite the high casualty rate, perseverance and firmly rooted resolve propelled them forward. By 3:00 p.m., they captured the first hill and planted the American flag. That small, but significant, victory boosted morale as the Allies pushed the Nazis farther back. In less than twenty-four hours, boys morphed into men, the timid were transformed into heroes, and all survivors would remember the longest day of their life.

OVER THE NEXT TWO MONTHS, they continued to propel Nazis into defeat across formerly German-held beaches in France. The Allies rallied with each victory as they smashed through German lines. By August 25, 1944 France was liberated and the German retreat was complete five days later.

William basked in the glow of the jubilant march with his fellow soldiers as French citizens celebrated escaping the oppressive enmity of Hitler and the Nazi Party. Riding on top of tanks through the streets as people cheered, hands were clasped in gratitude, and bouquets of flowers flung at the parading heroes. William was grateful to survive a grueling time fraught with danger, believing the worst was behind him.

After the major beachheads were overpowered, the Third Army headed farther into France toward Cherbourg to use its ports for troop and armaments fortification. Unfortunately, the city was destroyed by Nazis, and it took several months before roads and ports were rebuilt. The Allies persevered toward victory, but many would encounter a devastating shock when Hitler mounted one last major offensive.

Following the rigors of costly battles during the D-Day offensive, liberation of France, and a clear fracture in the Nazi hierarchy with the recent attempt on Hitler's life, the Allies believed the war was over. Hitler's Thousand Year Reich, lasting a mere twelve years, was nearing its end. Many soldiers, including William O'Malley, were transferred to the Ardennes region in Belgium for much-needed rest. Surrounded by heavily wooded areas and mountains, it was a relatively quiet zone where no major battles had been fought. It encompassed over four thousand square miles of difficult landscape traversing Luxembourg, Belgium, Germany, and France. American soldiers nicknamed it the Ghost Forest, since each morning greeted them with an eerie fog decreasing visibility as it rose above the mountainous terrain.

December 16, 1944, began as a routine day until snow began to fall in a white sea of turbulence, which swirled around William and his comrades. Air and land supply convoys with winter clothing and food were delayed as their failed attempts to navigate the formidable forest were hampered by the worsening blizzard and intermittent air attacks by the Luftwaffe. The soldiers, still in their summer uniforms and ill-prepared for the frigid weather, utilized any means at their disposal to maintain body warmth. Gazing around, William had an obscure but prophetic thought. *Sometimes, silence is the loudest thing you'll ever hear.* He questioned what it meant but didn't have to wait long for an answer.

"Hey, Dick," William called to the man shivering beside him. "Think we'll ever be warm again?" Sitting in a freezing foxhole afforded little comfort from nature's onslaught.

"N-n-n-o. My boots are leaking even after I stuffed them with newspaper from the last town before we arrived in this godforsaken forest."

"My boots are soaking wet, too. Boy, could we use overcoats. Even gloves or scarves would be a welcome sight." Overhead they saw nothing but overcast winter skies and William quipped, "Talk about FUBAR."

Dick laughed at the obvious sentiment felt by all soldiers barricaded in the freezing forest. "F'd Up Beyond All Repair is right." They both knew it would feel like an eternity before provisions could arrive at their desolate locale.

"This forest will be the death of us yet," William responded, without realizing his prescient words foretold hundreds of soldiers would succumb to the freezing cold and lack of food.

Dick pointed to bright lights topping the trees in a blinding display. "What's that? Think it's reinforcements with warm clothing?"

The floodlights served their objective of disorienting the Allies and gave the Ghost Forest an unrealistic glow.

"I don't—" William's response was cut off by the unmistakable stutter of machine guns and tanks navigating the intractable terrain, each equipped with howitzers capable of firing long-range cannons. Both men ducked in response, as shells hit close to their current location. But William's friend was frozen in place from shock.

"Quick, Dick, grab your rifle and let's make a run for it."

"Right behind you, buddy." Running in zigzag lines to the next foxhole, they were greeted with the horrifying sight of bodies riddled with bullets. But war had enured them to death as terror became the norm. They quickly removed supplies from their deceased friends to sustain them during their current hell.

"At least these boots don't have holes," said William before making the sign of the cross and whispering a silent prayer for the decedent. With the sound of gunfire never far behind, both men crawled on their stomachs across the frozen ground covered with freshly fallen snow, teeth chattering as they made their silent trek.

William looked back and momentarily stopped at the unbelievable sight on the horizon. Thousands of Nazis and tanks advanced on the Allies' sparsely numbered flanks. Feeling exposed, William called out, "Dick, watch your six and move to the nearest tree for cover."

"On my way, pal."

Laying on the ground and concealed behind thick tree trunks, William and Dick fought oncoming German troops until they ran out of ammunition. Forced to retreat until they could find fully loaded weapons, they quickly forgot the cold as adrenaline took over. Saving their lives became paramount.

For the next three days, it felt like the Germans were on the winning side, while he and Dick continued to defend their positions during the blitz. Hitler's victorious troops bulldozed the Allies, mowing down everything in their path as they advanced toward the Belgian supply port of Antwerp, considered one of the world's largest and most strategic harbors. English-speaking Germans infiltrated the dwindling Allied lines to corrupt their advance and conduct covert bombings, while providing misdirection by switching road and village signs.

During this short period, with casualties and fatalities reducing their meager defenses, soldiers lost everything important to any combatant: communications, command posts, sense of direction in the snow-covered mountains, and hope from pure isolation.

PRIOR TO THIS ATTACK, front-page stories back home included a pictorial aid of European towns depicting battle movements. Shaded areas, representing towns conquered by Allied forces, revealed an inward bulge as troops continued their trek from France toward Germany. Along with the majority of homes where a loved one was fighting in Europe, the O'Malleys kept a map to track troop movements. Families learned the names of many cities previously foreign to them and were proud of the progress made by the Allies. But Hitler's advance into the Ardennes revealed an astonishing new picture. The bulge on the map had reversed outward, indicating the Nazis were on the offensive and taking back lands previously occupied by Allied forces. Just when everyone thought the war was over, a wave of dread traversed Allied nations as the unthinkable became possible.

The Battle of the Bulge had begun.

109

By December 19, 1944, after fighting for three grueling days, the clouds opened up and aerial support bombed the German forces without mercy. William and his company cheered when supply planes dropped food, warm clothing, and ammunition to the Allied troops. Regardless of temporary German victories, General Eisenhower sent General Patton along with all available troops, including William's Third Army, to the Ardennes. He initiated a surprise offensive, where uncommon courage emerged from the ashes of despair. In spite of being outnumbered four to one, Allied troops bravely fought advancing Germans composed of soldiers and Hitler Youth conscripted in a last desperate attempt to win the war. Hitler's last-ditch offensive, considered by his top generals as insanity, was soundly defeated by January 25, 1945, with the surrender of German troops. The hubris of Hitler's master plan, based on an unpredictable weather projection of snow and inclement weather for ten days, would be reduced to a short-lived wish dying on the lips of their psychotic cocaine-addled leader.

Knowing the end of the war was near, William recalled the nightmarish sight of soldiers marching through the starless nights, driven by fatigue and anesthetized to the horrors relived behind closed eyes. Their outlines appeared as silhouettes against the backdrop of blinding fireworks from bombs exploding in the distance. Placing one foot in front of the other, moving by rote and bone-tired, each man prayed for survival. Days blurred into sleepless nights and fear abounded deep within—an unwanted companion taking up space previously filled with sparks of hope and peace.

William and his comrades wondered how they would one day reconcile normalcy after committing atrocities in self-defense and prevailing over the enemy at a high personal cost. They questioned if their souls were forever damned or if God's mercy would bless them with forgiveness they desperately craved. Despite paralyzing fear, each soldier arose each day to face unknown perils with valor. By performing their patriotic duty with steadfast determination, they would later earn the esteemed title as the Greatest Generation.

The war had taken its toll on William. His wiry frame became gaunt, and his green eyes appeared haunted by the misery burning into his brain. However, his wry sense of O'Malley wit became a finely tuned defense mechanism in combating the horror surrounding him.

110

Ellen prayed for William daily as did the remainder of the O'Malleys. But in the midst of worrying about her brother, Ellen and Frank received an expected surprise. Ellen was pregnant with her first child and her due date was January 25, 1945. She fervently hoped her brother would be home soon to welcome their new addition. Without knowing her brother's status, a slight pall was cast over the exciting news, but Ellen kept her concerns hidden to avoid diminishing Frank's excitement.

Frank helped Ellen in any way possible and treated her like a China doll, convinced she would break with any strenuous movement. Initially, Ellen found it endearing but knew she had to make Frank aware that being pregnant was a normal occurrence and he should save his strength to care for their newborn upon arrival.

When Ellen was five months pregnant, Frank almost knocked her over when she reached for her coat.

Taking a deep breath, Ellen said, "Frank, my darling, come sit by me for a moment."

He did as she requested, fluffing pillows behind her on the couch.

"I need you to understand that my pregnancy is an experience women have gone through for thousands of years. In some countries, a woman goes out into the field to continue her work right after giving birth."

Based on Frank's expression, Ellen was certain her husband had gotten the message.

However, Frank's eyes widened, and he replied, "Geez. I'm sure glad you don't work in the fields."

Ellen took another deep breath and grinned at the challenge she faced with Frank. Over the next several months, they shopped for baby supplies and decorated the nursery. Seeing the baby's room grow into a cozy and gentle space to welcome their child gave Ellen peace as she sat in the rocker and gently rubbed her expanding belly. Frank would enter the nursery, and his love for Ellen grew as the months flew by.

While Frank was at work, Ellen enjoyed visits with her sisters and commiserated similar experiences during their first pregnancies. Laughter and homecooked meals were the best medicine to offset worry and sleepless nights before their happy home increased from two to three. Surrounded by encouragement and humor pleasurably expedited the passage of time until the fateful day arrived.

In the early morning hours of January 21, 1945, Ellen began to experience contractions, and their system of what to do before going to the hospital, well- rehearsed many times, fell apart when Frank exclaimed, "I feel like I'm going to faint."

Ellen led her husband to a chair and placed a cold cloth on his forehead before another contraction hit her with the force of an avalanche gaining speed as it crested over a mountaintop. When Ellen doubled over in pain, Frank jumped up and roles were immediately reversed.

"Now what do I do?"

Ellen realized all their run-throughs left Frank's addled brain completely empty. "We need to call the doctor and hospital. Their numbers are right by the phone."

"That's right. I'm sure glad you're here, Ellen." The irony didn't hit Frank in his heightened state of fright, but it brought a much-needed grin to Ellen until the next wave of pain intensified. Watching Frank run out the door, grabbing Ellen's suitcase on the way, and backing the car out of the driveway, Ellen sat back and waited for his inevitable return.

Several minutes passed before Ellen exited the front door, closing it behind her, and stood on the front porch to await her husband. In between contractions, Ellen knew this would one day be an amusing story. Perhaps not today though . . .

Wearing a sheepish grin, Frank parked the car and carefully escorted Ellen into the front seat. "Did I mention it's a good thing you're here?"

Ellen just nodded, too exhausted to reply, as Frank drove his patrol car with lights flashing, at top speed to Fairview General Hospital.

"Frank, at this speed over bumpy roads, the baby will arrive before we get to the hospital." She looked over and saw Frank's terrified expression, and he contritely slowed his speed.

Frank kissed Ellen before she was placed in a wheelchair and taken to the delivery room.

Frank was placed in a room with other expectant fathers, but no one was sitting. They were either pacing, chain-smoking which created a dense cloud lingering in the air, or attempting to read mostly upside-down magazines. Frank knew he was in the right place.

After six hours, while Frank slept in a chair, a nurse tapped him on the shoulder.

"Your wife is recovering nicely from general anesthesia, but she's still asleep. Both she and your son are doing well. Would you like to see them now?"

"Is she all right? What about the baby? Wait, did you say son?" The nurse nodded sagely as she directed Frank into Ellen's room.

When Frank approached his sleeping wife, he kissed her forehead and pinned a note on her gown.

Congratulations Mom! We have a son. I'm so proud of you but I'm going home to rest. It's been a long night. I'll see you first thing in the morning. Love, Frank.

When Ellen woke up, she read the endearing note and smiled to herself. Seems she was the one to endure a difficult night but, when their son, James Francis, was placed in her arms, all the pain was forgotten.

When Frank returned early the next day, Ellen was nursing their son and teased, "You do realize this is one of the few times in my life that I've ever been early for anything." Frank smiled at the accuracy of her comment.

After Ellen completed her first nursing, with some assistance from the nursing staff, Ellen was exhausted. With a smile on her face, she drifted off into much-needed sleep. Frank held their precious newborn until the nurse came to return him to the nursery.

Ellen remained in the hospital for seven days, the customary length of confinement following a delivery. Despite the wonderful care and instructions by the nursing staff on feeding, bathing, and general infant care, Ellen was ecstatic when advised they could return home.

She looked forward to being in their charming bungalow on West 110th Street in Cleveland. Returning to their cheerful home was both surreal and heartwarming.

During her week-long confinement, Frank had decorated the nursery with beautiful WELCOME HOME signs, stuffed animals, a baseball and bat, and home-grown flowers in vases. Ellen thought of the movie *The Wizard of Oz* and fully understood—there really is no place like home.

111

Despite false hopes earlier, William was certain *this time* the war's end was in sight—a sentiment buoying everyone's spirits. Convinced their current insanity would soon end, they were completely unprepared for the brutality awaiting them.

A few months later, a new site of devastation would hollow William's faith in humanity to its very core. On April 4, 1945, as the Third U.S. Army and other companies were miles outside the Ohrdruf Concentration Camp, they were greeted by an unbelievable stench. With terror at what they might find, many retched and screamed as they encountered the lunacy of Nazi concentration camps, naïve to the extent of depravity from the Holocaust survivors awaiting the victors. When William approached one of the bodies, careful to cover his own face with a handkerchief to stave off the foul odor, he recoiled to discover the body was still warm. One week later, General Eisenhower demanded pictures be taken for posterity and proof of man's inhumanity to man.

With barely enough time to recover from the sight of barbarous acts committed by the Nazis at Ohrdruf, one week later William's company witnessed even more egregious atrocities awaiting them at Buchenwald Concentration Camp. It was larger than Ohrdruf both in size and degree of inhumane treatment; particularly the ominous brick ovens used to burn the remains of mass-murdered prisoners in gas chambers disguised as showers. Sensory overload burdened the soldiers as they became involuntary witnesses to man's capacity for grotesque acts when permitted to act unchecked.

William's face remained covered with a scarf as he quietly assisted the roundup of deceased skeletal remains for burial. The few surviving prisoners shook with gratitude as they attempted to walk toward their liberators, but their severely emaciated bodies refused to cooperate.

During one of his treks, William came across a young prisoner who appeared to be well-fed with a dazed look on his face. Completely blind to the deceit awaiting him, William gently approached the young man and inquired, "Can I do anything for you?"

His question was met with a bullet as the youth shouted in German. His firearm was quickly confiscated, and he was promptly taken into custody. Later, the imposter was forced to identify other Nazi guards using a similar disguise.

William passed out in the snow where copious amounts of blood tinged the snow a deep red. After several hours, soldiers hoisted him up and placed him on the truck with other fatalities. William's last thoughts were filled with tender reminders of the hours spent with Peggy and his wonderful family, fervently praying he would be spared to return into their loving arms.

112

Mary O'Malley wore the floorboards down to the subfloor by pacing each night to alleviate the pain of her precious William facing the horrors of war while she prayed constantly for his safe return. Ironically, Mary was not one to cast aspersions on others and didn't lament her first-born son was overseas fighting, while her sons-in-law remained stateside for a variety of medical reasons.

In 1945, when more than three months passed without a word from William, except a cryptic note heavily redacted, the O'Malleys clung to the possibility he was still alive. Each evening they gathered in prayer as the next few weeks were filled with alternating hope and despair as they anxiously awaited news. Ellen fervently wished her guardian angel would provide comfort but, on this matter, she remained silent.

On a warm summery day in 1945, Peggy had just finished preparing lunch, one of William's favorite dishes as she looked forward to his return. James and Thomas were setting the table when there was a knock on the door.

"I'll get it," Peggy replied, anxious to help the O'Malleys for their generosity in allowing her to live in William's room. But Mary glanced out the window and saw a Western Union truck outside 3104 Carroll

Avenue—a dreaded sight for anyone with a family member in the war signifying a soldier was lost in action or died.

When Peggy answered the door, she gasped in shock and stifled a cry in anticipation of dreadful news. Hearing his daughter-in-law's muffled sounds of anguish brought Michael rushing to the front door in time to catch Peggy as she fainted. Michael gently led her to the nearest chair as the telegram fell to the floor, and Michael picked it up.

With a quiver in his voice, Michael read the content aloud. "The Army regrets ta inform you that yer husband, William O'Malley, Sergeant U.S. Third Army, was killed in action in performance of his duty and in the service ta his country. The Department extends ta ye its sincerest sympathy in yer great loss. Ta prevent possible aid ta our enemies, please do not divulge the name of his last location, if known."

The weary messenger returned to his vehicle and continued his interminable mission of delivering additional notifications, leaving behind a wake of desolation.

Mary's stunned reaction turned into a heart-rendering scream as the dreadful news penetrated her soul and clutched her heart. Michael gently carried her to the couch in the parlor, covered Mary in a warm blanket, and placed a tender kiss on her forehead. Deathly pale and walking unsteadily toward the phone, Michael called Marge and requested she gather her siblings, and Peggy's parents, for a meeting at their home. Fighting a barrage of tears, Michael collapsed into the nearest chair when James and Thomas ran into the home.

"We heard Ma's scream a block away. What's happened?"

But looking into their father's face, they knew William would not return to their loving home. Their brave façade collapsed at the enormity of their loss, and they turned to comfort one another. Friends in the neighborhood received similar notifications, many to report loved ones never returned home or were lost in action. In a short period of time, the remaining O'Malley children and their families, including Peggy's parents, gathered around where hope died a slow death, and their vigil began a sad and unexpected new chapter in their lives.

With despair firmly ensconced in their hearts, grief could have buried their emotions in a deep cavern unreachable by mind or body. But instead of wallowing in depression, they relied on their inner fortitude and ever-present faith to face this tragedy with courage and conviction. Prayer continued to guide them by providing strength to overcome the anguish that hung over their heads in a collective cloud of melancholy. But the unassailable question on everyone's mind was, "Why do bad things happen to good people?" Peggy returned to William's bedroom for comfort as she reconciled a life without her beloved William.

To signify a wartime death occurred, the O'Malleys replaced the blue star with a gold star in their window, placed a back wreath on the door, and pulled down the shades. Throughout the week, neighbors dropped off casseroles and baked goods to the O'Malley home and offered heartfelt apologies for their loss. Since none of the O'Malleys had an appetite, food was placed in the parlor to be shared with friends who stopped by to offer support and prayers for the affable, quick-witted young man whose life was snuffed out prematurely.

Due to extensive injuries, his coffin was closed and a picture of William (in dress uniform with his officer's cap at a rakish angle and his signature lopsided grin) was prominently placed on top of the casket, a stark reminder of the hole in their lives now bursting with grief that resonated with each passing day. The siblings consoled their parents, Peggy, and one another as best they could until heartbreak immersed them in a sea of pain without respite. The family and neighbors prayed the rosary together and collectively experienced a remarkable sense of peace as the thought of William filled their hearts with a glimmer of contentment and the possibility of harmony.

113

William's funeral Mass was held at St. Patrick's Church, and Fr. McNally gave a moving sermon that comforted all in attendance.

"We are here to remember a remarkable young man who gave his life in service to his country. William O'Malley shared his gifts of love, laughter, and humility as an inspiration of what we should all aspire to become, especially in the difficult days ahead. He freely gave everyone his energy and talents without thought of recompense. William did not desire great wealth but strove to bring the richness of a life well-lived through his generosity of spirit to all.

"His ability to persevere in the grueling face of wartime, while maintaining his sense of humor and jovial nature, was evidenced in correspondence to family and friends. His efforts to preserve their spirit of hope in the future can be compared to a life-saving material dating back to the time of Christ. Salt in large quantities was essential for its preservative properties to ensure nations would not be plagued with hunger after harvests were gathered for storage. William's gift of preserving our faith is a testament to his strength in assisting one another in our own challenging demands. We must remember God made certain we are never truly alone, and His love is reflected in everything we see—the glorious sunrise, fertile soil providing sustenance, and faith to strengthen our souls.

"In the coming days, many will question God's decision to ignore our prayers to keep William safe and return him to his loving family. Although no one can know God's will, I'd like to tell you a story about my sister, Bridget.

"My mother had taken her to a local fair and Bridget desperately wanted to win a stuffed animal. Bridget prayed throughout her attendance at the fair and although she played many games of chance, was never able to win the prize she so desired. On the way home, my mother stopped at a store and purchased two bottles of milk. The rear seats were filled with assorted items, so she placed the bottles in the front by my sister.

"Bridget had an urge to do something she had never done before —she tucked her legs under her on the seat. After about fifteen minutes, the car hit an oil patch swerving abruptly to the right. The glass bottles shattered together and shards of glass were propelled into the front floorboard. Had Bridget's legs remained down, they would have been ripped apart by shards of glass. At that moment, Bridget realized her prayers had been answered, just not the way she expected.

"The same is true for us. Prayer is nothing more than a conversation with God and each prayer is answered, not always as we expect, but in the way God knows is best. If life were without any sorrow or problems, there would be no need to pray because a perfect life does not inspire us to seek help through God's intercession. But God wants us to seek His guidance and revels in our adoration. Although our prayers for William were not answered in the way we wished, he is no longer agonizing in the rigors of war and the horror of battle. Instead, William is at peace in the home of God waiting for us to join him.

"The devil wishes to turn us against God in times of despair as an act of solitary despondency. But we must remember God's love has a ripple effect that grows within each of us just as a wave builds in the ocean. Its tumultuous churning forward builds ever greater until it ebbs into the sandy beach. If we view our acts of kindness in their totality, they build in power until each of us is the beneficiary of its effect with a calm and refreshing feeling of rebirth. For love is not a finite commodity, but one that grows in strength and quantity each time we bestow it on others.

"By embracing life, as William did each day, we can reach those less fortunate by unlocking love's incredible power and forever transform the heart of another. Let us try to emulate William's warm and generous spirit. By doing this, we can defeat the devil and return God's love through our compassion toward others."

After Mass, the funeral procession slowly drove to Calvary Cemetery where William was buried with full military honors. At the graveside, Fr. McNally shared a brief message of consolation.

"Grief washes over you each day until the ache gradually lessens, never completely gone. Don't hold back, but cry those tears for the loss you bear. God will collect your tears and turn them into joy."

Absorbing Fr. McNally's message, each sound of the volley from the twenty-one-gun salute cratered an even deeper chasm in their already broken hearts. When the flag from William's coffin was crisply folded by the U.S. Army Honor Guard and solemnly presented to his wife with William's dog tags, a cry of despair escaped Peggy's lips and tears cascaded down her face. William was posthumously awarded the Distinguished Service Cross and three Bronze Stars to commemorate his service and bravery. Yet, in spite of overwhelming grief, the O'Malley's faith remained steadfast in knowing William's war was over, and his spirit was in God's hands.

114

Shortly after William's untimely demise, the war against Germany ended and they formally surrendered on May 7, 1945 to the Allied Forces. Three months later on August 14, 1945, the country was engulfed in celebrating VJ Day—Victory over Japan. Although the formal surrender would not occur for approximately two weeks, the war was finally over. But to the O'Malleys, the war ended with the loss of their cherished William.

The devastation of World War II touched everyone by depriving them of family, love, and everything decent in their world. Newsreels in 1945 portrayed humanity at its worst with victims mired in despair. It would be the first time the news media accurately depicted the suffering endured by millions in Europe involving crimes against humanity. During the news bulletin, gasps were heard throughout the audience. By the end, overt crying—including the men—was evidenced at the sight of human carnage.

The following day, talk in the neighborhood focused on the exposed Nazi death camps for what they really were—sanctioning slaughterhouses without regard for human life or dignity. When they had seen footage of people barely able to walk or move their skeletal frames, everyone felt sick.

Throughout the war, a silent death watch hidden and downplayed was so inconceivable—surely someone knew, yet the world stayed silent. It left a despicable stain on humanity known as the Holocaust —a new word in everyone's lexicon with loathsome images forever scarred into their memories.

Hitler's war claimed her beloved brother and initiated a Holocaust. Ellen needed to know how an entire nation could descend into madness leading to war and the premature death of millions, including her sweet William. She made several trips to the library, accompanied by friends with similar losses and a collective need to understand a foreign nation gripped by hatred.

Together, they expanded their search for the truth by reading new, and otherwise uncorroborated accounts contained within independent periodicals and magazines. Articles, especially those authored by two Germans who escaped Hitler's rule, noted the majority of Hitler's support was based on unemployment and inflation—a suitcase filled with Reichsmark was required to purchase a loaf of bread—and occurred long before his planned persecution of the Jews. If Jewish family members fought in World War I, they were lulled into security believing immunity was morally theirs, despite their religious background. Those with large estates thought their wealth was an insurance policy against evil.

Unfortunately, the rights of Jews in the New Germany were stripped away slowly, and they believed concessions were a passing phase—until it was too late. Ellen's band of researchers confirmed Germany's heinous crimes were actually known by many since its inception, yet this information was absent from Cleveland's two main newspapers in addition to many other well-known publications. One heartbreaking article was authored by two prisoners who miraculously escaped Auschwitz with an agenda to inform the world of the large-scale murders committed daily in the concentration camps. They besieged members of the Allied high command (including President Roosevelt, other world leaders, and the Pope) to bomb German railroads providing prisoner transports to the camps. But those in authority decided a better plan—without killing thousands of innocents on the trains—was simply to win the war. No amount of reasoning could change their minds and the executions continued.

Ellen and her friends also discovered methods of German brainwashing employed—books burned and banned as propaganda minister Joseph Goebbels's use of "The Big Lie" repeated constantly over Germany's only radio station and newspaper to cement the concept that Jews were worthless vermin. Heard often enough, the lie became an accepted truth. Germans were intent on being restored to their former power and stability. In the aftermath of World War I, lands including Poland, were disbursed among the victors, and all armaments were destroyed. Hitler made their dreams a reality by reestablishing armed forces and invading Poland on September 1, 1939, through an unprovoked attack on a sovereign nation.

Ellen and her friends realized when fear trumped anyone's instinct for basic humanity, moral depravity became the new accepted norm. Shaken by the Holocaust newsreel, Ellen's nightly prayers now included peace for the souls destroyed by Hitler and Germans lost to the bonds of malevolence.

115

Living in the O'Malley's back apartment, Eddie Collins was permanently laid off from GM when the returning GIs reclaimed their former positions. Veronica had every confidence in Eddie, but she was concerned about the added expense of a baby on the way.

"Don't worry, my dear," Eddie reassured her. "I talked to a friend about a new business opportunity, and we're meeting for breakfast tomorrow."

At the breakfast meeting with Eddie's friends, one of them mentioned working as a door-to-door salesman for Watkins products —first produced in Winona, Minnesota, during the late 1800s. Their product line included cooking extracts in a variety of spices and apothecary products, etc. But the best part of Watkins involved the creation of an unbelievable new incentive: a money-back guarantee. Watkins was looking for someone to take over a franchise in Cleveland, and after speaking to Eddie, they were eager to employ him. Eddie was a young man who possessed the exact qualities they were searching for—amiable and so confident he could turn a wrestler into a ballerina. After borrowing money from his parents, Eddie began his new career.

Eddie's franchise was located in a former A&P Supermarket and all profits were split in half with Watkins; Eddie had one employee: his wife, Veronica. Their store contained homemade liniment (a product with nationwide attention), household items, hard-to-find spices, a cookbook, and baking products. The ambitious couple stocked the entire store with Watkins products and were so successful, they eventually had a sales force of 150 people working solely on commission.

But after several years, the burden of providing leased transportation for product delivery to their store and the up-front cost of paying for items shipped became overwhelming. They sought another avenue of income and started fledgling Collins Realty. Selling residential homes, aided by their sales ability and sheer grit, became a career choice that served them well as their employees grew in number and Collins Realty became and extremely successful venture in a very competitive market. Following the birth of three children—Dennis, Kevin, and Marikate—all their dreams had come true.

116

In the days following their devastating loss of William, the O'Malley family would gather often to share their grief and exchange wonderful memories of their beloved William. As Mary O'Malley often told her children, a heartache shared is reduced by half, while a joy shared is doubled. Their faith would be tested as the rawness of William's passing triggered all five stages of grief—denial of his passing by pretending he was still overseas fighting and would soon return home; anger they were deprived of William's wonderful sense of humor and compassion; promises to be their very best in exchange for God's beneficence; depression that depleted the power to complete mundane tasks; and, finally, acceptance this was God's will best honored through prayer. But not everyone could reach this final step.

Ellen's depression lingered for months and repleted her energy until getting out of a bed became a chore requiring an insurmountable effort. She feared her broken heart had fractured into so many pieces they would be unable to find their way whole again. Ellen knew dealing with her grief would be necessary before she could return to being the wife and mother her family needed and deserved.

Ellen read an article in the newspaper that gave her a path toward recovery—one she knew William would heartily approve.

Sitting up in bed, abandoning all attempts to read, Ellen stated in a soft pleading voice, with eyes devoid of humor, "Frank, I need to ask you a favor."

He quietly replied, "Anything my darling."

With the sweetest smile, Ellen took Frank's hand and led him into the living room where they sat together on the couch. Gathering her courage, Ellen spoke rapidly before losing her nerve. "There's a program at The Cleveland Clinic where women can console and spend time with injured soldiers as they recover." Ellen paused for a moment as a wave a grief passed through her quickly similar to a freight train rushing to meet its deadline. When she was able, Ellen continued her request. "I'd like to volunteer two nights a week. Would that be all right?"

With concern in his voice, Frank inquired, "Are you sure you're up to it?"

Biting her lower lip, Ellen spoke in a quiet voice. "It feels as though William is telling me to do this. I'm not sure how or why I know, but I feel he's directing me on a path to deal with my broken heart." Brushing away a tear, Ellen continued, "I never could say no to my sweet William."

"Then it's what you must do. I can drive you there after work and pick you up when you're ready. Would that be all right?"

Ellen's response was a hug that took Frank's breath away as her eyes were filled with hope.

The following day, Ellen called the hospital and agreed to come in for two hours on Tuesday and Thursday evenings. For the first time since William's passing, Ellen felt her life moving in a positive direction and understood the help she gave others would, in turn, restore her back to normal.

The days dragged until her first visit the following week. Ellen began to hum as she did her chores and cooked Frank's favorite meals. She took comfort in the knowledge that God had never let her down and knew He would help her find her way once again.

117

Finally, Tuesday night arrived. Ellen was dressed and patiently waiting for Frank to return home. Mayme had agreed to watch James Francis until her sister returned.

Giving her a quick hug, Mayme whispered to Ellen, "Good luck." Ellen's reply of a smile filled with doubt and eyes tinged with hope brought a tear to Mayme's eyes.

With dinner in the oven and the home sparkling clean, Ellen was ready to face the challenge inspired by her brother. If she couldn't help him, perhaps she could ease the suffering of someone else. As soon as Frank walked through the front door, Ellen gave him a warm hug and passionate kiss before asking if they could leave for the hospital.

"Of course. I know how anxious you are. But I need to ask you one last time. Is this what you really want?"

Ellen picked up her infant and gave him a loving hug until James Francis squealed in delight. After placing him back in his bassinet, Ellen picked up her purse and gloves. Turning to her husband, she replied confidently, "Yes, Frank, it really is."

"Okay, then let's get going." Turning to Mayme, Frank thanked her for watching their infant.

The drive to the hospital felt interminable, and Ellen almost jumped out of the car before it came to a full stop.

"Thank you, Frank. I'll see you in two hours."

"All right, my dear. Be careful." Frank waited until Ellen walked through the front door and silently said a prayer for his beautiful and loving wife.

When Ellen entered the hospital, she went to the office where she registered for the program and was told to report to the fourth floor.

"Now remember," the woman told Ellen, "the men you'll meet are not only wounded on the outside but many carry deeper scars on the inside. Any act of kindness or simply reading to them if they can't or won't speak will bring them a long way toward recovery."

"I understand. Thank you." Ellen felt a surge of anxiety as she took the elevator to the designated floor and stepped onto the ward. Ellen slowly traversed the never-ending hallway filled with veterans in various stages of horror.

She recalled a childhood memory of her mother giving money to a war veteran—legless and propelling himself forward on a rolling cart using his muscular arms—offering to sharpen knives. At the time, Ellen didn't understand why her mother parted with much-needed funds when their knives were already sharp. But on this day, Ellen recalled her mother's words of wisdom were never more relevant.

"If we help one another, God helps us all."

This flashback in kindness freely given to others strengthened Ellen's resolve and gave her added strength of purpose.

Pausing momentarily while her senses adjusted to the sight of men bandaged and crying out in agony, Ellen grappled with her escalating fear. Approaching the nurse's station, located midway down the hall, Ellen introduced herself and asked where she should start.

"There's a young man in the corner who's never had any visitors. He was transferred to the Cleveland Clinic for their advanced cosmetic surgery program to reconstruct facial wounds. His head and neck are bandaged from injuries. We've never heard him utter a sound and don't know if he's capable of speech. I think a woman's attention would mean a lot to him. Here's a book if he would like to hear a story. His name is Declan MacLeod. With extensive facial injuries,

Declan has been seen by a specialist attending to his reconstructive surgeries. According to his military records, his family from Cleveland relocated to Wisconsin but they've been unable to reach them. They're continuing the search but, so far, no luck."

Ellen gulped and slowly approached Declan lying on his side in a fetal position. With a nod of encouragement from the nurse, Ellen gently tapped him on the shoulder and introduced herself. "Hi, Declan. I'm Ellen, and I'd like to keep you company. Do you mind if I sit in the chair next to your bed?"

The soldier hunched his shoulders, possibly the only way he could communicate. "All right then. I have a book that you might enjoy. Would it be all right if I read it to you?"

Another shrug gave Ellen slight encouragement. She began one of her favorite books by Charles Dickens, "It was the best of times, it was the worst of times . . ."

Two hours passed quickly and Ellen was startled when Frank tapped her on the shoulder.

"It's time to go home, my love." Glancing at the poor, unfortunate man, Frank patted him on the shoulder and said, "I'll bring my wife back in two days. Would that be all right?" The man slowly nodded.

When they got back in the car, Frank tentatively asked Ellen, "How was your first night?"

Her eyes bright with overflowing tears, Ellen replied, "I felt William by my side guiding me."

"I'm so proud of you." Frank kissed Ellen and they drove home in silence, each deep in their own thoughts.

118

Ellen looked forward to visiting Declan twice a week. She couldn't explain it, but her bereavement was inexplicably minimized knowing she was helping a fellow soldier. She felt William's warm embrace and lightheartedness envelop her each time she stepped onto the ward.

Ellen approached Declan's bed one evening surprised to see it was empty. Fearing the worst, she rushed into the hall and approached the nurse's station, where she breathlessly asked where Declan was.

"He's getting some tests done. Declan had a rough night, and we were forced to tranquilize him. He kept screaming, 'No, no!' Those are the only words he's spoken since he arrived."

Clearly upset, Ellen returned to Declan's room to await his return. Twenty minutes later, the groggy patient was delivered to his room, and Ellen smiled despite her inner turmoil. Until that moment, Ellen hadn't realized how much Declan impacted her own recovery process.

"Declan, are you up for a story tonight?" Ellen inquired in a soothing tone. When Declan shook his head, Ellen was at a loss. She closed her eyes to concentrate, and the answer came to her. She began to regale him with stories of life growing up in the O'Malley household, focusing on the happy times and childhood pranks. By the time Frank arrived to take her home, both were surprised to witness a teardrop escape from Declan's eyes. He reached for Ellen's hand and kissed it tenderly. Ellen softly patted his hand and said she'd return in a few days. Declan nodded in gratitude before he closed his eyes in exhaustion.

When they were finally alone in the car, Frank could see his wife was visibly shaken and held her in his arms. "Care to talk about it?"

"Declan's going through a difficult transition and didn't want me to read, so I told him stories from my childhood. I hope the stories didn't cause him further torment."

"My dear, I believe it was just what he needed to hear. You treated him as a friend, not a patient, and that can only improve the recovery process."

"I didn't think of it like that. Thank you, Frank." Ellen planted a loving kiss on Frank's cheek and rode the rest of the way home with her head on his shoulder.

119

O ver the next several months, Declan underwent multiple facial reconstructive surgeries with lengthy bouts of breathing tubes preventing verbal communication. Six months after Ellen first began her hospital visits, the nurse quickened her pace when Ellen arrived. Ellen was unsure if this meant devastating news or a much-needed improvement in Declan's condition.

"Declan began to talk! His voice was raspy but after asking a series of questions and a few simple tests, the doctor determined he has amnesia from head trauma. Ellen, if there's anything you can do to help him recover his past, perhaps there's family we can notify."

"That's wonderful, but I'm a little confused. If you already know his name, can't you find his family?"

"We tried the usual avenues to locate his immediate family in Milwaukee but came up empty. Perhaps there's extended family out there. You've developed a close bond with Declan. If anyone can reach him, I believe it's you. Although he's probably thirsty from protracted bouts of intubation and his vocal cords are sore from disuse, he's limited to occasional sips of water. Otherwise, it would be too much for his system."

Excited at the challenge but slightly intimidated by the task, Ellen promised to do her best. As usual, Ellen approached Declan with a warm smile and congratulated him on finding his voice. By this time, seeing his facial bandages no longer filled her with dread but hope as the extent of dressings lessened from the prior week.

"Feel good talk. Thirsty lots." Declan cobbled together the broken sentences with great effort and some discomfort.

Reaching for the water pitcher, Ellen poured a tiny amount of water, added a straw, and handed it to Declan admonishing, "Please drink it slowly and only take a few sips. They're rationing your water until your system is ready."

Declan slowly sipped through the straw until the small amount of water was gone. When he held the glass out for a refill, Ellen said that was all she could give him until the nurse instructed otherwise. While he was drinking the water, Ellen concentrated on the best way to draw out his personal information.

"Did you enjoy the stories I told you about my childhood?"

Nodding, Declan replied with difficulty, "Yes. Like mine."

"Declan, what do you remember?"

"Love. Friends. Happiness. Big blur." His voice drifted off in sadness at the starkness of his current situation.

"If we work together, perhaps we can recreate some of those memories. Would you like that?"

Lying in bed with a childlike innocence, Declan nodded enthusiastically but soon fell into an exhausted sleep as the thought of reconnecting with his former life and family seemed to overwhelm him.

Ellen sat and watched him with tenderness, knowing it would be a difficult task, but she was up for the struggle and could feel William encouraging her efforts. Now all she had to do was come up with a game plan. Sounded simple, but how exactly can you recreate another person's memories? Ellen couldn't wait for Frank to arrive, confident his exceptional detective skills would help solve Delan's mysterious past.

120

At Frank's suggestion, Ellen decided to bring her sisters to see Declan at The Cleveland Clinic when she returned the following week. But Ellen first stopped at the nurse's station with a special request. Although they were hesitant at first, they acquiesced. Ellen called her parents and asked if she could borrow McTavish when she returned to the clinic. Hesitant of interrupting Peggy's grief, Ellen contacted her sister-in-law but she was too fragile from the rawness of losing her beloved William.

Entering Declan's room with her sisters and McTavish, Ellen prayed her plan would help jog Declan's memory and assist in locating his family. The siblings agreed to meet Declan with an uneasy feeling. Each were dealing with torment in their own way but seeing a ward filled with soldiers in various stages of recovery exacerbated their apprehension. To their credit, all the sisters remained poised and ready to help the unfortunate young man who bonded with their sister and helped alleviate her suffering. Each of the sisters prayed for strength and guidance before the visit; Mayme agreed to stop at Carroll Avenue to pick up McTavish on her way. Before entering Declan's room, the siblings held hands and said a prayer for Declan's recovery and assistance in locating his family.

DECLAN COULD HEAR Ellen's footsteps—she had a familiar rhythm to her walk. He was eager to see her since his recovery process was advancing despite facial compressions from his latest surgery. But this night she wasn't alone, accompanied by three women similar in beauty and kindness. And, to his delight, a beautiful Irish setter.

"Declan, I'd like you to meet my sisters. And this young whippersnapper is McTavish. He's probably fifteen-years old but don't tell him. He still thinks he's a pup."

To everyone's surprise, McTavish, normally reserved around strangers, barked and jumped up on Declan's bed, licking his hands and any portion of his face not bandaged, until Ellen pulled him off.

"I'm so sorry. He's usually shy, but he's taken quite a liking to you." Ellen grinned and the tension in the room was broken. Introductions were made and Declan spoke up. His voice had traces of a raspy intonation from anxiety and prolonged inability to talk while plagued by the unknown.

Ellen could see Declan's surprise and happiness in meeting her family. She guessed Declan must have had a dog growing up based on his delight in seeing McTavish.

"It's wonderful to meet your family. Ellen, you're my own sweet guardian angel, now and always."

Hands shaking, Ellen asked tentatively, "Declan, would you mind if I checked your right ankle?"

With a puzzled expression but happy to comply with the simple request, Declan wisecracked, "It's not much to see, but sure. Go ahead."

Ellen gently pulled the sheet back and almost fainted at the sight of a shamrock-shaped birthmark.

Ellen and her sisters gasped as they, too, noticed the unmistakable birthmark.

Marge asked in an awestruck voice, "Ellen, how did you know?" Ellen explained the post-kidnapping remark whispered by William when he was fourteen—a memory she hadn't shared with anyone but one he just repeated exactly.

Seeing the expressions on the sisters faces, Declan quipped in a shaky voice, "What, am I that unsightly?"

Tears welled up as Ellen exclaimed, "Oh, William!"

Immediately hearing those miraculous words, memories came rushing back like an engorged floodgate finally releasing its contents. William's family hugged and kissed their long-lost brother. The sensation filled them with happiness and brought back memories of playing in the backyard together. Now it was William's turn to cry and kiss each of them in turn. They all believed in the power of miracles but never thought God would bestow the greatest gift of all— reuniting the family.

Marge ran out to the nurse's station and asked to use the phone, normally reserved for emergencies. After hearing the reason why, the nurse readily agreed. To relay the wonderful news, Marge called her parent's home where Peggy resided.

Peggy answered the phone. "O'Malley residence. Who's calling please?"

After Peggy hung up the phone, all the blood rushed from her face, and once again, Michael caught her mid-fall. "Ma and Da, it was Marge." Unable to continue while grappling with the incredible news, she managed to relay, "William is alive."

Mary's startled expression turned to one of complete ecstasy. "Oh, Saints be praised! Michael, 'tis grand news about our dear boy. He's alive! 'Tis a miracle." But a confused expression interfered momentarily with her delight, and she turned to Peggy. "But how is that possible?"

Peggy relayed Marge's message. Mary broke down in her husband's arms, and Peggy joined their circle, with tears intermingled as euphoria filled the room to capacity. With the commotion downstairs, James and Thomas ran downstairs to hear the astounding news. Michael instructed James to call the remaining family members before joining Mary in their bedroom to quickly don their Sunday best. James relayed the message from his father to meet at the Cleveland Clinic and ask for a patient known as Declan McLeod on the fourth floor. In less than fifteen minutes, the entire family was speeding toward a reunion with their dear William.

Within thirty minutes, the O'Malley clan was once again together, and William's room was filled with a joyous celebration at his remarkable return from the dead.

Basking in the glow of love, William realized he never completely lost hope or faith in being reunited with his family. He knew that reactions to any event resulted in consequences, including his initial despair and solitude, to test the mettle of even the strongest. William understood the measure of every person would be determined by their response to hardship—and this, in turn, defined their destiny. Although no one knows the future, facing life's daily challenges with courage and conviction assured a life well-lived.

Looking at Ellen, William asked how she knew it was him. Ellen relayed the story she told Marge and William knew his guardian angel hadn't forgotten him after all.

Ellen looked tenderly at her brother and teased, "You should have seen your funeral. It was a packed house and not a dry eye in the church."

William smiled, and his dry sense of humor emerged in his response. "I can honestly say, I'm glad I missed it."

Peggy walked over from where she was sitting on William's bed to give her father-in-law a warm embrace.

"Why me darling, whatever was that fer?"

"All the times you caught me when I fainted and held onto me until I was steady." Turning to William, she said, "Your father is a gentleman and wonderful source of support in a crisis. He reminds me so much of you."

Both men beamed at the high praise.

Peggy leaned over her husband and whispered in his ear, "When you are ready to unburden your soul, I would be honored to listen and help in any way I can. But for now, I just want you to heal. I'll remain by your side until they throw me out."

When it became apparent William's strength was waning, he received a hug and kiss from each family member. Peggy kissed William on the top of his head and with peace in his heart and a smile on his lips, William drifted off to sleep.

KISSING PEGGY before the O'Malleys left the Cleveland Clinic, everyone headed back to the family homestead, each believing the nightmare debacle involving William's identity would soon be resolved by the army. Mary felt like a schoolgirl as the constrictive bands surrounding her heart finally began to loosen. The euphoria felt by all at the unbelievable turn of events, especially after the agonizing months of William's absence, made the amazing outcome that much sweeter.

After two sleepless nights in a chair, Peggy finally went home to sleep as the O'Malleys took turns keeping watch over their dearest William, a true manifestation of God's love and the power of miracles. When Ellen returned home, she thanked her guardian angel for directing her path in reuniting the O'Malley clan.

News about William spread through the neighborhood quicker than a flash flood. Everyone loved to recount a true miracle. That weekend, the O'Malley family and their friends went into a local restaurant on West 26th Street, which offered air conditioning and, for this special occasion, a delightful Irish cuisine. They shared wonderful stories, drank, and joined in the celebrations of family and neighbors alike. On this day, secure in the knowledge William was safe nearby, everything was right in their world.

WILLIAM'S VOICE quickly returned to normal. His family provided pictures of William's pre-war semblance to his surgeons. The remaining reconstructive surgeries returned William to his normal appearance.

The family patiently awaited news of the army investigation, anxious to learn who was buried at Calvary Cemetery.

121

Unfortunately, William's return home would be delayed by a year when his condition deteriorated. He developed chest pain, shortness of breath, and a chronic cough producing blood-tinged sputum. He was diagnosed with tuberculosis and transferred to a VA hospital. The doctors surmised his TB was a direct result of lying on the freezing floor of the Ardennes Forest wearing only a summer uniform, a condition that remained dormant allowing his body to recover from multiple surgeries.

During his additional confinement, William regained his sense of humor as amnesia receded into the background. Peggy surprised William and brought Goosie, his childhood friend and Peggy's brother, for several visits to the VA as a special treat. As the two vets commiserated on their wartime experiences, it helped them both acclimate back into society and psychologically deal with the horrors of war. Peggy would often bring McTavish, who never failed to cheer William and aided his path to recovery.

The army investigation discerned the mix-up and discovered what had happened to the real Declan MacLeod. Born in Cleveland, Declan and his family moved to Milwaukee, but Declan's parents were deceased; he never married and there were no extended family members. Declan moved to Las Vegas where he incurred an extensive gambling debt with a consistent losing streak making him a prime target of the Mob. Declan joined the army to escape the inevitable bloody revenge for large unpaid debts. Fighting alongside William, he saw what he thought was a corpse, and Declan stole William's identity by switching dog tags.

The army investigator interviewed a friend of William's, a fellow survivor of his last battle, who recalled a stranger bending over William's body as if saying a prayer for the dead, not realizing his nefarious intentions. Another soldier mentioned he hoisted a body, identified by his dog tags as Declan McLeod, onto a cart with other corpses and was shocked when he heard a moan.

He screamed to other soldiers, "Hey, this guy's still alive." They quickly unloaded him from the truck and brought him to the hospital. Due to William's facial injuries, no one recognized the severely injured soldier as William O'Malley.

But for Declan, luck had once again deserted him. Death claimed him 400 feet from William's body. He stepped on a land mine and was ripped to pieces. When the O'Malleys heard this, they thought of the irony that a man causing them so much pain in his attempts to escape his dire fate would receive the exact outcome he was attempting to outrun.

Relying on the switched dog tags, the army mistakenly sent a death notification to William O'Malley's family and shipped the remains of Declan McLeod back to Cleveland, Ohio, for burial. After a full investigation, the remnants of Declan's body were exhumed from William O'Malley's grave and reburied in Milwaukee's Wood National Cemetery. Declan was returned to the home of his birth and buried alongside other soldiers. But this time, the grave was marked with the correct name.

122

During William's confinement to the VA, Peggy and family members visited him daily. Although his ordeal was far from over, they helped William gain perspective, strength, and continued hope for humanity. But he still woke up some nights screaming as events of the war replayed in his mind in a horror-filled loop of unforgiving footage.

A progressive-thinking VA physician arranged talk therapy sessions for William and, at William's request, Goosie was included in the meetings. Both battle-hardened vets received therapy twice a week to help them overcome nightmares plaguing their dreams. Gradually, they understood what is now known as PTSD from witnessing human atrocities and overcoming the death sentence suffered by too many before their time. With that knowledge and extensive therapy, they were able to grapple with horrors branded in their brains and understood the mechanism of survivor's guilt affording them self-forgiveness during their road to recovery.

After an arduous year, William finally returned to the family homestead from the VA. Veronica and Eddie still occupied the back apartment but, with the vacancy of his three married siblings (Marge,

Mayme, and Ellen), there was enough room for William and Peggy to live comfortably.

The next year, William applied for a GI loan and the couple purchased their first home with a lovely fenced-in backyard for McTavish to run. The family agreed McTavish, a positive force in William's life and recovery, would remain with William. McTavish, like all animals, had an innate sense of providing support to those in need. He remained by William's side until William could function without him. Six months after they moved, William was close to complete recovery when he noticed McTavish was moving slowly and losing weight. He and Peggy took him to a neighborhood vet, a friend of the O'Malleys.

"I'm so sorry William, but McTavish is in pain." The doctor knew of William's history and added thoughtfully, "I believe he's stayed around this long just to help you. But it would be a kindness to end his suffering." It was never easy for the vet to deliver this news, but his kind and gentle manner helped soften the blow.

"Could he receive pain medication now and something for tonight? We'd like to bring him back tomorrow morning so my family could be here."

"Of course. Would nine in the morning work?"

"Yes," replied William sadly, as he softly petted his loyal friend.

While brushing away a tear, Peggy gave her husband a hug and kissed McTavish's head. Returning home, William called his family, and everyone agreed to meet at the vet's office the following morning to say their farewells. None of the O'Malleys slept that night knowing tomorrow would be McTavish's last day before he went to dog heaven. At the appointed time, William held McTavish in his arms, surrounded by his family for support, as the doctor peacefully ended the life of a selfless and exceptional pet

But this story has a happy conclusion. The distressing loss of McTavish was offset by the birth of William and Peggy's only child the following year. He was named Michael O'Malley II, but his family called him Mike to avoid the confusion of two Michael O'Malleys.

As Mike grew, he was a handsome lad with large blue expressive eyes, brown wavy hair, an impish smile, and a sweet disposition with his father's wonderful sense of humor. He quickly became the center of their universe and William's intermittent despondency was forever lifted as he concentrated on his newest and best role—being a dad.

When Mike was five years old, his parents surprised him with a beautiful Irish setter puppy. Mike heard stories about the famous McTavish and when asked what they should call him, Mike scrutinized the tiny pup and promptly said, "L'il McTavish." His name was eventually shortened to L'il Mc and from the moment L'il Mc arrived, he and Mike were rarely separated. L'il Mc possessed the same sweetness as his namesake, and William felt McTavish smiling on them to infuse his gentle nature into L'il Mc.

Life had come full circle, reincarnating the absolute best of William's childhood friend into the next generation. William, while looking at L'il Mc, thought, *Gee life is swell!*

123

After all the upheavals and adjustments from the war, 1947 presented a wonderful gift for Frank and Ellen Szabo. Ellen was pregnant with their second child due on March 24. Slightly disappointed with the due date, Ellen came up with a brilliant plan to hasten her delivery one week earlier to St. Patrick's Day. After contacting her mother, who readily agreed to babysit two-year-old James Francis, Ellen concocted a plan that everyone believed was a spontaneous adventure.

"Frank, let's pick up Veronica and Eddie. We can ride around the countryside."

"Oh Ellen, are you sure that's a good idea in your condition?"

With a smile reminiscent of a favorite song to brighten your day, Ellen replied confidentially, "Of course. And let's make sure to take the country roads."

"But they're awfully bumpy, my love."

"I think I can manage."

Ellen turned her head to the side to hide her giddiness. The two young couples traveled the bumpiest roads in Cleveland, while singing contemporary tunes with gusto. With each thump felt over an uneven road, Ellen's smile grew wider, certain her plan would work. But as the hours passed, and they were running low on gas, they were forced to return home. Ellen's splendid plan was thwarted, and just as the doctor predicted, Thomas Michael was born on March 24, 1947.

As a premonition of the mischief to come with the birth of the newest Szabo addition, a storm ravaged the county and the hospital lost power. Following his initial intake of breath, Thomas Michael displayed a serene yet sublime smile that lit up the delivery room just as the electricity was restored.

Three years later, Eileen Marie was born, and three years after that, Mary Frances would round out the Szabo family. Just as Frank and Ellen discussed before their marriage, four children would be the perfect number, specifically two boys followed by two girls. This proved perfection could be achieved by hard work and a bit of good old-fashioned luck for the best dreams to come true.

124

After World War II, a new type of war appeared on the horizon. The Cold War began a tornado of fear cascading around the country in 1947 and continued for several decades. The threat of nuclear invasion from the Russians hung in the air, encroaching on a stable future and limiting the relief of surviving World War II. The country was thrust into the unthinkable: a war of mutual destruction. Everyone was doing their part. Even schoolchildren were taught to "duck and cover" under their desks in case of a nuclear attack.

Fearing complete annihilation, many families purchased a bomb shelter in their backyard. Depending on funds available, some were simple shelters while others had every extravagance available. And then there was Marge DuChez's shelter.

Marge attempted to convince her husband they needed to build a bomb shelter big enough to house the entire family.

"Lou, our entire family could be wiped out in one attack. Don't you want to prevent that?"

"Of course. But they're so expensive, and we may never need to use it."

"But what if we do need it and the Russians drop a bomb? Our family will be gone in the blink of an eye."

"I'll make you a deal. I will borrow one-fifth the total cost, but you need to come up with the rest."

Lou knew his wife would demand the best, which Lou discovered would cost $5,000. He assumed Marge would not be able to raise the remaining funds. But he forgot how stubborn Marge could be when she wanted something for her family.

Marge loved a good challenge and accepted. But when she called several companies, Marge couldn't find anything below $5,000 for what she considered the perfect family sanctuary to accommodate her growing family. She had no idea where she could find her share of $4,000 and called her siblings, but no one had the funds to help. Then Marge had a wonderful idea. She could raffle spaces in her new safe haven to cover the cost of $500 per person, convinced they could fit eight more people in their spacious shelter.

Marge took out an ad in the *NorthShore Post* that read, "Want to protect your family in case of a nuclear attack? Winning raffle tickets at a cost of $500 for eight lucky people will provide you a chance for a space in our brand-new, luxurious, top-of-the-line shelter. Meet on Sunday at 1:00 p.m. in the back of Manners Restaurant to sign up."

Infused with a rush of adrenaline, Marge woke up at 6:00 a.m. on Sunday and made a large breakfast to celebrate her wonderful plan. After the required fasting, they attended 11:00 a.m. Mass. Marge rushed home to fix a light lunch, freshened up, and headed toward the restaurant. Staying in her Sunday best to present a professional tone, Marge took a seat and ordered a cup of coffee. Glancing at her watch, Marge noticed she had five minutes before the throngs of people flocked to her table. If all went well, perhaps she should take a part-time job as a salesperson where she was certain a promotion to a managerial position would quickly occur.

Sitting at the table, paper and pens in front of her, Marge's confidence was on overdrive. When she finished her first cup of coffee and then her second, Marge began to doubt her magnificent strategy.

By 1:30 p.m., Marge was convinced her plan was a failure and she started to pack up her things to go home. Just as she was preparing to leave, throngs of people poured through the door, pushing past one another, everyone speaking at once. Watching the horde of people heading directly at Marge's table, she panicked and felt like her kid's pet hamster—running around its wheel in a hurry to get nowhere.

"Are we too late? There was a terrible accident, and we sat there for thirty minutes."

"Do you have any spaces left?"

"What a wonderful idea."

Marge was gratified to discover so many people believed her family protection plan was of the utmost importance. She circulated pens and passed out envelopes, each containing a sheet of paper to identify basic personal information. "I need everyone to fill out your name, address, and phone number. I also need a 10% cash down payment placed in your envelope."

Amazingly, everyone filled out the pieces of paper and returned the envelopes with a deposit to Marge without questions or complaints.

After an hour, Marge collected all the envelopes, placed them into a satchel, and headed toward home. She couldn't wait to share her secret with Lou and her children. Fortunately, Lou was at a football practice and her sons were playing outside. Marge emptied the satchel and opened a few envelopes, then sat back perplexed.

"Hmmm. This family only gave five dollars and listed fourteen members. Same thing with this family but they named twenty people."

Marge was confused as she opened the remaining envelopes. For $170 in deposits, Marge's grand total of applicants was 250! *What in the world happened?* Marge raced over to the coffee table and pulled the newspaper open to find her advertisement. Something about the ad looked wrong. And then she saw three glaring mistakes. There was no mention of a raffle for eight lucky people; the wrong price of $50 instead of $500 was listed; and it didn't mention the $500 payment was only for one person, not an entire family. Marge was relieved her family was outside and didn't see her project fail spectacularly. She wondered how she could put a positive spin on her mix-up so her plan would seem like a victory.

After supper, Marge made an announcement. "I was thinking about a bomb shelter."

Lou jerked his head up and couldn't hide his astonished expression.

"In the event of a nuclear attack, what good would it do if we are the only ones to survive but lose all our family and friends? Besides, there won't be any fresh crops or meat and no schools." Marge paused to give her sons "the look" when they hooped and hollered at that delightful possibility. "There also wouldn't be any churches, sports, or movie theaters. It makes more sense to accept each day as a gift and appreciate our lives with family and friends."

"That's an excellent way to view it, Marge. Now boys, isn't that a mature attitude?"

Their boys nodded in unison and the subject was mercifully over, except for the gazillion letters Marge had to write explaining what happened and return the deposits.

After the dishes were done, Lou sidled up to his wife and said, "So I guess your plan to raise money for the shelter didn't work."

With a twinkle in her eye, Marge said, "Actually, I raised enough money for 250 people." Seeing Lou's jaw drop, she added, "Of course that would only work if we each took up about one inch of space."

Lou started to laugh out loud.

"Obviously, in answer to your question, my project was a bust."

Lou kissed her forehead. But this venture wouldn't stop Marge from trying. Her ideas were always unique, but their execution didn't always go as planned.

125

The last two O'Malley children to fall into the web of matrimony were James and Thomas. Although both were determined to remain bachelors, they didn't factor in the intensity of love.

Following a routine eye exam in 1951, James was diagnosed with moderate amblyopia, also known as lazy eye. James was crushed. He would never be the flying ace he was destined to become. Luckily, he had a Plan B. He enrolled in airplane mechanic school and graduated at the top of his class. No surprise, since he had a lifetime experience in taking things apart. Now, however, he knew how to reassemble them as well. James was promptly hired by American Airlines and during his second week on the job, was hit by kismet.

Walking across the tarmac at Cleveland Hopkins' Airport, wearing a jumpsuit, scarf loosely tied around her neck, and sunglasses, was a slender woman in her early 20s. James gaped in astonishment. Her short, curly, brown hair, hazel eyes, high cheekbones, full lips with a captivating smile, and beautiful complexion without makeup infatuated James. He summoned his courage while attempting to come up with a line that would summon a mutual romantic attraction.

"Did anyone ever tell you—"

"I know. That I look like Amelia Earhart? I'm not a relation, but I'll take that as a compliment."

James tried to appear cool, but his heart was doing flip-flops. He was downright smitten. Thomas would have to continue their bachelorhood claim to fame alone. James told her briefly about almost meeting Amelia Earhart and Charles Lindberg at the Westlake Hotel when he was a young boy. He found his bait, and she was hooked.

"My name's Charlene Smith. And you would be——"

"James O'Malley at your service; or, should I say, your plane's service."

"Nice to know I'm in such capable hands, James."

"Equally nice to know you appreciate my hard work. Perhaps we can grab lunch sometime, and I could tell you more about almost meeting the famous aviators."

"I'd like that. I'll be working at Hopkins Airport next week. Do you have next Tuesday afternoon available?"

"Sounds perfect. I'll meet you at the hanger."

James would have been pleased to know Charlene's calm demeanor belied an underlying attraction to James with his wavy strawberry-blond hair, muscular build, and hazel eyes sparkling with excitement. Later on, it would be difficult to recall who was more enthralled—James or Charlene.

The pair became inseparable, and, to no one's surprise, James asked for her hand in marriage the following year. All his wishes had come true—a beautiful wife who resembled his idol, a companion who shared his love of flying, and a wonderful career of taking large planes apart into a gazillion pieces. To increase their joy, Charlene gave birth to Madie Katherine, named after the wise principal of St. Patrick's School. Her entrance into this world made each day a rhapsody of undiscovered pleasures. Life was paradise.

126

Since Michael and Mary, in addition to Frank and Ellen, were married on Thanksgiving—almost forty years apart—the couples celebrated their anniversaries on the holiday, not the actual marriage date.

The O'Malley children always observed their parent's anniversary with an extravaganza on Thanksgiving at one of the children's homes. Ellen didn't want to take away from her parents' festivities; instead, she celebrated with Frank and their family at their home that evening. In July 1952, the O'Malley children held a meeting to plan a party for their parent's upcoming anniversary.

"I know Da and Ma are expecting a really big party next year for their fortieth in 1953. You know what would really catch them off guard?" asked James.

"I give up. What're you thinking?" answered Thomas.

"Every year, it's always the same. We take turns hosting Thanksgiving combined with their anniversary. So, whose turn is it this year to host Thanksgiving?"

Marge raised her hand.

"Instead of waiting until next year to host a grand celebration for their fortieth anniversary, we could commemorate it this November, one year earlier. They'd never expect that."

"I don't know. It seems kind of unusual." Mayme's response mirrored her doubt-filled face.

"That's the whole point. They'll never expect it."

Gradually his siblings warmed to the idea of a real surprise party, and the planning began for the best celebration ever.

On November 27, 1952, the celebration of Michael and Mary's wedding would be the party of the century. All their children contributed funds for the gift and anniversary brunch to be held at the White Oaks in Westlake, a western suburb of Cleveland. This premium restaurant and former speakeasy during Prohibition overlooked a serene, wooded area. The large windows displayed nature's resplendent beauty offset by an artful display of lights and the occasional appearance of wildlife.

On Thanksgiving, Michael was impatient.

"Mary, are ye almost ready? Thomas will be here shortly. He wants ta take us fer a drive in his new car."

"Fer heaven's sake, Michael, we have almost thirty minutes."

"Best ta be early than late."

"Don't ye worry. I'll be ready before Thomas arrives." Putting on the final touches to her makeup, Mary skillfully transformed her long gray hair into a braid wound on top of her head like a crown. Satisfied with her appearance, Mary wore her new dress, an extravagant purchase but one that accentuated her lovely figure. Since visits from Thomas didn't occur every day, she wanted to impress her youngest son. Grabbing her purse and gloves, Mary walked downstairs.

Whistling, Michael admired his lovely bride of thirty-nine years. "'Tis a lucky man that I am."

Blushing through her carefully applied makeup, Mary replied in her usual self-deprecating manner, "Oh go on with ye. But I must say, ye look quite handsome, me darling."

Michael placed his arms around the love of his life and passionately kissed Mary. After almost forty years, they both could still ignite intense feelings of desire. Gently removing himself from Mary's soft and tender lips, they remained in one another's arms until they heard a knock at the front door.

Flustered, Mary called out, "Thomas, we will be with ye in a minute." She turned to Michael and said, "Perhaps we could continue this later?"

With a gleam in his eye, Michael nodded before placing a kiss on his wife's forehead.

Walking outside hand in hand, they admired Thomas's new car and felt like royalty as they drove toward Marge's home. "We'll take the scenic route, if that's all right with you."

"Of course, 'tis fine me boy," said Michael, thoroughly enjoying being chauffeured.

When they turned into the White Oaks parking lot, Mary inquired, "I thought we were going ta Marge's?"

"My watchband broke when I was here a few days ago. I called to confirm the watch is in their lost and found. Would you mind coming in with me? I can give you a quick tour, and it'll be warmer than staying in the car."

"We'd love ta, me darling," Mary said as Michael helped her from the car. They entered the establishment, unaware of the grand scheme planned months in advance.

In the interim, all the O'Malley offspring and grandchildren had arrived at the White Oaks shortly before noon and sat in their assigned seats designated by festive place cards. The party room was decorated for Thanksgiving in addition to a large HAPPY ANNIVERSARY banner printed in kelly-green letters and hung above the long stream of tables joined together. The fireplace provided warmth and comfort, while the candlelit tables lent ambiance to the ebullient atmosphere. Everyone waited in anticipation for the honored guests to arrive.

Michael and Mary followed Thomas into the party room where they were greeted with shouts and cheers by their children and grandchildren. The honorees were led to the place of honor, at the head of the tables and under the banner.

Their parents were flustered and truly surprised, just as their children hoped, assuming a large party would be held in their honor next year. Mary flushed when she realized they were the center of attention and, with her husband, made it a point to thank each person in attendance before taking their seats.

"Everyone has a choice of steak or lobster, sides are on the long table, and desserts will be brought out last." Rotating in her seat to get her parents' attention, Veronica said, "We've paid for everything, including gratuities."

"Dear girl, how expensive that must be fer such a fine establishment. How can we thank ye?"

"The two of you have devoted your lives to our happiness, and it's time we repaid the favor." With each person finally seated, Veronica continued, "Everyone, raise your glass for a toast." With all glasses raised, Veronica asked William to give the toast.

"How can I express the humility we feel when compared to the two best parents in the world? In leaner times, you've gone without to make sure we were fed. You've supported us through tribulations, picked us up when we were down, and given us unconditional love. You taught us right from wrong and set us on the right path when necessary. In short, we wouldn't be the people we are today without your loving guidance. So now we toast the best parents God ever made." Glasses clinked and laughter abounded throughout the meal.

Just as they were finishing their desserts, Mary spoke up in her quiet, lilting voice, "May I make a toast?"

"That would be the perfect end to a perfect meal," Marge said, as she helped quiet the grandchildren.

"Here, here," said Ellen, raising her glass.

"'Tis easy ta love children respectful and loving toward one another." Mary stopped and smiled at her beloved family. "Always be truthful with everyone fer 'tis the most powerful weapon in yer arsenal. Everyday experiences should not be viewed as either failures or successes without considering shades of gray in between. Try not ta box yerself into having only one viable solution ta a problem, fer success can be achieved by many different routes. If one path doesn't work, try another and ye may surprise yerself with an unexpected outcome. Reach fer the stars and always believe in yerself. Use yer resiliency ta strive fer perfection but allow yerself room ta make mistakes—fer that is the best way ta learn. Finally, love one another always and ask God fer help in times of difficulty. Yer father and I have every confidence that ye will live up ta our family creed of faith, humility, charity, and most importantly, love fer all." Reaching down for her glass, Mary made a toast to her family. "Yer father and I thank ye all fer this wonderful lunch and, best of all, the time we've spent together."

Everyone raised their glasses and clapped at the beautiful sentiments. But the grandchildren fidgeted. "Can we give them the surprise now? Please, please, pretty please?" asked Neil.

Their parents nodded yes and helped the younger ones with their coats and gloves. Mary and Michael exchanged quizzical looks.

Barely able to keep from laughing, Thomas said, "I'm getting a ride home with James."

"But, Thomas, ye brought us here. How will we get home?" Michael headed toward the pay phones to call a cab, when he noticed their grandchildren giggling and jumping up and down.

"Then I guess you'll need these." Thomas handed the keys to his father for the new Plymouth Cambridge.

"I don't understand. That's yer new car."

"No, Da. The car is our gift to you both. We all chipped in so you could have your first new automobile."

Mary buried her face in Michael's broad shoulders to hide her tears of joy. Hand in hand, they walked around the four-door sedan and admired its sleek lines. The body was mint green with a dark-green hard top, Mary's favorite color.

"Look, Da," said William teasingly, "it even has a clock and radio on the dashboard."

Michael chuckled as he recalled his very first Model T with a wooden dashboard, proclaiming it would never have anything as fancy as a clock or radio.

Michael and Mary hugged and kissed their children and grandchildren, while thanking them for their wonderful anniversary surprises. They carefully slid into their new car and, waving to their children, drove off to a new adventure and a destination they had never even considered.

127

Michael and Mary O'Malley promised themselves when the weather was warmer, they would have a special outing in their new car. That day arrived on an unseasonably warm day in mid-May, 1953. Under the warmth of the sun cascading down its sweet caress upon the earth with a feeling of spring in the air, they selected the perfect day to enjoy the gifts God bestowed upon them.

Their destination was the Cultural Gardens on Liberty Boulevard in East Cleveland, a particular favorite known for its beauty and diversity. Separate gardens were dedicated to individual nations that contained cultural symbols, floral displays, and landscapes unique to the separate eighteen ethnic gardens. Their favorite, of course, was the Irish Cultural Garden, a source of pride and serenity to all who graced its topography. In the summer, the Celtic cross would be surrounded by shamrocks, Irish juniper, lavender, and Killarney roses, with Shannon roses gracing the garden's borders. The flowers were beginning to blossom and filled the air with a sweet collection of floral scents, sure to lift the spirits of even the most despondent. After walking through the garden together, they returned to their beautiful car and drove toward Lozada's Restaurant on West 25th Street in Cleveland.

The entire day was a special treat to celebrate their loving marriage through times of adversity and immense gratitude for their wonderful children, who carried on their parent's legacy of faith, courage, and hope. After a delicious meal and wine to celebrate their love, they headed home in fine spirits. Mary's head was on Michael's shoulder, perfectly content.

"Michael, me darling, we are so lucky that God has blessed us with a wonderful life together and children ta be proud of."

"Aye. Considering we grew up in neighboring villages in Ireland but it took an ocean fer us ta meet, He has a strange way of working, doesn't He? Who knows where are next adventure will be?"

Michael bent over to kiss Mary's cheek. She sat back with a smile on her face thinking of the love they would share when they arrived home. But when Mary looked out the front window in horror, she jumped up in her seat and yelled, "Look out!"

A small puppy ran across the road, and Michael attempted to veer away from the tiny creature. He soon lost control of the car before it jumped the curb and rammed into an unforgiving tree. Still holding hands, they died a quick and painless death. Within an hour, Frank Szabo was called to the scene to provide an identification of the occupants, given his marriage to their daughter, and deliver the notification to his wife.

Walking into their home with a heavy heart, Frank performed the least favorite task of his CPD career—advising others of their loved one's untimely demise. Unfortunately, this time it was personal and agonizing.

"Why Frank, what are you doing home in the middle of the day? Playing hooky? I—" Ellen stopped mid-sentence when she saw Frank's expression.

"Ellen, honey, why don't you sit down? I have something to tell you."

"Frank, you're scaring me."

"It's about your parents."

"Are they all right? Where are they? Can I see them?"

"I'm afraid they were in a car accident. There's no easy way to say this." A lone tear escaped from his eye. "I'm so very sorry to tell you but . . ." He gathered his thoughts to deliver the unthinkable news. "Your parents are now with your grandmother, Elizabeth Ginley, and all the O'Malleys in heaven."

It took a minute to absorb Frank's statement before denial firmly took hold. "Maybe there's a mistake. It can't be them. I just spoke to them on the phone."

"I was called to the scene and made the identification myself so there's no mistake. My dearest, if it's any comfort, they died together holding hands."

Frank held his wife as copious tears and wracking sobs broke his heart. He felt so helpless and wanted to ease his spouse's grief. When Ellen's tears were spent, Frank guided her toward the nearest chair and brought Ellen a small shot of brandy. After much coaxing, Ellen drained the glass and was overcome with exhaustion from emotion and heartache. She was five months pregnant with their final child and told Frank she could feel a kick in her womb, signaling the baby's reaction to the distressing news.

Eileen Marie, their three-year-old, walked into the room, sensing a change in the atmosphere, and cried out for attention.

"I'll take care of her," said Frank, grateful for the distraction and. opportunity to help his grieving wife.

"No, I'll do it. It's Eileen Marie's naptime and snuggling with her will bring me comfort."

Frank helped his wife upstairs and convinced his daughter into taking a nap, promising a piece of candy if she was a good girl. Soon both mother and daughter were asleep. Reaching for the phone, Frank called the station to advise he wouldn't be in for the rest of the week. Their two sons wanted to understand what happened, but seeing the sorrow on their father's face and hearing their mother's cries, they didn't want to pepper their father with too many questions. "Dad, has something happened to Nana and Grandpa?" James Francis asked timidly.

Frank had the appearance of a man whose life had beaten him down and the weight of sadness was almost too much to bear. His sons gathered around him in support, as he replied in a mournful tone, "Your grandparents were in a car accident and now they're both in heaven."

By this time, Eileen Marie awakened early and joined them. Frank was able to comfort all his children while they cried. He gave them projects to deal with their pain and ease the heartache. "Why don't you boys write a letter to your grandparents telling them how much you miss them and that they're in your prayers. Eileen Marie, you can draw a picture of them as angels on their cloud, enjoying the beauty of heaven." Frank gave each of them supplies, and they quickly proceeded to pay homage the best way they could. Frank then called Ellen's siblings to advise them of the tragic news, an equally grueling chore.

The next few days were a blur of activity as Ellen and her family planned the double funeral at St. Patrick's Church in Cleveland, the same place where her parents exchanged marriage vows almost forty years earlier. Ellen's thoughts were incongruous ranging from panic—inability to locate her father's beloved pocket watch to place in the casket—to the physically painful acknowledgment that calling her parents for comfort was no longer an option. Ellen felt as though a nail pierced her heart and hemorrhaged her life force until it drained away into nothingness. Each time she attempted to rise from their bed, she slumped to the ground.

Ellen and her siblings, normally sociable, became introverted and withdrawn as desolation weighed down their hearts with a burden so heavy it was difficult to merely take a breath, let alone care for their loved ones.

The O'Malley children took comfort in the knowledge their parents died clasping hands and recollections of the fortuitous party the year before for their anniversary. Seeing them together basking in their love for one another and their family became the family's link to sanity. Nostalgic memories gave them respite as they mourned the tragic loss of the two most important people in their world.

128

The wake had continual visitors and the funeral Mass, held at St. Patrick's Church, was also filled to capacity with friends and family who shared in the profound anguish for the loving couple from Ireland who changed the hearts of so many.

Fr. McNally, a family friend for over forty years, gave the congregation a remarkable homily to provide solace to all who attended. "Love is limitless without constraints, barriers, or confines. It is an unburdened gift, without the expectation of recompense, forever present as a constant in our lives and available to all who seek its warmth and comfort. By its very existence, it has the potential to unshackle the normal drudgery of everyday life. The circumstances bonding Michael to his true love is a perfect example of its magical release. After growing up so close to one another in Ireland, they both immigrated to America as strangers. Michael would travel throughout the United States until he finally met his true love in Cleveland.

"But the beauty of God's love has an added brilliance in its simplicity. He made certain we are never truly alone—at night, we have a shadow that travels with us everywhere; in the daytime, we can see our reflection in mirrors or pools of water. These simple reminders, often taken for granted, serve as constant reminders of our existence in an ever-changing world. They're God's assurance we are forever in His sight and He is always with us. If we embrace the gift of life and truly value the bonus of awaking each day, we are filled with the potential of infinite possibilities to help one another. Our selfless acts and good deeds are unspoken prayers to God and an acknowledgment of blessings we each possess and can share with one another.

"I realize we all have problems that can feel insurmountable which cripples our ability to see a clear path. But learning to step outside our cloud of self-doubt and focus on the struggles of one another allows us to see God's light. He assists us in navigating our journey just as a lighthouse guides a small vessel caught in a tempest storm to a safe port. We must learn to see with our hearts and listen with our minds; only then can we follow God's illumination to witness the impact our actions have on others. With an open heart and spirit filled with compassion, we are able to incorporate the suffering of others into our hearts and ease their pain by unleashing the incredible power of love. All it takes is one person at a time to accomplish this miracle—just as Michael and Mary practiced daily. Through their actions, they exhibited courage and strength to face each day with hope and conviction. We should follow their example and live in the present by helping others fulfill brighter futures. Let us chart our own courses wisely and imitate the wonderful example of this loving couple returned to God's embrace as we pave the way for those to follow."

Sniffles and muffled sobs could be heart throughout the congregation. Yet a peace descended on the house of worship where God brought the beginnings of healing to the O'Malley family.

A WEEK AFTER THEIR PARENTS' demise, the O'Malley children gathered at 3104 Carroll Avenue to read the will, stored in a safe deposit box kept in the basement. Each child was given a choice—the large sum of $5,000 per family or the opportunity to maintain the Carroll Avenue home as a rental property.

After much discussion over the next week, it was finally decided that Frank and Ellen would assume the responsibility as landlords in lieu of the $5,000 payment. After each sibling selected prized possessions, including furniture, with personal significance from their childhood home, Frank and Ellen scoured estate sales to fill the fairly empty rooms (over the years, items had been given to each O'Malley child when they moved into their first home) with furniture and begin a new venture as custodians of 3104 Carroll Avenue.

129

Over the next year, after Sunday Mass, all the O'Malleys made the pilgrimage to Calvary Cemetery where they placed fresh flowers on their parents' graves and silently wept at the pain of their absence. Their only solace was that Michael and Mary were in God's loving arms always together, just as they had been in life.

Ellen knew the saying that time heals all wounds. But losing her parents, especially sudden victims of an unforeseen tragedy, filled her heart with a void that never truly went away.

The O'Malleys had now entered the next phase of their lives—learning to cope with the abrupt loss of their parents without the opportunity to say goodbye. It was one of the most challenging tasks they ever encountered. But even when the tears eventually dissipated, the emptiness remained a constant companion, as grief overwhelmed when least expected. But they knew their parents would be disappointed if they wasted precious time mourning and began the difficult chore of adjusting to their altered existence. It was grueling but each of the O'Malley children concentrated on raising their families in a way to make their parents proud.

The Szabos were fortunate to have an added advantage to help them cope with grief. Becoming landlords would prove to be a full-time job with a steep learning curve. Frank didn't complain because he knew it took Ellen's mind off her parents' demise, which he considered a blessing.

130

Although the Szabos rejected the $5,000 cash in lieu of becoming landlords, their experiences opened their eyes to assorted and diverse people, each with their own singular habits and routines. There were gypsies whose rent money smelled moldy because they stored their wealth in mattresses for fear of banks stealing their hard-earned money. Despite Frank's admonishments that a bank would be a much safer venue, his wise counsel was routinely ignored. Another couple was consistently late in paying their rent until they vanished in the middle of the night with their belongings and skipped out on the rent.

When Frank and Ellen initially established the price of rent, it didn't include utilities. They came to regret this omission when one particular family insisted on keeping the windows open all year round, even with snow freely flowing into the rooms. Ignoring Frank's warning that windows should be kept closed during winter, they were asked to leave after three months.

Despite occasional setbacks, Frank was particularly delighted when a family of tenants, whose only language was Hungarian, gave him a chance to brush up on his native tongue.

Each month, Frank and his youngest daughter, Mary Frances,

drove down to Carroll Avenue for rent collection. Mary Frances was particularly happy to spend time alone with her father. At times, there would be tenants with children, which helped pass the time for Mary Frances as her father discussed repairs and current events while collecting the rent. Afterward, he usually treated her to a local restaurant, which served the most delicious hamburgers in her humble opinion and limited experience.

But the Tudors, consisting of three members—deaf mute parents and their son, Hal—would become memorable tenants. Hal, close in age to Mary Frances, was a young man angered by the shame of his parents' disability, who were robbed of a normal life. When he first met Mary Frances, he exhibited open hostility, and she was taken aback. This would be her first experience handling enmity directed at her. She knew the reason for his cold and dismissive attitude was his feeling of inferiority—she was the daughter of their landlords who didn't have a disability. Ellen didn't know how to handle this type of behavior and decided to include him in her nightly prayers.

A few months after the Tudors moved into Carroll Avenue, the phone rang in the Szabo household at 3:00 a.m.

"Hello?" A groggy Frank spoke into the receiver after groping in the dark and knocking over a table lamp.

"Mr. Szabo?"

"Yes, this is he." Glancing at the clock and alarmed at the time, for nothing good happened this late, his voice rose in pitch as he queried, "Who is this?"

"This is the Cleveland Fire Department."

Frank sat upright in bed, and Ellen heard the distress in his voice as he echoed, "The Fire Department? What's happened?" He held up a hand in response to Ellen's queries and listened intently.

"We were given this number by the Tudor family."

"Is everyone all right?"

"Thankfully yes, but you need to come down as soon as possible."

As he quickly dressed, Frank informed Ellen of the scant information provided by the Fire Department. Fortunately, the streets were empty, and Frank arrived at Carroll Avenue in half the time. When he looked upward, he saw flames leaping up into the sky, refusing to be extinguished by fire hoses. By the time the fire was under control, the attic and roof were open to the heavens while the upstairs bedrooms, other than being soaked, were relatively unharmed. Frank saw the Tudors huddled together on the curb, sobbing at their near-death experience. Frank comforted them as best he could before he approached the fire chief.

"Chief, I'm Detective Frank Szabo."

"Pleased to meet you, Detective."

"Call me Frank."

"I'm Chief Williams and truly sorry about the circumstances. But at least everyone got out okay."

"Any idea how the fire started?"

"It appears an accelerant was used."

"You mean, it wasn't an accident?"

"No, this was intentional and you're very fortunate a neighbor was awake and called the fire department."

"Not the son?"

"He wasn't anywhere to be found."

When Frank explained Mr. and Mrs. Tudor were deaf mutes and unable to use the phone, a chill ran through him. "Where were the parents when you arrived?"

"They were asleep in their bed on the first floor. Their door was closed but stuck due to excessive heat in the hallway. Why? Do you think the son had anything to do with this?"

In Frank's line of work, he'd seen depravity exhibited by people of all ages. Unwilling to make a rash judgment and hoping he was incorrect, Frank replied, "I truly don't know. But I'll check it out."

Following a search of the neighborhood, the son was never found or heard from again. Based on unproven suspicions and no physical evidence, no case file was ever opened. The only fortunate aspect of this tragedy was the absence of tenants in the back apartment.

By the time Frank arrived home several hours later, the household was awake and anxiously awaiting news about the fire at Carroll Avenue.

"Sit down my dear and have a cup of coffee." Although Ellen was bursting with questions, she knew her husband would tell her once he composed his thoughts. His children, however, were impatient for details.

Impatiently speaking over each other with boundless curiosity, questions were hurled at their father.

"What happened?"

"Was anyone hurt?"

"Can we see the damage?"

Frank merely shook his head as he attempted to reconcile evil involving a disabled and unsuspecting couple, who barely escaped a premature death initiated by their only child. Ellen told her children to go upstairs and get dressed while their father had a chance to relax after his exhausting night.

With the children upstairs, Ellen patiently waited for Frank's response as she made him breakfast.

"No one was hurt but the attic and roof need to be repaired."

Ellen allowed her husband to fill in the details in his own time. Without realizing their youngest daughter sat on the top step listening to their conversation, he relayed his fears of Hal's involvement in the fire and attempted murder of his parents.

Although Mary Frances wasn't aware of all the details surrounding the fire, she knew Hal's involvement was a certainty based on her last conversation with him. He stated his parents were such an embarrassment and dreamed how much better his life would be without them. She waited for him to say he was kidding, but the words never came.

Mary Frances witnessed several occasions when Hal stood behind his parents mocking them as they attempted to communicate. Their primitive use of sign language was flawed because they lacked formal education and were unable to properly convey their thoughts. Mary Frances was grateful Hal's parents never knew he started the fire or his disdain and mocking behavior. She discerned his parents' strong loyalty and belief in their only child would be devastated if they knew the truth.

Luckily homeowner insurance covered the damage and furniture replacement. To Frank's relief, the Tudors moved shortly after the fire to a vacant house down the street. With the help of an interpreter, they communicated to Frank their horrific memories following the fire prompted the move, but they wanted to remain nearby for Hal's return. Ellen and Frank agreed to allow Mary Frances, knowing her acquaintance with Hal, to view the wreckage firsthand. Ellen recoiled at the devastation of her childhood home but was grateful no one was physically harmed. Mary Frances shivered at the thought Hal could be nearby laughing at the destruction he wrought. She knew the damage would be repaired but the lack of humanity inflicted by Hal could never be mitigated or salvaged—especially the lifelong pain his parents would be forced to endure.

While Frank and Ellen Szabo were learning how to be landlords—a blessing that continued to assuage their grief—William O'Malley's job at O'Malley Plumbing had drastically changed.

By 1947 William was sufficiently recovered and returned to work with his father alongside friends and neighbors. After the death of his father in 1953, William inherited the business but sorely missed the camaraderie and companionship shared with his wonderful father and best friend. Peggy was aware her husband was extremely unhappy with the daily reminder his father was forever absent and encouraged him to seek another job. William was relieved to have such an understanding wife and arranged a meeting with a group of Carroll Avenue workers employed by his father, some for more than thirty years.

Smiling to his employees, with a sadness he was unable to hide, William softly explained his dilemma to the workers he considered friends. "As you know, I've been having a difficult time since my parents died. Over the past month, it's gotten more difficult to come into work knowing my father wouldn't be here." William looked out at the faces of friends and neighbors—people he grew up with—and stopped briefly as he choked up before he could continue. His thoughts were jumbled as he attempted to choose his words with care. "I would like to sell the business."

A gasp was heard from his employees at the thought of losing their job and working for a complete stranger.

"Please wait. It's not what you think." Once everyone calmed down, William continued. "You know my father and I considered each of you as partners, and I would like to reward your years of service. I'd like to offer the business to all of you. The price will be fair, and you'll become your own bosses, each owning a portion of the business. All the profits will be distributed according to the work you generate and complete."

William felt a wave of relief emanating from his friends. Once they got over their shock, cheers rose from the crowd at the proposal. "I suggest you take the rest of the day off and discuss this among yourselves and give me an answer in two days."

William received a response the next day—a resounding yes. Paperwork was drawn up and the business was signed over to the coalition. A weight had been lifted from William but the resolution of one problem brought another to the forefront—which career path would interest him. He had sufficient cash reserves for about six months and decided to talk to his childhood friend and brother-in-law for advice.

Goosie was aware of William's unhappiness and hinted there was another venture available. Now that he made a final decision to leave, William contacted Goosie and they made plans to have lunch the following afternoon.

William arrived at Heck's Café, near Carroll Avenue and St. Ignatius High School, at 1:20 p.m. and secured a table by the window. Goosie arrived ten minutes later, and William flagged him down. After exchanging pleasantries, they placed their orders.

"How's my nephew since I last saw him?"

"Mike is such a happy young lad with the sweetest disposition and the biggest blue eyes. As you know, his dimples are so deep and adorable, he makes you smile just to be near him. And, of course, your sister is as sweet as ever."

"I'm glad to hear that. I talked to Peggy a few days ago, and I don't think I've ever heard her so happy."

"That's because Mike and I are the two luckiest guys in the world." William stopped when the waitress dropped off their meals. After taking a bite of his burger, William asked, "So, Goosie, what's this wonderful opportunity you think I would like?"

"As you know, I was honorably discharged around ten years ago when I was injured in battle. During that time, I took a job as a mailman in the ritzy neighborhood of Bay Village. To the people on my route, I've become a fixture. I know the original families living in the homes, their children and friends, and consider several families to be my friends."

"That's great, Goosie. But what's that got to do with me?"

"I took my real estate license a few years ago, and business is booming from referrals along my mail route. So, I'm the first person they think of when they're selling their home or buying a new one. But with my daytime job, I could use the help."

"I don't know. I've never sold anything."

"With your personality and wit, you'd be a natural. I checked earlier, and there's a test in Columbus next month. I brought my books for you to study, and you'd have a promising new career in no time."

"Well, it couldn't hurt to try."

"Thanks, buddy. You'd really be helping me out."

"And thank you for the career option."

They toasted each other with iced tea and conversed about events in their personal lives.

William studied for his real estate exam and traveled to Columbus, Ohio. He received a letter two weeks later from the Real Estate Commission advising that he passed with a near-perfect score. Peggy was overjoyed and so proud of her husband, she immediately gave him a passionate kiss that turned the tips of his ears a bright red, matching the high color in his cheeks. Once he was able to breathe, William called Goosie to let him know he was available to sit at an open house.

"I've got a cute little starter home in Bay Village, so you can get your feet wet. I have OPEN HOUSE signs that I can drop off at your home. I'll give you a copy of the address, listing sheet, and a few pointers. If you're okay to sit this Sunday, you can start your new business. If you're free, I can stop by tomorrow."

"Sounds great. I'll see you then."

After Goosie dropped off the promised items and provided selling tips, William's first open house was a hit. The home was beautifully decorated and the yard well-maintained. He sold the house the same day and called Goosie to thank him for the wonderful new career.

"That's fantastic. I'm working on a really nice house that should be ready in about a month or so. Are you okay to sit on a holiday? I'm not talking about the major ones like Christmas or Thanksgiving but maybe July 4th. Sometimes people don't have anyone to share holiday festivities, and instead of being alone, they want a free activity to fill the void of solitude."

"Sure, happy to help. Just give me the info for my next open house, and I'll be there."

"I knew I could count on you. I'll keep you posted. Give my love to Peggy."

"Always and thanks again for everything."

After saying their goodbyes, they hung up, and William ran into the kitchen to give Peggy the great news.

"Do you mind if I sit on July 4th? A large house for sale in Bay Village would certainly bring a handsome commission."

"Of course not, my love." After kissing his cheek, Peggy opened the oven door and surprised William with his favorite meal—pot roast marinating in a roaster with potatoes and carrots. "Here's a celebration to my successful husband."

"Yum, it smells delicious. No wonder I married you."

She swiped his shoulder with a potholder, and together they laughed. "Good thing Mike loves this, too."

"I called him to come downstairs while you were on the phone."

Right on cue, Mike entered the kitchen, and his mouth started to water at his favorite dish. "Looks terrific, Mom."

"Thanks son. Nothing is better than hearing praise from my two favorite men."

"And nothing is better than having you for a wife."

"And mother," Mike chimed in.

As they ate, anecdotes about school and work kept the conversation lively. William was unaware that his next real estate listing would impact his life and perspective of the legal system.

The time passed quickly before William's next open house on July 4, 1954. William couldn't believe the heavy Lake Road traffic on both sides of the street, including any spaces near his listing. Multiple police cars, reporters, television crews, a coroner's van, and noisy neighbors had taken up the entire block. William was prevented from putting up **FOR SALE** signs anywhere near the property, and it would have been impossible for any potential customers to approach the homestead.

William drove to the nearest delicatessen to call Goosie. "I don't know what to do, but something is happening on Lake Road." He explained his dilemma, and Goosie told him to call the owners and explain why they would have to wait until next week. When William called, they agreed with his assessment and rescheduled their first showing for the following Sunday.

After William got off the phone, he decided to return to the area causing the congestion. The closest parking spot was several blocks away, and enroute to the commotion, he was able to catch snatches of information.

"I don't understand. He was a prominent neurosurgeon, well-liked by his patients."

". . . and I heard a handyman killed her."

"What will happen to their son?"

"We were just there yesterday for their annual Fourth of July party. I can't believe it. What a lovely couple."

William walked back to his car and drove home, anxious to tell Peggy about the strange occurrence. But when he walked into their home, Peggy was watching television with special news coverage about the tragedy. Sitting next to his wife, William sat in astonishment at the after-effects of the tragedy he had just witnessed.

The television news reporter recapped the crime. "The Sheppard family held their annual Fourth of July party yesterday at their home at 28944 Lake Road in Bay Village. Dr. Sam Sheppard is a popular neurosurgeon working with his father and two older brothers at the Bay View Hospital. After the party ended around midnight, Dr. Sam Sheppard went for a walk on the shores of Lake Erie behind their home. When he returned home exhausted, he fell asleep on the couch. Around 5:00 a.m., he jumped up when he heard screams from his wife, Marilyn. Dr. Sheppard claimed he encountered a 'bushy-haired man' attacking his wife. When he attempted to fight the intruder, Dr. Sheppard was knocked unconscious.

"Police are collecting evidence and Mrs. Sheppard's bloody corpse has been picked up by the coroner. She was four months pregnant, and her husband was found to have a bloody lump on the back of his head. The only suspect so far is Dr. Sam Sheppard, who is undergoing extensive questioning. We will bring you more information as it becomes available."

William was shocked at the speed of the investigation and the almost-foregone conclusion expressed by newspapers and newscasts that Dr. Sheppard was guilty. "I can't believe I was there, but it sure feels as though they're railroading Dr. Sheppard. Hardly any time has passed and they're already accusing him, while investigators are completely ignoring his account of events. When I was there, it wasn't cordoned off and all sorts of people were traipsing over evidence. Curiosity-seeking neighbors and strangers milled in and around the house."

Two weeks later, Peggy agreed with William's evaluation. "The newspapers are all accusing only Dr. Sam Sheppard of murder. They're sensationalizing that poor woman's murder and not even making an attempt to investigate the husband's statement of events. To them, it's all about selling newspapers and nothing to do with justice."

"My heart goes out to him. If fate, happenstance, and perseverance hadn't been on my side when I was recuperating in the hospital after the war, we wouldn't be here together. If I've learned anything from my experience, it's that things are not always as they appear. I just can't shake the feeling he's not getting a fair break. His story hasn't changed, but it's being ignored."

"Why not call Frank? He's a detective and perhaps he has some insight."

"That's a great idea. I'll try right now."

William called the Szabo residence.

"Hello, Ellen. How are you and your family?"

"Why, William, it's wonderful to hear from you. Frank just got home, and all the kids are doing great. How's your family and new job?"

"Peggy is just as happy as ever, and Mike is running around the house. So far, everything's intact, but the day is still young." After the siblings shared a chuckle, William asked, "Is Frank available? I'd like his input on a strange occurrence involving my new career."

Although Ellen was curious, she didn't inquire. "Sure, William. He's right here."

"Hey, pal, how can I help you?"

"Hi there. I'd like your thoughts about something. I was supposed to sit at a Lake Road open house across the street from Dr. Sam Sheppard's home a couple of weeks ago. Due to traffic congestion and overall confusion, we rescheduled. Have you been following the Sheppard case in the newspapers?"

"We have, and it certainly was a gruesome murder. How can I help?"

"Peggy and I have been watching the news coverage of the murder, too. Is it just us, or do you think they're zeroing in on Dr.

Sheppard and ignoring what we believe is a plausible story by the husband?"

"The Cleveland detectives I've spoken to agree it's one-sided, and the newspapers are convicting Dr. Sheppard in the media. It appears the constant negative newspaper coverage is forcing the Bay Village detectives' hands by swaying public opinion toward convicting Dr. Sheppard. They're selling a sensational story at the risk of a man's life and preventing the police from properly investigating. But from what I can tell, their evidence collection, trampled by the entire neighborhood, was a joke."

"That's what Peggy and I thought. I just wanted a professional's opinion."

"Any time. Take care of your beautiful wife and son."

"Thanks for your time. Give my sister and your kids a hug from me."

After ending the call, William contemplated events surrounding the murder investigation. William felt a close affinity to Dr. Sheppard and the distorted rush-to-judgment he was forced to endure. It reminded William of the unfair circumstances he suffered at the end of the war when he was believed to be Declan MacLeod. If his family hadn't persisted in their quest for the truth, he never would have regained his memories or identity.

Over the next several months, William paid close attention to the one-sided presentation of trial evidence that morphed into a nationwide sensation and increased newspaper sales exponentially. Dr. Sheppard was convicted in the newspaper on a daily basis and judged guilty in a court of law. Not only was his pregnant wife brutally murdered, but he was also separated from his beloved son, branded a murderer, and dubbed a felon with automatic loss of his medical license.

Although William frequently checked investigation updates, it was painfully obvious very few articles addressed the probability Dr. Sheppard was railroaded by newspapers getting rich from their sensational accounts—yet, the incompetence of investigators was glossed over. The case would evolve over decades and his conviction would be posthumously vacated. Although William knew equitable treatment for some was an elusive concept, it increased his gratitude that justice for him was realized in his lifetime.

After Goosie resigned from the Post Office and real estate, William's real estate venture had become so successful, he formed the William M. O'Malley Realty Company serving him well until he retired.

133

In 1954, Mayme and Wilbur Staab took a break from their latest Broadway production. They gathered around their new color television as they reveled in being the first family on the block to watch TV shows in color. Their oldest, Kenny, was in awe and even the baby, William, was mesmerized by the sounds and colors coming from the strange box.

Unfortunately for the Staabs, their first program featured the sham hearings by Senator Joseph McCarthy. A shameful time in American government, "McCarthyism" played into American's fear of communist invasions by the Russians. McCarthy's hearings, formerly on the radio, became live television events in 1954. His committee lobbed accusations, mostly against the entertainment industry, without any proof they were communists.

At first, Mayme and Wilbur were spellbound at the sight of so many famous celebrities, writers, producers, and playwrights—many people they worked with in their careers. But it didn't take long for them to recognize the proceeding was nothing more than a facade.

Wilbur was disappointed in the programming from their newest luxury purchase and commented angrily, "They're asking rapid-fire questions and ignoring the answers, even if it comes from their attorney. And worst of all, the only way they'll excuse a witness is if he/she supplies the committee with a list of suspected fellow communists. It's nothing more than a kangaroo court."

The senator's voice droned on in his brutish and brash manner, a man of authority without respect for anyone who dared to disagree with him. Brandishing a piece of paper close enough to the camera for the audience to see, McCarthy said, "I have here a copy of the paper you signed to help Russians. That makes you a communist sympathizer."

"You don't understand—"

"I do understand. You, sir, are not a true American. You are a Russian sympathizer and, therefore, a communist."

When the witness refused to save his own career by providing a bogus list of friends purported to be communists, he was blackballed from working in his profession. Some received jail sentences and others, despite being skilled in their craft, were forever barred. Many were soon on the edge of bankruptcy as friends and former employers were suddenly too busy to answer their calls. Desperation for some drove them to suicide, ending empty days without purpose or hope.

Mayme asked their son, Kenny, to play in the backyard. Disappointed their new toy wasn't very exciting, Kenny happily complied. Mayme placed William in the bouncy chair, where he promptly fell asleep. Mayme sat back on the couch, wringing her hands.

Her face was pale as a snowdrift, and her eyes wide as saucers. "Mayme, what's wrong?"

"Did you see the form McCarthy held up to the camera? Didn't it look familiar?"

Wilbur shook his head.

"Well, remember that acting troupe in the 1940s collecting money for Russian refugees and asking us to complete that exact same form? We were unable to contribute since we were struggling financially. Wilbur, what if we had contributed? Can you imagine what our lives would be like?"

Now it was Wilbur's turn to shake as he realized how drastically the lives of their entire family would have changed. Mayme rose on rubbery legs and turned off the TV set before she sat down on the couch to hug Wilbur for support.

For the first time, Mayme was happy they were low on funds when they first started out and thought, *It's true. No good deed goes unpunished.*

134

Home entertainment by 1950 was forever changed when more than half of American homes owned black-and-white television sets. But that number jumped to over eighty percent by 1960. In addition to programs for all ages, it had the deleterious effect of upsetting many households as Marge DuChez ruefully discovered.

"Neil, what is that infernal racket? Would you please turn it down?" Covering her ears did little to drown out her teenage son's new favorite record, "Shake, Rattle, and Roll," performed on *American Bandstand*. But Marge had to smile to herself as she recalled her parents' reaction to her request for "boogie woogie" records as a teenager.

"But, Mom, it's *American Bandstand*. How will I ever know the most popular songs if I can't watch it? *Everybody* is watching this show. Besides, there's a school dance in two weeks, and I don't know the latest dances. Paleese." Neil was at his most persuasive, but when his mom didn't change her mind, it was time for a compromise. "I'll even wash the dishes tonight and clean the kitchen."

"Will you take out the garbage this week?"

"I'll take it out every week, if I can watch it until the school dance."

Of course, Neil had every intention of continuing to watch the program after the dance, but Marge was too smart. The day after the dance, she renegotiated their contract. Now he had to wash the dishes every other night and take out the garbage weekly.

ELLEN WAS EXPERIENCING SIMILAR PROBLEMS. On a Monday afternoon after her children returned home from school, she heard a racket coming from the living room and ran out to investigate the commotion. Her youngest and oldest were locked in fierce battle.

"No," said James Francis, "it's my turn to watch *American Bandstand*." He promptly changed the channel.

Tears spilled down Mary Frances's cheeks. "But I was watching *Barnaby*. He's going to have a special puppet birthday party and everything."

She jumped up and quickly switched the channel. The two siblings were flipping the channel selector around so quickly, Ellen was afraid the knob would break.

"That's enough, you two. Before we go any further, have you both done your homework?"

Mary Frances nodded vigorously because her first-grade assignments, if any, were usually short.

James Francis put his head down. "I was going to do it after my show. But I'm the oldest and should—"

"Sorry, James, but that's not good enough. Watching TV is a privilege, not a right, regardless of your age. So, we're going to establish rules."

She called to her remaining children. "Thomas Michael and Eileen Marie, I need you to come downstairs."

Within a few minutes, Ellen started at her four children sitting on the couch. "As I was telling James Frances and Mary Frances, we need to establish ground rules to use the television. First, no TV until your homework is done. Next, you need to compromise if your siblings want to watch a different program at the same time. Your brother and sister were flipping the channel selector so hard, I thought it would snap off. To be fair, we need to establish a shared TV schedule. For example, Mary Frances can watch *Barnaby* on Monday, Wednesday, and Friday. James Francis can watch *American Bandstand* on Tuesday and Thursday with a special program, perhaps sporting events, on Saturday. Sunday, after Mass, will be family entertainment chosen by your father and I. James Francis, is there a Saturday show you'd like to watch?"

"Sure, there's a great basketball game. I'm sure Thomas Michael would like that, too."

Thomas Michael nodded. "And if Dad's off, he'd probably watch it with us."

"That's settled. We can always switch the program lineup and in all cases, majority rules. If the four of you can't come to an agreement, there will be no TV for anyone."

Looking at the four, slack-jawed faces, Ellen knew the thought of no TV was unthinkable until now. "And it will remain off until either your father or I decide you're old enough for the honor of watching any programs. You can always listen to radio programs until we decide."

The fight was over, ground rules established, and a truce achieved. Ellen and her siblings were learning advances in technology presented unique challenges and compromise, or bribery, became their best tools.

135

Now that James and Charlene were married, Thomas was the sole O'Malley survivor of bachelorhood and proud to avoid the fate of others tied down by a wife and family obligations. His childhood stunt of climbing up five floors of the Higbee building's steel girders under construction, encouraged his subsequent career choice as a construction worker. He fearlessly climbed to great heights and was proficient at walking crossbeams in excess of twenty floors. He felt a surge of freedom as he stood on steel beams looking down on the ants rushing back and forth to work. Thomas loved his life and managed to make it thirty-seven years without getting married, until . . .

The end occurred on a normal summer day in 1964 with temperatures in the upper 70s and a gentle breeze wafting off Lake Erie. Thomas joined his brother and sister-in-law at the Cleveland Air Show, where a famous aerialist was scheduled to perform.

"Did you know the Cleveland Air Show is considered preeminent in the country with competitive air races dating back to 1929?" asked Charlene, not only a pilot but also an avid student of aviation history.

"Sounds like you've seen your share of aerial stunts, haven't you?" Thomas asked. His imagination was thrust into overdrive at the proficiency of anyone able to perform flying stunts in lieu of a normal desk job. According to Thomas, aerial ballet would be a perfect marriage of heights and freedom. He immediately panicked when he realized the "M" word crept into his thoughts.

"Sure have. But wait until you see my friend, Peg White, perform aerial ballet. There's nothing like it." Charlene closely watched her brother-in-law and hoped her match-making plans would be successful.

When Thomas glanced upward, he was captivated as he watched a biplane-wing walker whose flexibility and grace were unparalleled. She performed ballet moves while walking across the wingspan, executing perfect splits on the wing, and engaging in death-defying aerial stunts.

Charlene became animated when she saw Thomas's expression. Her carefully crafted plan to bring Peg and Thomas together might work, despite his confirmed bachelorhood. With his thick blond hair, sky-blue eyes, chiseled physique, suave demeanor, and ruddy exterior, it was his turn to enjoy the bliss of marriage.

"Thomas, I told Peg that James and I would take her to dinner after the show. Would you care to join us? We're going to eat at the new Top of the Town. Should be right up your alley on the thirty-eighth floor of the Terminal Tower downtown."

"Well, I have to eat. Sure, why not?" he casually remarked, although he had a strange feeling he was being set up. "We'll pick you up at seven tonight, if that works for you," said James.

"Sounds like a plan."

After Peg's show, Charlene informed her of Thomas's penchant for heights. Peg, a native Clevelander, was excited to dine at the newly opened Stouffer's Top of the Town Restaurant—a sumptuous and classic dining experience with a panoramic view of Downtown Cleveland. She wore a teal-colored dress, which accentuated her taut body, and matching high heels combined with just the right amount of jewelry to accent, but not overpower, her attire. She wore her chestnut hair in a French twist and at the last moment, added a flower from a bouquet in her room.

She took a cab to the restaurant and arrived ten minutes after the

O'Malley party was settled. Charlene smiled enthusiastically at Thomas's reaction when she entered the room. Although every man eyed her appreciatively, Thomas and Peg's eyes were locked on each other.

As the evening progressed, the chemistry between Thomas and Peg was unmistakable. They exchanged phone numbers at the end of the night and before long, were communicating daily with frequent dates. Much to Thomas's delight, Peg also shared his love of the sea. Over the years, Thomas's friends shared their boats with him for private excursions on the lake. Thomas was thrilled he now had someone to share his adventures. During the summer, many of their dates involved trips to Put-In-Bay, Kelleys Island, and romantic sunset picnics on the water.

Their mutual attraction and conviviality in dealing with even the most mundane tasks—added to shared passions of heights and the sea—led to the inescapable conclusion they were soulmates. Within six months they, too, were married.

Resistance truly was futile.

136

Ellen Szabo had a potential health scare in 1968 when she detected a lump in her breast while bathing. Ellen knew she had to see a doctor but needed moral support. She asked her sister, Mayme, and her daughter, Mary Frances, to accompany her to the doctor. Ellen made the appointment for the following Tuesday and mentally prepared herself for whatever the doctor would find.

Tuesday arrived and all three ladies marched into the Cleveland Clinic for her 1:30 p.m. appointment. Ellen signed the required paperwork and insurance information before she was taken back to an exam room. While her sister and daughter waited for her in the large waiting room, Ellen was told to disrobe and wrap a sheet around her body. Sitting in the freezing exam room, Ellen watched the clock as thirty, sixty, and finally ninety minutes went by. Mary Frances heard a commotion at the reception desk, and slunk down in her chair, covering her eyes, knowing her mother was making her displeasure known to all.

Mayme gasped. "Mary Frances, it's your mother." The teenager tried to slink down further in her chair, but she was almost on the floor with nowhere to go.

"Maybe she doesn't need our help."

"Oh no!"

"Now what's wrong?" asked Mary Frances, still afraid to glance backward.

"The sheet is wrapped around her like a toga. It's almost on the ground in the back, and it's sliding down even more."

They both jumped up and ran to help. The sheet was dipping dangerously, and everyone in the crowded waiting room pointed and snickered. Together they grabbed different parts of the sheet to pull it over her body and maintain some degree of modesty.

"I've been waiting for over an hour and a half and still no one has come in to see me. I'm cold and tired."

With those words, the sheet severely sagged in another area, and it took both cohorts to keep up with her disappearing cover.

"I'm sorry," said the receptionist. "But there are still five people ahead of you."

"Five people after this length of time? What did you do—triple-book appointments?"

"I'm sorry but you'll have to return to the dressing room, and the doctor will see you when it's your turn."

"It's been my turn for ninety minutes."

Again, an area of sheet plunged toward the floor. For a slender woman, she had a hard time keeping the sheet at a respectable level. Mary Frances glanced away for one minute—by now, her face was beet red—and the sheet plunged well below her waist, toward her birthday-suit best. The guffaws kept on coming.

"I'm not going anywhere. I'll stay right here until a doctor comes to examine me. I've tried to be patient, but after freezing for ninety minutes, I've had enough."

Within five minutes, a doctor escorted her back to the examining room and fifteen minutes later, the exam was done. With the ordeal complete, Ellen changed and walked out with her two escorts.

"The doctor said it was just a benign cyst."

"Hey Mom, are you planning on doing a strip-tease act for extra income?"

Ellen stopped in her tracks. "What?"

Mary Frances explained her mother's disappearing sheet and free anatomy lessons to everyone in the waiting room. Ellen laughed after receiving a recap of free entertainment for those also dealing with severely overbooked appointments. Ellen never told her daughter, but she was secretly aware her antics transformed the sea of gloom permeating the waiting area into smiles and short-lived levity. Ellen's shenanigans had worked their magic.

137

By 1972, Peg could no longer bear the toll of sleepless nights worrying about Thomas's work on high-rise buildings. She had quit her work as an aerial wing-walker once they had a child together, and Peg wanted two-year-old Bobby to grow up with a father. She devised a plan of preparing a series of delicious home-cooked meals and skillfully cajoled Thomas to change his profession to one without constant exposure to death-defying heights in all types of weather.

"I worry about you each day when you're up on the high-rise beams. I'm too young to be a widow, and our son needs his father."

"But I love the challenge. Where else could I find such excitement? You of all people should understand."

"With your passion for seafaring excursions, you could find a job working on the water. Several years ago, I had a friend who worked for the Oglebay Norton Corporation, based in Cleveland, to transport ore around the Great Lakes. He mentioned the pay was great and, just like you, loved maritime adventures."

Thomas was intrigued with the idea of being on nautical adventures to different ports—an occupation that could hold his interest and keep his heart racing. He applied to the Oglebay Norton Corporation and was promptly accepted. He found the work was stimulating, and he was eager to begin each day filled with new experiences.

As much as Peg loved Thomas, she often enjoyed the time to herself and taking care of their son, Bobby, without Thomas getting underfoot with his abundance of energy.

ON THE MORNING of November 9, 1975, Thomas was in Wisconsin, preparing to board a ship known as the largest freighter to navigate the Great Lakes—a hearty vessel in service since 1958. But to those who sailed her, she was affectionately called the *Big Fitz*. The ship was bound for Detroit then Cleveland, where Thomas would disembark, along with fellow Clevelanders, for a long-awaited vacation.

Before Thomas could board the freighter, he heard the overhead loudspeaker, "Thomas O'Malley, there's a call for you in the office."

Knowing only important calls were patched through to sailors before they disembarked, Thomas raced to the office and picked up the phone to hear a breathless Peg on the other end.

"Thomas, you must get home as soon as possible. Bobby has terrible abdominal pains and needs to have an operation. They think it might be his appendix. How soon can you get here?"

"Let me check with my boss, and I'll call you right back."

Thomas walked quickly down the hall to speak with his supervisor in the main steward's office. After knocking, Thomas explained his dilemma.

"You've earned time off. Take the next flight out and be with your family. We'll adjust your schedule when you're ready to return."

Thanking him for his understanding, Thomas called Peg before he sprinted to his bunk and packed his gear.

Unfortunately, he couldn't find a direct flight to Cleveland, and would be forced to endure several layovers. Thomas called Peg to inform her of his flight plans.

"I won't be in until late tomorrow afternoon. If his condition allows, could they schedule Bobby's surgery for the latest possible time?"

"I'll ask the doctor, and we'll do our best. Just get here. We need you."

"I promise, Peg. Can I talk to Bobby?"

Handing the phone to Bobby, his seven-year-old son's voice was extremely weak.

"Hi, Daddy."

"Hey, Champ. How are you doing?"

"I'm kinda sleepy. They gave me something that's supposed to help the pain."

"Then you just rest, and I'll be there before you know it."

"Okay, Daddy. I love you."

"I love you, too." Thomas had to hold the receiver away as he cleared his throat before he could continue. "Don't worry, son. God will watch over you. He has a special place in his heart for little boys. I'll be there as soon as I can."

Peggy spoke into the receiver. "Sorry, Thomas, he just drifted off to sleep."

"Well, that's good. At least he's not in pain right now. I love you, sweetheart."

Thomas heard Peg choke back a sob, but she managed to whisper, "And I love you, my big tough sailor. Safe travels."

When Thomas hung up the phone, he felt as though his knees would buckle. Saying a silent prayer for his son's successful operation and strength for Peg, Thomas steadied himself for the ordeal that lay ahead. He then resumed the task of packing and made his way to the airport.

Thomas didn't arrive in Cleveland until 4:00 p.m. the next day, and he rushed to Fairview General Hospital where he was able to visit Bobby right before he received the preoperative shot making him drowsy.

"Well, big man, your mom and I will be right here waiting for you. Everything's going to be just fine." Wiping a tear from Bobby's eye, Thomas held his son and kissed his forehead. "Remember, this will be over in no time. We both love you very much." Their only child was whisked away to the operating room.

"Peg, how are you holding up?"

"I'm a nervous wreck but so glad you're here." They hugged and kissed before making their way down to the waiting room. When they sat down, Peg rested her head on Thomas's shoulder and he placed his arm around her waist. Facing the TV set, they tried to drown out the extraneous hospital noise. Anxious and fearful as the hours ticked by, they were getting ready to grab a snack when a special broadcast caught Thomas's attention.

SPECIAL BULLETIN FOR NOVEMBER 10, 1975: Yesterday, the freighter *Edmund Fitzgerald* carrying over 26,000 tons of ore pellets left from Superior, Wisconsin, bound for Detroit and Cleveland. But there has been no contact from the freighter since 7:10 p.m. this evening after they ran into a November storm. Affectionately known as the *Big Fitz*, the crew was comprised of many Irishmen from Cleveland. At the first sign of trouble with winds gusting, the captain radioed the nearest ship but later cancelled the distress call when the weather seemed to improve. But a gathering storm quickly overtook the heavy barge and plunged it into the sea with its twenty-nine inhabitants. The Coast Guard search hasn't been able to locate the ship. The first aircraft has conducted an aerial flyover, but they were unsuccessful in locating the mighty freighter. Once again, our top story is the sinking of the *Edmund Fitzgerald* and the loss of twenty-nine people, many from Cleveland, Ohio.

THOMAS SAT down in the nearest chair and placed his head in his hands, quietly sobbing.

"Wasn't that the ship you were supposed to be on, Thomas?"

Nodding weakly as he thought of his shipmates doomed to a watery grave, Thomas was unable to form a coherent thought or respond verbally to his wife.

Peg held Thomas as he drew upon her strength and prayed the news reports were incorrect. Instinctively, Thomas knew his friends were gone forever. The gravitas of Thomas missing a fate similar to his friends combined with a sinking feeling in his gut consumed him until he felt he couldn't breathe. He rushed to the hospital chapel down the hall and sunk onto his knees as his shoulders heaved with a grief so profound it pierced his heart. Strangers moved away to allow Thomas space as he dealt with his intense anguish.

Peg allowed her husband time to mourn and stood as the doctor approached the clearly distraught mother. "How is our son, doctor?"

"It was touch and go for a while, but Bobby's going to be fine. He'll need to stay in the hospital for several days to monitor a possible infection. After that, he can be released to your care."

"Oh, Doctor, thank you so much. We appreciate everything you've done for our son."

"Bobby's a special young boy and very brave so it was my pleasure. If you wait here, you can go back and see him in about an hour. When he's awake, I'll send a nurse out. She'll take you to your son."

"We'll be here." Grasping the doctor's hand, Peg's eyes filled with tears of gratitude. "Bless you, Doctor."

Once the surgeon left, Peg entered the chapel where Thomas remained on his knees. Gently lifting him up and into her arms, Peg whispered, "Bobby is going to be fine. We can see him in a while."

Thomas thought his tears were spent, but the wonderful news about their beloved son brought a fresh round of crying with one definitive exception—these were tears of joy. Thomas felt overwhelmed by the simultaneous events from opposite ends of the spectrum—loneliness and grief for his friends but joy and hope for his son's recovery. Hand in hand, they returned to the waiting room, where they remained until the nurse took them to see Bobby. He was asleep, and the grateful parents remained in his room until their son began to rouse from sleep.

"Hey, Buddy. How are you feeling?"

Yawning, Bobby replied, "I'm tired, Daddy. Can I sleep?"

"Of course. Mommy and I will be here until you're stronger."

Peg and Thomas kept a careful vigil over their son until it was clear he was no longer in danger. Then Thomas boarded a flight to Detroit, Michigan, where he attended services at the Mariner's

Church for his fallen shipmates. The church bell rang twenty-nine times for each of the sailors lost to the sea.

A humbling and moving experience would become an annual pilgrimage to honor friends that Thomas came to love, respect, and mourn. When Bobby was older, he accompanied his parents on the yearly journey and thanked God his father was not among those claimed by the sea.

One year later, Gordon Lightfoot wrote the ballad, "The Wreck of the Edmund Fitzgerald." It quickly rose in the charts to become a number one hit. But for Thomas, it wasn't just a popular tune, it evoked painful memories of friends and shipmates lying in their submerged grave, frozen in time.

138

With the children of the O'Malleys all adults by the early 1980s, the O'Malley sisters, living in neighboring suburbs, made it a point to attend monthly luncheons to rehash old memories and relay new information. They alternated locations and took turns driving and it became driver's choice for restaurant selection. Everything was proceeding swimmingly until it was Mayme's turn to drive, a woman too proud to wear glasses for distance.

"I don't really need them," said Mayme, as she drove the wrong way down a one-way street. When she asked her mute passengers, "Is that a stop sign or a person?" someone had to act fast.

"It's a stop sign," Veronica replied, miraculously keeping the anxiety out of her voice.

But Marge was the quickest thinking of them all. "Mayme, I'm too hungry to make the long journey over to Corky & Lenny's on the East Side. Plus, the highway traffic will be heavy from the Cleveland Indians game. There's a wonderful deli just around the corner."

Ellen was in the front seat and passed a hand behind her to shake Marge's hand while Veronica gave Marge a gentle squeeze.

"That's a great idea. The food is delicious with very fast service," added Ellen, whose skin was white, mimicking a heavy snowfall.

"Okay, if you're really that hungry. And there's even a space in front where I can parallel park."

"No!" screamed her sisters without meaning to raise their voice.

Mayme gave them a peculiar look but pulled into the lot behind the restaurant. She led the way into the restaurant and turned to the first woman she saw in the restaurant. When Mayme inquired about a four-top, the hostess, sitting a few feet away, gaped at Mayme who was talking to a painting.

Ellen rushed ahead, explained to the hostess that her sister forgot her glasses, and requested a table for four. As the hostess led the way, Mayme said to her sisters, pointing to the picture, "Guess this lady can't help, but another hostess already led Ellen to our table."

Mayme headed off in the same direction but, just before sitting, dropped her purse. After retrieving her handbag, Mayme lost sight of Ellen and sat in the chair already occupied by a strange man. Marge and Veronica hurried forward and led Mayme to the correct table. Veronica went back to the stranger and apologized while Mayme complained Ellen was standing at the wrong table.

When all siblings were finally seated, they felt relieved until they realized they still had the return ride home. Three hankies were immediately pulled out and eyebrows dabbed as the trio of unlucky passengers knew the terror-filled drive awaiting them. To take their minds off the fright lurking in their immediate futures, the three sisters, despite being teetotalers, requested a strong drink. Feeling liquid relief, they spent the afternoon sharing humorous stories about growing up and child-rearing.

"I'm not very gifted in the athletics department," Veronica stated. "My oldest, Dennis, never did get the hang of swimming and usually preferred to stay in the shallow end. Amazingly he saved his cousin from drowning the week we spent at Ellen's rented cottage in Vermilion. Dennis swam out really far on Lake Erie when four-year-old Mary Frances floated out beyond the safety rope on an inner tube and screamed hysterically. It was even more surprising that he joined the U.S. Coast Guard and overcame his fear of water. He's such a brave and thoughtful young man."

All the sisters nodded in agreement.

Ellen shared a recent story about her grandson. "Mary Frances told me that Sean blew up his socks."

Ellen patiently waited for her sisters to overcome the shock before continuing.

"Mary Frances gave her son heated socks for Christmas. They contained an insert to heat in the microwave for thirty seconds at half power. When she was on the phone, he held up the socks for her to heat. She motioned to the phone and mouthed, 'Just a minute.' He became impatient and decided to do it himself. A minute later, there was a loud explosion and she ducked instinctively. Sean heated both socks without removing the inserts at full power for a minute. When she opened the microwave door, she was greeted with a toasty scent of feet. It took her an hour to clean the residue but most food still tasted like feet for several days."

Ellen was laughing so hard tears ran down her cheeks. Veronica gagged on her tea, and Mayme spit out her bite which, regrettably, landed on their waitress as she passed their table. For "some" reason, it took forever before they got coffee refills.

Once they were composed, Marge asked, "How's your acting career, Mayme?"

"It's wonderful. I cut down performances when the kids were younger. But Wilbur and I will be starring in a play down at Playhouse Square. We start rehearsals next week, and I can't wait."

"Just be careful. A friend of mine is on Broadway right now, but she took a misstep and fell into the orchestra pit. She broke her arm and leg and can't return for at least a year."

By now, their lunch was gone and with no more delays, D-Day was upon them. After their bill was paid, Mayme once again led the way. Unfortunately for her, someone was getting up from his seat and Mayme tripped over his foot. She twisted her ankle, and it swelled to the size of a grapefruit. She was given an aspirin and an ice pack. Her foot was elevated until the swelling was reduced. Silently her sisters thanked God for intervening to prevent another daredevil ride home. Ellen drove Mayme's car to her home, where their cars were parked. Her sisters helped Mayme from the car onto the couch, and Wilbur gathered supplies and placed them within her reach.

Over the next two weeks, the sisters discussed how to handle Mayme's next turn to drive but, without reaching a decision, fate intervened.

A week after their luncheon, Mayme made a surprise visit at Veronica's home to borrow a cake dish.

When Mayme arrived and Veronica opened the door, she was pleasantly surprised to see her sister wearing glasses. "Oh Mayme, your new glasses are beautiful."

"Thanks, I wasn't sure I liked them."

"They accent your face beautifully."

Mayme was hooked and always wore her new specs when she drove. Veronica didn't mention this to her sisters. She wanted to see their expressions. When it was Mayme's turn to drive, wearing glasses proudly perched on her face, her siblings wanted to break into a happy dance but refrained. Mayme told them she ordered contacts for stage use, but they wouldn't be in for another week. Mayme pivoted to face Marge and added, "I wanted to make sure I wouldn't fall off the stage during rehearsals or performances." Marge smiled, thoroughly pleased her sister listened to her older sibling's warning, proof yet again there truly was a higher power to guide everyone.

139

Days became whimsical over the ensuing years as the symphony of life played out its tender notes. Life, laden with memories over the vestiges of time, repeated itself as the O'Malleys experienced the beauty of living through their children and grandchildren.

Time had taken its toll after decades of being landlords for the O'Malley homestead. Frank spoke the words Ellen had been expecting but dreaded.

"Since my retirement from the police force, I think it's time we sell your home." Carefully watching his wife's expression, he added, "Are you okay with that?"

Despite Ellen's sadness, Frank's suggestion was timely and would permit them to fully enjoy Frank's retirement and travel. "I agree, Frank. I'll call my siblings so they can have a final tour to say goodbye to their happy childhood and make peace with their memories."

After her siblings returned to the family homestead for their last trip, Frank and Ellen made plans to clean out the home before placing it on the market, leaving behind select pieces of second-hand furniture. Dressed in jeans and T-shirts, they began the arduous task of cleaning.

"Frank, can you please bring me the Murphy's Oil soap to clean the floors?"

"Coming right up." Frank had just cleaned out the back apartment and entered the front home with additional cleaning supplies.

Together they cleaned out the chimney, and Ellen giggled when she looked at Frank, covered in soot. In response, he held up a mirror and Ellen saw her own disheveled appearance and burst out laughing. Ellen firmly believed a relationship could not survive without laughter. It's inherent ability to share joy with loved ones was a precious gift never to be taken for granted.

"I'm going to clean out my parents' room."

Ellen had a catch in her voice at the thought of the formidable task before her. Frank gave her a wonderful bear hug, keeping Ellen's tears at bay. Her thoughts were filled with pride in her Irish heritage: Grace O'Malley, the sixteenth-century pirate queen known for her prowess on the Western Coast of Ireland and respected by hundreds of men under her command; Elizabeth Ginley, her grandmother who braved two famines and raised three children while working two farms despite the loss of her husband and infant daughter; and Mary Ginley O'Malley, her own mother who braved homesickness while facing challenges of custom and language when she emigrated to America.

Ellen smiled as she recalled her childish thought that her legacy of fame was a surety because her middle name of Grace demanded it. She realized marrying an exceptional man and rearing four wonderful children, while not a claim to fame, were certainly achievements that enriched the world through their accomplishments. She surmised fame would only be in her grasp if someone wrote about her but dismissed this thought immediately as juvenile musings.

After completing her chores, Ellen observed the nightstand was unsteady and struggled to pull the table free. She glimpsed something under one leg embedded in the floorboard and reached down to retrieve it. Ellen's heart pounded furiously as her fingers felt its rounded contour and familiar notches. Memories of long-ago flashed before her like a sepia-toned movie of timeless adventures and memorable events.

Tears ran unchecked down her face while she held her father's beloved pocket watch, not quite as shiny but every bit as majestic. Clasping her fingers tightly over the much-loved heirloom, Ellen closed her eyes and fondly reminisced about her father's weekly habit of polishing the antique to a brilliant sheen. Its luster, more brilliant when catching the sun's rays, glistened and shimmered on everything it touched. This cherished recollection brought serenity to Ellen, easing the inner turmoil of relinquishing her childhood home. No longer did she feel anguish; instead, Ellen's spirit was refreshed, similar to drinking a cold glass of water quenching a powerful thirst after an airless day in the blazing sun.

Ellen unclenched her fingers and remembered her father's belief the timepiece had magical powers. Reflecting on her life, Ellen realized it was the second time when she was the custodian who benefited from its magical powers: the first was her teenage bout of congestive heart failure when doctors predicted she would die before her twentieth birthday; and today, the same mystical force intervened to mend her broken heart.

When she heard her mother sing the Irish lullaby "Too-ra-loo-ra-loo-ral," Ellen questioned her sanity. Slowly opening her eyes, Ellen received a priceless gift from Heaven—more precious than a pirate's bounty of gold and rare jewels. Time stood still while the air lovingly dispersed droplets of tranquility and serenity in a cloud surrounding Ellen.

Quicker than a heartbeat, the atmosphere morphed from its surreal quality to reveal her parents standing before her, in the glory of their youth. Kneeling down with head bowed in prayer, Ellen was thankful her parents transcended time and space to deliver a miraculous gift of fortitude, ever present to all with an open heart. Ellen could feel the infusion of an invigorated resolve coursing through her body. Surety filled her soul that she could handle any hurdles life dispensed—for she had the strength of her nana and all the O'Malleys who paved the way before her.

Michael gently lifted his daughter up and held her in a soft embrace filled with love and healing as he bestowed a gentle kiss on Ellen's forehead. Standing next to him, her dear sweet mother radiated pure love as she whispered, "Me darling Ellen, we are so proud of ye and yer siblings. But remember, no matter what, do not fear the hardships ahead. Hold close ta yer heart the joys, fer they will surely give ye courage ta endure life's burdens. Be sure ta celebrate each day as a gift and in times of doubt, always look ta God fer the answer."

Mary's hands, no longer chapped and red from household chores, were replaced with a velvety softness reminiscent of a rose petal. Her silken touch, brimming with the warmth of a mother's love, gently caressed Ellen's cheek to brush away a solitary tear. Gazing at her parents, a treasured memory was permanently embedded in Ellen's soul—a gift she would draw upon throughout her life to access courage buried deep within.

Just as her mother's lilting brogue began to fade in the dissipating mist, Mary imparted her final words of wisdom carried on the whisper of a delicate breeze. "Always hold yer head high, fer even in yer darkest days, ye are never alone. We are always by yer side." Before the apparition disappeared from sight, Ellen's mother softly hummed their childhood lullaby until silence broke the spell.

Ellen stood transfixed and didn't notice Frank standing in the doorway until he gently coughed. Startled back to the present, Ellen noticed Frank's confused expression.

"I didn't mean to surprise you. But I thought I heard singing and decided to check."

Speechless, Ellen's rapturous expression of peace answered Frank's question without a spoken word. She ran into Frank's loving arms and he lifted her head for a tender kiss.

"My darling, you are never alone. I will always be by your side."

Ellen was startled at Frank's declaration that, unknowingly, reinforced the power of her parents' visitation. Still clutching her father's watch, Ellen placed her head on Frank's shoulder as they exited the front door. Glancing backward, Ellen experienced a remarkable insight. A house was merely a construct of wood and brick, inconsequential by itself and devoid of anything meaningful. But, over the years, Ellen's family residence at 3104 Carroll Avenue was lovingly forged into a home through heartwarming memories forever etched in her soul.

With each step forward, Ellen could feel the constrictive bands around her heart slowly lifting the long-buried storm raging within since her parents' untimely demise. Until today, she never had a chance to say goodbye. Thanks to their appearance, not only had Ellen been gifted with the miracle of closure, but the world around her achieved a heightened difference—the flowers smelled sweeter, colors had a luminous effect, and the burden she unconsciously incorporated into each task had been lifted. Life truly was grand!

'TIS THE END

ALSO BY MARY FRANCES FISHER

From Mary Frances Fisher comes her debut novel, *Paradox Forged in Blood*, a compelling work of historical fiction based on true events and stories passed down from the author's family.

A murder on Millionaire's Row. A killer's chilling words, "Shh. I know where you live." A woman tormented by her guilt-ridden past.

A historical murder mystery, *Paradox Forged in Blood* is set in Cleveland, Ohio, during the late 1930s. Four decades after the murder of socialite Louis Sheridan, the cold case is resurrected with the receipt of new evidence that transports detectives back to Nazi Germany. The only living witness, Ellen O'Malley, must confront a haunting secret and her complicit actions.

ABOUT THE AUTHOR

Mary Frances Fisher, a lifelong resident of Cleveland, OH, has spent the majority of her career as a legal nurse consultant and was a commercial print model with Pro Model & Talent Management. With Germaine Moody and writer contributions from over 100 countries, she coauthored her first published work in 2013, *50 Seeds of Greatness* (www.50seedsofgreatness.com). In 2016, her award-winning historical murder mystery novel, *Paradox Forged in Blood*, was published.

Her additional writing experiences include several short stories published by Transcendent Publishing: "Earning My Wings" in *Touched by an Angel: A Collection of Divinely Inspired Stories and Poems*, October 2013; "Mercy's Legacy" in *Best of Spiritual Writers Network 2013*, December 2013; "Be Careful What You Wish For" in *The Best of Spiritual Writers Network 2014*, January 2015; "The Gift" in *Finding Our Wings: A Collection of Angelic Stories and Poems*, March 2016; and the second-place winner for "Leap of Faith" in *The Best of Spiritual Writers Network 2016*. She has also written a screenplay based on "Mercy's Legacy" and in 2023 won the Firebird Honorable Recognition for "Earning My Wings."

Both her novels, *Paradox Forged in Blood* and *Growing Up O'Malley*, won first place in The Firebird Book Awards for their respective categories: Fictional Murder Mystery, and Family Saga Fiction.

Mary Frances lives in a suburb of Cleveland with her family.

www.maryfrancesfisher.com

ACKNOWLEDGMENTS

As with my first novel, I was amazed at the number of people who assisted and provided me with encouragement to author a compilation of stories and experiences encompassing a century. Despite my attempt to make this list as comprehensive as possible, I may have inadvertently omitted someone and if so, you have my sincere apology. Also, recreating a time period dating back to the 1880s, it's possible there could be inaccuracies, no matter how diligent my research efforts. Therefore, any mistakes are mine and mine alone.

MY SON, SEAN PATRICK, assisted with website updates to include people, places, and events noted in *Growing Up O'Malley (GUOM)*. His overall strength and encouragement, a gift from God, became mainstays during the loving, but sometimes arduous, task at hand.

MY BROTHER, TOM, assisted daily as I recovered from multiple back surgeries. I don't know what I would do without you and my gratitude is immeasurable!

LORRAINE FICO-WHITE OF MAGNIFICO MANUSCRIPTS, is hands-down the world's best editor and a wonderful friend. Working her magic with laser-focused precision, she delivered a novel that is a true work of art. Lorraine is an absolute force of nature in the editing community.

MICHELE ORWIN, a professional proofreader and author of *Waiting for Next Week* provided insights and thoughtful commentaries to polish my manuscript until it "shone like a duck's foot" (favorite expression of my grandmother, Mary Ginley O'Malley).

FAMILY MEMBERS WHO PROVIDED SELECT STORIES FOR *GUOM* INCLUSION: All the O'Malleys, especially my parents (Frank and Ellen), Margaret O'Malley DuChez, and Mayme O'Malley Staab. I would be remiss if I didn't mention my wonderful cousins: Louis "Buddy" DuChez, Ann DuChez, Peg Collins, William Staab, Lynn DuChez Bycko, and Marikate Collins Wazevich. Special consideration to Ann DuChez for her recommendation of *The Newspaper Axis: Six Press Barons Who Enabled Hitler*, focusing on their support of Hitler by downplaying the Holocaust.

Additional Holocaust source can be found at : *Facing History & Ourselves*, 08/02/2016, "What Did the World Know," facing history.org. This article contains of summary of how the British and Russians learned of the holocaust as early as 1941. Correspondents from America, via the United Press, first documented German atrocities in 1942. The *Los Angeles Times* wrote: "Nazis kill million Jews, says Survey" - facts supported by the New York *Journal American*.

ANTHONY MORA COMMUNICATIONS: The trio of Anthony Mora, Ann Convery, and Lindsey Blick are powerhouses for the introduction of *GUOM* to a multitude of media outlets through media training, presentations, interviews, and digital PR.

HATS OFF TO THE STALOCH FAMILY FOR THEIR WONDERFUL DAUGHTER, EMILY, an avid reader with astute and creative input to advise book elements appealing to a younger audience, specifically with emphasis on the Irish Pirate Queen, Grace O'Malley.

CLEVELAND MEMORY PROJECT AND THE MICHAEL SCHWARTZ COLLECTON for images capturing important events in *GUOM* for inclusion in the website.

FATHER MICHAEL GURNICK AND SCOTT MENIGAN OF ST. PATRICK'S SHOOL for permissive use of church and school photos added to the website.

MR. PAULIUS NASVYTIS, FORMER OWNER OF THE VELVET TANGO located in Ohio City, is the same neighborhood as the O'Malley residence. Well-versed in the history of the location, Mr. Nasvytis was instrumental in providing background of this area known as "Duck City" in the 1920s-1930s—a name derived from bootleggers "ducking" into this establishment during Prohibition raids. At that time, Cubars was a barbershop in front with a hidden speakeasy in the back where William O'Malley worked as a teen. Today, the former barbershop has been converted into a beautiful restaurant, with a renovated speakeasy, known as the Velvet Tango Room. It remains at the same location and still has bullet holes in the walls from raids by Eliot Ness! This historical landmark has a secret entrance (through a closet in the restaurant into a gorgeous speakeasy, which transports all who enter back to the era of Prohibition).

MOOSEHEART CHILD CITY: An orphanage run by the Loyal Order of the Moose (LOOM) who provided my uncle, Louis DuChez Sr. and his siblings with lodgings, food, clothing, education, and various outlets. The astonishing fact was the free provision of all services despite their father having made only one donation to the LYOM before he died (their mother passed away years earlier from TB). My heartfelt gratitude to the generosity of spirit and kindness provided by this phenomenal organization. Many thanks for permissive rights of Mooseheart information and pictures for the website by Gary Urwiler (Executive Director), Scott Hart (Director General of the Moose Fraternity), and Colleen Morgan (Assistant to the directors of Mooseheart Child City and School, Inc.)

GERALD GURLEY, MD, AND DAVID RYAN, MD in addition to their fantastic staffs as they guided me through a lengthy period of lumbar surgery, procedures, and pain treatment. Without your outstanding expertise, this novel would never have been completed. Go team!

THE DOUBLER FAMILY: The Doublers lived next door to my family in West Park, Ohio, and their children became fast friends with my siblings and I. Mrs. Doubler grew up in Germany during World War II, and when I was a child, she told me stories about life in Germany. One memorable event occurred when Mrs. Doubler's mother visited from Germany. She sat mutely in a rocking chair while gazing out the living room window and remained devoid of any expression while exhibiting only limited movement. Because I was young, I didn't understand her behavior but could sense an innate and profound sadness. I remember asking Mrs. Doubler why her mother had numbers tattooed on her arm—it was my first introduction to the Holocaust and Germany's concentration camps (not just reserved for Jews, but anyone who opposed Hitler's New Germany). This knowledge ignited my imagination that remains to this day.

THE UNITED STATES HOLOCAUST MEMORIAL MUSEUM, an outstanding source of information at www.USHMM.org.

JAN WELLEN for the picture of Pervitin added to my website (used by the Nazis to create "supermen" fighting blitzkrieg-style warfare).

ANNE CHAMBERS, author of *Granuaile: The Life and Times of Grace O'Malley*, Wolfhound Press in Dublin, published 1979, an excellent resource of the infamous Irish Pirate Queen, Grace O'Malley.

CAROL LOFTIS OF MULRANNY TOURIST OFFICE & COUNTY MAYO provided links to census records of the early 1900s for Michael O'Malley.

ALL THOSE WORKING AT THE OHIO BMV for their assistance in researching Ohio driving laws in the 1930s.

PATRICIA RULLO of the Firebird Book Awards—you have my eternal gratitude for elevating both my books into award-winning novels: 2023 *Paradox Forged in Blood*; 2024 *Growing Up O'Malley*.

DR. CECILIA MYLETT and MARK PATRICK CAINE for sharing their beautiful photos of Grace O'Malley's castle in County Mayo on my website, www.maryfrancesfisher.com.

www.ingramcontent.com/pod-product-compliance
Lightning Source LLC
Chambersburg PA
CBHW020257180726
47994CB00028B/1734